Badger Valley Publishing

BadgerValley.com

The Treasure of Namakagon

Badger Valley Publishing
BadgerValley.com
45255 East Cable Lake Road, Cable, Wisconsin 54821

ISBN-13: 978-0615631097   ISBN-10: 0615631096

The author expresses sincere gratitude to the Sawyer County Historical Museum, the Wisconsin Historical Society, Lac Courte Oreilles Community College, and Forest Lodge Public Library for aid in researching the foundation for this story. Assistance and encouragement from my wife, Sybil Brakken, support from friends, and indispensable guidance from my critique group, the Yarnspinners chapter of the Wisconsin Writers Association, helped bring this story to life.

The Treasure of Namakagon is inspired by many true events that occurred in northwestern Wisconsin during the late nineteenth century when timber harvest methods were rushed and wasteful. Today's loggers practice sound conservation methods, knowing this is best for both environment and economy. This book is neither a criticism of today's loggers nor of contemporary timber harvest techniques. However, it does shed light on the questionable business practices, appalling forest management methods, and outright greed employed by most 19th and early 20th century lumber companies.

Other than Chief Namakagon and Governor Jeremiah Rusk, no characters in this book are meant to represent actual individuals. Any similarity to real persons, either living or dead, is unintentional and coincidental. Every attempt has been taken to make this book an historically accurate reflection of life in the lumber camps and northern Wisconsin communities in the 1880s.

This book is dedicated to the Ojibwe people who, for many centuries, prospered in our vast white pine forests until insatiable lumber companies turned those noble trees into mere timber bound for the mill. This book is also dedicated to the many thousands of strong-hearted lumberjacks who found their way to the western Great Lakes States' pinery where they worked from light of dawn until dark of night all winter long under deplorable, dangerous conditions. They brought great wealth to the lumber barons, put Wisconsin on the national economic map, and left us with immeasurable culture and historical wealth. Finally, this book is written in honor of the man known by a few as Ogimaa Mikwam-migwan, but by most as Chief Namakagon.

The Treasure of Namakagon

James A. Brakken

The Treasure of Namakagon Chapters

Endnotes and Glossary

The Treasure of Namakagon

James A. Brakken

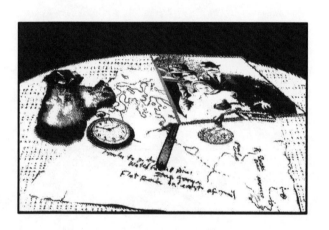

The Treasure of Namakagon
James A. Brakken

Prologue
May 18, 1966
Early morning

"It's hard to throw away all these memories, Grandpa," I whispered into the empty room.

I dumped another wastebasket of his faded papers into the woodstove and struck a match. Almost a hundred years of records, receipts, memos, and other notes from the long-defunct Namakagon Timber Company were finally being put to rest. The cast iron woodstove in the old man's workshop, once the lumber camp blacksmith shop, was perfect for the task. Two ladies from the church were on their way out to help. For now, though, the job was mine alone.

My grandfather, Tor Loken, had passed away in his sleep on a frigid January night at the age of ninety-eight. Now, on this cheerful spring morning with birds singing and bees dancing across the lilac blossoms in the front yard, I faced the inevitable chore of cleaning out my grandfather's home.

This grand, old lumber camp lodge and all of my Grandpa's land would be mine to protect just as the old Norwegian had done for so many decades. With my parents gone, I was next in line. It was my responsibility. I hoped I was up to the task.

The bedroom had two closets. Grandma's clothes hung in one. Neatly arranged by seasons, they remained untouched since her passing, three years earlier. I left that chore for the women from the church. In Grandpa's closet hung several suits, an assortment of shirts and trousers, and, wedged against the wall at the far end, his red and black wool mackinaw. In the pocket, rolled up and wrinkled, was his old felt hat. I pulled the coat off the hanger and tried it on to find the elbows nearly worn through and the cuffs and collar threadbare. Stepping back, I looked into the mirror as I put on the hat. There, staring back at me was the spitting image of my grandfather, Tor Loken, when he was much younger, as strong as an ox, and the bullheaded boss of the once-thriving lumber camp.

I gazed at the image in the mirror for a few seconds before reaching far into the closet, pulling out an old deer rifle. "Your first Winchester, Grandpa Tor," I said softly. "I wonder how many men you fed with this back in the big timber days." I opened the action, checked the chamber, and admired the rifle for a moment before putting it on the bed.

Next from the closet came the double-barrel twelve-gauge Grandpa used when he took me partridge hunting. I was just a boy then. "Those were great days, Grandpa. I wish we could have one more hunt. You taught me so much."

1

Forcing back tears, I reached again into the corner of the closet, finding the old fellow's Remington twenty-two pump, and, finally, his father's walking stick, made for Great-grandpa Olaf by an Indian hermit who lived on the lake. He was the man who, according to the Ashland Daily Press, had paid for supplies using silver from a secret mine. The walking stick was made from ironwood, carefully whittled, top to bottom, by the steady hand and sharp knife of the old Indian chief. Images of birds and mammals wound around the shaft. A whitetail buck could be seen escaping from two wolves. A bear reached high for wild currants. A fisher chased a snowshoe hare. Ducks flushed from nearby cattails. An osprey carried a fish through the air as other animals looked on. The top of the stick was adorned with a bald eagle. Its tail feathers and head were inlaid with hand-tooled silver, now black with tarnish. I laid the stick, the shotgun, and the twenty-two on the bed next to my grandfather's Winchester. They were all part of his life in the north woods. I would not let them go. I couldn't.

High on the closet shelf were two fedoras—hats I'd seen men wear in the old movies. "Rather dressy for you, aren't they, Grandpa Tor?" They showed little wear. I could almost hear Grandma Rosie telling him to be sure to put on his Sunday hat for one of their rare trips to the Twin Ports. Once or twice each year, he would gas up the big Buick and drive the seventy-five miles to Superior, then cross the old wooden bridge to Duluth. Grandma would go straight to the Glass Block, the big Superior Street department store that featured the latest fashions. His preferred stop was the Captain's Table, a downtown cafeteria where he could load up his tray with huge amounts of roast beef, pork, potatoes and gravy, carrots, squash, stew, baked beans, bread and coffee—lots of hot coffee. And pie! They served apple, peach, custard, blueberry, pumpkin, and cherry pie. Grandpa had to have one piece of each, always inviting comments from Grandma about making a public spectacle at these meals—meals not altogether different from those taken in the cook shanty of the old lumber camp decades before. The tough, old lumberjack remained thin—a wonder, considering how much food he could put away.

I tossed the two hats and his three neckties into a cardboard box for the youngsters at Cable High School where they might be used in some future school play. Next, I pulled down a wrinkled shopping bag from the closet shelf, finding a pair of old work boots. I pulled them from the bag and flipped one over. The sole and heel were studded with small spikes. "Calked boots—these definitely go to the museum, Grandpa."

A battered, wooden box, its green paint worn thin with age, was the last item on the shelf. I took the box into the kitchen and placed it on the table. Inside were two buckskin pouches. They were dark with age, dried out, and cracked. In one was some old tobacco. "Grandpa, you didn't smoke. So, why did you save this old tobacco pouch?"

Pitching it into the wastebasket, I untied the second, larger pouch. Out came a strange assortment of items including an odd-shaped, tarnished, silver *ring that almost matched the silver wristband Grandpa gave me years ago—the one I always wear. I also found an old pocketknife with one broken blade, a battered silver pocket watch, an old gold medal. Next, a short length of light blue ribbon and an old tintype photograph of a man and a woman holding an infant. The man was tall with broad shoulders. He sported a large mustache and a wide, endearing smile. I flipped the photo over to find 1867 scratched into the metal. "So, Grandpa Tor, who is this?" I stared at the image of the young couple. Then, as though my grandfather were whispering in my ear, it came to me. "Why, this is you, isn't it, Grandpa! You with Great-grandpa Olaf and his wife, just after they came to America. This must have been taken well before your pa came to Wisconsin to build his lumber camp." I put the photograph on the table, quickly picking it up again when I realized this was the only photo I had ever seen of my great-grandmother.*

"Great-grandma Karina. You are the one who died in that Ohio train wreck—or was it Indiana? I just don't remember any more."

I stared at the attractive, young woman in the photo trying in vain to recall some of the old stories I'd heard from my grandfather and his brother, my Great-uncle Ingman. "Oh, Karina, there are so many things I don't know about you and Olaf and your little boy—my Grandpa Tor. Your lives, your experiences, I know almost nothing about you. Here it is, ninety-eight years after this picture was taken, and I know so little of your life back then. Sure wish I knew more. Too late now," I said, "your stories—all lost and gone."

After studying the photo for a few seconds, I returned it to the table. In the bottom of the green box, tied together with white cotton cord, were two bundles of what looked like old, black and white, college theme books.

"More records from the lumber camp, Grandpa?" Before the words left my mouth I saw these were something else. The first book said "The Chief and Me by Tor I. Loken. 1938".

I opened the book. From inside the front cover fell a sheet of age-browned paper. It was a bill from a grocer in Morse, Wisconsin. "Morse?" I said, remembering the once large, busy lumber town had declined to a few, small houses among many over-grown foundations and abandoned homes. Its depot and sidings were gone, as was the enormous sawmill and planing mill. Gone, too, were the many stores and taverns, the bank, the huge hotels, and boarding houses. Like so many other large, lively timber-trade boomtowns that prospered in northern Wisconsin toward the end of the nineteenth century, Morse was now little more than a ghost town.

The date on the bill was September 29, 1884. Edges crumbling, I handled the bill carefully as I read the list out loud. "One barrel pork at six dollars and fifty cents; One barrel beef at four-fifty; Fifty pounds prunes at six cents per pound; Twenty-four fifths Old Crow at thirty-five cents each; Two-hundred pounds beet sugar at five cents per pound; Six-hundred pounds flour at two cents per pound; Twenty-five pounds tobacco at thirty per pound; Three pair wool drawers at one dollar each; Three pair suspenders at fifty cents each;

3

Three pair shoes at a dollar-twenty-five ..." The list went on with "Paid in full" marked at the bottom. "Odd you'd keep this old invoice all this time, Grandpa Tor."

As I was about to put it into the box for the historical museum, I turned the receipt over. There, on the back, in pencil, was what looked like a map. The faded lines and discolored paper made it hard to decipher. In time, I made out Lake Namakagon and the old Namakagon Lumber Camp where I now stood. I made out Jackson, Diamond, and Crystal Lakes, above. To the left were East Lake and nine-mile-long Lake Owen. A dotted line ran north beyond Lake Namakagon. "This line must be the old Indian trail leading north to Madeline Island, right Grandpa?" The log walls and hewn timber rafters absorbed my words as I studied the sketch. An X marked an island and another X lay well to the north, beyond Atkins and Marengo Lakes. Other notes on the bottom of the map were too worn and faded to read.

I heard a car pull in and the slamming of two car doors. Laying the old receipt on the table next to the photograph, I said, "The ladies from the church are here to help, Grandpa. I guess I'd better stop talking to you now. First thing you know they'll be hauling me away, too!"

I opened the door saying, "Come in, come in. Thank you for coming all this way."

One of the two ladies placed a large pan of cornbread on the table next to the photograph. I poured them each a cup of coffee and offered some instructions on what to take, what to leave, and what to burn. Eager to satisfy my curiosity, I went back to the black and white theme books.

The women began boxing and removing kitchen items for the upcoming church bazaar. Knowing I would be well out of their way, I retreated to the main room of the lodge, theme books in hand. I settled into Grandpa's well-worn easy chair near the fireplace, the old gentleman's favorite reading spot. I opened the first book again. The handwriting was Grandma Rosie's. I kicked off my shoes and put my feet up on Grandpa's footstool to read their words.

The Chief and Me
by Tor I. Loken. 1938

Chapter 1
Dark Visions

We know what we have left behind. The great mystery lies beyond the next bend.

Each stroke of the Indian Chief's paddle was strong and steady. His canoe glided silently along the shore, leaving only a gentle wake. He headed westward along Lake Superior's southern shore, not knowing where his journey would end—a journey that began with a dark, dark vision.

September, 1831. Weeks before, he was in the best graces of Major Lewis Wilson Quimby, commander of the United States Army post at Sault Ste. Marie on the eastern end of Lake Superior. An Ojibwe scout in his younger days, the chief contracted with the United States government to explore and map the many islands in Lake St. Claire and the forests far to the north. The Ojibwe surveyor and the Major quickly formed a friendship based on mutual trust and respect. He was one of a select few who shared the Major's dinner table. His association with the Quimby family brought him excellent reading and speaking skills. He thoroughly studied most of the books in the Major's home library. He'd also gained social skills exceeding those of most others on the post.

The chief came to the Sault a solitary traveler. Years earlier, when he lived near the shores of Lake Owasco in the State of New York, he fought bravely alongside the Americans against the British in the war of 1812. Like his father, he was chosen by his people to be their leader, the ogimaa, the chief.

But smallpox, that dreadful gift from the white man, claimed too many of his people, including his wife and sons, and brought too many tears. The chief needed to journey from this place. His travels took him far from his first home, far from the pain. Keeping memories of his loved ones close to his heart, he moved farther and farther from his former home to Sault Ste. Marie and the friendship of Major Quimby and his family.

The chief was tall, strong, had sparkling eyes, a warm smile and a warmer heart that led to frequent invitations to share the elders' tobacco. Seeking to learn and to share his knowledge with those he visited, he became known as a trader of wisdom. Each journey, village, and person increased the chief's insight as he traveled from Hudson Bay to Gitchee Gumi, the big lake the whites called "Superior."

The chief was a man of vision, understanding the differences between the Indian's life and the white man's way. He also understood that more and more white men would come to the northern waters just as his people, following another vision many years earlier, traveled beyond Gitchee Gumi.

His ancestors sought a new home and a new life. They discovered both in the land called Ouisconsin, a place with many lakes and rivers filled with menoomin, the good grain that grows in water and gives life. The whites called it wild rice.

One evening, after sharing dinner with the Major and his family, the chief's life suddenly changed. Following an enjoyable meal of smoked pork, buttered squash, and flat bread with molasses, he retired to his lodge. Hours later, he had the dream. Perhaps a nightmare, perhaps a vision, he knew Wenebojo, the Anishinabe spirit, presented it to him.

The chief dreamt of a fire. Edora, the daughter he adored, perished in the flames. He was wrongly blamed, put in chains, and sentenced to be hanged.

The chief escaped, in this nightmare, fleeing into the forest, the Major and his soldiers close behind. A life or death clash ended with the chief looking down on his friend, a knife sunk deep in the Major's chest.

Wenebojo then woke the chief, who now lay in a cold sweat, his heart pounding in the dark.

As in many dreams, he saw no reason, no rhyme. Making no sense of it, he drifted back into his troubled sleep. Wenebojo brought him a second vision—two shining stars in a sparkling sky, the chief there with them. Wenebojo whispered, "Thirteen days you must travel westward along the southern shores of Gitchee Gumi. Only there will you find your peace—only there."

The chief rose from his uneasy sleep, knowing what he must do. Well before dawn, with no one else about, he gathered his few belongings, took them down to his canoe, and silently paddled west. He would seek out the two stars. There would be no fire at the post. The vision had been broken. The horrible events foretold now dissolved, vanishing like northern lights chased by the early morning sun. The chief would never again see the Quimby family or the land he came to think of as his home.

Each silent stroke of the chief's paddle left small whirlpools of cold, Gitchee Gumi water spinning behind. As his canoe glided swiftly along the shore, two eagles watched from the top of a tall white pine. "Is that you, Wenebojo?" he asked the eagles. An otter followed him, diving and surfacing, again and again, curious about this rare sight of man and canoe. "You, Otter," he whispered. "You follow me and watch me. Surely, you are Wenebojo in disguise."

A doe and two fawns watched him from the shore, motionless. "You don't fool me, Wenebojo. You are keeping your eyes on me, waiting to play your tricks."

Stroke after stroke, the chief moved away from Sault Ste. Marie and closer to his new life, new home, and many new friends, each with stories of their own.

The mystery of what lie ahead began to unfold. And, across the land of the northern lakes, the *Treasure of Namakagon* would become legend.

Chapter 2
A Dollar and a Dime

A cold, penetrating rain fell on Chicago this April, 1883 morning. The air hung heavy from a mix of smoldering coal smoke and stockyard stench, making each breath hard to bear. A black, horse-drawn cab worked its way through the dark, wet city streets. A shaggy, wet, stray dog watched as the cab rounded the corner, pulling up to the door of the LaSalle Street Christian Boys Orphanage. The rain-soaked driver set the brake, climbed down, and opened the passenger's door bearing the words CHICAGO RIVER FUEL AND DRAY painted in gold letters. A tall man stepped from the cab, pulled his coat collar up, his hat down, and walked quickly to the door of the orphanage.

The *clack, clack, clack* of the brass knocker echoed off the wet, soot-darkened buildings across the street. The door opened and the man quickly disappeared inside. A boy with sandy-colored hair greeted the visitor who now dripped puddles onto the foyer floor.

"Good morning, sir. Can I tell Mr. Halder who is calling?"

"Yes. Tell your headmaster Mr. DeWilde is here, young man. Go!"

The boy hurried off. Ignatius R. DeWilde removed his hat and coat. Draping the coat over one arm, he looked around the small foyer, noting the cracked window nearly hidden by faded, green drapes, the peeling wallpaper, the worn spots in the carpet runner that trailed down the hall. The building's mustiness added to the unpleasantness of today's Chicago air.

The headmaster burst in. "Mr. DeWilde, how nice to see you. What brings you to our home today? Can I bring you coffee? Tea?"

"No coffee. No tea. Your office, Ernie. I am here on business and time is short."

DeWilde stepped past Ernest Halder, the orphanage headmaster. Halder was short, stout, with bushy, black eyebrows. He wore a wrinkled suit and black tie. His large red nose revealed his excessive taste for cheap wine.

"I need another clean-out boy," DeWilde said. "Today. Right now."

Halder walked to the back of his desk and dropped into his oak chair. He folded his arms across his large belly and stared in silence.

"Well?" said DeWilde.

"What of the Endelman boy?" shot Halder. "What happened to him? Did he run off? I told you he'd run off, you know. He was a strong worker but I told you he'd run off, Mister DeWilde. I told …"

"He didn't run off, Halder," DeWilde interrupted. "Who do you have for me?"

"See here, Mr. DeWilde. I cannot have two of my boys residing with you. I need to keep my beds filled to get paid by Cook County. They will not pay for empty beds. You know that. One boy is all I can cover up for. You will just …"

"He is dead, Halder," snapped DeWilde. "There was an accident at the plant yesterday. He died late last night. My men tried, but could not save him. You will get the coroner's report today. Find me a boy, Halder. I will make it worth your while."

"Dead? He is dead?" The headmaster put his hands to his head. "Mr. DeWilde, you cannot expect me to deliver another poor child to you. First the Swenson boy, now Johnny Endelman. I cannot do it, Mr. DeWilde. I won't."

"You will, Halder, and I will tell you why. I support you. You bill Cook County for coal to heat this firetrap building of yours, despite my providing that coal to you at no charge. Last winter that put almost one hundred dollars into your pocket. One hundred dollars. Now find me a boy. I am in a hurry."

"Mr. DeWilde, I simply cannot. Both the church and the county inspect the books of this orphanage twice each year. What do I tell them?"

"I do care neither what you say nor to whom it is said! Here, this should answer their questions." He pulled a roll of bills from his vest pocket, peeling off three twenties. "Here is twenty for the church and twenty for the county inspector." He threw the bills on the large oak desk. "And this is, shall we say, for the orphans?" He reached across the desk and stuffed the third twenty into Halder's shirt pocket. "Now, Mr. Headmaster, find—me—my—boy!"

"But how will I know the next boy will not also die in your coal yard? Certainly you can't expect me …"

"Do not presume to tell me what I can or cannot expect. Get my boy or return my sixty dollars and find someone else to keep you and your brats warm."

Halder reluctantly pulled a large, thin book from a drawer. He hesitated, looking at DeWilde.

"Tell me you will keep this one safe. I cannot have this on my conscience."

"Find me the right boy, one who is tall, agile, strong, and smart. Give me a boy with a good head on his shoulders this time—a boy who is smart enough to follow directions. If you do, there will be no problem. Tall, agile, strong, and smart, Halder."

The headmaster paged through the book. Dipping his pen into the inkwell, he began a list on a scrap of paper. "Tommy!" he shouted. The boy with the sandy-colored hair appeared in the doorway. "Here, take this list. Bring these boys here at once. Hurry!"

Minutes later, three boys entered the room, each appearing to fit DeWilde's description.

"Boys," said Halder, "this is Mr. DeWilde. He is looking for a good, strong, hard worker. We are going to help him out."

DeWilde studied them. "The lad I choose will have his own room, good food, a dollar a week to spend as he wishes."

The boys replied at once. "Please, I'll go!" "Me! Take me!" "Me, too!"

DeWilde studied them again. Clearly, these boys were strong. Their thin frames would enable them to do the specific job he had for them. But were they agile? Smart?

"Turn toward the wall, boys. I have a contest for you," he said. They obeyed. DeWilde pulled a silver dollar from his pocket. "You will hear a dollar drop. When you do, the boy who gets it first gets to pocket it."

DeWilde flipped the coin. The dollar rang out as it hit the oak floor. The boys turned and dove, sprawling across the floor as the coin rolled under the desk. Arms and legs flew in all directions. The space between desk and floor was only a few inches, but the boys' bodies were soon underneath. The desk bounced and shook as though in an earthquake. In an instant, the boys scrambled out, huffing and disheveled. One boy held the silver coin high above his head, grinning. Another boy jumped toward him, reaching for the dollar, but the blonde victor snatched his hand away and his rival fell to the floor.

"You have it, my boy," said DeWilde. "The coin is yours. You are strong and quick. But as Mr. Halder knows, I am looking for a worker who is also smart. So I have another test. This time I will throw many coins on the floor. The winner will be the boy who shows me not the most coins, but the greatest sum. Face the wall again."

As the coins hit the floor, the boys scrambled. But the blonde boy stopped short. He stood up with a single dime in his hand. Stepping back, he watched the other two fight for the coins to the final penny.

"You, Son," demanded DeWilde of the last boy. "Show me your coins."

"Two quarters, a dime and, um, two pennies, sir," the boy replied.

"And what is the sum total?"

"Um … Fifty, no sixty, two. Sixty-two cents, sir."

"And you, boy? Count up your fortune."

"I got plenty, sir. Look, I have all these." He pointed at the five nickels and ten pennies. "See?"

"And what, pray tell, is the sum of your coins, Son?"

The boy stared mutely at the coins.

DeWilde turned to the blonde boy. "You, why did you not go for the most coins?"

"Well, sir, when I hit the floor and grabbed this ten-cent piece, I saw less than a dollar in coins left. With Billy and Zach fighting for them, well, I knew my silver dollar and this here dime would win. You did say, sir, the winner this time was the boy who shows up with not the most coins but the greatest sum. That's what you said, sir. I got myself a dollar and a dime—a buck ten, sir. No point in getting all busted up if I already won."

"What is your name?"

"Tor, sir."

Halder flipped through his record book. "This, Mr. DeWilde, is Tor Loken. He's been here nigh onto two years now. Just turned sixteen years. Came from New York with his mother. They were on their way here to meet his pa who came ahead to find work in Wisconsin, so they told me. There was a train wreck near Cleveland. His mother was killed. They sent the boy on to

9

Chicago to join with his father, but his pa never showed up at the station. Two days later the county brought the boy here, all his belongings gone. Stolen, I suspect. Later on we got word his pa was killed in a logging accident up in the Wisconsin pinery. Lake Superior country. Nary a word since."

"Well, Tor Loken, looks as though you are my new clean-out boy. You will do just fine. Yes sir, just fine." DeWilde looked the boy over again. "You others both did well. Keep your coins. You earned them. Spend it or save it as you like. And Halder, don't you take it from them. It is theirs to save or squander as they please. Tor, gather your goods. You are coming with me."

The three boys left the room. Tor returned carrying a coat and hat, all he owned other than the stub of a pencil in one pocket, a silver dollar and a dime in the other.

A moment later, Ignatius DeWilde and Tor Loken stepped quickly through the drizzle toward the cab. From across the street, the shaggy, rain-soaked, stray dog looked on as the heavy door to the LaSalle Street Christian Boys Orphanage closed, echoing down the dreary, wet, Chicago street.

Chapter 3
The Smell of Money

The black cab with the gold-lettered doors wound its way through the gloomy streets to the gates of the Chicago River Fuel and Dray. The black, steel gates were wide open as horse-drawn wagons of coal left while empty wagons returned. The horses' hooves splashed black, muddy water from large puddles in the enclosed yard.

Seeing their employer and his passenger, the teamsters pulled back on their reins and stopped, allowing the DeWilde cab to enter the coal yard.

"Here we are, Tor," said DeWilde. "This, my boy, is your new home. Right up there are the offices," he said, pointing to the second floor windows of the huge, brick building. "That is where you will bunk. You and Big Jake Riggens, our security guard, are the only two who have quarters in the plant. Mrs. Ostralder, my office lady, will bring you a dinner each day. There is a canteen one block down the street if you want breakfast, but that is up to you."

Tor Loken, orphan, and Ignatius DeWilde, coal yard owner, continued into the huge complex.

"Over there is where the coal is unloaded from the railroad cars." DeWilde pointed again. "Men work all day and all night moving the coal into those tall silos. When one of our wagons pulls up alongside a silo, another worker, the wagon loader, opens the chute and fills the wagon.

"That's where you come in, Tor. You have two jobs here at Chicago Fuel and Dray. One job is to sweep out the offices, clean the stairs, and such, make the place shine. The other job is to help the wagon loader if his chute gets jammed. You see, Tor, the chutes have to be very narrow in order to control the flow of the coal. Sometimes the coal gets jammed up and the only way to get them working again is to climb inside the chute and jar the jam loose. It should be an easy chore for a strong, smart, wiry boy like you. It is an important task. I know I can count on you to do a good job of it."

The coach pulled into the carriage house. Sounds of coal dropping into wagons, steel-clad hooves striking wet brick streets, and distant rumblings of neighboring factories could be heard over their footsteps as they climbed the staircase to the second floor office. When they reached the office door, DeWilde stopped and turned, pointing across the coal yard toward dozens of tall, blackened, brick smokestacks in the distance. Some were barely visible through the heavy mix of fog, rain, and smoke. Each chimney spewed a thick column of black smoke that stood out against the steel gray sky.

"See those smokestacks, boy?"

"Sir?"

"Over there," he said. "Those are the mills, factories, packing houses, and plants that make this city run. And, Tor, they—all—buy—my—coal. All the stores and most of the homes in this part of the city, too. Think of it, boy. They give me their money and I give them my coal. When their coal is burned up, they come back with more money looking for more coal to burn. It has made me a very rich man, Son."

"But the smell of the coal and all that smoke—it makes it hard to breathe, Sir. Hard for everyone in the city."

"Only on days like this. Most other days the smoke goes high and the wind takes it away. Frankly, it is not such a bad smell, boy. It is the smell of progress. To me it is the smell of fortunes being made, the smell of money. And you, Tor, you are now an important worker in my enterprise. Why, you are as important as any man in my employ. You will soon learn to appreciate the smell of coal smoke. Do a good job and you will always have a place here at the Chicago River Fuel and Dray."

"Yes, Sir. My pa always told me to do my best. I don't remember all that much about him but I do remember that. Sir? Someday I want to find out what happened to him. I have an uncle, too. Pa's brother. He's the last of my family. I never met him. Someday I want to find him, too."

"All in good time, boy. All in good time."

They stepped into the bustling office. The dark, filthy coal yard stood in contrast to this clean and orderly workroom. Four big roll-top desks stretched across the back wall of the large room. Each was manned by a clerk and had many pigeon holes filled with slips of paper. The desktops each had wire baskets stacked high with papers. Above each desks stretched a thin, white cord connected to a pulley. Tor watched as a clerk reached up, clipped a form to the string, and pulling the cord, sent it to the desk farthest from him, declaring, "Fourteen ton to Mercer and Peckworth by noon today," in a loud, clear voice.

Instantly the slip was snatched from the line, stamped by the man at the receiving desk and thrust onto a spindle. This clerk quickly recorded the order on another paper, folded and inserted it into a small cylinder. He opened a vertical tube mounted to the side of his desk and put the cylinder into the tube, sending it to the floor below. In the same motion, he pulled a cord on the wall next to his desk. The loud, clear ring of a bell could be heard from the floor below. "Order out, Mercer and Peckworth, fourteen ton," called the clerk.

As these men tended to their work, two other clerks, each wearing white, collarless shirts with gartered sleeves, sorted other papers. They placed them into baskets and bins on a worktable. Neither man spoke. Their attention was focused only on their work. As DeWilde and Tor walked across the room, one of the clerks noticed his boss, stopped abruptly and shot out, "Good morning, Sir!" Hearing this, each of the others repeated the greeting.

"Sorry to interrupt you, men," said DeWilde. "This is Tor Loken. He is our new clean-out boy. You'll be seeing him around here from now on."

Ignatius DeWilde escorted Tor through another door as the clerks returned to their work routine.

The next room was Mr. DeWilde's private office, neat, comfortable, and quiet. Before DeWilde could reach his mahogany desk, another door swung open. In walked a large, muscular man. Around his waist was a wide belt carrying a sheathed hunting knife on one side, a nightstick on the other.

"Tor," said DeWilde, seating himself behind the desk, "this is Big Jake, our plant security man. He will show you to your room. If you have any questions about your work, see Big Jake."

DeWilde pawed through some mail on his desk as Big Jake Riggens escorted Tor out of the room and down a short hallway. They entered a small room with one small window looking onto the coal yard and the nearby factories. An old jacket and hat hung on one of several spikes driven into the wall. A single chair stood next to a small table. A pocket knife lay on the table. In the corner stood a small stack of books next to a plain, metal cot with a straw mattress and one blanket.

"Here's your bed, boy. There's some picture books in the corner. You can get rainwater from the cistern at the end of the hall. It gets piped down from the roof. Or, if you like, you can carry water up from the barn. No matter. Use the pitcher and bowl in the cupboard to wash up. Throw your wash water out the window. You won't hit nobody. It's just coal down there. If you want to take a bath or scrub your clothes, there's a washtub at the bottom of the stairs and troughs in the horse barn. Use the privy outside the barn. It's for the workers. You will find a chamber pot under the bed. It will save you a walk to the privy in the dark of night. You'll appreciate that more, come winter. You following me on all this, boy?"

"Yes, Sir."

Big Jake stepped to the table and picked up the knife opening one of the two blades. He examined it, felt the edge, and closed it again. He opened the second blade to find it broken off halfway from the tip.

"Here, boy. You might as well have this. The other boy don't have no use for it no more."

"Thank you, sir. Where's the boy who left it here?"

Jake Riggens was silent for a moment. Then, "He don't work here no more. He didn't do a good enough job and now he don't work here. He was a good boy, a real good boy, but not a good enough worker, that's all. No more questions about him. Come with me."

They walked down the hallway. Jake opened a closet door revealing several brooms, a dustpan, mop and bucket, and a wooden box containing cleaning rags. A dozen Fels-Naptha soap cakes were neatly stacked on the top shelf. Two feather dusters lay on the second shelf.

"These are the tools of your trade, boy," said Jake. "You'll use these to keep all the halls, stairways, and rooms clean, mornin', noon, and night. There's a push broom for the sidewalks. When you're low on supplies, see me. Don't bother anyone else. Clean every room every day, including yours," he said. "Now about the clerks' office, Tor. They work from seven in the morning till six at night. You are not to enter their office while they are working. Never. You'll have to clean the clerks' office after supper. And, Tor, this is important—do not ever go into Mr. DeWilde's office unless you are told. Mrs. Ostralder cleans it

13

for him. You stay out. If you see Mr. DeWilde, don't speak unless spoken to. Never. He don't need to be bothered. Now, come this way."

At the end of the hallway they descended a narrow stairway taking them out to the yard. Again, the acrid stench from the slaughterhouses, mixed with the odor of coal smoke, cut Tor's nostrils. "The smell of fortunes being made," he remembered.

A long line of empty coal wagons led to a series of four-story, concrete coal storage silos. The teamsters, wet from the weather and black from the dust of earlier loadings, directed their horse teams toward the bottom of the silos. There, four wagons could be filled simultaneously. At each loading dock, a coal-blackened worker controlled a long, slender, metal chute. As the sturdy wagons entered each coal dock, this man would pull on the shorter of two chains to direct the coal chute over the wagon. Then, pulling the long chain, he would open the chute's top gate. Both the teamster and the fill men would cover their noses with rags as coal and billows of black dust spewed from the chute.

Tor watched as one of these wagons was filled beyond the top rails in a matter of seconds. The chain was slacked off, the coal stopped, the teamster gave a *giddup,* and the coal-blackened team of four workhorses pulled the heavy wagon forward. A *whoa* from the teamster stopped them.

Two men, one on each side of the wagon, lowered a screed board onto the wagon rails and leveled the load. The excess coal fell to the black concrete. As the teamster drove toward the gate, the two men used wide shovels to clear the area for the next wagon.

Above and across the yard, a narrow gauge steam locomotive labored to pull a procession of small, stout coal cars up an incline toward the top of the coal silos. Another train of empty cars was working its way down the grade on the other side of the yard, having unloaded its cargo. Beyond and below, a larger railroad track disappeared behind one of four gigantic piles of coal. Men with shovels kept the loading dock clear of excess coal. Another man watched over it all, occasionally using his shovel to clear a small amount of spilled coal.

Big Jake Riggens escorted Tor to the loading crew foreman, shouting above the noise of the steam engine, "Wadalski—Wadalski! This is your new clean-out boy. Name's Tor Loken. From the boys' home down on LaSalle."

"Iss kinda tall, but he'll have ta do," yelled the foreman. "Iss dis pup got da goods?"

"DeWilde picked him out himself. Says he's strong and plenty smart, Wadalski. Smarter than most, I'd say. You just take good care of him. You don't want DeWilde to call you in. You don't want that, Wadalski,"

"You listen here. Iss not me vaht says how da cards play out, Riggens. Dat last boy's fate vas on you, not me, in spite vaht you say. You iss to blame!"

Big Jake shouted back, "It happened on your watch, Wadalski. These things always happen on your watch and you know it."

Instantly, the foreman's nostrils flared and he swung his coal shovel toward Big Jake's head. The security man's nightstick left his side and flashed

14

through the air, deflecting the shovel. In another fluid movement, the nightstick caught the foreman in the chin, knocking him to the ground. Riggens pointed the stick at Wadalski's face as he stepped on the fallen man's right wrist, pinning it to the ground.

"A fool's move that was, Wadalski, a fool's move. I could get you sacked for that! But I'll do you a favor. I'll keep you and your family out of the poorhouse this time 'round, but I won't forget this, Wadalski. You dasn't test me again. And, mister, you owe me now. You and your missus and your young'uns owe me big for not reportin' this. By rights you should be gettin' your walkin' papers." He leaned forward putting more weight on the fallen man's wrist. The foreman grimaced but made no sound. "Now you damn well best keep this boy safe and sound and whistlin' cheery tunes, Wadalski. I want to hear him whistlin' cheery tunes every mornin' from his pigeon-roost up there. Every mornin'. Say it, Wadalski. Say I'll be hearin' Tor whistle a cheery tune every mornin'." Big Jake thrust the nightstick closer to the foreman's face.

"Ya, ya, every mornin', Riggens."

Work stopped in the yard as the teamsters, loaders, screed men and shovelers looked on. Big Jake shot a glance around the yard and all returned to their work, many with wide grins after seeing their supervisor put in his place. Jake turned away and walked toward the horse barn as the yard foreman came to his feet and made a futile attempt to brush some of the wet coal grime from his overalls. He stared briefly at Tor, then picked up his shovel and went back to his work.

Tor had watched and listened intently. Things he had heard and observed at the orphanage, in DeWilde's office, in his new room, and now, near the coal docks told him something was wrong. This fight disturbed him, as did the words that came before and after the blows. And the broken knife in his pocket—where was the boy who owned it before? What happened to him?

"What have I gotten myself into? What am I gonna do?"

15

Chapter 4
The Place of the Sturgeon

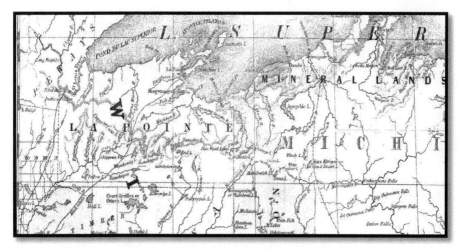

It had been thirteen days since the chief left Sault Ste. Marie and those disturbing visions. That terrible dream of his dear friends trapped in their burning home haunted him, as did the image of being in chains before the gallows. Paddling westward along the south shore of Gitchee Gumi, he steadily distanced himself from the nightmare.

He found his way to LaPointe on the island named by the French as Magdalene, then, later changed to Madeline. The weary traveler was welcomed into the lodge of one of the elders. The weather had turned cold and the warm fire felt good. A late fall storm had blown in. Snow squalls danced across Chequamegon Bay from the small settlement called Bayport to the Apostle Islands and beyond.

His host, Old Bear, told many stories about this western corner of Lake Superior. Many French fur traders had come and gone. Many of his people provided beaver pelts and other furs for the French and later for the English. But the beaver were almost gone now, having been all but trapped out and their hides shipped to Europe where they were made into top hats for gentlemen.

Old Bear wore his gray hair in a single long braid. His shirt and pants were made from the hide of a moose. Around his neck hung a string of bear teeth and a shiny, diamond-shaped silver ornament. The two men shared tobacco. Old Bear told the chief of a nearby lake teaming with fish and wild game and surrounded by dark forests of tall white pine.

"This lake has many sturgeon," said Old Bear, "and muskellunge and other fishes. There are small streams that bring water to the lake and a fast river leaving it. This river will take you through the waters we know as Pac-wa-wong. There you will find plenty of menoomin and a small village of our Ojibwe

16

brothers. You will find many friends there, and, though it is past time to harvest rice now, my friends at Pac-wa-wong will give you rice for the winter. If you travel south, you will come to what the French call Lac Courte Oreilles, a large Ojibwe village. Speak my name and you will be welcome."

"The lake you spoke of, what do you call it?"

"Namakagon," replied Old Bear, "the place of the sturgeon."

Snow, wind, and rain continued through the night. By noon the sun shone brightly against a cold, blue sky. A stiff, north wind helped push their canoes southward across Chequamegon Bay. The chief and Old Bear and two of Old Bear's dogs, worked their way up a stream. They portaged, paddled, and portaged again. At sundown, with only hours to go, they chose to complete their journey to the lake rather than make camp along the way.

"My lodge waits for us there," said Old Bear. "It will be dark before we rest, but inside it will be warm and dry through the night."

Canoes overhead and dogs in the lead, they continued on the trail, a trail deeply worn by the feet of countless thousands of travelers who had crossed it for centuries. As the first stars appeared, the chief gazed at the heavens. Two bright stars stood out against the darkening, blue sky.

"Two stars," said the chief, recalling his vision. "Wenebojo told me to watch for these, but I did not know if I was being fooled or if he was showing me the way."

"Wenebojo, yes. You never know with him."

"You have seen his tricks?"

"Oh, yes, yes. Many times he has played his games on Chequamegon Bay and in our forests and streams. Let us hope he is not watching us now, waiting to play his pranks."

The air grew colder. Old Bear and the chief slid their canoes into the waters of Lake Namakagon as a half-moon appeared above the eastern shore. The dogs jumped into Old Bear's canoe. The men paddled across a bay and down a channel to the main body of the lake. Now, as they crossed the still, black waters, they passed a small island and soon came ashore on a long, wide beach. Both dogs jumped from the canoe.

The moon illuminated a small, birch lodge beneath the sheltering limbs of large white pines. The travelers, fatigued from their trek, pulled their canoes onto the beach. Turning back toward the lake, the chief saw another island. Reflected in the mirror-like waters, now, were thousands of bright stars.

"Old Bear, look," he said pointing down at the lake's glass-like surface. "Two shining stars in a sparkling sky, and I among them. These islands are the two shining stars in the sparkling sky of the lake. This was my vision. This is the place I shall call home."

"Yes," said Old Bear. "I have long known this water would one day be the home of a chief from far away. This will be a good place for you. My lodge will keep you warm and dry through the winter. The lake, the forest will give you plenty of food and wood for your fire. This will be a good home."

17

"Yes, Old Bear, this *will* be a good home."

"Then you must take the name of this lake. All will know you as Chief Namakagon."

"Namakagon," said the chief. "Namakagon. It is a good name. Yes. This is the place I will make my home. And I shall take the name Namakagon."

Soon, a fire warmed the lodge, and the travelers shared smoked venison and many stories. Then, flanked by the dogs, they curled up under their robes, sleeping soundly.

The next afternoon, hoping to fill the need for winter venison, Old Bear and Chief Namakagon traveled north to a place where two swamps merged. The chief concealed himself near a deeply carved deer trail. The wind was in his face. Far behind, well out of sight, Old Bear softly grunted into a birch bark call, mimicking the sounds of a rutting buck. Old Bear called, waited, called again. The old hunter broke a dead branch from a nearby pine. Hiding between balsams, he scraped the branch against an oak, mimicking the sound of a buck marking a tree with his antlers. He grunted again, then waited in silence.

Chief Namakagon saw something move far down the trail. It vanished into the brush and boughs of evergreens. Old Bear grunted softly again and up the trail came a fine buck, head down and ears back in a posture of challenge. As the deer passed behind a large pine, Namakagon raised his bow, drawing the arrow. When the buck was no more than six steps away, Namakagon released.

The feathered, cedar shaft flashed through the air, then through the deer's heavy chest, planting itself deep in a spruce on the far side of the trail. The buck spun and vanished beyond the balsams.

Namakagon knelt, whispering words of thanks to the Earth Mother before tracking his quarry. Soon the dressed buck was hanging near the lodge.

"Tomorrow I return to LaPointe," said Old Bear as the men prepared their dinner.

Chief Namakagon skewered a piece of tenderloin with his knife and held it over the small fire. "I don't know how to repay you, my friend. You have given me a wonderful gift by leading me here. I will forever be in your debt."

"No," said Old Bear, "you owe me nothing. I have long known you would come. This lodge is my gift to you. I have enjoyed much time here, but I am old and will not see this lake again. You will live here in my place. My time has passed. It is your time now."

"Old Bear, you have many seasons left."

"No. You are wrong. I have seen in my dreams that I will not enjoy the warm days of summer again."

The two friends sat in silence before Old Bear spoke again. "Namakagon, my people, those who came here long before us, had another gift from this land." He removed a small buckskin pouch from his belt and shook a piece of glittering metal into Namakagon's hand.

"For many, many years, my people used this metal for decorations. When the French and the English saw it, they wanted us to trade it for their

18

goods. They called it silver and tried their best to learn where it came from. But Gitchee Manitou told us to not share it with them. He said they would take it all away and scar the land. I am the last to know where it is found. I must pass this knowledge to you."

"But, why should I be told of this place?"

"Namakagon, my dreams told me you would come and you would choose to live on this lake. My visions told me you would keep sacred the knowledge of our gifts from Mother Earth. My friend, I do not wish to burden you with this great responsibility, but the spirits have talked to me. We have no say in this. Tomorrow, before we part, I will show you the way to this place where we find silver."

"Old Bear, you have bestowed upon me the gift of this home. You have graced me with your friendship. And now, you have honored me with your trust. I will protect these with all my heart, as I do all gifts from Mother Earth."

The following morning, Old Bear and Namakagon canoed north, far up a narrow stream until brush and windfalls blocked their way. They portaged to a small lake, crossed it, and portaged again, this time skirting a pond. There, they left their canoes and crossed another creek. The terrain was changing. Steep ridges with rocky outcroppings now framed the narrow trail.

"We are near," said Old Bear. "Come," he said, leading away from the creek and up a narrow gorge. An eagle flew just above the trees along the trail. They continued up the gorge. "The eagle guides us, Namakagon." Tall white pines stood as sentinels above them. Deep in the pines they saw a large bear. It stood, watching them as they moved down the trail, a white, diamond-shaped blaze on its chest.

"Look," said Namakagon, "the makwaa carries the same sign as you, my friend—the shape of a diamond, there on his chest. Were I superstitious, I would say this might be the work of Wenebojo."

The old man grinned as the bear ambled off. "This is the place."

The chief looked, but saw no silver, no cave, nothing unusual. Old Bear pushed aside the branches of a small balsam tree to reveal a large, knee-high flat rock with an opening under it. He knelt, raised his hands to the rock face, and whispered a prayer. The old man then dropped to his belly and wiggled through the small opening. Chief Namakagon followed.

Slowly, the dark interior of the cave began to take form. Old Bear used a flint and steel to ignite some tinder and birch bark he carried. Each time he struck the steel and flint, light from the spark bounced off the cave walls, reflecting countless veins of metal. The spark finally took. The tinder began to glow. Old Bear blew life into the coals and the birch bark flamed brightly.

Namakagon looked into the tall, narrow cavern. Light from the flame reached far into the cave, reflecting off more and more metal protruding from the walls. He reached above his head, grasped a piece of the silver and, bending it back and forth, broke it off. He scraped it with his knife, then rubbed it on his deerskin-clad thigh. It glittered and glistened when Namakagon held it near the flame. He stared far into the cave to see more and more silver.

"This is a wonderful gift from Gitchee Manitou," said Old Bear. "You see why it must be protected."

"Yes. This secret must be kept. Count on me, Old Bear."

Outside the cave again, the two men made their way back to the creek and Namakagon's canoe where they said their farewells.

"Take this, it is yours now," said Old Bear as he removed the diamond-shaped silver ornament from his shirt. The old man lifted his canoe over his head and started up the north trail toward Lake Superior. His dogs sat by Namakagon's feet.

"Old Bear, wait. Your dogs!" shouted the chief.

The old man stopped. Without turning, he said, "I raised them for you, my friend. They are your dogs now. You will need them to pull your sled, find your game, make you smile. Watch over them. They are good companions."

Moments later, Old Bear disappeared beyond a bend in the trail.

Chief Namakagon returned to his new home on the shore of the lake that provided his new name.

The sun was low in the sky as he came ashore and carried his canoe over the sand onto the grassy forest floor. His dogs followed him into his lodge.

The chief removed one of the buckskin pouches from his belt. He opened it, pulling out the long, slender piece of silver. Namakagon bent it into an oval shape, polished it, and then placed it on his wrist. He squeezed it together, forming a wristband, then studied it, turning his hand from palm down to palm up and back again.

This sole resident of the lake stepped out of the birch lodge. His two dogs ran down to the sun-warmed beach, freshly decorated with bright autumn leaves. Far out in the bay, the late afternoon sunlight sparkled off gentle waves.

He wondered if he would see his friend, Old Bear, again in this life.

Namakagon's thoughts then drifted to his former homes and the people he left. They, too, were friends he might never again meet in this life. He gazed at the small island to the west, realizing the visions sent to him by Wenebojo, along with the prophecies of Old Bear, meant he, Chief Namakagon, had much more to do with his life. He knew, too, Lake Namakagon was where he was meant to be.

Chapter 5
The New Clean-out Boy

Emil Wadalski, yard foreman, placed a thumb and ring finger to his lips and gave out a piercing whistle. Every worker in the yard looked his way.

"Tor Loken!" he shouted. "C'mere! Make haste!"

"Yessir," shouted Tor, running full speed to the foreman.

Wadalski leaned his shovel against the wall and waved off the coal chute tender who let go of the chains and stood by. The teamster held his wagon steady. Foreman Wadalski pulled on the short chain to position the chute, then gave a sharp tug on the long chain. As a half-ton of coal dropped into the wagon, black dust billowed up, filling the air. He then directed the chute toward the rear of the wagon and dropped another half-ton of coal. Tor pulled his shirt up over his mouth and nose.

"See dat, boy?" Wadalski said. "Dat's how it should verk. And it does, mosta time. But, once in blue moon, da chute she jams up. Ven dat happens, only fix iss boy shinnyin' up da chute and clearin' da jam. Dat's vy you iss here. Tink you can do dat, boy? Tink you can shinny up to da toppa dat chute?"

Tor looked up. Twenty feet from bottom to top and many tons of coal resting above, waiting to fall, able to crush anything in its way.

"I asked you question, boy! Can you climb up dere?"

"Yessir, I believe I can. But what if the chute opens?"

"You don't need virry. Once you up dere, your job iss only to clear out coal stuck in gate. Da gate von't open by self. It takes pull on chain. Ain't nobody pullin' chain till you clear outa da vay. See? Now give it try. You climb up chute. You touch gate. I hold steady."

Tor took off his dust-covered shirt and shoes. He hopped into the wagon, ducked under the open chute and entered headfirst, pressing his hands and bare feet against one side of the chute and his back against the other. He climbed the twenty feet to the top in less than a minute, touched the gate and slid back down again, dropping out of the bottom.

"Vaht's a matta, boy?" said the foreman. "Couldn't make it? Iss too much fer ya?"

"No, Sir," replied Tor as he reached for his shirt and shoes. "I got to the top, touched the gate, and slid down again, Sir."

"Ya? Vel den, I'd say ve have new clean-out boy. You listen for my vistle, boy. Ven you hear it, come a-runnin'. You'll be helpin' ta keep da line movin' and da coal delivered on time."

In the horse barn, Tor found a washtub, set his shoes and shirt aside, and filled the tub half full from a hydrant near the stalls. He stepped into the ice-cold water, scrubbing at the stubborn black of the coal before drying off, using a horse blanket for a towel.

Tor crossed the yard, climbed the stairway, and returned to his room. With shirt and pants hanging on the wall pegs, he wrapped himself in his blanket. He sat on the bed wondering about his new life. Sure, the LaSalle Street Boys' Orphanage was not where he wanted to stay. The boys worked from dawn to dusk every day. The food was always the same and never very good. Here, at the coal yard, he had his own room but no friends. Here he had an important job to do. Was it too dangerous? And what happened to the last boy? Why were Big Jake, Foreman Wadalski, and Mr. DeWilde not willing to speak of him?

With the sounds of horse-drawn wagons moving through the coal yard in the background, Tor's thoughts strayed back to New York, to his mother. How excited they had been to be on their way to Wisconsin to join his father who left four years before. He struggled to remember what his father looked like. Although Tor had a few clear recollections, like his deep voice and strong bear hugs, other memories of his father were hazy. He could picture his mother with ease, right down to her long hair, bright smile, and the blue calico dress she wore on the train. But memories of his father had faded.

The roar of coal dropping into a wagon jerked Tor's thoughts back to Foreman Wadalski. How long would it be before he heard that shrill, piercing whistle of his? And what could, what would it bring?

As time went on, Tor fell into his work routine with ease. Occasionally, Big Jake Riggens would check up on him. One day Jake brought him a new shirt, britches, and leather work-boots.

"Can't have you lookin' like you ran away from some Chicago orphanage," laughed Big Jake as he piled the clothes and boots onto Tor's outstretched arms. "You take good care of these, Son. They're store-bought. They will have to last you a long while."

"Yes Sir, Mr. Riggens. Oh, thank you. Thank you! I will keep them neat and clean, Sir."

"I bet you will, Tor. I believe these will be among the few clean clothes ever found in this dust-laden coal yard. You and me and the clerks and Mr. DeWilde will be the only ones fit to appear in public." Big Jake laughed as he walked back down the stairs. Tor was eighteen days in his new home and job at the Chicago River Fuel and Dray when he heard the loud whistle from the lips of Foreman Wadalski. Leaning his mop against the wall and moving the bucket out of the way, Tor raced up the stairway, down the hall, and into his room, stripping off his shirt as he ran. Within seconds he was in his old britches and out the door.

Tor dashed across the yard. Three workers and Emil Wadalski surrounded chute number three.

"You need me, Mr. Foreman? Was that whistle for me?"

Wadalski turned, saying, "Ve got jam, boy. Dis iss good chance to earn yer keep. Git up dere and save da day, boy. I steady chute. You clean out good."

Before the words were out of his foreman's mouth, Tor Loken was into the bottom of the tube and on his way up. Again he pressed his bare feet and hands against the inside of the cylindrical tube, bracing his back against the

22

wall behind him. He quickly worked his way to the top, finding it blocked by a large chunk of coal. In the blackness above him, he felt for something to grip. A second wedge-shaped piece was tightly trapped between the large piece and the protruding head of a steel bolt. Tor pushed and pulled but nothing moved. As cramped as the space was, he was able to pull out his pocketknife. Tor worked the stub of the broken blade between the two coal pieces. Wiggling it, he noticed a slight movement in the larger piece of coal. Moving the knife with one hand and pulling with the other, he forced both pieces to shift. Then gravity took over. The coal fell, striking him in the face and shoulders. Tor lost his grip and slid down the chute and into the bed of the wagon, coal chunks and dust following him. Wadalski grabbed his arm and pulled him clear just as several more large pieces of coal fell.

"Vell done, boy. Vell done!" shouted Wadalski. "You got jam cleaned out. Ve're back in business, boys," he shouted to the teamsters and tenders men. "Da boy saved da day!"

It took Tor a few moments to collect his wits and realize what had happened. He was black from head to toe and had coal dust in his eyes, ears, nose, hair and pockets. Wadalski handed him a rag to wipe his eyes.

Tor turned to leave and then turned back. "My knife," he shouted. "Where's my knife?"

Wadalski used his shovel to search. Tor spotted the knife, blade still open, and snatched it up.

"Dere's knife, boy. Now off mit ya to da horse trough. Youse look like wharf rat at midnight."

Tor folded in the blade, slid the knife into his pocket, and left. Now he knew what this job was all about and how dangerous it could be. He saw how one pull on the long chain could drop a thousand pounds of coal chunks into a wagon. He knew if the gate opened at the wrong time, he would be dashed twenty feet to the wagon below and buried.

Tor entered the horse barn, filled the washtub, and, grabbing a small chunk of soap he had placed there earlier, began scrubbing up when he heard Big Jake Riggens' voice.

"You all right, Tor?"

"Yes, Sir, Mr. Riggens. I didn't think I could break the coal free. Next thing you know I'm flat on my back and black as molasses. But I got the jam cleared out, Mr. Riggens."

"Good for you, Tor. Good for you. Mr. DeWilde will be proud of you boy, and so am I. You told us you'd do your best and, by golly, you held true to your word. Good for you, Tor Loken."

"Mr. Riggens, I would like to know about the boy I replaced. What happened to him?"

Big Jake Riggens was silent.

Tor pressed. "Mr. Riggens?"

"There was an accident, Tor. I will say no more. There was an accident and we needed someone to do his job. We needed someone like you, Tor. That's why you are here and he is not. That's all I can say about it. It's all you need to know."

Big Jake left the barn. Tor returned to his room to change clothes. He resumed his cleaning chores, hoping not to hear the sound of Foreman Wadalski's piercing whistle.

Two days later, first thing in the morning, the shrill whistle cut the air. Within two minutes, Tor entered chute number one. As the foreman steadied the chute, Tor reached the top and felt around for the cause of the obstruction. Again several large coal chunks were wedged in tightly and held fast behind a protruding bolt head. All it took was a pull on one chunk and the jam was freed. This time Tor was ready. He protected his face and pushed the black chunks past him to the wagon below. He then slid down and into the blinding sunshine.

"Good virk, Tor," the Foreman said, handing him the rag. "Now off mit ya, boy. Keep an ear out fer me vistle."

No more coal jammed in the chutes during in next three weeks. Dry weather came to Chicago and the coal was more cooperative in the lower humidity. Later, after some rainy weather came in, Tor cleared three more jams within two days. This last steamer of coal, he learned, was an inferior quality with many large chunks in each load. He heard the men talking. They said Mr. DeWilde was angry about this and the supplier would suffer for the mistake. Tor had no trouble clearing the jams.

Early one morning, Tor, wearing his freshly washed clothes, waited by the front door to the office with a broom and dustpan in hand. He had a plan.

As Ignatius DeWilde stepped out of his private cab, he said, "Why, Tor, good to see you. I am told you are doing a good job for us, a good job, indeed."

"Thank you, Sir," replied Tor. "Sir? I know I'm not supposed to be a bother, but I think I know how to make the loading go better."

"Better? Well you don't say! Just how would you go about that, boy?"

"Well, Sir, I've been at the top of every one of your loading chutes. Each time, I find the coal chunks are not just jammed up with each other, but they are also getting caught on the heads of the bolts holding the chutes to the collar."

"Bolts?"

"Yes, Sir. There are six bolt heads sticking out far enough to catch the coal as it goes by. I think I have the answer, Sir."

"And what might that be?"

"It's right here, Sir," he said, pointing to the running board of DeWilde's coach. "See these bolt heads here? These bolts are rounded off so they don't catch on anything, so you don't trip or tear the cuffs on your britches. You could put bolts like these in place of the others, and the coal won't catch as it goes flyin' by. I know it will work, Sir. I've been up in those chutes and I've seen the coal hung up on those square bolt heads. I just know it will work, Sir."

"Well, boy, it is good to see you're trying to improve our system. I'll tell you what I will do. I will ask our shop foreman to look into it. Maybe it can't hurt to try out this idea of yours."

Tor grinned. "I know it'll help, Sir. I just know it!"

"We will see, boy," said DeWilde as the coach pulled away.

At the end of the day, Tor noticed workers removing chute number one. He sat at his table, eating his supper, watching the men through the window. Later, in the twilight, he could see the chute being reassembled.

A month later, and after seven jams in the other chutes, Big Jake Riggens said DeWilde ordered all coal chutes fitted with carriage bolts. Tor's idea worked. Chute one had not jammed since being refitted with round-headed bolts. The change would be made on Sunday, the only day of the week when the yard closed. Tor was anxious, hoping the carriage bolts would end the jamming problem and spare him from more trips up those dangerous cylinders.

Saturday afternoon, Tor heard Wadalski's shrill whistle. He was ready to climb in minutes. Wadalski steadied the chute. Tor climbed to the top.

This jam was different. In the total blackness he could feel two large coal chunks wedged against each other and the bolt heads. Tor worked to loosen them but couldn't. He reached for his knife, but, in his haste, had left it in his new britches. He probed with his fingers for any handhold on the coal.

"C'mon, boy. Ve need dis chute virkin'," shouted Wadalski. "Open 'er up, boy."

"I can't get a grip. I can't get hold of it." Tor scratched and pulled as best he could but couldn't manage to move the coal.

"Let's go mit you. Clean 'er out, boy! Vaht's da matta mit ya? Let's go!" yelled the foreman.

Tor dug the nails of his left hand into one of the coal pieces, noticing slight movement.

"Tor! Ve got vagons to load! Vat ya doin' up dere? Let's go! Clean 'er out, boy! Vat's takin' so long?"

Tor slowly loosened the piece. Growing angrier, Wadalski tried shaking the tube from his position on the ground. It shook and swayed, making Tor's work harder. As the foreman shook, the long gate chain swung out and wrapped around the side of the chute.

One violent shake later, the chain swung around again. Its momentum caused a wave in the chain. The wave rose to the top. S*nap,* the gate opened just as the jam came free.

Tor felt the force of the coal as the gate hit him in the side of the face. Like a ball from a cannon, he was thrust down the length of the chute. He slammed into the wagon. A load of coal followed, pinning him to the bed. Buried, he tried to breathe. The weight of the coal on his chest would not let him. He heard the sound of a shovel. He tried to move his arms, legs, and head.

He couldn't. Now he heard two shovels as they slashed into the half ton of coal. Closer and closer they came. Tor suddenly felt a sharp pain in his side as a shovel sliced into him.

"Here," shouted Wadalski. "Dig here."

By now, four men were frantically clearing away the coal. One reached into the pile near where Wadalski's shovel struck Tor. He grasped the boy's arm. Another man found an ankle. Between them, they pulled the boy free. All four workers carried him from the coal pile, laying him on the ground.

"Water. Get some water!" screamed a workman.

Tor gasped for air and spit coal dust onto the ground. He tried to stand but the pain in his side from the shovel wouldn't let him. He looked up at the men who had pulled him out.

"Thank you," whispered Tor, mustering his loudest voice.

"Don't talk now," said one of the workers. "Here, drink some water. Wash that coal dust down."

Tor took a big gulp of water but didn't swallow. He spit it out along with coal and coal dust. He closed his eyes as he felt a wet rag wiping his face and neck. Tor then drank a sip of water as the man with the wet rag wiped the cut made by Wadalski's shovel. Wincing with pain, Tor pulled away.

"Not too deep. Should heal," he heard someone say.

Sitting up, Tor looked back at the wagon, the scattered pile of coal, and Foreman Wadalski, apparently unconcerned with what had happened. He struggled to his feet, then, feeling the gash in his side, collapsed. Dazed, Tor looked up to see Big Jake Riggins.

"Tor, you all right?"

"Me? Oh, uh, I'll be fine. I better wash up. Mr. Riggens, one more day and we won't see another jam. One more day."

"Sylas, Cal," said Riggins, "you get the boy over to the barn. We'll have Doc Williams look him over, get that cut stitched up."

As the two men helped him cross the yard, Tor looked back to see Big Jake Riggens confront Emil Wadalski. He couldn't hear the words exchanged, but he could tell Jake was not pleased. As he watched, Wadalski's shovel suddenly swung toward Riggens. Just as on the boy's first day in the yard, Big Jake's club streaked through the air. This time, though, it caught the loading dock foreman solidly across the face. Teeth flew into the air and the shovel fell harmlessly to the ground with a clatter, Wadalski following.

"Calvin, I will wager you a week's wages we'll have a new foreman by Monday morning," said one of the men.

"No bet, Sy. No bet."

Chapter 6
The Great Makwaa

A thin, white wisp of smoke ascended straight into the cold, blue October, 1831, sky. It came from the campfire at Chief Namakagon's lodge.

Slabs of venison hung high above the fire. The smoke would preserve the meat for winter. Stretched over willow frames, two large deer hides hung in the white pine branches overhead, well out of reach of Namakagon's dogs.

The chief had soaked the deer hides in a mix of salt, water, wood ash, and crushed acorns. He had scraped the hair from each hide. Now they would be smoked. During the cold winter nights ahead, the hides would be removed from their frames and softened by working in suet from the same deer. From these hides he would make a new shirt and moccasins, among other necessities.

Today, after tending to his dogs, he would hunt.

"For breakfast, my friends, you will feast on fresh venison." He placed a birch basket of scraps before them. "Fill your stomachs, then spend your day guarding these hides. Keep the ravens away. In trade, I will hunt for more food to keep you fat and happy through the winter." The dogs sat at attention until a wave of his hand sent them to their food. The hunter set out for the woods.

Later that day, Chief Namakagon, bow in hand, followed the tracks of a large bear through a dark cedar swamp. He had seen the bear from his canoe two days before, high on a ridge south of the lake. He hiked up the ridge. The sign left by the bruin was evidence he was feeding on fallen acorns. The bear would be spending these cold, November nights in its den, unlike earlier months when he slept in the open. The hunter needed to find that den.

The sign also told the chief this was a heavy bear. He left a good trail. It took the chief across a small stream, then through a stand of birch. Namakagon looked beyond the bare branches overhead. The sun was high. He had about six hours of daylight left. The bear's trail rambled down the ridge, entering another swamp. Namakagon found the tracks were fresh and the trail well-worn. The bear's den was near.

"Where do you rest, my big friend?" whispered Namakagon. "How far will you lead me from my warm lodge?"

As the trail entered the swamp, balsams became so thick the chief could see only an arm's length ahead. Slowly, stealthily, he followed the bear, each step carefully chosen. Reaching down, he pulled a handful of moss from the forest floor, stuffing it into his quiver to prevent the cedar shafts from announcing his approach. Silently, he followed the large tracks, and step-by-step they took him deeper and deeper into the dark balsam swamp. "Where, great makwaa, are you taking me?" the hunter whispered.

Broken ice now showed the way. Namakagon followed, the icy water coming up to his knees. The sign soon left the swamp, entering a stand of tall white pines. Looking far ahead, the chief saw a single, giant pine leaning against another, likely the result of a severe windstorm, he thought. Its roots were half-torn from the earth, forming a large mound of wood, moss and soil. From fifty steps away, Namakagon could see the bear's trail disappear under those roots. He had found the bear's winter den.

"Makwaa, you have taken me far into this forest," he whispered, "but now, if Gitchee Manitou allows, I might have you. Yes, you and I shall meet."

But the slight breeze from the southwest was not in his favor. Although he was sure the bear lay in his den, the hunter turned and quietly walked away. He would wait for a better time.

The hunter explored the ridges to the east, finding a longer but drier route back to the lake. The sweet aroma of fall filled the crisp, clean air as he returned to the small bay where he had left his canoe. Strong, steady strokes from Namakagon's paddle soon brought him to his lodge.

Chief Namakagon rose before dawn. He stepped from his birch lodge to find the air cold and the sky ablaze with northern lights drifting in brightly colored waves above the night-blackened lake. They filled the sky above his camp, drifting and dancing so close he felt they almost reached the tops of the pines surrounding his lodge. To the south, the stars were bright.

"Makwaa, did you stay in your den tonight? Are you lying there, staring up at these beautiful heavens the spirits have painted for us? Or have you taken another trip to the oaks to fill your belly with acorns before the snows?" His dogs stared at him, looking confused. He stood in silence and in awe of the brilliant colors floating above him. "There is only one way for me to know, makwaa." He reached for his bow and quiver.

Namakagon placed four thin, green, maple logs on the glowing embers of the fire outside his lodge. "My friends" he said to his dogs, "this will keep the smoke flowing across our venison until I return. I need you two to keep the crows and ravens away for one more day."

He walked down to the shore to find twenty feet of ice ringing the lake. The hunter stepped one foot into the canoe and grasped the gunnels tightly. With the other foot, he gave a good push, sliding across ice that cracked, snapped, and yielded under the weight of his craft. A push on his paddle and he drifted into quiet water. With one stroke he turned the canoe. Namakagon looked back toward the eastern sky to see the faintest glow of early morning light. He paddled south and soon stepped again onto the shore of the quiet bay.

Up the ridge, through the forest, and toward the distant white pine stand he trekked in the pre-dawn light. When he approached the leaning white pine, he silently moved parallel to the trail until nearing the balsams where he had stood the day before. Namakagon leaned his bow against one of small trees and pulled his knife from its sheath. He cut two short balsams, placing them in front of him to form a blind. Next, he picked up a dead pine branch from the forest floor. The hunter walked the nine steps from his blind to the bear trail, taking care not to step on the trail. The northern lights faded now, chased by the increasing glow in the eastern sky.

"I will give your tongue a special pleasure, great makwaa," the hunter whispered. He pulled a piece of venison tallow from the small buckskin pouch he carried over his shoulder and attached the tallow to the pine branch, then reached high, hanging the baited branch above the trail.

An owl called from a nearby pine.

"Not for you, Owl," he whispered, "nor your enemy, the raven."

Back in his blind Namakagon chose the straightest of the seven arrows in his quiver. He knelt on one knee with his bow in his left hand, the arrow lying across a balsam branch in front of him. He reached down to confirm his knife was in place, ready to be drawn quickly. Then, he waited.

The soft morning light brought songs from the birds. A red squirrel came from its nighttime hiding place, scurrying up one of the giant pines and onto a limb. The quiet of the morning was broken by its chattering.

"Little squirrel," Namakagon whispered, "are you trying to alert your neighbor, the big makwaa? Bizaan! Bizaan! "Leave, little red squirrel—or are you really Wenebojo in one of your clever disguises?"

Soon other red squirrels replied from other distant pine limbs. "Now you have done it, red squirrel. You *must* be Wenebojo. You have awakened the whole forest!" A pair of blue jays added their screechy calls to the scolding chatters of the squirrel above him.

An eagle flew above the treetops, heading for the lake to find a fish for its morning meal. Crows, angry to see the eagle so near, cried out warning calls. The woods came alive with the sounds and sights of animals beginning another day. Surrounded by all this noise, Namakagon waited silently as frost formed all around him.

"Where are you, Makwaa?" he whispered. "This cold morning air urges me to move along. How long I can kneel here before I must take its advice?"

Namakagon heard something coming down the trail. He reached for the cedar shaft on the balsam branch before him, fixing the arrow's nock onto the bowstring. Shifting his weight slightly, he readied for the shot. A slight breeze drifted up from the swamp below. From under the balsams came a large fisher. It loped down the trail, stopping only to inspect leaves, twigs, and old animal tracks left behind. Namakagon relaxed.

"You there, Ojiig!" he wanted to shout. "Go away! This is no time to linger here."

When the fisher neared the branch holding the tallow, it stopped to sniff the air, then sat back on its rump and stretched, seeking out the source of the scent. Its eyes locked on the bait.

"Ojiig, go now! This small feast is not meant for you."

The fisher crouched, paused, then sprang high into the air, almost reaching the tallow. It landed on all fours and looked back at the prize. Again the fisher crouched low to the ground, as if it were winding a great internal spring. Up it flew, again almost achieving its goal.

"Leave, rascal, before you spoil my hunt!" Namakagon felt like shouting. He contemplated sending an arrow toward the animal to scare it away.

The fisher gave up its attempt to reach the delicious smelling prize by jumping. It now circled the trunk of a nearby pine. Digging its claws into the rough bark, the agile animal climbed. Chief Namakagon watched as the fisher, now in the wrong tree, looked below at its breakfast. The ojiig hung on the side of the tree for a long moment. Suddenly, it sprang through the air, missing the bait by several feet and tumbling across the forest floor.

Namakagon could not contain his laughter. The fisher heard him and stood on his haunches, looking for the source of the slight noise. It sniffed the leaves and thick bed of pine needles on the forest floor. When his nose met the spot where Namakagon's moccasin had touched the earth an hour before, the fisher spun around and raced back up the trail. It quickly disappeared into the balsams. The chief relaxed, waiting in silence again.

As time passed, the hunter's muscles became stiff and sore from the cold. "Could it be, Makwaa, you are fast asleep in your den? There is no snow. You should be filling your belly for the long winter sleep. Perhaps I should leave. I, like others in the forest, must prepare for winter."

Still kneeling, he picked up his arrow and began to slide it into his deerskin quiver when he heard a faint sound. He pulled the arrow out again, nocking it onto the bowstring. The hunter waited. More soft sounds came from the trail.

"Are you Ojiig, the fisher, again? Are you another wandering animal? A deer? A raccoon? Or could you be the great bear? Maybe you are just Wenebojo, tricking me into shivering here for a few more minutes." Namakagon closely watched the trail where it wound its way into the balsam swamp. "Come, show me what you are," he wanted to shout.

The hunter heard the soft swishing of balsam boughs rubbing on fur. Then, not fifty steps off, lumbering toward the hunter, sniffing the still morning air, came his quarry. His thick, black coat glistened in the morning sun. The bear's large paws made almost no sound as they carried him down the trail, closer, closer, and closer to the hunter.

On this quiet, frosty morning in the tall pines south of the lake that now shared his name, Chief Namakagon and this great makwaa were about to meet.

30

Chapter 7
The Man in the Black Derby Hat

Tor Loken's work at the Chicago River Fuel and Dray was less exciting now that the coal chutes were working well. The new foreman had not called for him in three months. His daily chores became routine. Tor read all of the books left in the corner of the room. Some he read twice. The hot summer of  1883 was almost over. More and more, his thoughts strayed back to his previous home in New York. He thought of his mother, his father, and his uncle.

One morning in early October, after sweeping out the back stairway, Tor returned to his room to continue reading one of the books. He glanced out of his only window to see a tall, muscular man with a red moustache approach the steps leading to the front office.

The man was dressed in a new, black suit. His derby hat, cocked to one side, matched it precisely. His footwear did not, for below his trouser cuffs were a pair of well-worn leather work boots. He gave the distinct impression of someone out of his element but trying hard to fit in. This tall, mustached man in the black derby hat climbed the marble steps and disappeared into the towering Chicago River Coal and Dray building.

Hearing the commotion in the clerk's office, DeWilde threw open the door to see two of his clerks blocking the entrance to his office.

"Here, now. What is the matter?" he said in a stern voice. As the clerks turned to reply, the caller pushed past them.

"If you are in charge here then I want to speak with you," said the man in black derby. The two clerks grabbed his arms. The brawny intruder easily shook them off.

"Step into my office. We can do our business in here, and my men can get back to their duties," DeWilde said, motioning the caller in. "Have a chair, Mister …"

"Loken. My name is Ingman Loken," he said with a heavy Norwegian accent. He remained standing. "I am uncle to a boy sent here from the boys' home over on LaSalle Street. His name is Tor, Tor Loken. I have been looking for him for over two years. Do you know where I can find him?"

DeWilde was silent for a long moment. Then, "Perhaps, uh … well … Mister Loken, is it? Well, you must understand, Sir, I … uh … I have many, many employees. Tor you say? Tor. I do not recall anyone…"

Suddenly the back door to DeWilde's office swung open, and Big Jake Riggens stepped in with his right hand on his nightstick.

"Everything all right here, Mr. DeWilde?"

"Everything is fine, Jake. Right, Mr. Loken? But Jake, stay here a minute in case we can help this gent with his problem."

"I am here for my nephew, Tor," said Ingman Loken in a booming voice as Big Jake stepped closer. "I know he was sent here. I wish to see him. Exactly what must I do to get your cooperation?"

Down the hall in his room, Tor heard the disturbance.

"Now, see here, Mr. Loken," said DeWilde, "calm yourself. How do I know you are related to this ... Tor, I think you said?"

"Tor Loken," said Ingman. "He is sixteen years of age and the son of my brother Olaf Loken and his wife Karina. Yust where is he?"

Tor crept up the steps and listened from the hall.

"We have a number of sixteen-year-old boys here, Loken, not one Tor in the bunch as I recall. How about you, Jake? Are you aware of a boy with that name?" The security man remained silent.

"You're talking about me," said Tor, entering the room. "I am Tor Loken. My pa was Olaf, Karina was my ma, and I have an Uncle Ingman. Is that you, sir?"

"Now hold fast!" snapped DeWilde. "I am not going to let some fellow come in off the street and claim my workers. Jake, take the boy back to his room."

"Yust you wait a minute," said Ingman, stepping between Big Jake and Tor. "I have proof. I have a photograph of my brother, his wife, and their son right here." He opened a pocket book and pulled out a well-worn tintype photo. He looked at it, then at Tor, and then showed it to DeWilde.

"The boy was only one when they had this likeness made, but you can see it is him and his folks. And you can see the resemblance between me and my brother, Olaf Loken—Tor's pa."

DeWilde looked closely at the photo, then at Tor, then at the photo again, wrinkling his brow.

"I am not convinced," he said. "Look here, now. You cannot expect me to let a youngster go with just anyone who comes in off the street with an old photo and a made-up story. I will not have it. Jake, take the boy to his room."

"No!" shouted Tor. "This *is* my uncle. And that's my ma and my pa in the photograph. I know it! Mr. DeWilde, you have to let me go with him. He's my only kin. You must let me go."

Ingman stepped over to the boy and turned back toward DeWilde and Big Jake who now had a menacing scowl on his face.

"My nephew and I are leaving now and won't be coming back. There is nothing you can do to stop us. He is my family, and he is going with me."

"Jake," said DeWilde, "I have no more time for this foolishness. Send this man on his way."

Big Jake Riggens, right hand grasping the handle of his nightstick, reached for the collar of Ingman Loken's new suit. Ingman's arm came up to deflect it.

Instantly the nightstick flashed from its sheath and sliced through the air. Ingman ducked as the stick flew past. With his left hand he struck a strong, solid blow to the security man's right side, snapping several ribs and sending him to the floor where he struggled to breathe.

DeWilde jerked open a desk drawer and reached inside. Tor's uncle threw himself, head-first, across the top of the desk, slamming the drawer closed and smashing the coal merchant's fingers. Ingman held the drawer closed, trapping DeWilde's crushed right hand.

"I believe you were yust reaching for my nephew's back pay, ya?" said Ingman. "I'm sorry if I inyured your man over there, but I wasn't given much choice in the matter."

Tor's uncle eased up on the desk drawer, allowing DeWilde to pull his hand free. He raised his bloodied right hand into the air. With his left hand, he reached into his pocket and pulled out a handkerchief. He shook it open and quickly wrapped his damaged fingers, holding them tightly.

"Damn you, Loken," he cried. "And damn your brat nephew to boot."

"I do hope your fingers are better soon," said Ingman. "Tor, get your belongings. Like I said, we are leaving now and we won't be back."

Tor ran down the hallway to his room, returning in seconds with his coat, hat, pocketknife, and his savings, five dollars and thirty-two cents.

Big Jake was stirring now, trying to catch his breath. He grimaced from the pain in his side.

"Mr. Riggens?" said Tor. "I am sorry if I caused you any problems. You were good to me. I thank you for looking out for me."

Riggens, clutching his side, looked up at Tor but remained silent.

"All right, Loken," said DeWilde, "Take the boy. Take him and leave here." He reached into his pocket with his left hand, pulling out a few coins. "Here is your pay, boy," he said, tossing the coins on the floor. "This is how we met and this is how we part."

Tor picked up three quarters, just enough to cover the wages he earned since payday. He left the rest on the floor.

"This is all I'm owed and all I shall take."

Tor's uncle pulled open the desk drawer, taking out the small pistol laying there. "I will see to it you get this back, DeWilde." Ingman backed his way toward the door. Tor opened it, and they quickly crossed the bustling office. The clerks, still focused only on their duties, busily stamped papers, shouted orders, and continued with their work.

As he neared the front door, Ingman flipped open the cylinder on the revolver, ejecting all five cartridges into his hand. He tossed them into a wastebasket, dropped the pistol, and kicked it under a nearby file cabinet.

Tor and Ingman left the building for downtown Chicago. They soon blended into the midday crowds of pedestrians. Ingman checked out of his hotel and they headed to the station. By one o'clock, the Lokens were seated in a passenger car on a northbound train.

Belching black smoke, the steam locomotive soon crossed the Illinois border, roaring past cities, towns, woodlands, and fields. Ingman and Tor Loken were on their way to a lumber camp on a lake in far northwestern Wisconsin.

33

Chapter 8
Ogimaa Mikwam-migwan

A coal-black raven flew above the hunter and his prey, calling out an alarm. The huge bear did not heed the bird's warning.

Namakagon's blood pounded in his ears as the bear, much larger than he had previously thought, came closer and closer. A slight breeze on his face assured him the bear would not catch his scent. But it did catch the smell of the venison suet he had set for bait. The bear looked in every direction, but poor eyesight prevented it from seeing the motionless hunter who knelt behind the balsam blind a short distance away.

Chief Namakagon's bow was now fully drawn. When the bear reached the point directly below the suet, it stopped. The hunter's heart was pounding harder and harder now, but he could not shoot. The angle was wrong. He might only wound the great animal if the arrow hit the shoulder bone rather than entering the chest. He waited in silence at full draw, arms trembling.

The bear sniffed the air, looked up, and saw the suet above him. He stood on his hind legs, his belly and great black chest facing the chief, not ten steps away. The hunter put more tension on the bowstring, took final aim, and relaxed the fingers of his strong right hand.

Just as the enormous bear plucked the tallow from the branch, the arrow flashed through the crisp, morning air and pierced the bear's hide. The sharp, steel arrowhead snapped a rib, and then cut through the bear's great heart. He grunted a loud *ooof* as he spun around and bounded aimlessly off the trail.

Namakagon's eyes opened wide as he watched the giant makwaa charge straight at him. The bow fell from his hand as he reached for his knife, but before he could pull it to defend himself, the great bear crashed through his balsam blind and bounded across him, smashing him to the ground below its huge front paws.

The bear never saw the hunter, who was now looking up from under a tangle of balsam branches, wet with bear blood. He watched the bear run through the tall pines, taking long strides as it flashed between the huge trees. When almost out of sight, the enormous animal crashed to the ground.

Namakagon stood. He picked up his bow and quiver, and looked back to the trail where his arrow had met the bear's black chest. The suet lay on the ground. He left it there for some unknown animal that shared these woods with his bear. He stretched his sore muscles, before silently approaching the dead bear. Namakagon opened his tobacco pouch, sprinkled some across the bear, and chanted a prayer of thanks to the bear, to the woods, to the earth, and to Gitchee Manitou.

As always, the satisfaction of this successful hunt was mixed with a great, hollow, personal sadness. One of nature's beautiful creatures would no longer walk through the forest. Instead, it would make way for another of its kind. It would grant nourishment and provisions to the hunter and live long in stories told near future campfires. A great animal when alive, the makwaa would remain great in memory.

By late afternoon Namakagon had skinned out and quartered the bear. He wrapped the hindquarters in the large skin and tied it onto a simple travois he fashioned by lashing together some nearby maple saplings. The front quarters and rib cage were hung from an overhanging pine limb. The ravens would find the meat before he could return, but maybe they would spend their time on the pile of innards rather than the meat in the tree.

The last, lingering smoke from his campfire was blowing to the west as the chief pulled his canoe onto the beach. His dogs greeted him and his cargo excitedly.

Namakagon looked at the rising smoke and the thick clouds gathering in the eastern sky. The weather was turning. He pulled his canoe under several tall white pines in anticipation of a storm. There it would sit until spring, overturned and protected by the limbs of the pines.

"You have been a good partner for another season," he said to the birch and spruce canoe. "The lake will freeze over soon. I will wake you in the spring."

Three more green logs on the fire would finish smoking the venison. He carried the bearskin and hindquarters up to his lodge after tending the fire.

That night, the east wind strengthened. Snowflakes appeared. By morning's light, the forest floor was blanketed with a foot of snow. And it continued to fall. As he cut the smoked venison from its place above the cold campfire, he looked across the lake. The dense snowfall masked the opposite shore, not a quarter mile away. Namakagon returned to his lodge to wait out the storm.

"The crows and ravens won't wait," he said to his dogs. "They will be happy to have a breakfast of fresh bear meat." He peered out at the falling snow. "I should go. But now I must travel by land. It will take me a full day to go there and return. If the snow continues, it will take longer, and I will have to sleep in the forest overnight. Should I wait or should I go right now, before it is too late?" he wondered, staring at the falling snow. "No. I will stay. If Gitchee Manitou decides the animals need the meat more than I, then so it must be."

The old chief built a small fire in his lodge and spent the rest of the day trimming fat from the bear hide, preparing to tan it in better weather.

The late November snowfall continued all day and well into the night. He heard the wind switch to the north, then slow, then stop. He felt the temperature drop. By morning an inch of ice covered the lake. The snow in the woods was knee-deep.

As the sun peeked over the treetops, Namakagon hitched up his dogs. They took the trail south. Each exhaled breath made a white cloud in the freezing air. The near shore ice was strong enough to hold them as they crossed onto the mainland and followed the shoreline to the south, then west. As they struggled to climb to the top of the ridge, the chief saw the tracks of two other men heading east. "Hunters," he said to his dogs. "They must also be looking for extra food for the winter months." At the top of the ridge he turned west again, finding the stand of giant white pines where he had killed the bear. He circled to the trail leading into the balsam swamp. Two ravens flew up from the ground and into the branches above. The bear meat he left hanging from the pine limb was frozen as solid as stone. Birds had knocked most of the snow from it but had devoured little meat. Protected from freezing by the snow lay the last of the innards, nearly consumed by ravens.

Namakagon untied the rope and dropped the two front quarters and large rib cage into the sled below. The heavy load in this deep snow would be a challenge. Off they went, the dogs following their own trail back toward the lake. The burden was heavy. The hunter pushed from behind as his dogs pressed on under a cold, clear sky.

The chief was steaming with sweat by the time he neared the lake. In the frigid air, moisture from his breath froze, making icicles on his beard and hair. On the trail ahead he saw two Ojibwe hunters who left the tracks that morning. They dragged a large doe and waved as he approached.

"Boozhoo!" shouted the chief, with a friendly motion.

"Boozhoo!" came the reply. "Where are you going with such a heavy load, Mikwam-migwan?"

"To my lodge, the lodge of Old Bear," said the chief. "But why do you call me Mikwam-migwan?"

Grinning, they pointed at the frost on Namakagon's face and hair. "The ice you have made on your whiskers looks like the feathers of the osprey," one man laughed. "You will scare our friend Old Bear out of his wits!"

Namakagon smiled, feeling the ice around his face. "Old Bear is no longer here. He has given me his lodge. I have taken the name of the lake as my own."

"Then, Mikwam-migwan, we will let our people at Pac-wa-wong know we have met Namakagon, the tall man with ice feathers. You must come visit us when you can. We are near. One-half day by canoe in summer, one day walk in winter."

"I will come to your camp soon," said Namakagon "Look for me when the river ice will carry the weight of my sled and dogs."

Two hours later, as the bright November, 1831, sun descended over the western shore of the lake, Ogimaa Mikwam-migwan, known, too, as Chief Namakagon, built a fire in his lodge to cook a fresh bear steak for his supper.

Chapter 9
Oshkosh, Chippeway, and Northbound

The steam locomotive's whistle cut through the fall air as the train raced northward on this October, 1883 afternoon. It pulled twenty-eight cars including the passenger car carrying a sixteen-year-old boy and his uncle.

"My father ... Uncle Ingman, tell me how he died."

Ingman Loken looked into his nephew's blue eyes. "How he died?" He paused. "Tor, your pa is not dead. He's waiting to see you. Your pa sent me to find you. Why, he has had me searching for you ever since you and your mother were in that train wreck and your pa got laid up. I've spent yust about every spare minute scouring the land from here to Cleveland seeking you out. We never thought you would have been sent west to Chicago."

Tor was stunned. "My father is alive?"

"Oh, yes! He was badly hurt when his horse team bolted and the load of lumber he was deliverin' flipped over. We found him pinned under the wagon, barely alive. But your pa is mighty tough. The local doctor saved his life. He's been on the mend ever since—in a Hayward boarding house."

"But they told me ..."

"They didn't know. The Chicago police and the man at the boys' home knew nothing about your father, other than he was inyured. Nobody bothered to look for your pa or any family you might have. Easier for them yust to say your pa died."

Tor stared out the window in silence for a moment. "It will be so good to see Pa again. How bad was he hurt?"

"Well, Olaf has been mending for quite some time. Most of his inyuries have healed up. But ... Nephew, he's bound to a wheelchair."

"Pa can't walk?"

"He spends much of his time yust starin' out the window. But his mind is quick as ever, and he is still strong of will and has the same spirit–the same Olaf Loken as before. He yust can't walk."

"Will he ... ever?"

"Oh, the day will come when your pa can leave the boarding house and live at the camp again. But for now, he needs to rest up. You coming home to him will be wonderful for his health—and for his heart!"

"I can hardly wait, Uncle Ingman."

The locomotive's whistle sounded again.

"Uncle, what is the camp you speak of?"

"Oh, ya, I suppose you don't know about the lumber camp. It's called the Namakagon Timber Company. We cut white pine all winter, then float it down the river come spring. Sometimes all the way to the St Croix and the Mississippi to the lumber mills in Stillwater, St. Paul, and LaCrosse. Some of our pine even went as far as St. Louis last spring. Our camp is way back in the woods where the pines are tallest and the men are toughest, or so we claim."

"When your pa first came to the north woods he had yust enough money saved to build a small sawmill and hire a few fellas to log off sixty acres north of Hayward. They put in a hard winter's work and, wouldn't you know, yust before he went to sell his timber, the market turned for the better. The pine brought a good sum. Your pa was able to sell both the timber and his mill for a good profit. He used the money to start up his own lumber camp near a big lake called Namakagon. Olaf's camp was small at first, but soon grew into a gol dang good outfit. Some say we have the best crew in the north."

"Crew?"

"Ya. When the snow flies, men come from all over to work for us cutting timber. We have bunks for eighty-eight workers in our camp. Eighty-eight men all working to bring the timber out of the woods, downriver to the mills. The money is good and the work is honest. Ya, it's a good outfit. And you will fit right in, Nephew. Why, you'll be a lumberyack in no time!"

"But I know nothing about it."

"Oh, you will learn. Don't you worry 'bout that. We work yust like the other camps in the north—Michigan, Minnesota, Manitoba, Wisconsin, everywhere you find tall white pines you'll also find lumber camps like ours. As soon as the fall harvest is in from the fields down south, the farmers and their boys come north to the pinery. By fall the lumber mills are yust about out of timber, too. Many mill hands come north lookin' for winter work. Other lumberyacks come from all parts of the country to work in the pinery.

"Each man has his own yob to do. We have sawyers who fell the trees. Then come the swampers. Their yob is to cut the limbs off and clear the way for the teamsters who use horses or oxen to skid the logs out to the sleigh trails. Workers load up the logs onto the big sleighs so the teamsters can take the sleighs down to the lake, unload, then come back for more."

"Each log gets stamped with our own mark, NTC—Namakagon Timber Company. It's a good outfit, nephew. Big, too. So big that we hire on three or four hands yust to feed the crew and two more to feed and tend to the oxen and horses. We hire on a blacksmith and a carpenter, too. And another man whose only yob is to keep the saws and axes sharp. Ya, it's a good crew, Tor. A gol dang good outfit!"

"What job do you do, Uncle?"

"Me? Why I keep the whole she-bang runnin' smooth. I'm what you call a woods boss. I see to it the crew is woke up before five o'clock. After the men eat their mornin' meal, I get them off into the woods before daylight.

38

They cut and haul pine till noon. We give them a good dinner, either at the cook shanty or out in the woods, depending where they are cutting. Then they work through till dark. Each night they return to camp hungry for another meal. After supper, it's off to the sleep shanty to dry the sweat from their shirts, socks, and boots and to smoke their pipes. They tell a few tall tales and maybe sing along to the tune of a fiddle and a squeezebox before turning in."

The train whistle blew two longs, one short, and another long. Ingman looked out the window at the passing landscape.

"By the time the swamps freeze up solid in December, we already have hundreds of loads of white pine to move. Some of our sleighs travel through the woods for many miles before finding their way out onto the frozen lake where the pine is rolled off onto the ice. In the spring after the ice goes out, our men take the logs over the dam and downstream. River pigs, they call us. Dangerous work. When the pine gets to the sawmills it is pulled from the river, tallied up and sawed into lumber for homes and businesses. The mills then pay your pa and he sees to it the men get their pay."

The engine's whistle sounded again. The train slowed as it approached the Oshkosh station. It pulled alongside the depot and came to a stop. A single long whistle gave the all clear to disembark. Ingman and Tor entered the depot. Ingman stepped up to the telegraph window. Minutes later and hundreds of miles to the north, Tor's father would read these words:

OLAF LOKEN ... STOP ... RINGSTADT BOARDING HOUSE ... STOP... HAYWARD WISC ... STOP ... WILL ARRIVE TUESDAY WITH TOR ... STOP ... HEALTHY AND SHARP AS TACK ... STOP ... WHOOP IT UP ... STOP... INGMAN.

From the telegraph office Ingman and Tor went into the depot restaurant for a hot meal while the train crew took on water and coal. Soon, the locomotive sped north again, stopping in Neenah, Menasha, Appleton, Stevens Point and Marshfield.

By late afternoon the train neared the immense Chippewa Falls railroad yard. Tor saw row after row of freight cars on the sidings. Most were stacked high with lumber. Others were filled with huge pine logs. Two switch engines were moving cars to make up the next trains leaving town. Another long train, laden with timber, was departing eastward. As they crossed the Chippewa River trestle, Tor saw logs floating down the river. Some were directed into a sluice that took them to lumber mills along the shore. Others floated over the falls. Men gingerly walked on top of the logs, pushing and pulling them with long, spiked poles.

"River pigs," said his uncle, nodding towards the window. "They use those pike poles to sort and send the right logs to the sawmills."

"Uncle, how do they keep from falling in?"

"Oh, they take a dunk now and then. Yust part of the yob."

Smoldering, volcano-like sawdust piles spewed smoke high into the air. More smoke came from tall sawdust burners. The pungent smell of the pine smoke soon filled the passenger car. As the train neared the station, Tor surveyed the lively city of Chippewa Falls with its new brick buildings. Overhead wires connected new electric streetlights, an innovation found only in the most modern of cities, as his uncle explained. The train rolled up to the depot. Tor saw hotels, taverns, and stores under construction as carpenters and masons raced to get them closed in by winter.

"Yust think, Tor. This is all paid for by the work being done in the lumber camps. Pine is making men rich and, right here, from the Chippewa River Valley to Lake Superior, lays the single biggest stand of white pine on dear Mother Earth, and we're right in the midst of it! Big, beautiful white pines, Nephew. Some are three, maybe even four hundred years old. And you, me, and your pa, well, we are right, smack-dab in the middle of it all. It's a great place to be."

The train pulled to a stop at the Chippewa Falls depot. Tor, coat in hand, and Ingman, clutching carpet bag, stepped out onto the platform. The setting sun gave the yellow, orange, and red trees a warm evening glow.

The Lokens stepped up to the ticket master's window. Ingman paid the fare for the next leg of their journey north before checking into a hotel for the night.

At dawn, Ingman and his nephew ate a large breakfast before boarding the northbound for Tor's reunion with his father.

Clouds of steam rolled out from behind the engine's huge drive wheels. Thick, black, coal smoke spewed from the locomotive's stack, rising into the air. The smell of the smoke brought Tor memories of the coal yard he left the day before. He was glad to be on his way to see his father.

As the train rolled north through the new lumber towns of Eagle Point and Bloomer, the color in the hardwoods intensified. At the Cartwright station, the train picked up four lumberjacks and twenty-two flat cars.

Rumbling north again, with stops in the new lumber towns of Chetek, Cameron, Rice Lake, Haugen, and Chandler, Tor saw large stands of maple, oak, and birch passed over by the logging companies for the more profitable pine. Their red, yellow, and orange leaves glowed on the distant ridges. He listened to more stories over the rhythmic sounds of the wheels rolling on the steel rails as they passed through Superior Junction, Veazie, Ames, and Stinnett Landing. Tor watched the brilliant autumn landscape pass by.

"Nephew, we are comin' into Hayward," said Ingman, gazing out the window of the passenger car. Two long whistle blasts, one short, and another long echoed off the nearby hills as their train approached the new community. Tor looked out to see mile after mile of tall stacks of white pine lumber drying in the sun. As the train rounded a curve he got his first glimpse of the lively lumber town.

The sweet smell of pine soon flooded the car. Beyond the track, the dusty road was busy with horse-drawn wagons hauling lumber to waiting boxcars. Just as in Chippewa Falls, when the train approached the station, the fresh aroma of pine was replaced by the pungent smell of smoldering sawdust. Smoke from the huge sawdust burners filled the air. The train pulled into the Hayward yard.

"Right on the button," Ingman said, checking his watch. "Ready, Nephew?"

They stepped off the train into the warm, fall sunlight and crossed the large, wooden platform, descending the steps to the crowded plank walkway. Turning west, the Lokens headed straight for Iowa Avenue, the busiest street in this young city. A horse-drawn wagon loaded with hand tools passed them, raising billows of dust. Other horses were tethered to wooden rails that stood before a large hotel on the corner.

Ingman led his nephew around and up the street. Far ahead, atop the hill, Tor saw men nailing cedar shingles onto the cupola of a new courthouse.

The Lokens worked their way up the street, past several stores, a bath house and barber shop, two banks, another hotel, a photographer's studio, nine busy taverns, rooming houses, and a sparkling new church. Ingman led the way up the next block where they rounded the corner to Mrs. Ringstadt's Boarding House. In the front parlor, seated in a wheel chair, waited Tor's father, Olaf.

"Tor! Ingman! Come in! Come in!" he cried, laughing with joy. He tried to stand, but slumped back into his wheelchair.

"Father!" shouted Tor, rushing in. "Father!" The two hugged somewhat awkwardly because of the chair. Olaf kissed Tor on the forehead.

"Tor, my boy! Let me look at you! Oh, Tor, how I missed you. Why, look at you! By gosh, you're tall! Taller than me—even if I could stand up. And you're built strong and straight like—like a Loken man! Oh, it is so wonderful to see you again Tor. So, so wonderful!" He hugged his son again.

"Father, I thought I would never see you again. They told me—they said you—you had been killed."

"Killed? No, Son, I'm still kicking! We Lokens are too hardheaded to give up without a good fight."

"Ingman!" Olaf reached toward his brother. "Ingman, how in tarnation did you do it? How did you find our boy? Oh, Lord, such a wonderful day! Such a wonderful reunion! We must celebrate. Yes! The Loken boys are all in town. It is time to strike up the band, to raise the roof!"

The jubilation and excitement attracted others to the room. Adeline Ringstadt's three daughters peeked from the kitchen.

"Who is that boy, Mama?" whispered Rose Ringstadt.

"He's Tor Loken, Olaf's son. You know, Rose, the boy Ingman has been looking for."

"*He* is Olaf Loken's son? Why, Mama, from the way Mr. Loken talked, I thought he was just a little boy."

"He was very young when Olaf saw him last. Olaf told me Ingman

41

found Tor in Chicago. Can you imagine that? Chicago." She brushed past her daughters.

"Adeline," shouted Olaf. "Come meet my son, Tor. Adeline, doesn't that sound wonderful? My son, Tor—Torvald Ingman Loken, right here in your parlor! He had us worried for so long, but now he's back. Yesiree Adeline, Tor Loken is back to stay!"

"Oh my, my!" said the landlady. "You are the image of your father, aren't you. Yes, another eye-catcher you are, handsome as your father. Oh, mercy me, it is so good to finally meet you. We are all so happy to see you back with your family."

"I'm pleased to meet you, too, Ma'am."

"Mama," came a loud whisper from the kitchen doorway. "Pssst. Mama."

"Oh, my, yes," said the apron-clad woman. "Tor, you must meet my daughter." Then, turning toward the kitchen, "Rose, dear, come meet ..."

But before she could finish, Rose Ringstadt stood in front of Tor. Her younger sisters followed close behind. "Tor, this is my daughter Rose Ringsta ..."

"Rosie," she exclaimed, reaching out to shake Tor's hand. "You may call me Rosie. All my friends do."

"I'm Daisy," interrupted Rose's younger sister, pushing in between Tor and Rose. The youngest daughter, Violet, stared up at Tor but said nothing.

"Daisy," snapped Rose. "Mother," she pleaded, pushing her sister aside. "Please remind Daisy to mind her manners."

"Now, Daisy, Rose is right," said her mother, "you shouldn't ..."

"Tor," interrupted Rose again, "will you be staying with us long? I'd love to show you around our town. Maybe you'd like to meet my friends."

"Well, uh, I don't know how long we're staying, Rose. Father? Do you know ..."

"Rosie," insisted the pretty, dark-haired sixteen-year-old. "You simply *must* call me Rosie! All my good friends do!"

"We will be here a time, Tor," said his father.

"But not a long while, Nephew," countered Ingman. "If it's all right with your pa, you and I will be heading up to the camp in two days. There are supplies waiting for us at the depot in Cable. It's a lumber town between here and the camp. Tomorrow I will send a telegram arranging to have those goods loaded into wagons, and Thursday we will be on our way."

"Ingman," Olaf said, "I have come to a decision. I will be going with you."

"Oh, I don't know, Olaf. It's a long, hard ride from Cable out to the camp. You're not ready for that kind of yourney."

"Ingman, I know very well just how tough that trip is. You will do well to remember I made it far more often than you, up until my accident. I can make the trip without any trouble to you. It will be good for me to get back to the camp. It doesn't matter where this wheelchair sits—here in Hayward or up at the camp. It matters not a fiddlehead and that's that."

Mrs. Ringstadt interrupted. "Good for you, Olaf. Good for you. It's time you got back into the midst of things again. No point in you sittin' around here. But don't you think twice if you feel you want to come back, Olaf Loken. You will always be welcome in my home. Welcome as a cool breeze in August."

"Father, I will help you. I'll be your right hand man, if you'll have me."

"Then it's done!" shouted Olaf.

"Well, it seems I am out-numbered," said Ingman. "So, come Thursday mornin', we will be on the train north. By nightfall we will be back in the pines, back at the Namakagon Timber Company camp. Tonight, though, we celebrate. Adeline, don't bother settin' places at the table for us Loken boys tonight. We'll be paintin' the town red. And, Adeline, if we don't turn up for breakfast, yust send someone down to the Sawyer County yailhouse to throw our bail!"

Chapter 10
Chief Namakagon: More than a Man of the Woods

The train was officially known as the Chicago, St. Paul, Minneapolis, Omaha, and Northwestern, but everyone called it the Omaha. The morning northbound pulled out of the Hayward yard with Tor, Ingman, and Olaf Loken on board. By the time they reached the iron trestle, Conductor Clyde Williams had inspected and punched their tickets.

The sixteen-mile train ride to Cable took them across the Namekagon River. Ridge after brilliant ridge displayed tiers of brightly colored trees. The blue of the clear, fall sky was reflected in the small lakes and streams they passed. This blue, along with the deep greens of the pines, contrasted with the reds, oranges, and golden-yellows of autumn.

Near Mosquito Brook, the train passed through a section of cutover pine. Huge, dark stumps were all that remained of what had once been a majestic white pine forest. The rust-brown tops and limbs of dead trees were scattered across the landscape.

"Look," said Tor. "What happened there?"

"That, Nephew, is the handiwork of the Muldoon Lumber Company. It's one of biggest timber outfits in these parts. They don't leave a pretty sight."

"Most camps don't," added Tor's father. "Most outfits take every stick of wood and leave the land in a shambles. Their only goal is to make the most money they can. Then, to steer clear of taxes, they let the cutover land go back to the government. They make so much profit off the timber that they don't care what happens to the land. There's even a name for it—cut and get out. It's a gol dang, dreadful thing to do to these beautiful woodlands and waters."

"Waters, Pa? How is it bad for the waters?"

"With no forest cover left at all, the rains wash the soil into the creeks. The muddy water ends up in the lakes and rivers, usually killing the plants and animals that have thrived there for thousands and thousands of years. Son, if I could walk, I'd take you to creeks and ponds that, just two years ago, were teaming with big, beautiful brook trout. Now those waters are all but dead. Muddied up and dead."

"We do not work that way," said Ingman. "The Namakagon Timber Company takes only the big pines and leaves most of the small pines and hardwoods to grow. The only time we clear-cut is when we need to build a road, a landing, or a new camp. We get plenty of profit from the big pines without wasting the land. In twenty or thirty years, when the virgin pine is all gone from this country, we will be able to come back and cut our woods again. That clear-cut land you see out there, well, it'll take a hundred years, maybe two, for those pines to recover."

"It's a shameful way to treat these magnificent woodlands, Son. Most of the big outfits have no interest in the future of the north country. They don't care about tomorrow, just the money they can reap today. It is a sorrowful way to treat Mother Earth."

Tor watched as they passed mile after mile of cutover. The Omaha crossed another iron trestle and made the last bend before Cable. The engineer opened the throttle to make the uphill climb and thick, black, coal smoke spewed from the stack.

"We're almost there, Son," Olaf said, patting Tor on the shoulder.

The engineer eased off on the throttle. The train slowed and soon pulled into the Cable yard. With the fireman ringing the bell, the engineer released the pressure, locking the air brakes. A long, piercing *whoosh* sounded as the steam shot out below the locomotive. One long whistle blast gave the all clear to disembark. Conductor Clyde Williams stepped from the passenger car, ready to assist departing passengers. Tor and Ingman helped Olaf out of the car and onto the platform just as the stationmaster stepped from the depot.

"Oscar!" shouted Olaf. "Oscar, you old pine knot!"

"Well, I'll be. Look what the damn cat dragged in!" replied Oscar Felsman, rushing to meet his friend. "Good to see you back in town, Olaf."

"It's a marvelous day to be here. Say, Oscar, this strappin' young man here is my son. Tor, meet the gol dang stubbornest, most irritable, and ornery pinochle player betwixt Chippeway and Hudson's Bay. But he keeps the trains on time and always has another four bits for the card table."

"Well, well, Tor Loken. I wondered if ever I would meet you. Welcome to Cable, Son. It is a pleasure."

"Pleased to be here, sir, and pleased to meet you, too."

"Found him in Chicago," said Ingman, "workin' in a big downtown coal yard, he was. His boss was not all that willin' to set the boy loose. I had to sort'a pry young Tor from his grip, you might say. But we showed those coal peddlers not to come between us pinery boys, right, Nephew?"

"They found out Uncle Ingman can be very persuasive."

"Tor, Olaf, you catch up on the news with Oscar," said Ingman. "I'll ready the wagons and meet you at the general store. We need to be on the trail before noon if we hope to make it to the camp by dark."

Wheeling his father across the platform into the crowded depot, Tor sensed the freshly painted walls and spotless waiting room were the pride of the

45

stationmaster walking with them. Oscar's blue-gray uniform was neatly pressed and its brass buttons brightly polished.

Tor also noticed an Indian among the others in the waiting room. He sat on a bench near the south window reading a book. His buckskin clothes were clean and neat. A diamond-shaped silver medallion was neatly stitched onto his shirt. A dark belt around his waist supported a sheathed knife and two buckskin pouches. His moccasins were tied above his calves. Next to him was a canvas pack. Leaning against the wall near him was an ornately carved walking stick. Two large dogs, one black and one white, lay at his feet.

Tor found it hard not to stare. This was the closest he'd ever been to an Indian. He had seen photos in books and he saw several at a distance in Hayward, but they were clad in loggers' clothes, not in buckskin. This man seemed to carry something special with him—something from nature—from the past—something mysterious.

The Ojibwe looked up from his book. He gave a friendly nod, acknowledging Tor's presence in the room. Tor nodded in reply.

"That fellow is Chief Namakagon," said Oscar. "Come. I know him well. You must meet him." They crossed the waiting room. Namakagon stood. He was broad-shouldered and a half-foot taller than anyone in the room. With a snap of his fingers, his dogs jumped to attention.

"Chief Namakagon," said Oscar, "this is Olaf Loken and his son, Tor. They are headed for their lumber camp, not far from your lodge. Olaf, here, is the proprietor of the outfit.

"Ah, yes, the Namakagon Timber Company. A good camp. One of few."

"I have heard of you," said Olaf, shaking the chief's hand. "My men often tell of the adventures and perils of the great Chief Namakagon."

"It is a pleasure to meet you, sir" said Tor as they shook hands.

"Your father treats the forests and waters with respect." He turned to Olaf. "The men in the lumber camps tell many tales on long, winter nights. I hope words spoken about me offer a hint of truth. I am but a man of the woods, no more and no less."

"Ha! You, sir, are far more than just a man of the woods," exclaimed Oscar. "You, sir, are known to all in the north as a great and noble man who respects both Mother Nature and the people who have come here to work and live. True, you are a man of the woods, but you are also a man of the people."

Namakagon was quick to reply, "First I am a man of the woods, Oscar. The forests, the lakes, the streams have given us many gifts. Perhaps they will continue to grace us with beauty and bounty, but only if the people who come here show respect for nature. Our woodlands and waters are first in my heart."

Outside, the southbound train pulled up to the platform. The bell rang and a single blast from the locomotive's whistle let everyone know it was time to board. Tor spoke to his father as the Ojibwe man prepared to leave, then said, "Mr. Namakagon …"

The chief interrupted. "I am known as Namakagon and I am known as

46

Chief Namakagon. I will call you Tor. No need to call me Mister. Mister is what Oscar cries out when he shoots at a doe." The stationmaster scowled, but in jest.

"Yes, sir," said Tor. "Chief Namakagon, if you are able to join us at the camp … well, ah, sir … we'd like you to come to our lumber camp. Maybe you could join us for supper someday?"

"I would be pleased to break bread with you. Today, I am off to see friends in Lac Courte Oreilles. When I return I will come to your camp."

"That's mighty fine, sir! We'll watch for you."

"And I second that," said Olaf, "as long as you don't bring this old curmudgeon of a pinochle-playing stationmaster with you!" He laughed as he tugged at the blue-gray sleeve of Oscar's uniform.

"Now Olaf, why in the world would I take that long, miserable ride across that moose path you call your tote road? Why in tarnation would I give up a clean, comfortable home in town for a crooked, old shack in the woods filled with mosquitoes, woodticks, graybacks, bears, wildcats, wolves, and who knows what other critters who all crave to feast on me?" Tor's eyes widened. "No, sir," he continued, straight-faced, "you won't get me out to your camp anytime soon, unless there's cards on the table and whisky in the jar!"

Oscar turned, handing a small box to Tor. "Young fella, I have a welcome home gift for you. You will want one of these to make sure you don't miss dinner, unless your pa's doing the cooking."

Tor opened the box to find a silver pocket watch. The cover was missing. The crystal was scratched. Dents, scuffs, and worn plating showed hard use. Still, holding it to his ear, Tor heard ticking. No boys at the orphanage ever had such a treasure.

"Oh, thank you, Mr. Felsman. This is the only watch I've ever had!" Delighted, he again held it to his ear.

"Well, Son, it isn't much. But it served me well for eleven years. And it keeps good time, if you remember to wind it, that is."

Chief Namakagon left to board the southbound train. Tor wheeled his father down the freight ram onto the walkway that took them through a small, town park surrounded by a neatly trimmed, cedar hedge. They passed a new, white gazebo and stepped out to the main street. Tor looked up and down the dusty road.

"This is Cable, Son, your new home town. Two hotels, one general store, one dry goods store, a livery over there, a park right here in the middle of town, a feed store, a blacksmith around the corner there, and eleven taverns, not counting the ones in the poker rooms and the hotels. The taverns and poker rooms are here for the lumberjacks, miners, and railroad workers. Son, you ought to see this town on a twenty-below-zero Saturday night in January. You would wonder how, in the stone-cold dead of winter, a town can be so alive!"

A horse-drawn buggy rounded the corner down the street and passed the two Lokens. The horse was as white as snow. The driver wore a tall top hat and black coat and tie. The lady next to him was dressed in a long, navy blue dress. She wore a white, wide brimmed hat adorned with blue ostrich feathers and tied under her chin with a blue silk scarf. The driver pulled up to a large, white building across the street. He was greeted by a boy who took the reins, tying them securely to the deck railing.

"Land speculator," said Olaf. "Here to buy up the cutover so he can sell it back in the old country. Livin' awful high on the hog, I'd say."

The driver of the buggy stepped down, tossed the boy a coin and escorted his companion up the wide steps of the large hotel. A dozen others enjoyed the midday sunshine from their chairs on the second story porch.

"See that fancy building, Son? That's the Merrill Hotel. It sits where the Cable House stood before it caught fire two years back. Now *that* was a hotel. Twice the size of Joe Merrill's place. The Cable House surely was the finest hotel between Chippeway Falls and Ashland. Our own Namakagon Timber Company provided all the white pine and oak in that building. That was my first big sale and the one that really set your uncle and me up in business."

"It looks like brand new, Pa."

"Everything in Cable is new. Three years ago, this town didn't exist. They started building in 1880 when the railroad got here. A year later the streets were lined with new homes and businesses. That's when the Cable House burnt to the ground. Most of the town went up in flames with it. What you see here today is all new.

"The railroad only got here three years ago?"

"Ya, the Omaha-Northwestern line built the depot, put in a siding, a water tower, and, because this was the end of the line back then, they built a turntable for the locomotives. Then it came time to name the town. Some folks called it Gunderson, after the new postmaster. But the railroad company figured since they provided the lumber for the new depot, they had the naming rights. Named it after one of the big shots in the Chicago head office—a fella by the name of Ransom Reed Cable. They put a sign on the depot reading *Cable* and that was that. The name stuck. Good thing, too, 'cause ol' Gunderson turned out to be a crook. Walked off with the whole works and ended up in prison, or so they say.

"I have heard that Ransom Reed Cable has not even bothered to come up to see the town that bears his name. And, mind you, he rides the train for free. His brother came once. That's what they tell me. Came to town, got off the train, walked through the park, looked up the street, looked down the street. He turned right around, walked back to the depot, and boarded the train again. Apparently he didn't appreciate small towns tucked away in the wilderness. You know, Son, some people have no appreciation for the beauty and solitude of the great north woods. Thank the good Lord for cities so folks like that have someplace to hang their hats!"

"Pa, which way is the store where we're meeting Uncle Ingman?"

"Down there past the hotel—the big, whitewashed building with the large window panes."

48

They started across the street. The wheel chair was hard to maneuver in the rutted sand. Next to the huge store, Tor saw two wagons, loaded and covered tarped. Each wagon had a two-horse team. A man sat at the reins of one.

"That fella is Buck Taylor, Son. He will help us get these supplies out to the camp."

Tor and Olaf entered the store to find Ingman paying for the supplies. He saw them come in and made one more request of the clerk.

"Hand me one of those Winchesters, Roy."

"What caliber?"

"Forty-four-forty."

The clerk studied a rack of twelve rifles, taking down the third lever action rifle from the left. With the muzzle pointed up, he pulled the lever forward to open the action, looked inside the chamber, then closed it again with a solid *click-snap*. He eased the hammer down and handed it to Ingman.

"Twelve dollars and two bits, Mr. Loken. Our best seller. Shoots straight right off the rack. Buckhorn sights. Company claims it'll never jam up."

"Twelve dollars and twenty-five cents? Roy! Twelve dollars for a deer rifle? Pretty gol dang steep, ain't it?"

"That's the goin' price. Ain't nothin' cheap in these modern times no more. Cartridges went up, too. Thirty-five cents per box."

"Awful gol dang steep price for a deer rifle, Roy."

"Well, you could wait until you get back to Chicago," said the clerk. "I'm sure you could save a dollar or two down there."

"Chicago? I dare say I won't be going to Chicago any time soon. There is a big Irishman in Chicago who curses my name every time he takes a breath of that foul air! No, I would yust as soon not see him or his city for a time."

"I watched him take a swing at my uncle with a billy club," said Tor. "Uncle Ingman gave him a fist in the side. I could hear the bones snap, I swear!"

"Busted a couple of his slats, did you, Ingman?" said the clerk. "Maybe he'll know better than to cross a pinery boy next time around."

"Tor," Ingman said, "how much money you got?"

Tor reached into his pocket, pulled out a blue kerchief, set it on the glass display case near the cash register and unfolded it, revealing his savings.

"Six dollars and seven cents, Uncle Ingman."

"Olaf," said Ingman, "deer season's 'round the corner and we're going to need to put up plenty of venison for the camp this winter. The boy need's a good rifle. What do you say we give him an advance on his pay?"

"Really, Uncle Ingman?" Tor said, looking up at his uncle.

"I think that's a great idea, Ingman! Put it on the bill along with four, no, six boxes of shells. Tor, you wrap up that silver of yours and keep it in your pocket. You can draw the full amount on your first month's pay. Son, I would buy the rifle for you outright, but a man needs to pay for his first deer rifle with his own earnings. It's the way it's done. Roy, hand that rifle to its new owner."

"Gol dang!" said Tor. "My own gun?"

"Rifle," said his father, "your own rifle. Or, if you want, your own Winchester. And mind your language, Son."

"Yes, sir! My own Winchester! Pa, I can't wait until you show me how to shoot it!"

"All in good time, Tor," said Ingman. "Believe me, by this time next month you'll be a crackshot and we'll have venison in the salt barrels to show for it. Roy, you did load the salt I ordered, ya?"

"On the second wagon, Ingman, nearby the sacks of beans."

"My own Winchester! Pa, Uncle Ingman, thank you!"

"No need for thanks, Son," said Olaf. "You will earn it fair and square."

The three Lokens left the store. Olaf rode with Buck. Tor and Ingman helped him to his seat and tied his wheelchair to the back of the wagon. They climbed onto the lead rig and Ingman gave a snap on the reins and a soft giddup.

"Uncle, what did Mr. Felsman mean when he said we had something called woodticks in our house?"

"Woodticks? Oh ya, I suppose you don't know about woodticks. Well, you see, they're these big blood-sucking bugs that bite clear through your hide when you're not payin' attention. They're about the size of apples. We don't have many at our camp, though."

"We don't?"

"No, sir. Lucky for us the mosquitoes are big as crows. They carry the woodticks off and fry 'em up for breakfast." Tor's eyes widened again.

"Naw. You're joshin' me, Uncle."

"Yust you wait and see, Nephew. Yust you wait and see."

"Pa!" Tor shouted to the next wagon, "How big are the mosquitoes around here?"

"Four, maybe five pounds apiece," Olaf shouted back, straight-faced, "'cept for the big ones."

The horses pulled the wagons down the sandy street past small tar paper shacks, a horse barn, and the blacksmith's shop. Soon they were on the east trail under a clear, blue sky and warm, October sun. The party forded the Namekagon River and Five Mile Creek, named, like other area streams, for its distance from the Cable station. The Lokens were bound for their lumber camp on the east shore of Lake Namakagon.

Chapter 11
The Loken Camp

Although the first eight-mile leg of the wagon ride to camp was rough on Olaf Loken, he uttered not a word of complaint. The elation he felt, finally returning to his home on the lake, far outweighed the difficulty of the journey.

To Tor, the trip was a great adventure. Around each bend he saw more wonders of nature. He also heard more from his uncle about the woods and waters he could now call home.

The rough, rutted trail followed the river, snaking through the forest and crossing several creeks. All four travelers were pleased to reach the fork near the dam. It meant they were at the halfway point. It did not mean the traveling would be easier.

They took the south road. It narrowed again. The ruts were deep. They held tight to their hats and ducked under branches hanging over the trail. Still, they made good time, according to Ingman.

Then, through the trees, the lake appeared. "There she is, Tor!" shouted Olaf. "Lake Namakagon. Oh, how I have longed for this sweet sight."

Tor jumped from the wagon as Ingman pulled back on the reins. He ran down the short path to the lake. A southern breeze formed small waves that sparkled in the afternoon sun. As Tor reached the shore, a Great Blue Heron flushed and flew across the bay bawling out a loud *whaaahk*. Tor watched it glide over the water and land on a low oak limb near the opposite shore. The branch bobbed up and down under the bird's weight.

A late hatch of dragonflies zipped here and there above dark green cattails. One landed on the edge of a lily pad in front of him. Tor knelt to look. As he did, a large bluegill sucked it from sight with a pop, a splash, and a swirl. It quickly devoured the insect as another big bluegill tried to steal it away.

Tor stood again, scanning the landscape and taking in as much of this beauty as his senses would allow. The scene was breathtaking with tall, majestic white pines, yet untouched by the lumberjacks, lining the shores to the east.

Turning to the north, he saw a different scene. Large chest-high pine stumps and thick underbrush were all that remained of the old-growth forest beyond the shore. It had been clear cut. The contrast between the awe-inspiring, pristine, natural view across the lake and this harsh scene of forest destruction to his left was

unsettling. He turned away.

Tor picked up a stone and threw it far out into the quiet bay. He watched as the concentric ripples expanded, eventually disappearing into the surrounding blue water.

"All aboard," shouted Tor's uncle. "Next stop is Loken's Namakagon Timber Company. Make haste, Nephew!" Tor ran back up the path to the wagons. With one, smooth motion he was up and onto the seat next to Ingman. A twitch of the reins, a soft giddup, and the wagons began the last leg of the journey started only days before in Chicago.

Deep ruts from earlier wagons, pushed and pulled the Loken rigs, rocking them and their passengers from side to side. Brush on both sides of the trail leaned in, often raking across the men. Occasionally the trail would open, but soon the brush would close in again, often worse than before.

The horses trudged forward, the twisting trail crossing a narrow creek and stretches of wetland. Small diameter logs had been laid side-by-side across the bog, making it passable by wagon. The rigs shook with a rhythmic shudder as they crossed this corduroy road before proceeding up the slope.

Tor looked ahead. The trail was blocked by a windfall. They pulled up to three large, fallen pines. Tor, Buck and Ingman climbed down. Tor held the reins, steadying the horses. Buck drew two double-bit axes from his wagon. Without a word, he handed one to Ingman who climbed across the logs to the far side. Tor's uncle felt the edge of the blade with his thumb. He then pulled a pair of leather gloves from his coat pocket. Ingman grabbed the ax and started swinging. Soon each chop was throwing large chips of pine into the air. Within minutes the two men cut through the trees and were moving down the logs to make the next cuts. Again the chips flew as Buck and Ingman chopped. Buck returned to the wagon, lifted the corner of the tarp and pulled out a picaroon. He stepped back to the pine, swung the tool into the end of one log and heaved back, turning the log. Twice more he drove the tool into the log and pulled, rolling it off the trail. Ingman was now through the third log. Breathing heavily, he wiped his brow with a handkerchief. Grabbing both axes, he returned to the rigs. Buck rolled the last log off the trail and the wagons were on their way.

"Sure didn't take you and Buck very long," said Tor. "I thought we'd be here till nightfall."

"Till nightfall? Why, those were yust toothpicks! Hope we don't run across any big trees blocking the road. Nephew, years ago, your pa and I were on a road quite a ways west of here one stormy day. The wind came up and this big, ol' pine fell right, smack-dab in front of us. It was so gol dang big, why we knew we couldn't cut it before winter set in. Well, Tor, we yust took out our shovels and covered it up with dirt, then went right over the top. Nowadays, they call that the Rocky Mountains." he said, straight-faced.

Tor shook his head. "Yarn or no yarn, Uncle, your ax sure made short work of those trees."

"Good thing these were yust pine. A big oak or maple really brings the

52

sweat out of you."

Tor readied himself for another tall tale but, instead, heard advice from the seasoned logger.

"Tor, any good bark eater will tell you it isn't as much about muscle as it is about brains. First thing you need is a good double-bit ax that has been sharpened right. The man in the file shed can make a woodchopper's life miserable or he can make it a breeze."

"Next, you need to know how to swing and where to hit in order to bring out the biggest wood chips with the least effort. A good lumberyack knows how to fell a tree with the fewest swings so he has plenty of vim and vigor left over for the next tree. I'll give you a lesson after we have been in camp for a spell. You will soon know how to both sharpen and swing an ax, though I don't see you using one much. We will have better use for you, I 'spect.

"Now, a good, sharp, crosscut saw will take down a pine with far less effort than an ax," Ingman continued. "Buck and I used axes on those windfalls because it would have been hard to get a saw in there. Out in the woods, though, you will see two sawyers working a crosscut saw to fell the tree. Then they will usually cut it into sixteen-foot logs while another fella, the swamper, uses an ax to limb the tree … er … trim off the branches."

"Next, a teamster brings in his ox or his horse, wraps a chain around the end of the log and skids it out to the tote road where it can be loaded onto a timber sleigh. The sleigh brings the logs out onto the frozen lake where they lay all winter. Come spring, when the ice melts and the water levels are high, we drive the whole she-bang on down the river to the sawmills in Hayward. If we get a better offer from some other buyer, we might drive them downstream to a different mill. Maybe all the way to Stillwater or even St. Paul or LaCrosse."

"So, Uncle, what will I do at the camp? What will my job be?"

"You? Well, let me see. What task do we have for Tor Loken? Hmmm. How are you at peeling spuds?"

"I had plenty of experience at the orphanage, Uncle, though I never really took a liking to it."

Ingman laughed. "Well now, Tor, I don't suppose we will have you skinnin' the hides off of spuds for eighty-eight yacks. My guess is you will be your pa's right-hand-man. He will need you to be his legs, too. You and Olaf will likely run the business end of things and I will oversee the men. Your father knows more about the lumber trade than most of the big shots in the biggest outfits. He has a mind for this business and a feel for the pine. Ya, Tor we Lokens will make a good go of it, by golly. We're gonna have the Namakagon Timber Company runnin' like a ten dollar watch. You betcha!"

As the horses negotiated the rough trail again, holding on became more tiring, especially to Tor's father. The four men talked less. After a few more rough miles of ruts, brush, and corduroy, Tor noticed the road was widening. Here and there, a few white pine stumps could be seen among the smaller pines, balsams, cedar, and spruce.

"Tor," called his father from the second wagon, "you are now on Loken land. This is part of our holdings."

"Ya, ya" said Ingman. "The Loken land runs from the lake to two miles north of here and yust about three miles east. It's a fine piece of property. There's enough timber left for at least one more season of cutting. Your pa and I are planning to bid for some more nearby land, too. If we get it, we'll be in business here for a good while longer."

Within minutes, the wagons rounded a bend and climbed a slight grade into the lumber camp. The road widened into a large yard surrounded by log buildings. To the right was a small structure with a lean-to roof and open front. Inside, Tor could see a massive stump supporting a huge anvil and an assortment of large and small tools. This was the blacksmith's shack. Next to it stood the filing shed where one of the workers would be kept busy all winter keeping the crosscuts and axes razor sharp. In the pinery, this man was known as the camp dentist, although the only teeth he fixed were on the saw blades.

A flock of twenty chickens ran across the dusty, lumber camp yard in front of the wagons as the travelers ambled past a big garden and cabbage patch. Hundreds of pumpkins and squash could be seen in a clearing behind.

Ahead was a large barn. A half-dozen horses and a white colt could be seen behind the barn near a chicken coop and a pigpen. Across from the barn stood a long, low, log building with a portico and a double doorway. Tor saw two skylights, one on each end, but not one window. Three black stovepipe chimneys poked out of the roof. The chimney on the near end of the building, Ingman explained, was for the single woodstove in the sleep shanty, where the workers would be bunking in two months. The two chimneys on the far end came from the huge, cast-iron kitchen stoves in the cook shanty. Inside, the cook's pantry also housed the wannigan. There, the workmen could get tobacco, wool socks, and other necessities, all charged against their spring paychecks. Behind the cook shanty stood a large lean-to, stacked to the rafters with a winter's supply of firewood.

At the far end of the yard, overlooking the lake, stood the only two-story building in camp. This was a grand, handsome, log cabin, large enough to contain the company office and the living quarters for the Loken family.

"Tor," said Ingman, "your pa built this home for you and your ma. It deeply hurts him that only part of his dream for you and your ma came true."

As they neared the lodge, tears came to Olaf's deep blue eyes. This was a bittersweet return. He was overjoyed to be returning home after more than two years away. He was thrilled to have his son by his side again. At the same time, he was saddened, wishing fate had taken a different turn. How he longed for Tor's mother to be there with them to enjoy this homecoming. He remained silent about his grief and regret. Olaf Loken wiped his eyes, resolved to move on, to do his best to make this a good home for his son.

Closer now, Tor got a good look at his new home. Above the lodge door was a hand-painted sign reading *Namakagon Timber Company*. Below, *Olaf*

Loken, Prop. The grand log building had a tall, stone chimney and large windows facing the lake. A broad porch stretched around three sides. Two log benches flanked the large double doors. The doors were blocked open to let fresh autumn air flow through the handsome lodge.

"Hello in the camp!" shouted Tor's father as their wagons approached the office. Seconds later a short, round man wearing a white apron came through the office doors onto the porch. He was waving with one hand and holding a large wooden spoon in the other.

"Well, my Lord in Heaven, look what didn't blow in, and, wouldn't ya know, just before supper," shouted the stout man from the porch. "Olaf Loken! It is genuinely wonderful to see you back," he said.

"Sourdough!" shouted Ingman. "This young man is Olaf's boy, Tor." Then, "Nephew, this fellow here is the most important man in camp. Name is Mieczyslaw Kczmarczyk but we yust call him Sourdough. He is the one and only fellow in camp who can silence all the other men three times every day!"

"Pleased to make your acquaintance, sir," said Tor.

"Welcome to camp. Had I knowd your Uncle Ingman was bringin' you and your pa and Buck today, I would have butchered an extra dang mule or two. But don't you never mind me, I will have supper for the lot of you, as usual."

"We're having mule for supper?" Tor asked his uncle, wide-eyed.

"Sourdough," said Ingman, "the way you spout off, it would seem we wouldn't have a single mule left in Bayfield County! They'd all be butchered to make that watered-down stew of yours!"

"Ingman, you old Norski, now don't you start up! Not two minutes in camp and already you're complainin' 'bout my cookin'! Why, I could serve you up mule, mink, or muskrat and you would *still* eat twice your share and ask for the bones to gnaw on!"

"We really havin' mule for supper, Pa?"

"Pay no attention to your uncle. Sourdough's not such a bad cook, be it mule, muskrat, or whatever he puts in the stewpot." Then, "Buck, you take care of the wagons. Meet us in the lodge for supper. First, though, give me a hand getting off this dang bone shaker. I've had enough travelin' for a while."

Buck climbed from the wagon seat, brought Olaf's wheelchair around, and helped him down. Tor wheeled his father onto the porch. Olaf took control of the wheels and spun the chair around to look across the yard, hearing only the sound of the light breeze drifting through the bright, yellow tamaracks.

Olaf squeezed his son's hand. "It surely is good to be home, Tor. So good to be back here in the Loken camp with my son and my brother. There were times I thought I might never see this day. But here we are. The Lokens are back. Back home and ready to make timber."

"Pa?" whispered Tor, "Does Sourdough really serve mule meat for dinner?"

Chapter 12
The Whitetail

The first two weeks in the lumber camp kept Tor busy. He learned some of the ins and outs of the business, harvested thirty bushels of cabbages, and helped Sourdough put up large crocks of sauerkraut in anticipation of the many hungry men who would descend on the camp in a few weeks.

Tor spent one day cruising a woodlot to the north with his uncle and another brushing out the trail around the south end of the lake. He and Ingman increased the size of the corral to accommodate more horses this winter. They did the same for the ox pen. Blisters on his hands soon turned to calluses.

Olaf taught Tor how to safely handle a rifle. Each day he practiced shooting his uncle's twenty-two and each evening he listened to the stories told by his father, uncle, and Sourdough over hands of pinochle. Some of the stories were true. Some were clearly not. Most fell somewhere in between, often leaving him perplexed.

The stories he heard made him eager for his first hunt. He would not have to wait long. In late October the whitetail rut would start, and they would begin a quest to put up enough venison for winter.

Nine days before the hunt, Chief Namakagon appeared at the office door. He joined the Lokens for supper in the lodge.

"Olaf," the chief said, sampling a piece of Sourdough's mincemeat pie, "I thank you for inviting me to your camp."

"Good you could join us, Namakagon," said Olaf. "We hope you'll stay on a while. Please consider our camp to be your camp."

"Say," said Ingman, "Sourdough, Tor, and I are planning to strike out into the woods next week to put up some camp meat. You can yoin us if you want. We can always use another hand."

"I usually hunt alone. The deer are less anxious when a single hunter walks the woods. But, yes, I will join you next week. I can share with Tor some of my knowledge of the whitetail—if this is acceptable to you," he looked toward Olaf.

"Wonderful!" replied Tor's father. "It will be a good experience for this tenderfoot of ours."

"Chief Namakagon, I have my own Winchester! It's a forty-four-forty. Pa says I'm a crackshot with it, too"

Namakagon laughed. "In my youth, many hunts passed before I learned to trade my excitement for patience. Soon you will know what I mean, young man. A hunter must learn these lessons out in the woods, in the presence of his prey. It is knowledge discovered by young eagles, young wolves, young cougar, and young men when they first hunt. Soon, Tor, you will know the way of the whitetail—and more about yourself as his predator."

The evening meal ended with the elders recalling past hunts and a salute to the whitetail made by Chief Namakagon. He stepped before the fireplace. His voice was somber and he gestured with his hands as he said, "To the whitetail."

"Softly treading the forest floor,
Wary and wild, quick of mind,
He surveys all that lies before,
With one eye on the trail behind.

Caution is his way of life,
Foiling death, again and again.
His senses are keen as the sharpest knife.
He's Nature's reward to worthy men.

Go, hunters. Trek from camp to field.
Search the forest where he runs free.
For you, his freedom he might yield,
If Nature says it's meant to be."

"Hip, hip, hurrah!" shouted Ingman, raising his glass high in the air.

A week later Sourdough, Tor, and Ingman made final preparations for the hunt. It would begin in the cutover near the north end of the lake. As they made their plans, Olaf remained in the office, checking ledgers and reviewing timber value estimates Ingman had gathered during his earlier inspection of the government land east of the lake. Olaf longed to be with the hunting party, but his legs would not let him. He would have to be content looking on from his wheelchair as the others prepared for the hunt.

After supper, the party made their final arrangements, laid out their gear, then turned in. The anticipation of the next day's hunt kept Tor awake longer than the others. He finally drifted off to sleep with incoherent dreams of a whitetail buck with antlers as large as those hanging high above the fireplace in the lodge.

Sourdough was up first, both from habit and by his profession, cooking sausage, eggs, and biscuits. He tucked three extra biscuits and several smoked sausages into the pockets of the red, wool mackinaws hanging near the door.

In the darkness, the three hunters took to the field. Mackinaws buttoned against the cold pre-dawn air and rifles in hand, the hunting party soon skirted a large stand of oak, just north of the lake. They would begin their hunt near a narrow swamp between two oak ridges.

In the dim morning light, Ingman posted Tor on a good stand. It overlooked a deer trail crossing the creek and leading from the swamp. He chose a spot on the opposite ridge. Sourdough would slowly work his way through the oaks to the north.

Tor stood on a large pine stump in the cold, morning air. He watched as the sun slowly revealed the woods around him. Soon the first rays of sunlight edged over the ridge. The warmth of the sun on his face felt good. He wished his toes could enjoy some of this warmth. The young hunter remained silent and still, watching the landscape below him for the slightest movement. A white-footed mouse darted out from under a log and rustled in the leaves a few feet away. Then all fell silent again, other than the call of a raven in the distance.

A single, sharp rifle shot rang out, echoing off the twin ridges. His uncle's rifle had shattered the silence, startling Tor. It woke a nearby red squirrel who chattered in disapproval.

Tor stayed on his post, wondering if the shot was good. Another shot rang out, muffled and much quieter than the first. This second, muffled report, he recalled, from his father's hunting stories, was probably a mercy shot, meant to quickly dispatch a mortally wounded animal. They would be bringing home at least one deer, he thought. Tor remained on his post as he was told. He waited and watched for the next three hours.

Biscuits and sausage long gone, Tor's morning wore on without sight of a single whitetail. He wanted to move, to roam the woods in hope of seeing deer, but he forced back his impatience, remembering advice from the others.

The sun was high now. Tor's hands and feet warmed. He sat as still as possible, leaning back on the big barber's chair projecting up from the wide stump chosen for his post.

Three spruce hens walked past him, unaware of his presence. A hawk with a red squirrel in its talons passed overhead, then landed in a dead pine out in the swamp. Tor watched the raptor peck at its meal, remembering Namakagon's earlier words about predators and prey.

Around ten o'clock, Tor saw something move near the creek, something small coming down the deer trail. A fisher. Wait. No. A fox. Straight toward him. It crossed the creek then stopped, looking back down the trail.

Tor, only yards away, watched in silence. It didn't take a skilled woodsman to know the nervous fox had another animal behind. A moment later Tor saw more movement down the trail. The fox bolted toward him, nearly running across his boots. When it realized its blunder, it flared and streaked across the forest floor in a red-orange flash.

Looking back down the trail, Tor saw something brown in the underbrush. It moved, then stopped, and then moved again. Tor saw the legs, the body, then the head of a whitetail doe. She crossed the creek, following the bank upstream into the swamp. Tor raised his Winchester.

The doe stopped, looking back. Tor gently cocked the hammer, making a soft click, hardly audible to his ear, but as loud as a Sunday church bell to the doe. She snorted and dashed through the brush, a fawn close behind.

Tor eased off the hammer, relieved, yet anxious—upset with himself for missing this first opportunity. His heart pounding, he took a deep breath, lowering his rifle.

He heard a slight crack in the brush. His eyes darted back toward the creek. Something else was on the trail. It came closer. It came fast—running—a blur through the trees—clearer now—there! A deer—yes, definitely a deer—a big deer—running fast—a buck—a big buck—rifle up—buck moving fast—very fast. The hammer came back. The deer kept coming. Tor saw an opening for a shot. He bore down on the sights with his right eye as the buck passed between two oaks. Tor squeezed the trigger. The rifle stock pounded against his shoulder.

The crack of the rifle, barely noticed by the hunter, shook the woods. It echoed off the surrounding hills as Tor levered another round into the chamber. It did not matter. In a handful of heartbeats, the big buck had come and gone.

"Dang it all!" Tor shouted, easing down the hammer, heart pounding with excitement. Pulse racing, he wished he'd acted sooner, shot better. "My first shot. My first shot at a buck and I missed him clean!" He tried to imagine what he should have done, what he might do differently if the buck came down that trail again. He knew it would not. It had to be a half-mile away by now. Maybe it would go past his uncle. His uncle wouldn't miss. "Uncle Ingman is a better hunter, a better shot."

Tor felt disgusted for shooting too soon. No—not shooting soon enough. No, not that, either. He didn't know what he'd done wrong. Silently, he swore he would pay closer attention next time, react sooner, make the shot count. Relaxing a bit, his mind wandered back to Chief Namakagon's poem. "If Nature says it is meant to be," Namakagon had said. "Maybe it was not meant to be," Tor whispered. "Maybe next time."

He wondered what Uncle Ingman and Sourdough would say. What would his father say? If only he could do it over. He imagined hearing Sourdough's words.

"Well, didja git 'im, boy?" Sourdough might ask. "Why that buck must've been close enough to spit on! Didja git 'im? Must've been a twelve or fourteen pointer!"

"Missed him clean," Tor decided he would reply. "Should have had him, Sourdough, but I missed him clean."

Tor knew he would take a good ribbing for this. "But I did all I could do, didn't I?" he thought. Now feeling disgusted and depressed, he remained perched on his post overlooking the creek bottom.

"Good morning, young woodsman," a voice whispered.

Tor jumped, startled by Namakagon, standing a few feet behind him.

"Oh! Chief Namakagon. How did … where did you come …"

"Shhhhh. I heard you shoot. I knew your uncle would post you here. I did not mean to startle you. I try to not announce my presence when stalking."

"Startled?" replied Tor. "No, I wasn't start …"

Namakagon quietly interrupted. "I came to help you dress out your animal."

"Missed him. Missed him clean," Tor confessed. "Should have had him, but I missed him clean."

"Tell me the story."

"Well, first, I saw this fox come down the trail and cross the creek, then a doe and a fawn, then a nice buck. I thought I had a good shot through those two oaks there, but I missed. I couldn't get a second shot. He ran into the brush along the creek."

"First, a fox. I have seen this many times. The fox is smart. Often first down the trail when man enters the woods. First the fox, then the deer. Probably running from Sourdough. Your first lesson today—When the fox crosses your path, watch next for the deer."

Namakagon silently stepped toward the oaks. He carried only a bow. A quiver of arrows was slung over his shoulder. "Where did the deer cross?"

"It came right down here. Ran between these trees and into the brush."

"Big buck," whispered the chief. "You can tell by the depth of his track." He looked back toward the barber-chaired stump where Tor posted and then turned, peering into the woods before stepping forward.

"Your bullet hit here," he said quietly, pointing to a small pine with a notch taken out of the trunk, "not too high, not too low." He studied the pine, the tracks, and looked back at the barber-chair stump again.

The distant report of a rifle shattered the quiet air. It came from the cutover where Sourdough was hunting. Tor and the chief looked at each other. Another shot rang out and then another, followed by a fourth.

"Sounds like Sourdough got one," whispered Tor.

"Not likely, young woodsman," said Namakagon. "My elders have a saying: One shot, deer; Two shots, maybe; Three shots, miss! I have seen this hold true more times than not. Back to your stand now, quickly."

They watched the trails leading from the cutover before turning their attention back to the sign left by Tor's buck.

Namakagon looked at the notched pine again, then at the grass and plants below it. He reached down with his right hand and picked something up, placing it in his left palm. He studied it for a moment and then turned to Tor, saying, "You hit your mark, young woodsman."

Tor looked at Namakagon's outstretched palm and saw a tuft of brown hair. "I did? I hit him? But I was sure I missed."

"Shhhhh. Until the deer is ours, we must remain quiet—both to save ourselves a longer search and out of respect for the animal. Tor, lesson two. After *every* shot you must *always* look for sign of a hit. You owe this to the animal. Men unwilling to do this are neither fit to be in forest nor field."

The skilled hunter slowly stepped forward, his eyes scouring the plants at his feet. "Blood," he whispered. Then, "good blood." He took a few more steps forward, studying the alders and the ground below. He turned back toward Tor who was close behind.

60

"Look. There is blood on these alders and on both sides of the trail. Your bullet has passed through the deer."

Namakagon stretched out his hand to Tor. "Congratulations, young woodsman, on your first whitetail buck."

"You—you mean I got him?"

"Shhh! Yes. We will find him within a hundred yards," whispered Namakagon, again inspecting the blood trail, "probably much closer. He is now yours. Here is the sign. You follow it. Go slowly. There is no need to hurry. Try not to disturb the sign, young woodsman."

As he followed the blood trail, Tor listened to tracking advice softly spoken from behind. The sign became easier to follow as they moved farther from Tor's post. Soon the blood could be seen on many of the nearby stems of grass, on leaves, and on the thin tag alders. Soon the blood seemed to be everywhere along the trail. Then the sign diminished, making it harder to follow. The chief reminded Tor to not disturb any sign. Soon, the blood stopped. Tor scoured the trail.

"Kneel down," came words from behind. Tor handed his rifle to the chief, then knelt to study the leaves. There, before him, was a small speck of blood. Soon another drop revealed itself in a deer track. A few feet ahead, another. Then, again, nothing.

"Now, young woodsman, you will see why it is so important to not disturb the blood sign," said Namakagon. "Your quarry has backtracked. Behind us, where you saw all the blood, that is where he stood watching to see if he was being pursued. This was ten, maybe twenty seconds after you shot. Seeing no threat, your buck continued down the trail. As he became weaker from loss of blood, he stopped again. He then turned for another look down his back trail. Again he saw nothing. He felt no pain, just weakness. He walked slowly back toward you as you stood on your stand. When convinced he was not threatened, he looked for a place to rest and slipped into the thickest brush. Find the new trail and you will find your buck."

Tor knelt again, carefully studying the leaves, grass and twigs. There, on the back of a blade of grass was another speck of blood. He found another drop, then another. More followed. The tracking was easier. Tor looked ahead, seeing thick tag alders, brown marsh grass, and a large boulder in the underbrush. He looked down again to the blood trail.

Namakagon placed a hand on the boy's shoulder. "There."

Tor looked up. Just beyond the large, smooth, brown rock, a single, forked antler curved upward. This was no rock at all, but the body of a large deer lying on the forest floor. His heart racing now, Tor led the way through the brush, approaching the buck.

"Wait!" Namakagon warned. "Look first at the eyes. They will tell you if it is safe."

Tor stepped around the deer, trying to get a better view of his buck. It lay on its side with one antler half buried in the soft soil. The other forked into

61

four long, points. The eyes were open but glazed and lifeless.

Namakagon gently prodded the deer with the end of his bow. "His spirit has left him," he said. "The whitetail is yours to keep forever in your memories and to share at your table. He lived well. He did not suffer. Now his spirit will continue its journey, just as we continue ours."

Namakagon lifted the head of the buck by the antler. "Look. Five points on one side, four on the other. This bark on his brow tines shows he has been marking his territory, warning other bucks to leave his does alone."

"Nice buck," said Tor, trying to hide his excitement in the presence of the somber, collected elder. "Just look at those horns."

"Antlers, young woodsman. Antlers are shed off each year. Horns are not. This buck has shed his antlers many seasons. We will dress him out and take him to the tote road. First, though, we must honor him for his gift to us. We must also thank Nature for letting us share in her abundance once again."

Tor watched as Namakagon motioned skyward. Chanting softly, he reached down to his belt, opened a small pouch and removed a pinch of tobacco. He passed his hands over the handsome animal, letting flakes of tobacco fall onto the deer. Sunlight filtered through the trees, onto the hunters and the deer.

Both Tor and Namakagon were silent now. The songs of nearby birds and the soft rustling of the leaves in the trees were the only sounds to be heard.

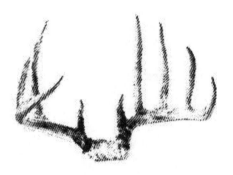

Chapter 13
Rogues and Scoundrels

The antlers of Tor's first buck were hung high in the gable end of the Namakagon Timber Company office. Olaf proudly pointed the trophy out to anyone who entered the lumber camp headquarters.

"My son took that nine-point," he'd say. "One shot, clean and quick."

Tor was proud as well. In just four days, the party of four hunters brought in a total of nine bucks, one doe, and a bear. The chief took three of the deer and the bear with his bow. Two lumberjacks who came into camp a few weeks early were put to work helping Sourdough and Tor butcher, salt, and smoke the meat. Chief Namakagon traded the hides for a hundred pounds of sugar and a barrel of molasses for the camp kitchen. Sourdough would have extra sweets for the shanty boys this season.

Winter was coming. In the barn, the sleighs, harnesses, and chains were being inspected and repaired. The haymow was stacked to the roof. The oat bin was full. Every stall for more than forty head of oxen and horses was lined with fresh straw for the animals soon to arrive with their teamsters. The skid trails from the new cuttings were brushed out. Wilbur Johnson, the camp dentist, had every saw and ax sharp and ready.

The camp blacksmith, Gust Finstead, and Louie Thorpe, carpenter, were finishing three new sleighs to haul logs from the cuttings to the lake. In their skilled hands, wood and iron became the runners, beams, bunks, sway bars, whiffletrees, and tongues making up each sleigh.

The cook shanty had plenty of pork, venison, onions, apples, squash, and pumpkins put up. Gunnysacks of potatoes and beans were stacked to the storeroom ceiling next to fifty-pound muslin sacks of flour, sugar, and salt.

Sourdough rendered three drums of lard for frying, baking, and for making soap. The last of the turnips, carrots, and rutabagas were being harvested from the garden and put up in the large root cellar dug into the hill behind the cook shanty.

Olaf had his ledgers ready, pencils sharpened, and the ink well filled. The Namakagon Timber Company was primed for another winter's cut. The only things lacking now was a foot of snow and a full company of lumberjacks. Although most of the men who worked at the Namakagon Timber Company the previous year would be returning, room could be found for more.

Olaf knew it wouldn't be hard to find good workers. Hayward was crowded now with men looking for pinery work and the Loken camp was one of the best outfits around. Olaf was known as a good head push, Ingman, a good woods boss, Sourdough's food was the best to be found, and, although some camps failed to pay up at the end of the season, the Lokens were known to be honest and reliable.

Working for the Namakagon Timber Company was one of the best bets in this part of the pinery in 1883, in spite of the nation's poor economy.

Sawyers and swampers could count on good wages—thirty dollars a month and a bonus if the timber sold high. Teamsters made the same wages, unless they brought their own teams. If they did, their pay was almost doubled.

The weather turned cold now, and the first good snow couldn't be far behind. A few farmers trickled into camp during the next few days. Back home the crops were in, and the families were set for winter, allowing the men to find pinery work. With most sawmills now closed for lack of timber, many mill hands were also looking for work in the lumber camps.

Men first in camp got the best bunks. The ones too close to the door might shiver all night when the outside temperature fell to forty below zero. The bunks nearest the stove at the end of the shanty were often too hot for sleeping, especially in the milder months. The veteran lumberjacks prized the middle bunks so much that they were often won and lost at the poker table.

Tor's uncle left camp right after breakfast one early November morning. That afternoon he boarded the southbound train. He was on his way to Hayward to recruit more lumberjacks.

Ingman had another task to tend to while in town. He and Olaf were hoping to expand. His first stop was the state land office where he placed bids on several sections of land near the camp. From there he checked in at Johnny Pion's hotel across the street. At dusk, he returned to the land office to learn he had been outbid. He shared the disappointing news with his friend, Pete Foster, owner of Foster's Saloon, next door to the land office.

"The Muldoon outfit beat us out by four dollars an acre, Pete. Four dollars! I don't see how they expect to make a profit. Must be plannin' to scalp the land clear."

"They are crooks, Ingman. King Muldoon has made a fortune by shavin' the whiskers off thousands upon thousands of acres southwest of here. He cheats the government when he buys the land and then he cheats his men when it comes time to square up in the spring. Muldoon is buyin' up more and more. Somebody needs to put a stop to it." Pete poured him another beer.

"Not much I can do about it, Pete. Small outfits like ours yust don't have the capital to swing the big timber sales. Ya, I guess Phineas Muldoon calls himself King for good reason."

"Ingman, you and I have been acquainted for a long while, and I don't mean to butt into your business, but, well, I think there is a way to get the land you want. And it's all on the up and up, at least as far as the law is concerned. At the same time you might teach old King Muldoon a lesson about makin' his fortune on the backs of hard-workin' folks."

Twenty minutes and two beers later, Ingman left Foster's Saloon with a plan. At six o'clock when the land office closed, Ingman was there. The clerk stepped out, thrust a skeleton key into the keyhole, and locked the office door.

"Say, now, Mr. Thompson," Ingman said as the clerk pocketed the key, "yoin me for a beer at the hotel?"

"Oh, Loken. A beer? Well, I don't know, now. I … I think I should really be on my ..."

"Now, Mr. Thompson, surely you have time for a friendly glass or two. You put in a full day for the government today. My treat!"

"Loken," replied the clerk, "I believe I will join you. It has been a long day, and a beer would taste good. And call me Bob."

The two men crossed to the hotel. Ingman put a silver dollar on the bar and ordered two glasses of beer. Two women were talking to three men at the far end of the bar. Other than Ingman, the clerk, and the bartender, the only other person in the bar was a man with his head on a corner table, apparently fast asleep. The bartender placed a plate heaped with fresh pork rinds and a small bowl of salt before Ingman and Bob. The clerk sprinkled a pinch of salt into his beer, then grabbed a pork rind, dipped it into the salt, and bit into it.

"That was some bid King Muldoon put in on the land up by Lake Namakagon, eh Bob? They must think those pines are pure gold!"

"Oh, yes. You know, Ingman, that weren't no honest bid."

"No?"

"No, Muldoon has figured out a system for swindling the state and beatin' out the competition. It's a clever, slippery thing he does."

"If he's cheatin' the state, well, shouldn't something be done?"

"Something should be done, alright" said Bob. "I wish to hell I could stop him, but what can I do? Some shyster must have told him how to get away with it. Why, I'll bet Muldoon cheats the government enough to pay a hundred shysters. It's not right when the big outfits cheat the public in order to make their fortunes. If they were caught cheatin' at poker, they could get shot, but when they cheat the State of Wisconsin on these land deals, all they get is rich."

"Ya, you're right, Bob. Wish someone had the nerve to step in."

"Scoundrels!" said Thompson. "Rogues and scoundrels, that's all they are. If only we had a way to stop them." He tipped up his second glass of beer.

Ingman noticed one of the women down the bar looking their way. Placing his arm around the clerk's shoulder and leaning in, Ingman said quietly, "Bob, a fella once said, 'Where there's a will, there's a way.' Ever hear of that one? Where there's a will, there's a way?"

"Yeah, I heard of it," the clerk replied. "What good does it do? Gol dang scoundrels." He dipped another pork rind in the salt and bit into it with a loud crunch. "I told the state inspector about this last spring. You know what he told me? You know what he said, Loken? He said his hands are tied. He said if we complain we could lose our jobs. Lose our jobs, Ingman! There must be somebody upstairs gettin' paid off. It sure ain't me. I can tell you that much. I can't even afford decent Sunday clothes for my wife and little ones."

"Let's you and me put our heads together. I'll bet we can figure a way to put a stop to this. Where there's a will, there's a way, Bob. Whadaya say? Let's you and me show 'em that cheatin' the public does not pay after all."

"You got cards up your sleeve, Ingman?"

"If I don't, I'll figure a way to put them there. Now tell me how their scheme works, start to finish. Maybe then we'll find a hole in their plan big enough to drive a sleigh full of logs through, Bob."

The clerk finished his fourth beer. "Well, it's pretty simple. First they come in with a low bid just like everyone else. Then, right before bidding closes, they enter a second bid, four, maybe five dollars more than the land is worth. At the same time they put down the ten dollars needed to guarantee the bid. That gets them the sale. Then, next thing you know, they come in and cancel their damn bid, giving up their sawbuck. Ten bucks means nothin' to these scoundrels anyway. Hell, Ingman, they can get three to six bucks at the mill for a good pine saw log! What's a dang sawbuck to a crook like Muldoon?

"Keep goin', Bob. What happens next?"

"Well, now, with their bid off the table, the land parcel goes up for sale again. But now, Ingman, nobody but Muldoon and his men know about it, see? Nobody. You followin' me on this, Ingman? There is no one out there to bid against him!" He took another drink of beer. "Well! Next day Muldoon's man sends a telegram to the state land office in Madison offering the bare minimum that the State of Wisconsin will accept. That's a dollar and a quarter an acre, Ingman. A lousy ten bits for each acre of land including every stick of timber and even the mining rights! King Muldoon gets the whole damn she-bang, Ingman! Gol dang pot-lickin' scoundrel, that's what he is, by gum!" He took another long draw from his mug.

"Yeah, looks like they have a good swindle goin' on, all right. A very good land swindle. Tell me, this telegram, who does it go to?"

"The state land office. That's all I know."

"I'd sure like to know who they contact there."

"They telegraph someone in Madison. I don't know who. I get word back the next day that the deal is done—signed, sealed and delivered."

The two women and three jacks down the bar were quieter now. Ingman grew concerned they might overhear his conversation with the clerk.

"Bob," said Ingman in a whisper, "I have an idea. I think we might be able to turn the tables on Phineas Muldoon. Maybe we can beat him at his own game, if we work together."

"You'll keep me out of it?"

"Don't you worry, Bob. Nobody will know."

"All right then. What can I do, Ingman?"

"I'll be here in the hotel tomorrow. I will sit at the table next to the window so I can keep an eye on your office. You yust give me a wave when Muldoon's man cancels their bid on that land up by Namakagon. That's all you have to do. Yust get word to me that the deal's off. I will do the rest."

"Nobody can know I played a part. We're clear on that, right, Ingman?"

"Clear as gin, Bob. Clear-as-gin."

66

Chapter 14
Turnabout

Ingman was up at dawn. He shaved at the dry sink near the door, donned a new shirt, added a starched collar and tie, put on his new wool trousers, socks, garters, and boots. He then slipped on his vest and suit coat, fastened his watch fob to his waistband, and dropped his gold watch in a vest pocket. He fastened his tie with a gold pin, donned his derby hat, and stepped in front of the mirror on the dresser. Three minutes later, Ingman sat at the table near the window overlooking the state land office across the street.

While Ingman was finishing his sausage and biscuits, he noticed his new friend, Bob Thompson, unlocking the land office door. Ingman motioned to the waiter.

"I'm in room seven," he said. "I need you to hold this table for me. I'll be right back." He placed a nickel in the palm of the waiter's hand. The waiter nodded with a wide smile.

Seconds later, Ingman was in the land office.

"Mornin', Bob."

"Oh, Ingman," said the clerk, looking up, "I didn't hear you come in."

"How ya doin' this chilly morning?"

"Good as can be expected after all that beer we drank."

"Now, Bob," Ingman said, "about our conversation last night. Are we still gonna give those scoundrels what for? Are you still with me on this?"

"You're dang right I'm with you. I will hail you from the window just as soon as I hear the Muldoon bid is canceled."

"All right. That's what I wanted to hear. I'll be across the street, watching for a signal. I have some work to do that will keep me there all day. You give me a sign, Bob. I'll take the reins from there."

"Like I said, though, you keep me clear of it, Ingman. I have a wife and two daughters to support. I can't afford to lose this job. I won't risk my life workin' in the woods. No, sir. I'm no shanty boy and don't intend to become one."

"Don't you fret. Like I said last night, I'll keep this all under my hat."

Ingman left the office, crossing the boardwalk and the rutted, frozen street to the hotel. He sat down at his table with a day-old copy of the *St. Paul Pioneer Press*. Within a few minutes four, big men approached him.

"You be Loken?" one asked.

"I am Ingman Loken. And you?"

"Name is Leonard Lewten out of Mankato, Minnesota. Me and me brothers, we're up here lookin' for work. Sign at the depot says you're hirin'."

"You fellows have any experience workin' in the woods?"

"I got two years under me belt as a cross-hauler and river pig," he answered. "Brother Norman, here, he got two years in as a swamper. Me other brothers, Thomas and Clem, they got no time workin' in the pinery, but they are

67

both strong as bulls and willin' to do all what's needed. Our Pa taught us to work hard. And, like I said, I been a river pig. I been on two log drives, and I can show me brothers the ropes. Us Lewtens don't mind workin' in the cold. Don't matter none if it's thirty below in Febrary or if we's neck-deep in the river in April."

Ingman pulled a small notebook from his inside coat pocket. "You boys drink much?"

"Only on Saturday nights, Mr. Loken. Never in camp, if that's the rule of the outfit."

"It is. Hard and fast. Pay is thirty a month guaranteed, plus a bonus if the timber sells high," said Ingman. "You'll be in the woods from first light until dark, six days a week. Three meals and bunk included. You'll draw your pay when the timber gets to the mills, yust like everyone else. Anybody caught stealin', cheatin' at cards, or fightin' in camp will be given his walkin' papers on the spot. Any man who decides to yump camp to work up in the mines or yoin up with some other lumber outfit, well, he'll get none of the pay owed him. Not a penny. Leonard, we are good to our men, and we expect them to be loyal to us. Any questions?"

"Them terms are agreeable. Sign us up, Boss."

"All right boys," said Ingman, writing four names in his notebook. "You're in the camp. You'll need to go north to Cable. You can walk or take the train. Seventeen miles. From there you'll take the tote road eastward along the river to the dam. It's a good eight mile walk. There's a fellow there with a boat who will row you across Lake Namakagon to the camp or you can walk around the south trail, your choice. It's a half-day on foot. When you get to the camp go straight to the office and tell my brother, Olaf, that I hired you. Your pay and your work starts the next mornin'.'."

"That's fine, Boss. We'll be there fit and ready to work."

"Your brothers have anything to say?"

They looked at each other without speaking. Leonard said, "No, sir. I don't think they do." Grinning, the four Lewtens left the hotel bar.

With an eye on the land office across the street, Ingman went back to his paper. A tall, broad-shouldered man approached. He wore calked boots laced to the top. Hand-knit green wool socks stretched almost to the knees of his black, wool britches. His green and black plaid wool shirt and black suspenders looked new, but his red mackinaw showed many seasons of use. A sweat-stained felt hat shaded his dark eyes, three-day beard, and heavy, black eyebrows. On the right side of his face lay the telltale pockmarks left after being kicked with calked boots. Overall, he had the look of a hard-living, hard-working, hard-fighting lumberjack. He walked straight to Ingman.

"Your name Loken?"

"Who's askin'?"

"Jackson's the name. Mill foreman's my trade. Lookin' for winter work."

68

"We sold our sawmill near to three years ago," said Ingman, glancing out the window. "Try A. J. Hayward over at the new dam. Maybe he can put you to work."

"He's full up. Thought you could put me somewhere else. I can get good hard work out of men, if hard work is what you want."

Ingman noticed two men entering the land office and then looked back at Jackson.

"Woods boss yob is filled. Our barn boss yob is open, but I can see that's not for you. Been on any spring drives?"

"In seven years I worked seven log drives on the Wolf River for the Paulsen outfit down near Fremont. Quit when they pulled up stakes and went down to Fond du Lac. That's when I got the mill foreman job in Oshkosh. When the mill burnt to the ground I thought I'd give it a try in the pinery again. I gotta tell ya, though; I don't have much good to say about driving logs on fast water. Loken, I seen men die on them drives. One wrong step and a man can disappear in that ice-cold, muddy water. Nothin' left but his hat floatin' twixt the pine. Ain't no way for a fella to die."

"Well, Yackson, you can fell or swamp if that's your likin', or I can try you out on a chain-haul team. You would be top-loadin' sleighs. Yob pays thirty-a-month if you want it. You show me your mettle during the winter and, come spring, maybe you can help head up our drive—if you got the gumption. Fifty-dollar bonus, provided you stay with the yob till the logs make the mill. If you yump camp, Jackson, don't expect to be paid. And, Jackson, no liquor, no guns, no brawlin' in camp."

The big man nodded in approval. "I'll take that top-loader job, Mr. Loken. One more thing, I don't mind a scuffle now and then. You ever need someone with some backbone, you can count on me."

"Good to know, Yackson. We all get along pretty well in our camp but you yust never know what's around the next bend."

"Boss, I'll turn up in camp in a couple a days. I need to inspect the local scenery here in Hayward first. Might be the last chance for a long while to waltz with the young lassies instead of some ripe-smellin' shanty boy."

"Take your time. Yust be in camp before the snow flies." Reaching for his notebook, Ingman added, "You got a first name, Yackson?"

"I go by Blackie."

The big lumberjack turned and left, ducking as he passed through the hotel doorway. Ingman looked again at the land office window, saw the two men leave but no sign or signal from the land clerk. Ingman watched Blackie Jackson cross the rutted street and enter a tavern.

"Blackie Yackson," he thought. "Seems I've heard that name before." He glanced again at the land office window, then returned to his newspaper. "Blackie Yackson." He flipped back through several pages. There, in a small, page-three article he read, *INFERNO DESTROYS OSHKOSH MILL*. Ingman read on.

69

"A fire has burnt to the ground the Fox-Poygan lumber mill in Oshkosh, Wisc. The Oshkosh City Fire Department dispatched its new hand pumper but to no avail. Water pumped from the river was no match for the flaming pine, the smoke from which rose well into the sky as the fire blazed both day and night. Only the foundation now remains. A blacksmith shop aside the mill was also lost in the blaze, but other nearby mills were spared from the fiery conflagration. The Fox-Poygan mill foreman, who was recently demoted for mistreatment of a workman, is missing and presumed deceased and lost to the fire. Oshkosh police and the Fire Marshall tell this newspaper that they will search for the body of Irving Jackson Black, the missing mill worker, when the embers from the devastation are stone cold."

"Well I'll be gol danged!" muttered Ingman. "Blackie Yackson. Now don't that take all the beer and the bucket, too!"

Five Ojibwe men came in carrying a letter from Chief Namakagon. Ingman hired them on the spot. The Namakagon Timber Company, like many of the camps in the north, counted on the skills of the Chippeways, as the French called them. Ingman assured them that, unlike most of the other camps, a good day's work would net them the same pay as the other men received.

It took the Norwegian woods boss a while to write their names in the notebook. He sounded the names out as best he could and jotted them down as he thought best. He then numbered the five names in his book and looked up.

"Remember these numbers," he said, pointing. "You are Yoe-one, you are Yoe-two, you are Yoe-three, you are Yoe-four and you are Yoe-five."

Four of the Ojibwes laughed at Ingman's inability to pronounce their names. The fifth man did not.

"I am Misakakojiish," he said, sternly, "not Joe-five. You write Misakakojiish or you write Angry Badger or you write nothing. *Not* Joe-five!"

"Angry Badger it is," Ingman replied, scratching Joe-five from the list and making the change. "I'll see you fellas in camp."

Ingman finished his newspaper and pulled his watch from his vest pocket. Half-past nine. He glanced across the street to see a well-dressed man approaching. Ingman watched him enter the land office. The same man stepped back into the morning sun moments later. He pulled a cigar from an inside pocket, struck a match on his boot and lit the cigar. Tossing the spent match into the street, he headed for the depot. Seconds later, Bob Thompson appeared at the window, pulled out a handkerchief, shook it open and blew his nose.

Ingman stood up to let Thompson know he saw the signal. Gulping down his coffee, he tucked his newspaper under his arm, pulled a quarter from his pocket, and dropped it on the table saying, "Hold this table for me again, ya?" He left the hotel and followed the well-dressed man into the depot.

The cigar smoker crossed the waiting room to the telegraph window. "I need to send this message," he said, handing the telegrapher a note. Ingman sat on a nearby bench, opened his newspaper, and listened.

The telegrapher wore a collarless white shirt. Garters held the sleeves and cuffs up and out of the way of his nimble fingers. He was a younger man, perhaps twenty-three or four. A green visor shielded his eyes from the single, electric light bulb hanging above. He read the note, made some pencil marks on a sheet of paper, and said, "That'll be nineteen cents, sir."

The man counted out the coins, laying them on the sill of the barred window. "... Seventeen, eighteen, nineteen. There you are, Sonny."

Ingman strained to hear the name of the recipient of the message. He could not. He hadn't counted on the message being on a slip of paper. He needed that name if he hoped to make his plan work.

The man puffed on his cigar as he crossed the waiting room and left the depot. Ingman remained seated, wondering what he might do to get that name. He could hear the clicking and tapping of the telegraph operator's key.

Seconds later, the depot door swung open. Cigar still in hand, the man approached the window again.

"Sir?" said the telegrapher.

"I need a receipt, Sonny."

"Yes, sir. Right away, sir."

The telegrapher dipped his pen into the inkwell and began writing. "Let me see ... message from Muldoon Lumber Company, Hayward, Wisconsin ... to Marvin ... Ambruster, Wisconsin Timber Sales Office, East Washington Street, Madison, Wisconsin .... A total of fifty-seven words ...and a cost of, let me see... nineteen cents. There you are, sir!"

Ingman pulled his notebook from a pocket as he watched the man again leave the depot. He made a note in his book, tucked his paper under his arm, and returned to the hotel to watch the land sales office across the street. Within minutes he saw a telegraph boy deliver a message to Bob Thompson. Ingman knew Muldoon's bid from the previous day had been canceled.

At ten before noon Ingman was back in the depot. He sat down in the same seat near the telegraph office window. He re-read his paper and watched the large clock on the waiting room wall while listening to a switch engine move carloads of white pine in the railroad yard.

When the minute hand of the depot clock reached twelve, a lumber mill whistle sounded. Ingman heard the peal of a church bell and saw the telegrapher stand, pull on his topcoat, and leave his post behind the window. Another man sat down in the tall chair behind the window.

Ingman watched and waited as the telegrapher left the depot through a side exit, pulling the collar of his long wool coat around his neck as he met the frigid air. Ingman tucked his paper under his arm and approached the window. The noon attendant looked up.

"I wish to send this message," Ingman said, handing him a slip of paper.

The new telegrapher read the note out loud. "Disregard earlier message. We have been found out." He looked at Ingman. "That's all? No signature?"

"That will be enough," replied Ingman. "Ya, quite enough. Send it to a Mister Ambruster, State of Wisconsin Timber Sales Office, West Washington

71

Street in Madison."

"Very well. Eleven cents, sir. Receipt?"

"No need," replied Ingman, sliding a dime and a penny under the barred window. "Here's for the telegram." He slid two more dimes under the window. "And this is for you. I'd like you to keep this under your hat, friend. We don't want to embarrass anyone."

"I understand, sir. Thank you very much. Very much, indeed, sir!"

By the time Ingman returned to the hotel, nine more men waited for him, all hoping to become Namakagon Timber Company lumberjacks. He interviewed them, explained the details of their new jobs, and jotted some of their names in his notebook. The waiter took his order for pork roast and johnnycake with gravy, a bowl of canned peaches, and a glass of beer for dinner.

About one twenty he returned to the telegraph office. The young telegraph operator was again on duty. Ingman approached the window.

"Yes, sir? Can I help you?" said the telegrapher.

"I would like to send a message to Marvin Ambruster, Wisconsin Timber Sales Office, East Washington Street, Madison, Wisconsin."

The telegrapher jotted the recipient on his pad. "And the message, sir?"

Ingman paused, looked over his shoulder to make certain no one was listening, then spoke slowly, pausing to let the telegrapher jot down the message.

"Olaf Loken's Namakagon Timber Company," he began, "offers one dollar and sixty cents per acre … for outright purchase of all acreage … within sections five, six, seven, eight, seventeen, and eighteen … of township forty-three north and range five west … including all rights. Stop. Total acreage is three thousand eight hundred and forty. Stop. Total price is six thousand one hundred … and forty-four dollars. Stop."

Ingman looked over his shoulder again, turned back, and continued. "Deposit of one hundred dollars will be made … on acceptance of this bid. Stop. Payment in full within eight months. Stop. Ingman Loken, Agent."

Smiling, Ingman left the depot. He stopped at the Lumberman's Bank before returning to his hotel table. Minutes later he saw the telegraph boy running down the boardwalk and into the land office. He knew his plan had worked. As soon as the telegraph boy left, Ingman crossed the street to pay the one hundred dollar deposit on the six sections.

"We did it, Bob," Ingman said as he folded the receipt and placed it in his wallet. "We hornswaggled King Muldoon."

"Looks as though we did, Ingman. I don't reckon I'd want to be in the Muldoon Company office when they figure this out."

Ingman gave his new friend a hearty handshake. With his left hand, he stuffed a twenty-dollar bill into the clerk's jacket pocket.

Thompson looked at the bill. "That's a month's wages, Ingman. I can't accept …"

"That's not for you, Bob. It's for your wife and your daughters. Buy them some new Sunday clothes, my friend"

Ingman checked out of the hotel the next morning. He caught the first train to Cable. By late afternoon, he was relating the tale of his land purchase to his brother and nephew. They both rolled with laughter at his outrageous ingenuity.

Olaf pulled the cork from a bottle he kept in his desk and poured two glasses of the amber liquid. He glanced at Tor, looked to Ingman, and with a nod and a smile, poured a third glass, handing it to his son.

"To the new Loken pinery," he said. "May it share with us both its bounty and beauty for many years to come!"

The three Lokens touched glasses and Tor got his first taste of brandy.

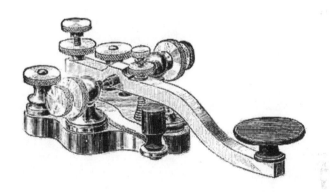

Chapter 15
Into the Deep Woods

Mid-November brought a string of ten-below-zero nights and five inches of snow. The loggers welcomed the freeze-up. Swamps and creek bottoms could now be crossed and timber sleighs moved with ease. All across the north, the lumberjacks were back to work in the pinery.

"Tim-berrr!" came the call from another sawyer. It echoed off the ridges near the Namakagon Timber Company camp and across the frozen lake. The warning was followed by the thunderous crash of another giant white pine falling to the frozen ground. From dawn to dusk these sounds could be heard throughout the pinery as the majestic trees gave up their long lives in the forest and fell to the earth.

Two of the new sawyers, Klaus and Ernst Verner, young men from Maine, took the honors for most trees felled and bucked. It took two swampers, Frank Rigby and Pete Van Evenhaven, both from St. Louis, to keep up with these veterans. Pete and Frank used their razor-sharp double-bit axes to trim off all branches, clear the brush and ready the logs for the chainer. Spike Andersen, a teamster, brought his own plow horses to the woods for the season. The camp's best chainer, Thomas Winslow, rounded out the crew. Winslow was one of many Oklahoma cowboys who took work in the pinery after barbed wire came to the southern cattle country, putting an end to open range grazing.

The other lumberjacks did their best to match the number of logs this hard working team brought to the lake, but few came close. The Verner boys knew their trade well. Neither wasted a minute of time nor any of their seemingly endless energy. Rigby, Van Evenhaven and Winslow fit into the Verner boys' crew like parts of a well-oiled machine.

Frank Rigby was the only married man in the bunch. Frank's twin sons, Zeke and Zach, were hired on as cookees to help out with the many kitchen chores. At thirteen, they were the youngest in camp—and the least-paid.

Lake Namakagon was already capped by four inches of clear ice, a lot for mid-November. Latecomers to camp could now avoid the long winding narrow tote road by crossing the ice, only a half-hour's trek with no hills or windfalls to negotiate. Those with horses and oxen still came by way of the woods, wary of the early ice and not wanting to risk their lives and the lives of their animals to the icy depths of the lake.

The Lokens' four, large birch bark canoes and several smaller canoes brought in by Ojibwe lumberjacks were pulled up on shore, hidden from the elements under the protective boughs of the balsam trees. There, they would remain all winter, upside-down, waiting for ice out. The two, big camp rowboats had been pulled on shore and covered with oiled canvas tarps. Weeks earlier these boats carried load after load of feed for the animals that skidded the logs and pulled the heavy sleigh loads of pine down the ice roads. Soon the hay and oats could be hauled across the ice by horse-drawn sleighs.

A twelve-hundred-gallon, round wooden tank, mounted above ironclad oak runners and pulled by two Clydesdale horses, was already busy spraying lake water on the ice roads. This tanker, its horses, and the teamster would work almost every night until the spring thaw. Without ice in the ruts, the sleighs would not move under their many tons of timber. With roads properly iced, horses or oxen could move the largest of loads with ease.

Smoke drifted up from every chimney in camp. All eighty-eight bunks in the sleep shanty were taken. Each had a mattress made from gunnysacks stuffed with oat straw. Some of the men brought wool blankets for the cold northern Wisconsin nights. Most slept in their clothes, using their mackinaws as blankets. Each man had three pair of socks—two to wear during the day in the cuttings and a third to wear at night while their daytime socks dried near the stove. The stench of unbathed workmen and unwashed socks mixed with the strong smell of pipe tobacco smoke to give the room a dreadful odor. Folks in town swore they could tell when a shanty boy was coming from ten miles away if the wind was wrong. The odor and crowded conditions, along with the bite from graybacks and bedbugs, made the bunkhouse a poor accommodation.

Olaf Loken's purchase of the extra six sections of timberland resulted in Ingman hiring a dozen more lumberjacks than the previous year. The Loken outfit now employed one hundred men—one hundred and four, counting the Lokens and Chief Namakagon. With the sleep shanty full, the extra workers had to sleep in the horse barn. Although colder than the shanty, the heat generated by more than forty horses and oxen made the barn bearable.

Some of the lumberjacks preferred the barn. If a man covered himself with enough straw, he could stay warm on the coldest of nights. Smoking wasn't allowed in the barn—no blue stench from tobacco smoke, unlike the bunkhouse. And light sleepers could get a better rest without the endless roar of eighty-eight snoring shanty boys.

One of the men Ingman hired, John Kavanaugh, was a widower from the farm country near Mazomanie in southern Wisconsin. John worked as a teamster and came with his own pair of oxen and his youngest son, John Junior. The same age as Tor, Junior was hired at half pay to help out in the barn and cook shanty.

"Ma died of the small pox," Junior told Tor one evening in the barn. "It took her and Grandpa and Grandma last year. Took a whole lotta folks in our town. I caught it too, but the doctor said it wasn't my time. I guess what saved me is when he smoked the disease out of our house."

"How did he do that?" asked Tor.

"Well, Pa said he put something on our house called a quarantine. I don't know what it was. Never saw it. But I know he did. Pa said. Then the doc closed all the windows and doors and he took a tin bucket, filled it half full of coal, doused it with fuel oil, and put a match to it. He set it atop the kitchen stove, and when it was going good an' hot, he poured on this stuff from a bottle he had in his doctorin' bag. It made this thick green smoke that went through the house and drove out all the small pox. Pa and I had to stay inside and breathe the smoke. Ma did too, but it was too late for her. She died."

"Ya? My ma was killed in a train wreck," said Tor. "We were on our way here. One more night on the train and we would've made it."

"You were in a train wreck?"

"Ya. I didn't get hurt much but Ma did. They couldn't save her. They sent me on to my pa, but he got laid up when his lumber wagon turned over on him. They told me he died, too. Plunked me in an orphanage in Chicago. I was there pretty long till my Uncle Ingman found me and brought me to camp."

"Golly. I guess I didn't have it so bad, then. You got any brothers or sisters?"

"No. You?"

"Ya. I got me a big brother named Billy. Billy Kavanaugh. Pa says he's down in a place he called Ha-van-nie. I think it's by Mexico—or maybe Texas. Pa says Billy's a big shot. He goes from island to island and buys up bananas and sugar and coffee and such. Then he puts it all on ships going to New York and New Orleans and other places. He's a big shot, all right. Pa says so. Someday I'm gonna go with him and be a big shot, too! Yep, I'm goin' with him some day."

"He sells bananas?"

"Bananas, oranges, cocoa beans, Billy buys and sells lots of things. Once he sold a whole boatload of shoes to an island full of natives who always went barefoot. Billy told them that leather shoes was what the fancy people in New York all wore. Within a few days, everyone on that island wanted his shoes. In a wink they were all gone. Billy ended up with a whole boatload of baskets, melons, straw hats, and other goods to ship back. Those islanders all got blisters so bad that Billy dasn't go back there anymore. Says he's worried that they'd cook him and eat him. But, boy oh boy, does he make the money! I seen him pull out a big roll of double sawbucks last time he was in Mazomanie. That was before Ma died."

"Junior, you think they'd really cook him and eat him?"

"Why, sure, Tor! Them islands down there is plenty dangerous. White folks get eaten alive all the time, Billy says. Well, I better git some sleep. Pa wants me to turn in earlier than the men 'cause ol' Sourdough gits me up so dang early to help with breakfast. My brother Billy doesn't ever git up early. Big shots don't have to. Yep, Billy's a big shot an' I'm gonna be one too, someday. Yes, sir, I am!"

"If the natives don't cook you and eat you, Junior."

76

"I ain't worried, Billy being a big shot and all. He'll show me the ropes."

Tor left the barn and crossed the snow-covered yard. The sky was clear. He stopped for a moment in the center of the yard, looking up at the millions of bright stars. He stood motionless, his exhaled breath the only movement in the yard. As he stared into the sky, the clear howl of a timberwolf came across the frozen lake. A moment later, another wolf replied from the ridge just behind the camp. Even though Chief Namakagon convinced him to not fear wolves, the nearby call sent chills down his spine. He returned to the lodge quickly, wondering if it would be worse to be eaten by island natives or timberwolves.

Tor opened the large door and stomped his feet to knock off the snow. He pulled off his choppers, stuffing them into the pockets of his mackinaw. After hanging the coat and his hat, he kicked off his rubber shoe-pacs, noticing a walking staff leaning against the nearby wall.

With his long, wool socks still pulled up to his knees, Tor stepped into the large, open room. A single oil lamp hung from a hook near the stairway. Across the room his father and uncle sat near the fireplace. Light cast from the flaming maple logs played upon nearby walls and the faces of the men. Each had a glass in hand. Sitting with them, his face hidden by the wing chair, was Chief Namakagon. His two dogs, Waabishki and Makade, lay at his feet.

"Son, come greet our guest." The chief leaned forward.

"Chief Namakagon! Welcome, sir."

"Boozhoo, young woodsman. How are you taking to your new life in the pines?"

"No place I'd rather be! Today I helped Charlie Martin ice down the sleigh trails. Must've covered fifteen, twenty miles or more. Even made it up to the new cuttings. Sure is a lot of big white pine up there. Saw a bull moose cross the trail ahead of us, too. Antlers wide as the filing shed."

Namakagon smiled. "It is good to see you are learning the ways of the woods. And learning to spin yarns like the men. Tor, small tales become tall tales in the lumber camps during long winter nights."

"No, really. It was a big moose. Huge antlers. I swear it. He was a-prancin' and a-dancin' across the cranberry bog west of the creek. Charlie said he wished he had his deer rifle. That moose would have made for many a good meal in camp."

"I believe the moose would tell you that he prefers to run free." Namakagon turned to Olaf. "Good to see there are still a few moose. There have been three bulls up there since last spring. Like your lumberjacks on a night in town, they try their best to impress potential mates."

"I'm surprised we don't see more moose around here," said Ingman into his glass.

"The timberwolves control the size of the moose herds," replied the chief. "Wolves are skilled hunters. They work together. Not even the largest bull moose is free from the eye of the timberwolf. Only man can kill with greater efficiency. But, unlike many hunters, the wolf will stop hunting when he is no longer hungry. Too many hunters have not learned this. When the deer and moose are almost gone, perhaps they will understand what the wolf has always known and take only what they need."

"Like the buffalo out west?" said Ingman.

"Yes, the buffalo. Millions a decade ago, now there are few." Namakagon waved his hand and both dogs sat up to greet Tor.

"Tor," said his father, changing the subject, "the chief is going to Hayward for some supplies at daybreak. I want you to go with him."

"Sure, Pa!"

"You can take the small cutter in to Cable and leave it at the livery. The morning train will have you in Hayward before noon. Stay at Mrs. Ringstadt's Boarding House overnight. She'll be happy to see you."

"Well," said Ingman, "it's high time for me to hit the haystack. Breakfast comes mighty early in the cook shanty and I know better than to show up for breakfast two minutes late. Sourdough is yust about as ornery as a woodchuck down a well when you show up late for breakfast."

Laughing and nodding in agreement, Olaf turned his wheelchair toward his bedroom. Tor grasped the chair back and helped him to his room. His father lit a candle and shouted out a "good night" before closing the door. Tor and his uncle made their way up the stairs, Ingman carrying the oil lamp.

Chief Namakagon watched as the two disappeared into the shadows of the loft. Only the dim light from the coals in the fireplace lit the room now.

Speaking softly, Namakagon thanked Gitchee Manitou for another good day among good friends. He then rolled out a green, wool blanket before the fireplace, placed a small log on the coals, and soon drifted off to sleep, his two large dogs curled up beside him.

Chapter 16
Yellowjack, Blackjack, and Flapjacks

Sourdough, his two cookees, Zeke and Zach, and Harry Green, the bull-cook, were always first to rise. Harry had already stoked up the stoves and pumped water for coffee, tea, and cooking. Meanwhile, Sourdough sliced enough smoked pork for a hundred men. The pork now sizzled in four huge cast iron pans on the two big Monarch wood-fired ranges while water boiled in the reservoirs built into the stoves. Roaring fires inside each range made both stovepipes glow a deep red in the dim light from two oil lamps.

Harry used a two-foot-long wooden spoon to stir a large bucket filled with yellowjack batter. He ladled several cups of pork fat from the frying pans into four enormous cake pans, swishing it around before pouring in the cornbread batter. Next, he transferred boiling water from the stove reservoirs to pots and tossed a handful of tea into each pot before opening the oven door to remove three more big pans filled with steaming blackjack. The yellowjack pans went into the oven in their place. Harry moved the blackjack to the chopping block, flipped it out of the pans and cut it into four-inch squares. Trays stacked high with the hot blackjack squares were set on the tables.

Next, Harry dished the pork onto large platters and scooped the hot pork fat into bowls. The cookees distributed the platters and bowls to tables already set with pots of baked beans, bowls of molasses, tin plates, cups utensils, and the blackjack.

While the cookees and Harry attended to the daily breakfast duties, Sourdough was mixing batter, pouring, flipping and stacking golden brown flapjacks onto tin platters. Each was the size of a plate and a half-inch thick. Two of these, along with the baked beans, blackjack, yellowjack, and smoked pork would satisfy even the hungriest lumberjack on this cold winter morning.

"Time to rattle the bear cage, boys," shouted Sourdough, " and don't take no guff. Get those lazy bums out of their bunks and tell 'em to leave the graybacks where they be."

"Yes, sir, Sourdough!" shouted Zeke. He and his brother set out the last bowls of hot pork grease before Zeke ran down to the end of the bunkhouse, turned, and cried out, "Five o'clock! Chow down or go hungry till dinnertime."

Some men stirred. Others grumbled obscenities at the boy who walked the row waking the workers. "Day's a-wastin', bark eaters. Food's on the board, hot and ready to go."

Sourdough looked up from his work. "Harry, watch the oven. This time, don't burn your dang johnnycake. I don't want to be blamed for your mistake again today."

Using a washrag to protect his hand, Harry opened and closed the oven door. "Still needs another two minutes, Boss."

"Yellowjack, blackjack and flapjacks, get 'em while they're hot, lumberjacks," Zach cried out, ducking a shoe-pac thrown by one of the men.

"Up and at 'em, bark eaters," Zeke shouted, throwing it back.

Harry pulled his pans of Yellowjack from the hot ovens. He then crossed the room and propped open the large double door to cool down the cook shanty. The hot, humid air escaping into the frigid, black December night immediately turned into a great cloud of steam before rising.

"Must be ten, fifteen below," complained Klaus Verner, returning from his walk to the latrine.

"Them pines don't care how cold it is, boys," hollered Blackie Jackson. "Don't matter to them and, by God, it shouldn't matter to you, neither."

"Ya, Blackie, but that don't mean we gotta like it," yelled Tex Ketchum from the far end of the bunkhouse.

"Move it along, shanty boys," bellowed Sourdough. "You'll enjoy the cold more if you have your bellies full, And what you don't eat I throw to the hogs. It's them or you, and it don't make no matter to me!"

Within moments the benches along the long oilcloth-covered tables were filled. The men ate in silence as Harry and the cookees shuttled hot coffee and tea to them. Only the sounds of knives and forks against tin plates could be heard.

Up and down the tables, food disappeared from the large serving plates and bowls, all placed within reach of every group of four men. Hot pork grease and molasses were poured over the flapjacks. Sourdough supplied more flapjacks as the lumberjacks emptied the platters.

Barely awake, Junior Kavanaugh, stumbled in from the barn, oat straw on his hat, coat and britches. Ingman Loken was right behind him. "Daylight in the swamp, men!" shouted Ingman. "You can't earn your pay by sittin' here sippin' that shoe polish ol' Sourdough calls coffee!"

Sourdough looked up from the stove. "*Anyone* here who don't like my coffee don't have to drink it," he bellowed, staring directly at the woods boss.

Grinning, Ingman sat down at the table nearest the cook stove just as Tor and his father entered through the cook shanty door. Tor pushed his father's wheelchair up to the table. They filled their plates as some workers, hats pulled down and clad in mackinaw coats, filed out into the dim morning light. The side door opened again, and Chief Namakagon entered the room.

"Boozhoo," muttered Namakagon. "Sourdough, what delicacies have you prepared for us this fine morning?"

"Delicacies? Oh yes, delicacies, let me see ..." The camp cook slapped a big tin plate heaped with flapjacks onto the table. "Sautéed salamanders, pickled porcupine, fried frog feathers and field mouse pie!" Then, pouring hot coffee into their tin cups, "And here's some sparkly champagne to wash it all down your gullets, moin-sewers."

"Doesn't smell half bad in here, Sourdough," said Ingman. "Don't tell me you got the boys to wash their socks."

"Wash their socks?" replied Sourdough. "These roughneck bums? Never! Ingman, the sweet fragrance of my good cookin' mixed with the smoke

80

from this leaky old stove is what covers up the fumes from them foul-smellin' shanty boys of yours." Then, "Junior, fetch that bowl of butter from off the window sill for the boss and his guest. And bring over the maple syrup, there."

"Junior," said Olaf, "how are you getting on here in camp?"

"Good, sir. Real good." he replied, setting the butter on the table. "Better than danged ol' farm work! And when ol' Sourdough ain't lookin', I get my fill of pies."

"Hey, you skinny little whippersnapper, you best not be pilferin' my pies!" griped Sourdough. "I'll kick your skinny butt into section thirty-seven!"

"You'd never catch him, Sourdough," said Ingman. "You got forty more years on Yunior and two hundred extra pounds." Sourdough grunted.

"Junior," said Tor, "Chief Namakagon and I are taking the mornin' train to Hayward to pick up some supplies."

"Well, ain't you the lucky pole cat," exclaimed Junior.

"We need some more stove lids here," said Ingman. The cookees brought a fresh stack of large pancakes and another platter of smoked pork.

Tor spread butter on his second plate of flapjacks and poured the hot molasses over the flapjacks, the baked beans and his corn bread. He stabbed a piece of pork so large that he almost had to drag it from the platter to his plate. Harry poured more hot coffee into their tin cups.

"Tor," said Sourdough, "can you bring me two quarts of lemon extract from the grocer? I'm plannin' on making up some lemon pies for Christmas day. And a pound of nutmeg, too."

"I surely can, Sourdough," replied Tor.

"Need anything else, Sourdough?" asked Olaf. "Now's the time to speak up."

"We're pretty well stocked up for now, Boss," replied Sourdough. "If I put much more in the cupboard, there won't be any room left for the mice."

Ingman gulped down his coffee and stood up.

"On that fine note, I think I best catch up with the boys," he said, pulling on his mackinaw. "I have two crews movin' into those pines along the creek today. I need to blaze a skid trail across the swamp for 'em. No way they can cross that ridge." He opened the door, then turned back into the room. "Oh, Tor, I'll see to it that the cutter is hitched and ready for your trip to town."

Ingman headed toward the horse barn. Olaf, Tor, and Chief Namakagon finished breakfast and returned to the lodge. Harry Green and the cookees started the breakfast clean-up as Sourdough measured out ingredients for twenty-five loaves of bread. Junior helped for a while, before returning to the barn to start his daily chores.

Back in the lodge, Olaf wheeled over to his desk. "Tor," he said, handing his son a letter, "I want you to take this note to the Lumberman's Bank as soon as you get to town. The bank president will prepare a canvas wallet containing some money for you to pick up just before you return tomorrow. Now Tor, it's important for you to keep to yourself on your way back. I've already talked this over with Namakagon. He'll stay close by until you return."

"All right, pa." Tor said, buttoning the note into his back pocket, "Can I ask what the money is for?"

"Well, Son, there's been good snow and cold temperatures. The boys have been working plenty hard and we are already well ahead of the game. I decided it's time we gave the fells a chance to blow off some steam. I'm going to give them an advance on their spring wages so they can go to town Saturday night. You'll have five hundred dollars under your care, Son. I don't expect you'll have any problems. A young boy and an Indian aren't likely to attract attention. Just keep to yourself, stay near the chief and all will be fine."

"Olaf," said Namakagon, "Bury your concern. I will keep close watch on your son and his cargo."

The new snow squeaked sharply under the weight of the cutter's runners. The ride across the lake went quickly and the travelers came into Cable just as the southbound locomotive was pulling into the rail yard. They bought their tickets and waited near the depot's pot-bellied stove.

"Well, Chief Namakagon, Tor Loken. It is good to see you, my friends," exclaimed Oscar. "My clerk mentioned you were here. Tell me, how are things coming along at the Loken camp? Your father, Tor, how is he doing?"

"Pa? Oh, Pa's doing great, Mr. Felsman. He's happy to be home and running the camp again. Pa and Uncle Ingman have the camp just a-buzzin' along like a beehive. Every man is hard at work and each crew is trying to out-cut and out-haul the next. Pa is happy as a dang fisher in a chicken coop!"

"Your father has a fine lumber camp, Tor," said Namakagon. "Hard-working men and good employers. I believe your pa's lumberjacks are quite pleased to be part of the Loken outfit."

"Well, they should be," said the stationmaster. "The Lokens treat their men well and offer the best pay around. I suppose it doesn't hurt that Olaf has the best cook in the pinery working for him either. I am told your outfit is the only camp around that pours coffee instead of tea." He glanced down at his clipboard as the locomotive's whistle blew. "Well, I see you are off to Hayward."

"Ya," said Tor. "We're going' to the city to pick up some ..."

"Supplies," interrupted Namakagon. "Sourdough is short of some Christmas fixings, and we are proud to save the day!"

"We're coming back tomorrow," said Tor.

With a metal-to-metal squeal, the huge, black locomotive slowly rolled past the depot platform. It slowed to a stop with a rush of steam, a whistle blast, and its bell ringing. Namakagon with his walking staff and Tor with a knapsack, they stepped onto the train. Seven other men and four women boarded the same car. Soon the train left the station, sending a huge cloud of smoke and steam into the icy morning air.

"Tor," said the chief, "your manner of speech, is very good. How did this come to be?"

"Well, sir, my folks moved to America right before I was born. Mother was an English teacher back in Norway. When Pa left for Wisconsin, Ma stayed in New York and got hired to teach English to others from the old country. She taught me to read and write and such. You think I learned pretty well?"

"Quite well. It is not often you hear proper English in the north woods."

"And what about you?"

"I, too, had good instruction—by a close friend, the Commander of a United States Army post. He, his wife, and daughters won my heart. Taught me reading, writing, and language skills. I studied every book in their family library. I read, learned, and read more."

"Do you ever see them?"

"No. Circumstances have steered me far from them. I have never returned. Perhaps one day ."

The train crossed the Pac-wa-wong springs, Mosquito Brook, and soon rumbled across the large iron railroad trestle north of Hayward. The train's whistle told them they would soon pull into the Hayward station.

They later walked through the large front door of the Lumberman's Bank. Tor approached the teller, asking to speak with the president.

"I am sure Mr. Forbert is busy," said the teller with indifference. "What is it you want, Sonny."

"My father told me to give this letter to the bank president," said Tor, holding up the letter.

"And who might your father be, boy?"

"Olaf Loken."

The teller's eyes widened. "Oh! Yes. I see. Yes, I will deliver this to Mr. Forbert myself." He walked briskly toward the door behind him.

Seconds later, a well-dressed man accompanied the teller to the window.

"Please come in, young man!" he said. Tor and Namakagon walked around the end of the tellers' windows toward the office door.

"Wait," said the teller. "The Indian is not allowed."

Both Tor and Namakagon stopped. Forbert turned. An awkward silence loomed in the bank lobby.

"Tor, I will be right here when you are finished with your business," said Namakagon in a measured voice.

Tor followed the bank president into the office. In a moment, Forbert rushed out exclaiming, "Chief Namakagon, please accept my apologies. I didn't know it was you, sir. Please step into my off ..."

Namakagon spoke slowly. "If, Mr. Forbert, you are not willing to let any other of my people enter your office, then I, like them, will not enter. I am my people and they are me."

"Dearborne!" snapped the banker angrily, "Why in the name of the Almighty did you not tell me this was Chief Namakagon? Why do you think I keep you employed here?" The teller was silent.

The bank president returned to his office. He read the letter and assured Tor the money would be ready to be picked up at eleven thirty on the following day so they could make the noon train to Cable. Tor and Namakagon left the bank after hearing another apology from the banker.

Several horse-drawn wagons trudged down Hayward's snow-covered Main Street. A half-dozen horses were tied to posts in front of the Hotel Pion, and a woman carrying several packages walked down the plank sidewalk across the street. Her stylish long wool coat and scarf contrasted with the wide-brimmed, wool hat she had pulled over her head. Tor and Namakagon walked down the block, crossed the street, and headed up the hill past the new courthouse. Adeline Ringstadt met them at her boarding house door.

"Why, of course you can stay here. Please, please do! I have a room at the top of the stairs all ready for you, and supper will be served promptly at the strike of five."

Chapter 17
Spilt Milk

"Mama," Rose whispered. "I want to sit next to Tor at the supper table tonight. Can I? Can I please?"

"You girls will be helping me in the kitchen and with the serving, just as always, Rose," said Adeline Ringstadt.

"But, Mama!" Rose protested. "Just this once? Please?"

"Well, perhaps it would be good for you to get to know the boy. He has so few friends. But you'll have to take over the kitchen chores after dinner. Don't expect your sisters to do all the work."

"Yes, Mama. I'll take care of all the dishes after supper! Thank you Mama! Thank you!" Rose said, giving her mother a hug.

"That's not fair!" whined Daisy. "Why should Rose get to sit next to him at dinner? What makes her the Queen of Persia? Mama, you're not fair."

"Daisy Lou! You watch your tongue, young lady! Rose can sit with the Loken boy at the supper table and that's the end of it. Now hush!"

Daisy turned and stomped back into the kitchen with Violet, the youngest of the three girls, stomping out right behind her. When isolated from the others by the kitchen door, Daisy turned to Violet. "Rose always gets the gingerbread and we get the crumbs!" she whispered. "Well, we will see if ol' Rosie-Posey gets the gingerbread tonight, Violet. We'll see!"

"What you gonna do, Daisy? Mama said …"

"Just you never mind what Mama said!" snapped Daisy. "I should get to sit next to Tor just as much as anybody, including Rose! You just wait."

Namakagon and Tor left the Ringstadt home, headed for the dry goods store. The big storefront windows were thick with frost. Inside were two narrow aisles. A clerk stood behind the counter near the door. Shelves crowded with boxes, tins and bagged goods extended from floor to ceiling all around the large room. Most of a twenty-pound wheel of cheese sat on the counter next to a large roll of brown wrapping paper and the cash register.

Tor ordered the two quarts of lemon extract and nutmeg for Sourdough. The clerk fetched the nutmeg from one of the tin boxes kept high on a shelf. He tore a sheet of paper from the roll, wrapped the nutmeg, then, reaching up, he pulled a length of string from a cone-shaped spool hanging overhead. He quickly gave the package two wraps of string, knotted it and broke the string with a snap of his wrist.

After checking the corks on the lemon extract bottles, he pulled a second and third sheet of brown paper from the roll and wrapped the bottles before pulling a third, larger sheet of paper from the roll. The clerk then laid the bottles and the nutmeg on the large paper, folded up the sides and the ends, then reached overhead and pulled down another length of the white cotton string from the spool. In one smooth motion the clerk put two wraps of string around the package, gave it a quarter-turn, and then put two more courses of string across the others. A quick overhand knot secured the small bundle.

"That will be ninety-seven cents," said the clerk.

"Make it eight bits," said Tor as he placed four quarters on the counter and grabbed six licorice twists. When the clerk pressed a key on the cash register, the drawer popped open, a bell rang, and a metal flag marked $1 popped up in the top of the register.

Chief Namakagon placed a tin of B and L Black pipe tobacco on the counter along with two nickels. The clerk took his coins and returned two pennies in change.

Their return to the boarding house took them past a sausage shop, a bathhouse, and the Rail Inn, a favorite tavern of the railroad men. Just as they passed by the tavern door, they heard a loud crash inside. The front window suddenly exploded into hundreds of glass shards as two men came flying through the large window frame, across the boardwalk and onto the snowy street. The two brawlers stood up, shook off some of the mud, snow and glass, then violently tackled each other again.

A crowd of men spilled through the doorway to watch. Some cheered, others just looked on. A man wearing a black wool shirt and red suspenders was taking bets on the fight. Several onlookers handed him dollar bills.

Namakagon and Tor moved up the boardwalk before turning to watch. The larger of the two brawlers pinned his opponent to the ground. The smaller man gave a mighty shove, throwing the big man off. Springing to their feet, they started in again, but it was too late for the big man. He had lost his balance and his confidence. The smaller man threw him to the street and stood above him with clenched fists, waiting for him to stand up again.

"Uncle," said the beaten man. Cheers came from the growing crowd.

"Let's have a beer. I'll buy you one," said the winner.

"No siree. You whipped me fair and square. It is my burden to buy."

"Which one of you drunken bums is gonna pay the bill for my busted window?" shouted the tavern owner. "That's the way it works here in Hayward, boys. Either pay the freight or you will be sittin' in the jailhouse till you do."

The big man pulled some money out of his pocket, counted out two dollars and handed it to the tavern owner. He looked back at the window and gave him another dollar before picking up his hat, dusting himself off, and, stumbling back inside. The owner smiled, stuffing the money in his pocket.

"Seems to be a fool's pastime," said Namakagon.

"I'll say. I don't see what they see in it. Seems pointless and painful."

"Most men around here, whether rails, miners, or lumberjacks, live for three things—liquor, women, and brawling. It is the way of the north."

Tor and Namakagon continued up the street, returning to the Ringstadt home. In the parlor, Rose was playing the family's upright piano. She was dressed in a blue and white calico dress buttoned up the back. The white lace collar was fitted tight to her neck and the lace cuffs fit tight to her wrists. A

86

light blue ribbon kept Rose's hair neatly behind her ears. Around her waist was a wider ribbon. She moved her fingers gracefully over the keyboard, playing Stephen Foster's *Camptown Races* for the small audience.

Two of Adeline's boarders sat at a small parlor table playing cards. Other guests watched Rose, tapping their feet to the beat of the lively song.

In the middle of the number, two of the borders popped up from their chairs and started dancing. The middle-aged couple rocked back and forth to the rhythm, laughing and kicking their feet as they locked elbows and turned around and around over the brightly colored, braided rug.

Both Tor and Chief Namakagon laughed as others in the room clapped in time to the energetic music. Tor joined in, clapping to the beat. When Rose played the chorus, the dancers sang, "Gwine to run all night! Gwine to run all day! Bet my money on de bob-tail nag. Somebody bet on de bay."

Rose and her audience were all laughing when Adeline entered the room, half walking, half dancing. "Dinner's on the table. Rose will play more songs for you right after she finishes her kitchen chores, if you please."

"If we please?" exclaimed the dancing man. "Why, Mrs. Ringstadt, this is without a doubt the best concert in Sawyer County since the chautauqua came to town last August!"

"Here, here!" shouted the card players, laying their hands face down.

Tor wanted to add his own compliment but couldn't find the right words. Rose finished the song with flair, then reached forward and turned the page on the sheet music and placed it in its cover folder. Tor watched as she stood and gracefully stepped around the piano bench. He was still speechless.

"Why, thank you for your nice compliments! I'm not very good at the piano but I try. I'd be happy to play some more after dinner, if you please."

"Yes," said the chief. "We insist."

Rose and the party of guests followed Adeline Ringstadt into the dining room. The oak table was neatly set with white plates, cups, and saucers, all flanked by well-polished silverware. The center of the table held large bowls of steaming squash, mashed potatoes, a beef and rice hot dish, and a mixture of boiled carrots, onions, and peas. Mrs. Ringstadt sat her boarders around the table, saving the chair nearest the kitchen for herself. She took care to place her daughter to her right, next to Tor. The chief, who sat to the left of his hostess, suspected Adeline was engaging in some matchmaking. He was right.

Pete Washburn, one of the two card players, reached for the potatoes.

"Now, now, Peter," said Adeline, "grace comes first, you know." The room became quiet. "Who will offer our words of thanks tonight?"

Namakagon spoke. "Oh Great Spirit, we thank you for the Earth, and the sky, the woodlands and waters—all you have placed in our care. We hope we will be able to protect these precious gifts so all who come after us will be able to enjoy their bounty as do we."

An awkward silence followed.

"Well, that is a simply wonderful prayer, Chief Namakagon," declared

Adeline, "although I must say, a bit unusual for our table. Rose, why don't you start the carrots around?"

"Yes, Mama," replied Rose, spooning some carrots and onions onto her plate and passing the dish to Tor.

Tense and self-conscious in the presence of this attractive girl, Tor was apprehensive his lumber camp manners might show.

"Thank you, Rosie," he said as he took the carrots, placed a heaping spoonful onto his plate and attempted to pass them across to the chief. Namakagon looked into Tor's eyes without reaching up for the bowl. He then glanced at the card player sitting to Tor's right, then back at Tor.

"Oh," said Tor. "These go this way, don't they?" He passed the carrots to the man on his right. "I'm out of practice. We don't pass dishes in camp. Everybody just reaches for what they need and hopes to get a bellyful 'fore it's all gone." Everyone laughed, including Tor, who wondered if what he said was funny or if they were laughing at him for being crude and ill-mannered.

"Many years ago," said the chief, "they tried passing dishes in one of the lumber camps. This worked fine for the men near the kitchen, but the fellows at the end of the table got nothing but drippings and crumbs. The resulting brawl got the cook, the men, the whole camp very deep in hot water. And, as everyone knows, the one thing a lumberjack loathes most is a good soaking in hot water!"

Everyone broke out in laughter again. More dishes went around the table, and the diners began eating. Tor nervously mustered the courage to speak to Rose.

"Rosie, you're quite the piano player.".

Rose smiled. "Thank you, Tor. I'm taking lessons from Reverend Spooner's wife. They might let me play the organ in church someday."

"I'd like to hear that," said Tor.

"Yes, so would I," said Willard Rogers.

"Tor, will you be coming to Hayward again soon?" asked Adeline.

"I can't say, ma'am. I'd sure like to." He smiled at Rose. "We usually go into Cable for supplies. We come down here to Hayward if we need to do some banking or company business. Tomorrow we'll stop at the bank …"

Chief Namakagon interrupted, "Mrs. Ringstadt, this is delicious."

"Why, it's my grandmother's recipe. It's the cinnamon that makes it special. I'm so glad you like it."

"Tor, I'd like to visit your lumber camp one day," said Rose, looking at her mother for approval.

"Well, now, I don't know," said Adeline. "That is quite a trip to make. And what about all those ruffians?"

"Perhaps after the spring drive," volunteered Namakagon. "Most of the men will be gone by then."

Tor hid his displeasure with the suggestion. He'd prefer to have Rose visit the camp much, much sooner.

Rose hid nothing, saying, "Spring? Why, winter is when the camps are busy. I'd like to see the camp in the winter. I know that Reverend Spooner visits the camps now and then. He's always looking to convert another Christian. He could take me along, Mama! I'll ask him tomorrow."

"All in good time, Rose, all in good time," said Adeline, patting her daughter on the back of the hand.

Rose turned to Tor and smiled, now confident that she could convince her mother to arrange for a visit. Tor returned the smile.

"More coffee?" said one of the card players as he lifted the coffee pot from the table.

"Oh my," said Adeline. "Tor, Rose, you have no milk. Oh, Daisy, Daisy," she called. "Daisy Lou!"

"Yes Mama," answered the middle girl, peeking around the doorway.

"Daisy, bring a pitcher of milk and two glasses."

"Yes, Mama," replied Daisy, backing out of the doorway. In the kitchen, Daisy spoke to Violet, the youngest, who was pouring a kettle of hot water into a white, enamel dishpan.

"I'll get even with Rosie now," said Daisy, lifting a milk-filled pitcher from the sill of the frosted window. She carried the pitcher to the cupboard where she picked up two glass tumblers before entering the dining room. Daisy placed the glasses between Tor and Rose, filling Tor's glass first. She smiled at him, then at her older sister. Rose's glass was filled next, but, when the milk neared the top, Daisy poured faster. As the milk flowed over the rim, she shrieked, fumbled, and dropped the pitcher into her sister's lap.

Rose jumped up with a shout of surprise and horror, bumping the table and upsetting two coffee cups and the half-filled gravy boat.

Tor, Namakagon, Pete, and Willard quickly slid their chairs away from the table. Tor held his milk glass in the air. Adeline reached for the empty gravy boat and bumped a nearby bowl, sending carrots and onions flying across the table and onto the floor.

"Egad!" shrieked Adeline. "Daisy Lou, look what you've done! Violet, bring some dishtowels. Quickly. Quickly!"

Daisy ran crying from the room, not to the kitchen, but across the parlor and up the stairs. When she was out of sight, she turned and peeked around the corner at the top of the stairway to inspect the results of her work.

The table was a mess. Milk covered the floor where Rose had been sitting. Adeline Ringstadt was using a dishtowel to sop up coffee, gravy, and carrot juice from the table. Tor was picking up carrots and onions from the floor. Rose ran into the kitchen so Tor and the adults would not see her in tears. Peter picked up his plate and fork and walked toward the parlor to finish his meal. Everyone's shock soon turned to laughter as all pitched in to help straighten up.

Namakagon slid his chair farther back from the table. At the top of the stairway he saw Daisy peeking down, now wearing an enormous, impish grin. "This," he said, "will be a dinner long remembered!"

Chapter 18
Hoodlums

Early the next morning, Tor and Chief Namakagon met the other boarders around the breakfast table. The table was well set with eggs and sausage, fried potatoes, coffee, and fresh corn biscuits with butter and honey. As the guests seated themselves, Adeline Ringstadt came from the kitchen.

"Good morning all," exclaimed their cheery hostess. "Fill up your plates. There's more coming soon."

Rose carried in a large glass of milk. "Good morning," she said to the breakfast party. She walked around the large table to Tor and placed the milk before him. "Tor, I'm dreadfully sorry about the disaster last night."

"Don't go fretting about it, Rosie," he said with a laugh. "Better cold milk than hot coffee when it's in your lap."

"Tor, you'll have to come back soon," she replied. "And when you do, I'll have another song to play, just for you."

Embarrassed, Tor replied, "I'll return when I can, but we have plenty of work to do in the camp."

"Oh, please do hurry back, Tor," pleaded Rose. "You need a break from all that hard work from time to time, don't you?"

"I suspect," said Namakagon, "Tor's journeys here will be frequent."

Rose beamed.

After the meal was finished, Tor and the chief said their farewells.

As they were leaving, Rose approached Tor. "Tor," she said quietly, "it was so nice to see you again. Please do try to visit us soon, won't you?"

"I'll do my best," he replied. "Maybe I can put some of the other men to work on my duties and get away."

"Oh, that would be wonderful!" She smiled and then pressed a light blue ribbon into Tor's hand. "Here," she whispered, "take this and keep it with you until you return. It's the ribbon I wore in my hair last night. Maybe it will bring you good luck and keep you safe in the woods."

"Ah, er, thank you, Rosie. I … I don't know what to say. I will keep it with me, always, Rosie."

As Tor and Namakagon left the boarding house, Rose's mother smiled at her daughter and whispered, "Rose, I used the same ploy on your father nearly twenty years ago—only *my* ribbon was red."

"I know, Mama. You told me that story a half-dozen times. I just had to try it out for myself."

They smiled at each other as they watched the departing guests through the parlor window.

"He is such a nice boy, Mama."

"I agree. He will be a fine, fine beau for some lucky girl."

"Oh, Mama, I *do* hope we can soon visit their camp. Please Mama?"

"Now, now, Rose, it is not proper to rush things so. Like I've always said, 'time spent apart will win a young man's heart, dear. Be patient, young lady. We shall see what we shall see."

"Well, I'm going to speak with Reverend Spooner this morning, Mama. I am going to let him know there are a hundred lost sheep up on Lake Namakagon, all waiting for a fine shepherd to bring them to salvation."

"Oh, I don't see a need to rush, dear. I have a feeling your new friend is just as smitten as you."

"But, Mama," Rose sighed, "I simply *must* see Tor again soon."

"All right, you may speak with the preacher when you see him. I see no harm in it."

"Oh, thank you, Mama, thank you!" Rose cried out as she gave her mother a big hug. They peered through the frosty parlor window, watching Chief Namakagon and Tor cross the street and walk from view.

Two inches of light snow made the small city look bright and clean in the morning sun. Tor and the chief passed the courthouse and turned down Iowa Avenue. They crossed at the corner, dodged a fast moving, horse-drawn cutter, and headed straight for the Lumberman's Bank.

"That young girl is quite interested in singing songs for you," said Namakagon.

"She sure can whip up a tune," replied Tor. Then, eager to change the subject, "Here's the bank." They entered.

"Mr. Dearborne," said Tor. "Please tell Mr. Forbert that we're here."

"Certainly, Mr. Loken."

Dearborne disappeared from behind his barred cashier's window, returning a moment later. "Mr. Forbert will see you now, Mr. Loken."

Curbing pride felt from being called Mister, Tor entered Forbert's office.

"Here you are, young man," said the banker. "Five hundred, all in five-dollar bills, just as your father directed." He flopped a neat stack of bills onto his desk along with a yellow-green, canvas bank wallet. Tor counted the bills and placed them in the wallet. He tied it tightly and signed the receipt.

"Mr. Forbert, could I ask you for another canvas poke?"

"Certainly." He pulled a second bank wallet from a desk drawer.

"Sir, are you done with that newspaper?" Tor pointed to a copy of the North Country News.

"Here you are," said Forbert.

Tor folded the paper and folded it again and again, before stuffing it into the second wallet. He tied the leather thong and shoved the wallet into his left coat pocket. The other went in his right pocket.

"Chief Namakagon told me to do this," he said. "I don't want you to think I was just looking for a free newspaper."

Tor stepped back into the bank lobby, pulled one of the wallets from his coat and slipped it to Chief Namakagon who dropped it into an inside pocket of his bearskin robe. They left the bank.

Heading toward the depot, they passed two lumberjacks conversing on

91

the wooden walkway. On his face, the taller man wore the telltale scars from being kicked with calked boots. The other man was short and muscular. Neither made any effort to move aside as Tor and Namakagon passed.

Tor purchased the return tickets, along with a copy of Harper's Weekly and the latest edition of the *St. Paul Pioneer Press*. He slid the magazine and newspaper into his knapsack next to the nutmeg and bottles of lemon extract. He and the chief sat down to wait for the next northbound train.

The depot door opened and the two lumberjacks they had passed on the boardwalk entered, bought tickets, and sat nearby.

The northbound train pulled into the station with a rush of steam and the bell ringing. A long whistle blast signaled time to disembark.

The conductor assisted four women passengers from one car while several men got off another. Mail and freight were unloaded from a third. The brakeman swung off the corner ladder of the caboose and onto the platform.

When they heard the conductor's call, Tor and Namakagon boarded, finding no other passengers sharing their car. The locomotive's whistle announced its departure. As the train began to move, the two lumberjacks crossed the platform and stepped into the same car, taking the seat behind Tor and the chief.

The Omaha rumbled up the track. Tor scraped frost from the window with his fingernails and watched the rail yard, blanketed with snow, pass by.

The big man behind Tor spoke. "You there! We don't want any trouble. Give us the money and you won't be hurt."

Tor and Chief Namakagon turned.

The man behind brandished a large caliber revolver in his gloved hand. "Do as I say. I want the money. Now!"

"Sam! What are you doing with that gun?" said his partner. "You didn't say nothin' about no gun."

"Shut up, you fool!"

Conductor Clyde Williams entered the car calling, "Tickets—tickets, please."

The thief hid the gun under his coat and offered his ticket, as did his partner. The conductor inspected both, smiled, nodded, then canceled the tickets with four clicks of his punch.

Tor reached for his ticket. Namakagon stopped him.

"We have no tickets," said the chief.

"No tickets?" replied the conductor.

"None whatsoever."

Conductor Williams scowled. The thieves remained silent. Namakagon, still wearing his bearskin robe stood up, pulling Tor with him.

"We had no money."

"Not true," said the shorter thug. "They got plenty of money, all right."

"Quiet!" said his partner.

"But, Sam..."

"I said quiet, Percy." repeated the man with the boot-scarred face.

"Take us to the station," said the chief. "I'll square up with Oscar."

"You know Oscar?" said the conductor.

"We both know Oscar Felsman," said Tor. "He's a close friend of ours and my father and my uncle, too."

"And just who are you?"

"Tor Loken. My father is Olaf Loken and Ingman is my uncle."

"Well, I'll be! I know Ingman. I know him well. Skinned him for three dollars and sixty cents at the poker table last time I saw him. I know your pa, too. Good fellow. Well, young man, there's no doubt in my mind that you're good for the ticket price. Just square up with Oscar when you reach Cable. How is your pa, anyway?"

"No!" Namakagon demanded. "You must take us there—straight to Oscar Felsman."

"And just who are you?" asked the conductor.

"I am Namakagon."

"Namakagon?" said the shorter bandit. "Sam, he's that Indian with the silver mine! You know ..."

"Seal your damn lips, you fool!" snapped the other thief.

"Sam, I'm tellin' you, this here is the old Indian they talk about—the one with the treasure. He has a secret silver mine. We could be rich, Sam, rich!"

"And I said seal your damn lips, Wilkins. We are here to collect a debt."

The conductor looked puzzled. Namakagon stepped into the aisle. Tor remained standing, his knuckles white from clutching the straps of his knapsack.

"Enough talk," said the larger thug as he brandished his pistol again. "Sit down, the both of yous. And give me that money!"

"What is this?" exclaimed Williams. "What do you think you're doing?"

"I'm collecting a debt," replied the thief. "This ain't your concern. The Loken camp owes my boss and we're here to collect, that's all. None of your business." He turned toward the chief and Tor. "Now hand over the damn money." He thrust the revolver forward toward Namakagon's chest.

"There will be none of this on my train!" shouted Williams. "Resolve your differences when you reach the station. Now put away that pistol, sir!"

"The money!" shouted the thief, ignoring the conductor.

The other thug stood up with a look of disbelief. "Sam, Sam!" he said in a forced whisper, "We were just supposed to get the money back. You didn't say nothin' about no gun. This is more than I bargained for, Sam!"

"Shut your dang mouth, Percy."

"I ain't takin' no part in no train robbery. This is the Omaha line, Sam. They'll have the gol dang Pinkertons after us!"

"Hush up, you fool," Sam said, now pointing the pistol at Tor. "Give me the money now or I'll shoot the boy."

"Not on my train!" shouted the conductor. The train whistle blew twice as they approached the trestle north of Hayward.

"Wait!" said Namakagon. "Tor, give this fellow the money."

Tor reached into the pocket of his mackinaw and pulled out the canvas bank wallet. He saw Sam's eyes get big and a grin spread across his face. Tor looked at Namakagon, then, with a sudden snap, threw the wallet to the far end of the car. As it bounced off the last seat, Sam turned, his pistol moving aside. Tor whipped his knapsack up and around, hitting Sam in the head, breaking both bottles of lemon extract. The knapsack then struck the henchman's gun hand and the revolver discharged with a deafening *pow!*

The bullet hit the gunman in his own left knee. He collapsed to the floor, holding fast to the pistol.

Namakagon stepped onto his forearm to stop him from raising the gun again. Percy Wilkins, the shorter of the two thugs, scrambled across the seat back, pushing Tor out of his way. Wilkins bounded from seat to seat, then into the aisle, running to the end of the car. He dove to the floor and grabbed the wallet, then sprang to his feet and reached for the train's emergency chain above the doorway. The air brakes on the train locked, slamming Namakagon and the conductor to the floor. Wilkins kept his balance by hanging onto a seat back, then scrambled out the door.

His arm now free, Sam brought the pistol up again. Both the conductor and the chief lay in the aisle before him. Instinctively, Tor whipped the knapsack up and around once more, hearing a *click* as the robber pulled back the hammer. But the flying knapsack knocked the pistol down again, just as the bandit's gun went off.

Pow! The second bullet struck the wooden floorboards next to Conductor Williams' head and ricocheted up and through the backs of two empty seats, lodging in a third. The gunman tried again to raise the revolver but, instantly, Namakagon's hunting knife flashed through the air. The sharp, steel blade cut through the back of the thief's gun hand, crunching bone and pinning it securely to the oak floor. The gun flew free, the thief screaming.

Conductor Williams scrambled to his knees and grabbed the gun. Tor jumped over two seats into the aisle and ran to the end of the car. He threw open the door and watched the escaping bandit disappear into a grove of cedars along the river, downstream from the railroad trestle. The door leading into the next car opened. Two lumberjacks, a man in a business suit, and two Ojibwe men stepped in looking for the source of the commotion. Both the brakeman and the switchman were right behind, trying to crowd through the narrow portal. They all followed Tor to where the fallen thug lay, still pinned to the floor and writhing from pain.

The engineer burst into the car, the air strong with the smell of spent gunpowder. "Who the hell pulled that dang emergency chain?" he shouted.

"Clyde, for Pete's sake, what in tarnation is going on here?"

"It's alright, folks," cried Conductor Williams, waving the revolver recklessly. "I have this all under control."

Namakagon snapped the pistol from the careless hand of the conductor and pointed it upward. In one, smooth motion he flipped open the cylinder and dropped the four remaining cartridges and two empty forty-four caliber casings onto the floor, some falling onto the defeated thief.

"Here, this is safe for you to wave around now," the chief said as he handed the revolver back to Williams, "as long as you don't reload it."

"Why, Sam Rouschek," exclaimed Albert Ross, the brakeman. "Sam, what the hell is going on here?"

The bandit, still twisting from the pain, made no reply. Namakagon reached down and pulled out his knife, causing the bandit to scream again. The brakeman grasped the chief's arm with one hand and drew back a clenched fist with the other.

Clyde Williams grabbed the brakeman's wrist. "Hold off, Bert. The Indian is not the cause of the trouble here. Him and the boy were on their way to Cable when they got stuck up by this here villain and the other fella."

Williams turned to the engineer. "It was that other scoundrel, his partner, who stopped the train. He made off into the woods with the money."

"Nothing but newspapers in that wallet he took," said Tor with a smile.

"But ..." began Williams.

"Not a penny," added the chief.

"Well, don't that take all," said the engineer. "A gol dang robbery right here on my train! And we upset their plans, right Clyde? We foiled a dang train robbery! Wait till the Chicago office hears about this. Good work, Williams," he said slapping the conductor on the back. "Folks, I have a telegram to send to the home office and a schedule to meet. Clyde, Bert, you take care of things here."

The engineer walked back toward the locomotive muttering, "Wait till Chicago hears about this."

Bert grinned. "Well, Sam, looks like you got yourself stuck neck-deep in the pickle barrel this time." Sam made no reply as he cradled his bleeding right hand.

Conductor Williams turned to the brakeman. "Just how do you know this fellow, Bert?"

"You mean Sam, here? Well, Sam was the only fella who ever had enough gumption to ask my sister to marry. She turned him down flat. Imagine that. Not much goin' for her, my sister, that is."

"What about the other bandit?" asked Tor. "He'll get away!"

"He won't move fast in the snow," said Namakagon. "I will find him. He will soon be in the Sawyer County jailhouse next to his friend, here."

"Mikwam-migwan," said one of the Ojibwes, "you go to Cable with the boy. We will track the thief. Meet us tonight. We will leave you a good trail."

"Thank you, my friends," said the chief. "Without snowshoes he will not move fast. Good hunting," he said, patting the shoulders of the other two Indians. The two Ojibwe men jumped onto the shoulder of the railroad grade.

Namakagon turned to the captured bandit. "Now, what is this about collecting a debt? For whom?" Rouschek pulled himself up to a sitting position. He grimaced with pain as he tried to move his leg. "I ain't workin' for nobody."

"How did you know … Who told you we had that money?"

"We just figured it out, that's all."

"I repeat, for—whom—are—you—working?"

"I already told you, I ain't workin' for nobody but myself!"

The brakeman interrupted, "I saw Ned Dearborne, the bank teller, talking to you in the hotel bar last night, Sam."

"The teller at the Lumberman's Bank?" demanded the chief.

"I told you," Rouschek insisted, "I don't work for nobody and I don't know what you're talkin' about. Nobody told me nothin'."

Namakagon turned to the brakeman. "Who else was at the bar?"

"Only other person at that end of the bar was Phineas Muldoon."

"King Muldoon?" asked Clyde.

"Yep, King Muldoon."

"Is that what this is about?" Namakagon demanded of the thief. "Did you do this because King Muldoon doesn't like the Loken family working near their holdings?" Then, louder, "Sam Rouschek, did you threaten our lives and try to steal our money because of that timber sale last month? Is that it?"

"So what if it is!" snapped Sam, still suffering pain. "I was offered a job and told to collect a debt, that's all. Muldoon said he'd give us each twenty-five dollars and steady work till breakup. I was just doin' my job, that's all."

"Well, sir," said the conductor, "You may have been sent to collect a debt. I don't know anything about that. But I do not believe your job extends to train robbery. No, sir. Society frowns on train robbery and so does the law."

"I ain't no train robber," muttered the thug. "We just needed work and came to collect what's owed."

"The circuit judge will have his own opinion on that," said Namakagon. "Mr. Williams, can you deliver this man to the Sawyer County Sheriff?"

"With pleasure, Chief. I will have him back in Hayward in an hour and ten. And I will see to it that Oscar telegraphs ahead to let the sheriff know to meet us at the station—with shackles."

Sam Rouschek groaned from pain as he cradled his bloody right hand.

"Just one more thing," said Conductor Williams, pointing to Tor and Namakagon with his ticket punch. "What about those tickets?"

Chapter 19
Tracking the Bandit

The Omaha arrived at the Cable depot twenty-two minutes behind schedule. Stationmaster Oscar Felsman was on the platform, pocket watch in hand. The train pulled to a stop with the familiar rush of steam, ringing of the bell, and squeal of the locomotive's wheels against steel rails.

Conductor Clyde Williams swung down and stepped onto the platform to meet the stationmaster. He told the tale of the holdup with much arm waving and gesturing as the passengers disembarked. The bandit, Sam Rouschek, shot in the knee and stabbed through the hand, remained on the floor of the forward passenger car. There was no reason to guard him. He was in shock, in pain, unable to move. Percival Wilkins, his partner, had escaped into the forest with what he thought was the camp payroll.

Tor Loken and Chief Namakagon, each carrying their knapsacks, crossed the platform to meet Oscar.

"Well, now, sounds like you two had quite a trip home."

"Yes, sir, Mr. Felsman, we surely did," replied Tor. "One villain is caught and now we're going back to capture the other who bolted into the woods. He thinks he stole our money but we sent him on his way with only last week's newspaper. Wait till Pa and Uncle Ingman hear." Tor placed his knapsack on a nearby handcart to button his mackinaw. "We'll surely have him captured by nightfall, Mr. Felsman."

"I am certain your father would prefer you come home," said Namakagon. "I know you'd like to be there to see this ruffian delivered to the sheriff, but, Tor, you must leave that to me. Your duty is to return to the camp."

"But, Chief Nama ..."

"You must complete your task. Your responsibility is to return to camp today. You must never stray from your responsibility, Tor, especially when others count on you."

"Dang it all, you're right," muttered Tor. "I'll deliver the goods to camp, then come back here to meet you."

"No. Stay at the camp. I'll be along in good time."

"Listen to Chief Namakagon, Son," said Oscar. "Let him deal with the bandit and the lawmen."

"Then I wish you good luck on the tracking," said Tor. "I look forward to soon seeing you in camp."

As Tor slung his knapsack over his shoulder, the smell of fresh lemons filled the air. His pack and all its contents were soaked in lemon extract. It dripped onto his boots and the platform.

"Looks like Sam Rouschek owes you a bottle of lemon juice on top of everything else," said the chief.

Tor held up the knapsack as the yellow liquid dripped out. "If Sourdough was the judge of him," he said, "I'd bet he'd get another five years

97

in prison for this."

"I'd best check on the scoundrel," said Williams. "I hope he don't leave me with a big blood stain to clean up. Lemon juice is one thing. Blood is another. I don't like to see blood stains on my cars."

"Say, Tor," said the stationmaster, "you tell your father I'm coming out on Sunday for a sampling of Sourdough's dinner fare and a hand of pinochle. Tell him and your Uncle Ingman, too, that I'm bringing along some of my home brew. We can celebrate the capture of these dishonorable louts."

"Yes, sir, Mr. Felsman."

"Call me Oscar, Son. Any man who takes part in the conquering of such ruffians is certainly man enough to call me by my first name."

Tor tried hard not to show the pride he felt from hearing such words. "Why, thank you, Oscar. Well, I'd best be off, then."

"Tor," said the chief, reaching deep inside his bearskin robe.

"Oh!" "I dang near forgot."

Namakagon pulled out the canvas bank wallet, handing it to Tor, who opened it and peeked inside.

"Tell me it is not last week's newspaper," said the chief.

Tor looked back into the bank wallet, then at Namakagon again. "You'll just have to wait until you get back to camp to find out."

Tor left with the canvas bank wallet tucked deep in the back of his mackinaw. He walked through the depot waiting room and out the east door, down the steps, across the siding. He followed the narrow concrete walk through the small park to the quiet street lined with stores, taverns, rooming houses, and homes. A horse drawn wagon filled with lumber turned up the street toward him. He crossed the snow-covered road and entered the general store on the corner.

Tor asked the clerk for two quart bottles of lemon extract and more nutmeg, knowing that Sourdough would have a fit if he did not get his supplies. As the clerk wrapped the order, Tor noticed a gold locket in a glass display case.

"How nice that would look on Rosie," he said.

"Young fella?" said the apron-clad clerk.

"Sir?"

"Did you have a question about the locket?"

"No. Well, not really—well, how much is it?

"Dollar-eighty-five," said the clerk, "but it's ten karat gold. So is the chain. Shall I put it on the Loken account with the lemon extract and nutmeg?

"No, sir! Don't you dare do any such thing! Can you imagine the razzin' I'd get? Why the whole camp would know of it and I'd never hear the last word from the fellas. No, I'll just have the lemon extract and the nutmeg, thank you."

Tor left the store with his order and hitched the horse to the cutter. An hour later he was at the dam on the west end of Lake Namakagon.

As the horse trotted out onto the ice across from the dam, Tor noticed two men on ladders hanging a new sign on the dam tender's building. He pulled back on the reins. The cutter came to a stop. Tor looked back at the tender's building to be sure he had read the sign correctly. *MULDOON & COMPANY DAM, King Muldoon, Proprietor.* With a snap of the reins and a *giddup*, he was off again, heading down the narrows toward the main body of the lake. The cutter rounded the point and crossed the lake, then turned north and followed the shore. The horse held a quick and steady trot. Tor looked back to see black storm clouds rolling in from the west. The December light was fading quickly but, soon he saw the glow from the oil lamps in the Namakagon Timber Company lodge. His horse followed the trail from the lake up the bank, across the yard, and straight into the horse barn. Harry Green was there to take the reins. Tor jumped from the cutter, grabbed his pack and ran to the main lodge.

"Pa, Pa!" he yelled. "Pa, you won't believe what happened!"

Olaf turned his wheelchair away from the large roll-top desk.

"Pa! We dang near got ambushed by two train robbers! They wanted the money from the bank." As he spoke Tor pulled the canvas wallet from his coat pocket and tossed it onto the table with a grin. "Oh, Pa, you should've seen us. We gave them what for and sent one to the calaboose with a bullet in his knee and his hand cut clear through by the chief's hunting knife. Why old Namakagon is chasin' the other bandit through the pines right now. Pa, it surely was something to see!"

"Slow down, Son. Slow down. You all right? Didn't get hurt, did you?"

"No, Pa. Not a nick or a scratch. Nobody got hurt but the one bandit. Name's Sam Rouschek. Big man with a waffled face! He was tryin' to rob us of the men's pay when I knocked his revolver down with my pack. Pa, it went off and he shot right into his own knee! Dang it all! I wish you could have seen it."

"Revolver?"

"Ya, Pa, forty-four. Shot himself right in the knee. Then when he tried to get another crack at us, the chief pinned his gun hand to the floor with his hunting knife. Stabbed clean though his hand and into the floor. Pa, you should've seen it!"

"You sure you're not hurt? I never should have sent you."

"Fine, Pa."

"Chief Namakagon is all right? Didn't get hurt?"

"Just fine, too, Pa."

"Anybody else hurt?"

"Nobody else harmed a bit. It all happened on the Omaha run back to Cable this morning. Down by the Hayward trestle. Oscar Felsman said he was dang proud of me for helping to spoil the plans of the hooligans. Oh, Pa, I wish you could have been there to see it all!

"Oh, ya, Oscar told me he's coming out Sunday to celebrate and that he's bringing out a batch of his home brew. Can I tell Sourdough to fix up a special Sunday dinner, Pa?"

"Ya, you better let him know," said the elder Loken. He wheeled his chair around the table and across to the stone fireplace. "First you take off your coat and have a seat by the fire. I want to hear the whole story, front to back."

Tor walked to the windowsill where the water bucket stood. He plunged the dipper into the cold water, took a long drink and dropped the dipper back into the pail. He tossed another log onto the fire, hung his coat on a peg and sat in one of the big wing chairs as Olaf pulled his wheelchair close. As Tor neared the end of his tale, he heard Harry Green blow the gabreel, calling the men into the cook shanty for supper.

"Tor," said Olaf, "your Uncle Ingman and the men will all want to hear your story. After the supper chores are done, you can fill them in."

Chief Namakagon did not catch up with his bandit-tracking friends until dusk. The fugitive, Percy Wilkins, was still ahead of his pursuers. He had made his way to an open creek and waded down the creek bed to hide his tracks. His pursuers knew better than to become drenched in icy water during winter. They followed the stream bank, hoping to find the track as he left the creek but doubled back after seeing no sign downstream.

Upstream, they found the thief's trail. His tracks showed he left the stream where it entered a large spruce swamp, crossing it before taking to the ridges.

"This man has the skills of the muskrat," the chief was told when he met up with the other trackers. "He has doubled back like a wounded deer trying to escape a wolf. He now follows the ridge tops where less snow lets him move faster. He is heading back to Hayward."

"There is a storm coming," said Namakagon. "No light from the moon or stars. He must stop.

"He is wet. He will make a fire," replied one of the trackers.

"Snow will soon cover his tracks," said the chief. "We should go on."

The thief's tracks were easy to follow even in the dim light. The three stayed on the track until too dark to see. A few large, soft snowflakes began to fall. Namakagon pulled a piece of bark from a dead birch tree and snapped off a thin oak sapling. He stripped off some of the oak branches and wove the bark into the rest. A strike of a match and the torch was lit. They stayed on his trail.

Three torches later, they found more of the fugitive's sign. The snow was well trampled.

"Look," said Namakagon, pointing to some tinder and kindling, "we interrupted the muskrat before he could light his fire. He is close. If he starts a fire now, we will see it. He cannot continue without light and he will freeze without fire."

Namakagon stared into the dark silence. Then he cupped his hands around his mouth.

"It is over, Percy Wilkins. All is lost unless you surrender." Namakagon's deep voice echoed off the nearby hills. No reply. Namakagon called again. "Now is your chance to live rather than die, Wilkins," he called. "Come share our fire. What do you say?" Again, no answer. "Wilkins, you can

100

keep your life if you come with us now. What is your reply?" More silence. The fourth birch torch burned out. Namakagon called again. "There is a storm coming. You are wet. You have no fire, no blankets, no light. Come share our fire now or we will find you frozen and dead in the morning."

The three trackers stood in the black silence. "We should make camp," said one of Namakagon's friends. The chief struck a match and lit another piece of birch bark, then tossed it into the fugitive's abandoned kindling. A flame soon burned before them. Light from the flames danced across the snow-laden limbs of nearby trees.

"There is no need for you to stay. This muskrat is wet, cold, and tired. He can have no fight left in him now and will have less tomorrow. You have brought me to the thief. If he surrenders, I will bring him in. If he does not, I will leave his corpse for the wolves and ravens."

Chief Namakagon watched his two new friends leave, the diminishing light from their birch torch flickering until it finally disappeared into the darkness. Ogimaa Mikwam-migwan was now left alone in the dark woods to wait either for the surrender of the bandit or for dawn. He kicked snow onto the fire until only a few embers were left to glow in the blackness. Steadying himself with his walking staff, he felt his way back down the trail around fifty yards. The chief wrapped himself in his bearskin robe and curled up on the snowy forest floor. Sheltered under a balsam tree, he would wait through the night. The storm came in. Heavy, wet snow fell hard as Namakagon slept.

Chapter 20
Junior's Wager

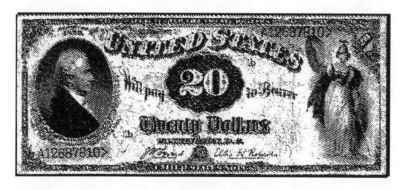

Back in the Loken camp, supper ended, the kitchen was cleaned up, and the men hung their socks to dry. Pipes were lit. One man played *Oh, Susannah* on his fiddle. Olaf and Ingman sat at a table near one of the kitchen ranges.

Word quickly spread through the camp that Tor had a story to tell. Uncle Ingman was eager to hear the tale. He grabbed one of Sourdough's empty stew pots and a wooden spoon. His *clang, clang, clang, clang,* brought the whole camp to attention.

"Listen up, men!" shouted Ingman. "If you are like me, then you're champin' at the bit to hear Tor tell us of his adventure. So light your pipes, open your ears, and shut your yaps so the boy doesn't have to holler."

Ingman sat down on a stack of flour sacks and wiggled in for a comfortable seat. A mouse scurried out from underneath. Sourdough rushed to stomp on it without luck. Several jacks moved in closer from the back end of the line of bunks, and the whole camp became unusually quiet as Tor Loken climbed atop one of the oilcloth-covered tables to tell his story.

A half-hour later, Tor finished his tale by telling the men Chief Namakagon was now out in the pines tracking down the escaped bandit. Tor stepped down. The camp remained silent as the men considered the boy's tale. Then, from the back, came a hearty laugh.

"That, young fella, is as grand a tale as any I ever heard this season! Even better than any ol' Paul Bunyan story, I'd say."

Laughter rolled through the room. Sourdough stepped forward and banged the spoon against the bottom of the soup pot again.

"You fellas can hoot an' holler all you want," he shouted above the laughter. "As for me, I believe that this ain't no tall tale."

"Who are you to say it ain't, Sourdough?" came a voice from the back. "The boy's got himself a good yarn there, that's all."

Tor jumped up on the table again. "This is not a yarn," he shouted. "I told you, I was there right in the middle of the whole ruckus. So was the chief. He'd tell you so if he wasn't chasing down that other pole cat."

"I ain't one to believe no wet-behind-the-ears cub!" shouted a man in back. "I'll lay two-to-one odds that the whole story is counterfeit."

Junior Kavanaugh jumped up onto the table next to Tor. The men watched as Junior said something to Tor. Tor replied, then Junior turned to the men, shouting, "I'll take those two-to-one odds, Elmer." The camp grew silent again. "I'll put seventy five dollars from my spring paycheck against it at your odds, and I'll lay the same bet for any man willin'." More silence. "Where's your courage, fellas? My money's good as yours, ain't it?"

"You're on for a double-sawbuck, young fella," replied Elmer, grinning.

"I'll take dat bet, too, Yunior—for ten bucks!" shouted Swede Carlson. "Yust so ve're talkin' likevise on dis, you're a-bettin' dat two crooks tried robbin' Tor on da train today und I'm bettin' dat it iss all yust a big fairy tale. Und you iss puttin' up you five dolla agin my ten-spot?"

"That's right, Swede," replied Junior. "Two to one odds. That's what I heard Elmer say. Payment guaranteed out of my earnin's come spring when we all get paid off."

"Okay, den. I'm in."

"I'm in for a sawbuck, too, Junior." "I'm in for twenty." "Me, too!" came shouts from the men. "I'm good for five." "Put me down for a sawbuck, too, Junior."

"Just a minute, fellas. I need someone to write this all down."

"I'll do just that, Junior," said Sourdough. "I'll mark it right here on the kitchen wall where everyone can see. Fair and square, boys."

Within minutes twenty-three bets ranging anywhere from two to twenty dollars were recorded on the wall, and Sourdough was still writing.

"Hold your horses, boys," shouted Blackie. "The way I figure, Junior can't pay off that much money unless he works here for three years or more."

Sourdough whispered something in Junior's ear. Junior nodded in return. "I'll back Junior up," shouted Sourdough. "I know young Loken here ain't no liar and I'm willin' to wager on it."

"Now wait just a dang minute there, Sourdough," shouted one of the men. "We ain't sayin' nobody's tellin' lies here. We're sayin' this is just a good ol' fashioned lumber camp tale—sort of like sayin' your bean soup is safe to eat." The whole camp broke into laughter.

Sourdough stopped writing bets on the wall long enough to scowl at the roomful of lumberjacks. He shouted above the laughing men, "I'm puttin' my money behind Junior! Place your bets if you have the gumption, shanty boys."

More bets came in. Sourdough kept writing until the betting stopped. "What's the matter, boys?" he shouted, "do you think your camp cook don't have the money?"

"Sourdough," called out one of the men, "if I had your money, I'd throw all mine in the cook stove just to help dry me socks."

Sourdough added up the tally. "We have thirty-seven bets in for a total of two-hundred and fifty-eight dollars. That's what Junior and me stands to

103

make if we win the bet. If we lose, we'll be out, let's see, that's one hundred and, uh, twenty-eight, no, nine—one hundred and twenty-nine dollars. That's quite a pot."

Junior had a big grin on his face as he and Tor stepped down from the table. He turned to Tor. "I surely hope you're on the level, Tor," said Junior. "You are, ain'tcha?"

"Junior, if I made this whole story up, then wouldn't I have also laid down a bet against you?"

Junior thought for a couple of seconds, then grinned a much wider grin.

Chief Namakagon, warm and secure under his bearskin robe and a seven-inch layer of snow, woke in the middle of the night. He lifted the corner of the robe enough to see the flickering of flames coming from the campfire.

"The muskrat!" he thought, "He has started another fire. He thinks he is alone." The chief carefully reached down and pulled his knife from its sheath, then moved more of the robe to better see the campsite, fifty yards away. Large, wet snowflakes were falling fast. He stared through the falling snow trying to locate the bandit. He moved just a bit, feeling the snow on his black, fur blanket slide off. He still could not see Percy Wilkins.

Namakagon slowly sat up to get a better view. He started to stand, then, *whoosh!* Something struck him in the back and, as he glanced up, struck him again in the back of his head. Namakagon fell face-first into the snow. The old Indian quickly rolled over to see the his own walking stick again coming down toward his head. He tried to scramble to his knees but slipped in the snow as it struck his right arm forcing his knife from his hand and into the snow. He rolled again as the staff came down once more, missing his head by less than an inch.

Now Namakagon sprang to his feet, but before he could catch his balance, it hit him again, slamming him to the forest floor, thick with snow. He tried to get up, but his old muscles would not do what they could in his youth. The woods fell silent now. The snow continued to fall.

Ingman Loken wheeled his brother Olaf from the cook shanty back to the main lodge. There, they found Tor putting logs on the fire for the night.

"Looks like we'll have some snow by tomorrow morning, eh, Son?"

"I only hope this snow doesn't make it hard for the chief out there in the pines."

"Namakagon will do what needs to be done, snow or no snow," said Ingman. "No thief is going to out-do that old rascal. No sir."

"I hope to my soul you're right, Uncle. Namakagon's pretty dang old to be out there chasing outlaws on a night like this. You know how old he is?"

"Over sixty, I'd say," said Tor's father. "Maybe sixty-five?"

"Naw, he can't be that old, maybe fifty-five," said Ingman.

"Well, you're both off the mark," said Tor. "He told me on the train that he was born in seventeen seventy-nine. That makes him more than a hundred."

"Boy, you are full of tall tales tonight," said Ingman.

"Full of tales? You don't believe me about the bandits? Why, Uncle, you think I made the whole thing up. Well, you are dead wrong. I am no liar. You should know that. You should know, too, that I would not leave my friend Junior Kavanaugh out in the cold. Maybe *you* should put up a bet against me. I'll tell you what, Uncle Ingman, I'll bet my deer rifle against yours. Now what do you say to that? We could have Sourdough write it on the wall."

"Tor!" snapped his father. "You mind your sharp tongue, young man. You cannot fault your uncle for questioning your story. It does tend to bear the qualities of a detective magazine tale, you know."

Tor was astonished. "Pa, you don't believe me either? Neither of you believe my story? You think I made this whole thing up? You think I'm lying? Say it! Say you think I am just another gol dang liar sittin' on the deacon's bench in the sleep camp, making up tall tales to pass the long winter night."

"Torvald Loken! I told you to watch your tongue." warned his father.

"I apologize, Pa. I am sorry how I spoke to you and you, too, Uncle Ingman. More sorry you don't believe me. Mr. Felsman did, you know. In fact, he said I could now call him Oscar because of my bravery. Chief was right there to hear it."

"Oscar told you that?" asked Ingman.

"Yes, he did."

Tor's father and uncle were silent.

"Oh, I see. Now you think I made *that* up, too. Well, Oscar said he was coming out to the camp on Sunday to celebrate the capture of the crooks. Now, do you think I'm lying about that, too?"

His elders remained silent.

"All right, try this hat on for size: I had to stop at the store to replace the broken bottles of lemon extract and nutmeg. I can prove it broke. Just take a good whiff of my pack."

His uncle and father still said nothing. Tor sighed. "Well then, if I'm just a low-down, no-good liar, then go ahead and bet the whole dang lumber camp against me. What have you got to lose? Go ahead."

"Torvald!" shouted Olaf. "Now I told you to watch that sharp tongue of yours, boy!"

All three Lokens fell silent now. Tor stirred the fire with a poker. "I'm sorry, father. I don't mean to show disrespect. It's just that I'm giving you the story straight as an arrow. I don't know what else would convince you that I'm on the level."

"In a few days we'll know, won't we, Son. When Oscar Felsman rides into camp, he will either make an angel or a devil of you, now won't he."

"If he rides in at all," mumbled Ingman.

Silence again. Tor was disturbed. "Say, Uncle Ingman, as long as we got our deer rifles on the table over this, let me try one more of my tall tales out on you. What do you say, Uncle?"

Ingman looked at Tor with an eyebrow raised. "Yust say what you're gonna say, Nephew."

"That dastardly hooligan you think I dreamed up … you know, the fella that I say got shot and stabbed?" Tor paused to consider his words, "Well, Uncle, he said he was collecting a debt. That's what he said, Uncle, collecting—a—debt. Now, don't you think those would be strange words to add to a fairy tale?" Tor paused again. Ingman said nothing. "And when the brakeman, Bert Ross, piped in," continued Tor, "he said he saw the same bandit, Sam Rouschek, sitting at the Hotel Pion bar near someone named King Muldoon. Now, that name made no sense to me, except, when I came through the narrows today, I saw a new sign going up on the dam with the same name on it. Now, do you suppose I made that up, too? Do you think I am as clever a yarn spinner as ol' Mark Twain, Uncle? Or Charlie Dickens? Well, if so, I guess I should be quite pleased to be so well-regarded."

"Who did you say?" asked Ingman.

Tor sensed a change in his uncle's tone. "Charlie Dickens."

"No, no. Before that."

"Mark Twain? Oh, no, you mean Bert. Bert Ross? Or Sam Rouschek?"

"No, no, the name you saw at the dam—on the sign," persisted Ingman.

"King Muldoon," replied Tor.

"Ingman, it was the Muldoon's outfit that you bamboozled on the land deal in October," said Olaf. "Maybe they figured it out."

"Could be they are spiteful we bought those six sections out from under their noses," said Ingman. "With all the land they own, I don't see why they would care much about a small outfit like ours buyin' up six sections."

"I know Phineas Muldoon's ways," said Olaf. "He could own rights to every acre of land and stick of timber in the State of Wisconsin and he would still go lookin' for more. Muldoon calls himself *King* for good reason." Olaf looked at Tor. "What's this you saw at the dam?"

"Two men on ladders were hanging a sign on the tender's building. It said Muldoon and Company Dam, King Muldoon, proprietor."

Again, the room fell silent.

"Tor," said Ingman, "I believe I owe you an apology and my Winchester to boot. I should have believed you when you first spoke."

Olaf leaned forward, reached out and grasped Tor's arm. "Son, seems I should have held more faith in you, too. I swear I will never again doubt you. I do hope you can forgive us."

"Of course I forgive you. It's hard even for me to believe this day's events and I was right there in the midst of it all."

"What are we gonna do about this, Olaf?" said Ingman. The fire crackled in the stillness.

Olaf broke the silence. "Muldoon and Company Dam, King Muldoon, Proprietor," he muttered. "Ingman, pay Phineas a visit. We need to find out exactly what the scalawag has in mind.

Chapter 21
The Desperado Percy Wilkins

Heavy snow fell across the Namakagon Valley through the night. By dawn more than two feet of new snow blanketed the ground. As the snow continued to fall, the wind turned from east to north and the temperature fell. Limbs of the tall white pines bent far down under the weight of the heavy snow and swayed in the wind.

The tracks of men there the night before had vanished from the ridges north and west of Hayward. The woods were silent, save for the occasional call of a raven searching for any scrap of food on the winter landscape.

Chief Namakagon lay motionless under the snow. As the morning light filtered through the tree limbs, the old Indian stirred. He slowly opened one eye, then the other, but, covered by his bearskin robe and buried by snow, he saw only blackness. He recalled the flickering firelight and the falling snow and the vision of the tree limb striking him again and again.

"Was this a dream?" thought Namakagon. "Was this a vision from Gitchee Manitou? Or did the trickster Wenebojo visit again?" He closed his eyes again and lay silent for a moment, then reached for his knife to find it still in its sheath. "My blade is secure," he thought. "Yes. It must have been Wenebojo. I have been tricked into dreaming this dreadful nightmare."

Namakagon gently pushed the corner of the fur robe aside. Snow and bright morning sunlight fell onto his face. Squinting, he saw the heavy layer of snow in the woods around him. He looked at his hand to see blood. He felt the back of his head finding a large lump where he had been struck the night before. He moved his left shoulder and grimaced, then groaned with pain.

"This was no dream," he muttered. "This was not Wenebojo's work. I was careless. I trusted that the darkness would keep me safe. I was a fool. The muskrat could have ended me here on this ridge." The old man lay still again. "But, why is my knife still in its sheath? How is it I am covered with my robe?"

Still under the warm bearskin, the old man began to move, stretching, trying to determine the extent of his injuries. He found his walking staff there next to him. Keeping the robe over his head and shoulders, he slowly sat up.

Chief Namakagon stood, snow falling from his robe. Blood-painted pine needles lay where he had slept. Stretching and moving, the chief felt pain, but he knew this was pain he could endure. He rubbed a handful of snow onto his face and neck, cleaning off the blood there. Another bit of snow went into his mouth. He spit it onto the ground. He melted more snow in his mouth, this time swallowing it. He straightened his robe, reached down for his hat, taking care to not touch it to the tender, swollen lump on the back of his head. The chief looked at his left wrist. The silver band he had worn for more than five decades was gone. He reached for his leather poke. This too was gone, along with the few coins he carried in it.

Namakagon shook more snow from his robe, adjusted it, and walked toward the depression left in the snow where Wilkins slept the night before. He looked up the trail, then down. "No tracks," he said. "Perhaps, Muskrat, you sprouted wings and flew to safety?"

Walking up the trail to a place where a large white pine protected the ground from deep snow, he saw moccasin tracks and knelt down for a closer look. "No," Namakagon said. "These are not right. You did not go this way, Muskrat." He turned, trudging through the deep snow down the back trail. There, under the protective limbs of another white pine, he saw the faint but recognizable track he wanted.

"Shoe-pacs," he said to the trees around him. "Muskrat, I have you now. You head back for the railroad grade where the snow has been thrown to the side by the locomotives and where walking is easy. You think I do not follow, but you know not Ogimaa Mikwam-migwan."

As the old chief followed the faint tracks, he wondered out loud. "Why did you not finish me with my own blade, Muskrat? Did you think about this deed? Did you stand there above me, looking down at my chest with my knife in your hand? Did you want to plunge the blade into my heart? Why did you not take my life? And why, Muskrat, did you cover me? Did you not know I might wake and come after you?"

Chief Namakagon flexed and stretched more as he followed the trail. His pain eased as he picked up the pace. He again wondered aloud about his quarry. "I was a fool to let you ambush me, Percy Wilkins. Are you a fool, too? Yes, you must be a fool. You were foolish to partner with Sam Rouschek. You were foolish to run. You were foolish to not surrender last night when you learned you had only newspapers, not money. And you are a fool now to think this old Indian will not hunt you down."

Following his quarry through the deep snow proved difficult for Namakagon. Still, he pressed forward and, soon, the trail told him he was nearing Wilkins. Unknowingly, the bandit was breaking trail for his pursuer. Far in the distance, Namakagon heard the whistle of a train.

"Ah, this is a welcome sound to your ears, Muskrat. You believe that train to be your salvation. You do not know I am behind you. Soon you will learn of your mistake. Muskrat, soon you will know more about old Mikwam-migwan, the man you left in the woods."

Namakagon shed his bearskin robe, hanging it on the limb of a white pine along the trail. He walked faster now. Through the trees ahead, he caught a glimpse of the fugitive, now trudging, plowing through the deep snow.

Percy Wilkins was much shorter than the tall Indian behind him. Wilkins had been breaking trail through the deep, wet snow since first light. Now, with the sun high, he had to stop to catch his breath after every third or fourth step. Namakagon closed in.

"You should imitate the whitetail and watch your back trail, Muskrat," whispered the chief. "You will not escape. You are tired, weak, not accustomed to such work. Soon, Muskrat, you will be at my feet."

The trail took them into a stand of snow-clad balsams. Leaving his walking stick behind, Namakagon drew nearer. Ahead, he heard Wilkins gasping for breath as he trudged through the deep snow. The chief stepped when his quarry stepped and rested when he rested.

When less than eight feet behind the weary man, Namakagon drew his hunting knife from its sheath. Silently, he shed his hat, letting it fall into the snow behind him. The fugitive, gasping for air, took two more steps, then leaned against a small birch.

Without a sound, Namakagon stepped within two feet of the thief. Slowly reaching out with both hands, he pulled back on a hank of hair as he placed his knife across the throat of the tired man. His head snapped back. Wide eyes looked up into those of the old Indian who held the blade to his throat.

"Percy Wilkins," said Chief Namakagon, "surrender or you will be food for the wolves."

The exhausted outlaw collapsed into the snow, Namakagon's knife still at his throat. Filled with terror, he stared up at his captor. The chief saw a mix of fear, surprise, and relief on his face. The man tried to speak.

"Don't," he gasped, "don't kill me. Please ... don't kill me," he gasped again.

Bending forward to keep his blade tight to the thug's throat, Namakagon said, "I will take my poke and my silver band now, Muskrat."

The thief fumbled with his belt, then delivered the Indian's buckskin pouch. Next he reached into his coat pocket, pulled out the silver wristband and handed it to his captor.

"Don't kill me," he pleaded, gasping again. "Please! I spared ... I spared your life last night," he said, gasping again. "Please, I'm beggin' you ... don't kill me."

"Why did you return my knife and cover me?" asked the chief, still holding the blade tight to Wilkins' throat.

"'cause I ain't no killer. I never would've give you such a beatin' if I thought I could make a good getaway. I was hopin' you weren't hurt bad. I figured before you froze, you'd come to. Please, please don't kill me. I could see you was old. I never figured you'd trail me after the beatin' I give you.

"I never imagined we'd get mixed up in no train robbery, neither. Sam and me was out of work. We couldn't find no outfit to hire us on. All the camps are full and the mines are cuttin' back. We got this here job collectin' a debt and was told just to get the money back, that's all. I never knowd Sam had a gun. I ain't no criminal and I ain't no killer. I just want to get back home to Iowa. Oh, I beg you, don't leave my dead body here for the wolves. Don't kill me. Please!"

Chief Namakagon stood, hunting knife clutched in his right hand. "Get up." The outlaw slowly stood. "Turn your pockets out." The man complied. A six-inch folding pocketknife fell into the snow along with some stick matches. "Take off your coat," demanded the chief. The man complied again. Namakagon searched through the coat pockets, finding only two cans of snuff and the empty canvas wallet. He returned the coat.

"Muskrat, put your arms around the birch tree." Again he did as ordered. Namakagon pulled a length of quarter-inch rawhide from his belt and tied the thief's hands together, binding him to the tree.

Wilkins watched as Namakagon headed back down the trail. "Wait! Where you goin'? You can't leave me here to freeze to death! Please, friend. Wait. Wait! Oh, God, no. Please don't leave me here to die."

Namakagon did not reply. A short time later he returned with his bearskin robe, walking stick, and hat. He untied his sobbing, shivering captive. They headed for the railroad grade, Namakagon behind and his captive again breaking trail and gasping for air. The wind picked up. Branches were shedding their thick cover of snow as the north wind rocked them back and forth.

An hour later the two men stood near the iron trestle north of Hayward, not two hundred yards from where the previous day's hold-up took place. They sat down on the rails facing each other. Drenched with perspiration, both men quickly chilled as the north wind whisked down the open railroad track.

Namakagon reached into an inside pocket and pulled out some pemmican. He took a bite, then gave a piece to Wilkins who devoured it. Hearing a distant whistle again, the men stood to face the oncoming southbound train.

When the Omaha came into sight, the chief climbed onto the snow bank waving his arms. The locomotive did not slow down. Seeing this, Wilkins joined his captor. Together, high on the bank above the track, they waved and waved, but the train maintained its speed.

When the engineer finally saw them, he threw the brake and sounded the whistle. The screech of braking wheels against cold steel rails pierced the air. The men would have their ride, but the train would be well past them by the time it came to a full stop.

Just as the locomotive was about to pass by, Wilkins dove down the bank toward the tracks shouting, "I'm goin' back to Iowa!" He bounded onto the railroad grade right in front of the moving engine, bounced off the cowcatcher, and landed on the other side of the track as the engine passed by. Now, with the train between the bandit and his captor, Wilkins would again try to make his escape.

Both the engineer and brakeman saw him jump. But, by the time they looked out the other side of the cab, Wilkins was gone.

The Omaha came to a full stop. Namakagon crossed the track but found no sign of his muskrat. Within seconds, the engineer, brakeman, switchman, fireman, flagman and conductor were in on the search. They looked inside and under every car from coal tender to caboose. A deputy, bound for Hayward, helped search for Wilkins, as did three other passengers. One man climbed to inspect the tops of the boxcars. Each hoped to spot the fugitive who seemed to have vanished.

Namakagon returned to where he saw Wilkins last. He found signs in

110

the snow along the track where the fugitive landed after jumping the track. He followed the faint footprints to the trestle. The chief looked down. Far below the wooden ties, on a steel beam, was a single footprint in the snow. He slid down the bank at the near end of the trestle, swung under the upper beam and looked up at the underside of the iron bridge. There, hiding far up in the shadows of the understructure, with his back, shoulders, and head tucked in tightly against the bottom of the ties, was the muskrat.

"You are not going to Iowa, Percy Wilkins." shouted Chief Namakagon. "You are going to the Sawyer County jail."

The other men heard this and soon covered both ends of the trestle in case the thief would try again to run.

Realizing he had no escape, the fugitive began to climb out. But he was tired, weak, and his hands numb from grasping the cold, steel I-beams. When he tried to find a handhold, he lost his grip. His feet slipped out and he flipped back, slamming his head sharply on a steel beam that rang out as Wilkins tumbled toward the river below. He landed headfirst, punching a hole through the ice and plunging into the moving water, instantly disappearing.

Namakagon stared at the hole in the ice, waiting for the man to surface. Only the slow, deep, rhythmic chug—chug—chug of the steam locomotive interrupted the winter silence. Chief Namakagon soon understood Percy

Wilkins would neither go to jail nor to his Iowa home. If the authorities could find his body after spring break-up, his corpse would likely be buried somewhere along the river, just as they did with the remains of ill-fortuned river pigs who drowned on many Wisconsin log drives.

The old Indian sang a sad, eerie chant to the waters below, to the surrounding trees, to the sky above. He climbed back up to the grade, gazed again at the hole in the ice below the trestle, and then boarded the train.

Chapter 22
The Widowmaker

Junior Kavanaugh had both of the big cook stoves stoked and the fires roaring when Mieczyslaw Kczmarczyk rolled out of his cot in the back of the cook shanty. The eight-inch stove pipes above the ranges glowed a deep red from the heat. Water in the ten large coffee pots was already boiling.

"'Bout time you came back from your voyage through dreamland, Sourdough," quipped Junior. "There's a hundred snarling jacks soon to be grumbling about your greasy gravy and bone-hard biscuits!"

"Humph," uttered the cook.

"Zeke and Zach and me got thirty pounds of pork cooking up in the oven, just the way you showed me, Sourdough. What do ya think about that?"

"What do I think, Junior? Well, I think I gotta water the petunias before anything, that's what I think."

The camp cook pulled up his britches and slipped into his shoe-pacs. He opened the cook shanty door to find more than two feet of fresh snow drifted against it. "By the holy jumpin' ghost of Jehosaphat, Junior! Look at all this gol dang, pot-lickin', snot-pickin' snow!"

"I got news for you, Sourdough, there's plenty more of it out in the yard and the woods. Gonna be a whole lot of angry bull cooks across the pinery when they see how much shovelin' they gotta do. Harry's out there now, makin' a trail to the crapper."

Sourdough tromped out, mumbling stronger oaths. A minute later, still cussing, he was back in the kitchen stomping his feet to shake off the snow. "What got you out of the barn so dang early, Junior? Graybacks chase you out?"

"Couldn't sleep much," replied Junior, pouring pancake syrup from a large kettle into a dozen tin bowls. "I had to get over here to count up all those bets again. I'm gonna be rollin' in dough, Sourdough. Up to last night I stood to earn about sixty dollars this winter. Now, if the fellas pay off, I'll have more than double that much in one pocket plus my wages in the other. Move out of the way, Mr. Andrew Carnegie, Mr. Junior Kavanaugh is takin' over!"

"Don't count your chickens before they's hatched, Junior," said the camp cook. "Ever heard of that?"

"Sourdough, not only is them chickens counted but they's already plucked, gutted and simmerin' in the stewpot."

Next door in the Namakagon Timber Company lodge, Olaf and Ingman sat across from each other at the table in the office. Ingman poured hot coffee from a blue, enameled percolator

"I suppose, then, we best invite Phineas Muldoon over to talk. No reason to postpone this, Olaf."

"We don't know that he will meet with us. Looks like he has the whole deck of cards on his side of the table and that dam is the trump card. I believe he intends to stop us from driving our timber."

"No man on God's good earth has right to claim control of the waters. The law's on our side."

"Law? In the pinery, Ingman, law is controlled by a handful of dishonest lumber tycoons who know which corrupt officials to pay off. Small timber outfits like ours haven't got a chance."

"Don't get me wrong here, Olaf, I agree with you. But it yust don't seem Muldoon or anybody else can decide how much water goes down the river. What if they did that with the mines up on the Iron Belt?"

"They do. The legislature allows the dang railroad to decide how many runs they'll make from the mines to the Ashland ore docks. That gives the railroad company control over who ships, when, and at what price. And where does the railroad company get its steel?" he asked rhetorically. "From their own mills in Buffalo, Pittsburgh, and Cleveland, that's where. Brother, the big mining outfits own not just the ore, but also the steel mills. The mines and mills are controlled by the railroads. They all work hand-in-hand. The small outfit does not stand a chance. You either pay their price, play their game, or sell out to them. In the final tally, they win. Seems Muldoon wants the same deal."

"Olaf, listen. If we could find a way to stop King Muldoon from controlling the river and our pine, stop him from forcing us out, well, shouldn't we do it? Shouldn't we do absolutely everything in our power to get our timber to the mills? To pay our men? To keep our camp and help protect the other small outfits from going bankrupt?"

"Well, of course we should."

"Then I say we set up a meeting with Muldoon. Then we set up another meeting, this time with the new governor. I read in the paper that he is very interested in the number of voters who now work in the pinery. Some say there are now more votes in the north than down in Milwaukee. Hell, there's more than twelve thousand lumberyacks between Hayward and Hurley alone. Maybe we can get some help from ol' Governor Yeremiah Rusk.

Junior Kavanaugh interrupted. "Burnt stove lids and woodtick stew in a quarter-hour. Harry is headed this way with his scoop shovel to clear a path. Otherwise you will need knee-high gumboots just to make it to the outhouse."

"Tor, get up! Get out'a the sack, boy," yelled Olaf. Then, to his brother, "Ingman, best you set up that meeting with Muldoon. Let's see what the slippery old shypoke has to say."

Minutes later the Lokens sat with the men in the cook shanty. Tor poured hot molasses over his pancakes, biscuits, and stewed pork. Ingman and Olaf watched as he devoured everything on his plate, gulped down a second cup of hot coffee, then filled his plate again.

"Son, you eat like a regular lumberjack. I hope you showed better manners at Mrs. Ringstadt's, yesterday."

"Yesterday? Oh, sure, Pa. I watched my manners. I didn't want … well …"

"Let me guess. You didn't want Mrs. Ringstadt's daughters to see you

113

eatin' like a north woods shanty boy, right?"

"No, well, maybe," said Tor, slightly embarrassed. "They're all nice folks there at her house. Guess I was representing the Loken Camp and I wanted them to see we're a real polite outfit." A man at the next table belched.

"Any daughter in particular?" asked his father. "Say ... Rosie?"

"Is she the one who plays the piano?" asked Tor, taking a bite.

"Yes, you know, the oldest daughter—your age—the pretty one with the dark hair and green eyes. Remember her?"

"Oh, sure. Was her name Rose? I was concentrating more on business. The bank and all, you know."

"Yes, business. Tor, I was thinking about inviting the Ringstadts up here for a Sunday dinner. Christmas is coming soon and it would be good to have something fairer to look at than your Uncle Ingman's ugly snout."

"And something that smells better than your old pole cat of a pa," Ingman snapped back with a grin.

Tor's eyes lit up. He fumbled his fork, dropping it into the syrup on his plate. "That would be fine. Makes no matter to me."

But inside, Tor was overjoyed with the notion of Rosie coming to the camp. "Rosie, right here, right in our lumber camp," he thought to himself. Then he looked down the table at the scores of lumbermen stuffing themselves, showing no manners, eating with their fingers, some grunting like hogs at the trough. Many were foul smelling. Most were foul-mouthed. Others were crude, rude, hard characters. What would his young, tender, innocent Rosie think about him, knowing he, Tor Loken, was part of the same company of men? The man at the next table belched again. Tor shook his head in utter disgust.

"Well, then," said Olaf, "let's plan on it. Oscar Felsman can telegraph Adeline from the station as soon as we get a message into town."

"I can take it in later today," offered Tor, forgetting to hide his interest.

"For a young fellow who doesn't seem to give a hoot one way or the other, you're quick to volunteer, Tor," quipped Ingman.

Tor took a big bite out of a large molasses cookie hoping he wouldn't have to reply.

Blackie Jackson, finished with his breakfast, grabbed a wooden step stool near them and sat down next to Tor. Sitting on the short stool, he was still taller than the others at the table.

"Mornin', Boss," he said to both Ingman and Olaf in his deep voice. "Looks like we got some snow to deal with today."

"Mornin', Blackie," said Ingman, as Olaf nodded hello.

"I'll run a couple of ox teams out to the cuttings to break a trail for the boys," Blackie said. "Skiddin' should be fine with this wet snow. She'll be plenty greasy on the sleigh trails. Gonna be a slow mornin' for the saw teams, though. Ain't no records gonna be set today, Boss."

"Blackie," said Ingman, "set Tor up with one of the ox teams. He can break trail back into those pines up by Sugarbush Creek." He turned to Olaf.

114

"Sound all right with you, Boss?" Olaf nodded, taking another sip of coffee.

"Dang right!" said Tor. "Long as I can ride on the back of one of those oxen, I'll break trail all the way to Lake Superior if you say the word."

"Our holdings don't go quite that far, Son. Not yet."

"Olaf," said Blackie, placing his arm around Tor's neck, "I've been thinkin' about this lad's adventure yesterday. Times are hard. There's some gol dang desperate men out there today, especially in this north country. You never know who might show up around the next bend or what he might have in mind. But them who get a look at me think twice about any foul play or foolishness. Boss, I just want you to know that if you ever need someone to tag along when there's business to be done, well, Boss, you can always call on me."

"I appreciate that, Blackie. I'll keep you in mind. You never know when we might need some help with this and that. Like you say, the world's not as safe a place now as when we were in short pants, right Blackie?"

Many of the men were finished and heading out the door into the thick snowdrifts. Strings of foul language could be heard as more men ventured out into the dark lumber camp yard. Blackie stood up, towering above the three Lokens. He returned the stool to its place near the cookstove and strode out the door into the deep snow. It would be a slow morning in the pinery.

Tor and his ox team were eight miles from camp by ten o'clock when the sun came out and the wind shifted. Now a warm, south breeze combined with the sun's rays to melt the snow. Tor's ox team dragged a three hundred pound v-shaped plow made from oak timbers. When he reached the timber landing at the end of the trail, Tor turned the oxen homeward. His return trip was faster, a pleasant ride through the woods on this sunny, mid-December day.

Near the camp, Tor met up with one of the saw teams. The two sawyers felled a big pine that missed its mark and now leaned into another tree. The top of the leaning tree was hung up in a tangle of limbs and branches. The cutting crew's attempts to free it were not working. They chained the butt of the log to their horse team but the horses could not budge the giant white pine.

"Looks like you got a good ol' widowmaker, fellas," called out Tor. "You're welcome to use my ox team if need be."

The swamper threw a chain over the oak plow pulled by Tor's team and hooked the other end onto the stubborn tree. The teamster and Tor slowly coaxed the two beasts forward. The five-foot-diameter butt of the tree began to move, then stopped again. Tor and the teamster urged both the oxen and the horses ahead once more. The animals strained, digging into the frozen turf beneath the snow and placing enormous strain on the chains.

High above them came a deafening *ca—rack!* A large limb sixty feet up in the other tree snapped violently and the gigantic pine plummeted toward the earth. As it fell, the thirty-foot broken limb sprung through the air and fell not three feet from Tor, missing his oxen but striking the horse beside him.

The huge workhorse reared up, snapping the harness. Both horses, crying out in fear, fell to the ground, hooves flailing as the tree slammed to the ground nearby. The oxen lurched forward. Both Tor and the teamster dove away from the animals, covering their heads. In seconds, the accident was over and the horses and men were getting back up.

"You fellas all right?" shouted the teamster. "Anybody get hurt?"

"I'm fine," called out one of the sawyers.

"Me, too," piped in the swamper.

"I'm all right," yelled Tor. One man didn't answer.

"Where's Mason?" shouted the teamster. "*Mason!*"

"Here—over here," called out the second sawyer.

Mason Fitch lay in the snow face up. A three-foot-long splinter, part of a larger pine branch, stuck out of his thigh. Tor and the other teamster plowed their way through the deep snow to the fallen man. Mason groaned as Tor slowly lifted his leg to find the splinter went all the way through. The swamper brought over his double-bit ax, and with a swift swing, separated the splinter from the branch. The injured lumberjack screamed in pain. Bleeding badly, he began slipping into shock.

"Tourniquet!" shouted teamster Henry Tilden. Immediately the swamper ran to the horse team. Using his razor-sharp ax as a knife, he cut a six-foot length of rawhide strap from the reins. The teamster tied a loop around the leg above the wound, inserted a two-inch thick pine branch and twisted it tightly. The bleeding stopped.

"Where'd you learn that?" asked Tor.

"I worked in a hospital back east during the war," Henry replied. "Virginny. I saw plenty of soldiers with their arms and legs dang-near blown off from Yankee mini balls. The soldiers who came in with tourniquets usually lived. The poor fellas who didn't have 'em, well, they just bled to death where they fell." He checked over his knot. Looking up at the injured logger he said, "Mason, let's get you back to camp so Sourdough can have a look at you."

"I don't want to lose my leg, Henry Tilden," cried Mason. "I ain't gonna spend the rest of my years with a stump. Promise me, Henry. Promise me that you will not let Sourdough take my leg!"

"Calm down, Mason. You ain't got such a bad leg here, just a good ol' pine sticker through it. Ol' Sourdough ain't gettin' no soup bone off you this time 'round." No siree. You'll be dancin' Irish jigs by Christmas Day."

Chapter 23
The Telegram

Mason Fitch lay on a table in the cook shanty, a thick, pine splinter protruding from both sides of his left thigh. Once again the head cook was drafted to patch up a lumberjack after a logging accident. Interrupted while butchering a hog, this amateur doctor wiped his hands on his apron before sliding his butcher knife up Mason's pant leg, slitting it to the crotch. He cut through the man's long johns, wet with melted snow and blood, and pulled back the layers of wool.

"Best loosen that tourniquet for a minute, Henry," he said.

"Don't take my leg, Sourdough," begged the pale, weak lumberjack.

Sourdough peered at him over his round, wire-rimmed glasses.

"Don't you worry now, Mason. Your leg will be good as new in no time at all." He stepped away for a moment, returning with a quart bottle of yellow liquid and a tin cup. He filled the cup and, with help from the others, pulled the wounded workman up to a half-sitting position. "Drink this."

Mason Fitch obeyed, choking down the medicine. "Dear God, Sourdough! You tryin' to poison me? What in tarnation was that?"

"Lemon extract," replied the cook, pouring another half-cup. "Here you go, Fitch. Have another."

Mason choked down the second drink. "Why you fillin' me with lemons, Sourdough? Ain't I suffered enough?"

"Stop your complainin', Fitch. There's more spirits than lemons in this stuff. Most bark eaters in camp would give a half-day's pay for a pull on this bottle. Stronger than that rotgut whisky they serve in town, Mason. I confess that I take a nip myself now and then—just to clear my sinuses, you understand."

After a third drink, the men helped Mason lay down again.

"Henry, Will, Tor, hold him tight now. Mason, we're gonna pull out that splinter. It's bound to hurt some so bite down on this rag," he said, plugging a dishrag in the man's mouth. "Now grab the edges of the table and hold on, Son."

Mason did. With a quick jerk, the head cook yanked out the long, blood-soaked, pine splinter. Mason bit down hard and didn't utter a sound.

"Good, good," said Sourdough. "Henry, grab that empty sauce pan off the counter and fill 'er up with snow. Tor, hand me my sewing kit—that green box on the shelf over the sink." Henry and Tor complied. Sourdough took a handful of snow, packed it into a ball and placed it on the open wound.

"Henry, you hold this tight for a minute. Push hard," he ordered. The amateur doctor then pawed through the green box until he found a large, curved sewing needle. He pulled three feet of cotton thread from a spool and snipped it off with a small scissors. Tipping his head back and squinting through his glasses, he threaded the needle. The backwoods doctor removed the bloodied snow, pitching it across the room, straight into his slop bucket.

"All right, Fitch," said Sourdough. "I'm gonna stitch up this side, first.

Might pinch a bit." He poked the needle through Mason's chilled hide. The others watched as the camp cook sewed the wound closed, tying each stitch securely. Mason grimaced with each push and pull on the needle.

"Thirteen stitches, Mason," said Tor. "Not so lucky."

"Lucky?" said Sourdough. "I'll tell you about luck. Mason, if you had been standin' a bit to the left, you'd be singin' in the Vienna Boys Choir. That's how lucky you are, pal." Then, to his assistants, "All right, turn him face down so we can stitch up the other side."

With help from his co-workers, Mason Fitch rolled over clumsily with a grin on his face now. "I think the lemons are wearin' off, Sourdough. How about another swig?"

"Nope. No more for you. Your damage ain't bad enough to warrant me givin' up any more of my bottled goods. Next time you taste my lemon extract will be in one of my Christmas pies."

"Don't make my leg look too ugly, Doc."

"I'll make it look so dang pretty that every dance hall queen in Cable will pay a dollar just to steal a look at my fancy needlework. You'll make more a night than they do."

Olaf Loken, stared into the lively, crackling fire. Ingman sat in a wing chair near him. He stuffed a chunk of cut tobacco into his pipe, then put it to his lips. Leaning forward, he struck a wooden match on the hearth, and lit the pipe. "Good thing nobody got hurt worse, Olaf. Could have been real bad. We could have lost a man today."

"We haven't lost a man since we started up. Neither mill nor camp. Few outfits can make such a claim. Not one man. I want to keep it that way."

"And, Ingman, what the hell was Tor doing there? He has no business being around that kind of work. Lord's sake! The boy is only sixteen years."

"Well, you know your Tor. He saw they had some trouble and yust wanted to do his part to help out."

"Ingman, I do not want him anywhere near the men when they're out on the job. Plenty of work to be done in camp that won't put him in danger."

"Well, now, brother, I understand your concern. But, Tor needs to learn the business. He's old enough to study the trade and he's plenty bright. Tor needs to be out in the cuttings if you want him to learn how to stay out of peril."

"Like today? Did he stay out of peril today? Ingman, look at me! I wouldn't be in this gol dang chair if I had the good sense two years ago to stay clear and let the men do the work. Look what it got me. Look what I have done to myself."

"You know as well as me that yours was a freak accident."

"They are all freak accidents. Wasn't today's a freak accident?"

"I know you want to protect your boy. I do, too. But we both know the best way to protect him is to teach him all there is to know about the lumber business. And he can't learn unless he's out in the woods—out in the cuttings

118

with the men. We yust have to drill safety into his head, day in, and day out."

"I suppose you are right. I just can't bear to think of him gettin' hurt. I lost his mother. I lost my legs. I couldn't bear losing my boy again."

"How about I put him on one of our most experienced crews—say, Mike Fremont's crew? Those men know the ropes. And I'm sure Mike would like the help. He'd see to it that the boy stays out of peril."

"You will guarantee Tor will be safe with them?"

"Olaf, you know there is no guarantee when it comes to pinery work. What I can guarantee is that there is no finer crew chief than Mike Fremont in our camp, and nobody more responsible." The fire crackled a bit louder, flamed up a bit, then settled back down.

"You arrange it with Mike, then," said Olaf. "I'll tell Tor he will be working with the Fremont crew in the morning. He can do half-days at first. At least that way he will be safe half the time," he muttered to himself.

The snow settled during the night. Tor joined Mike Fremont's team in the cuttings and helped swamp out twelve big white pines felled and bucked by the sawyers in the morning. Using a double-bit ax, he cut off the limbs and cleared any standing brush in the way of the teamster and his huge steeds.

Tor learned how to safely swing an ax and how one miss could put a razor-sharp blade into the frozen ground or, worse, your foot. One error would ruin the blade's edge, making your work harder. The second error would likely result in no more work that season. The young woodsman was careful to avoid both errors. Still, the camp dentist did not have good words for him when, at noon, Tor dropped off his ax at the file shed before heading for the cook shanty.

"Where's Junior?" he called.

"I sent him and one of the cookies up to the north forty with dinner for the men," answered Sourdough, chopping a pile of rutabagas for the stewpot. "They'll be back any time now. Have some stew and biscuits."

"How's Mason Fitch doing with that lame leg of his?"

"Fitch? Oh, he's in a whole lotta pain. Leg swelled like a pine stump."

"Sure was tough, getting stuck by that splinter," Tor said, ladling steaming stew into a tin bowl.

"He's damn lucky to work in your pa's camp," said the cook. "Most outfits would send him out the door, probably without his pay."

Junior opened the cook shanty door. "Tor! I thought you were swampin' today. Mike Fremont kick your hindquarters off his crew already?"

"Nope. I put in a full day's work by noon so I figured I'd enjoy the easy life that you and ol' Sourdough have each day." The camp cook turned from his rutabaga chore and scowled at Tor's words.

Ingman entered the kitchen, kicking snow from his boots. "Another beautiful day in the pinery, ay?"

"You betcha, Uncle Ingman."

The woods boss grabbed a tin bowl next to the cook stove and sniffed the hot stew in the big pot. "Any meat in this stew, Sourdough? Or is this yust

119

the same ol' everyday skin and gristle?"

"Gol dang it, Ingman, if you don't like it, then you can just leave it for the shanty boys."

Ingman winked at the boys. "Well, Sourdough, I'll try my best to choke some down. If Yunior here can stand it, well, maybe so can I."

No sooner were the words said than half a rutabaga zipped past Ingman, bounced off the table, and landed in Tor's lap.

Everyone but Sourdough was laughing now.

"Oh, what I'd give to once more cook for civilized folks—folks who really appreciate good food—instead of a hundred scavenging wild dogs who's got no culture."

"You want to cook for someone else, Sourdough? Looks like you'll be doin' yust that on Sunday," said Ingman. "Oscar and the ol' chieftain will be here." Junior looked at Tor with a big grin.

"Like I don't have enough gol dang ungrateful mouths to feed."

"Tor, how about you and Yunior here take a telegram into Cable this afternoon. Your pa has it on his desk."

"Sure! Junior, you hitch up the cutter. I'll meet you outside."

"You betcha!" said Junior, putting his bowl to his mouth and tipping his head back. "I get the reins."

Junior was out of the room in a flash. Tor headed for the lodge a few minutes later. He picked up the message and a quarter for the telegrapher, then went to his room.

Tor pulled a green box from under his bed, placed it on the patchwork quilt and flipped open the lid. Inside was his watch, a tintype photo of his mother and father, and the nine dollars and eighty-six cents he had saved. He dropped three silver dollars into a pocket, and slid the box back under the bed.

Warm temperatures the day before, followed by a cold night, left an icy crust on the snow. The long-legged mare had them skimming lightly across the frozen lake. Tor noticed two more cutters, one quite fancy, tied near the tender's building as they passed by the dam.

By mid-afternoon, the boys were at the Cable depot. Tor approached the ticket window with an envelope. Tearing it open, he read his father's message before handing it and the quarter to the clerk.

Mrs. A. Ringstadt. Hayward, Wisc. Join us for Sunday dinner. Bring family. Olaf.

"Rosie!" Tor realized. "Rosie will be at the camp on Sunday."

The clerk took the telegram and the coin, returning fourteen cents in change and a thank you. Tor left two pennies for a tip.

The boys jumped into the cutter, Junior Kavanaugh at the reins.

Chapter 24
Sporting Girls

The black mare trotted away from the Cable train station, the cutter gliding smoothly over the snow. Junior deliberately passed the road to camp. Tor looked at him, waiting for a reason.

"Let's take a quick look-see around town, Tor."

Junior's passenger did not object. Up and down the streets of Cable they flew, past snow-laden shacks, houses, and horse barns. A flip of the reins and the mare turned down the main street, passing the taverns, gambling halls, sporting houses, shops, and stores crowded together there. Junior suddenly pulled back on the reins and the cutter stopped before the largest hotel in town.

"Let's go in for a beer, Tor."

"Who do you think you're joshing, Junior? We are *not* going into the hotel bar for no beer."

"C'mon, Tor! I ain't never been in a tavern without my pa. Let's go have ourselves one beer just so as we can say we did."

"Junior, use your dang brains. My pa would tan my backside and your pa would tan yours. We are not going and that's that!"

"Well, I'm goin'," Junior said, dropping the reins and springing out of the cutter. "You can wait for me here, yella belly."

Junior ran across the rutted street, bounded up onto the boardwalk, and disappeared behind the doors of Joe Merrill's hotel. Tor hitched the mare to a nearby rail. He crossed the street and soon found Junior sitting at the bar with two large mugs of beer before him.

Five men sat around a poker table in the far corner. Two were well-dressed. Three wore work clothes. Two sporting girls, dressed in fashionable, revealing clothing, stood nearby, watching the game. They all turned to watch Tor enter the room and join Junior at the bar.

"I figured you'd see it my way, Tor," said Junior. "Here, this one's for you." He slid one of the big glasses to Tor who ignored the offer.

"Junior, just what the heck do you think you're doing?"

"Ten cents," said the bartender.

"You'll have to pay up, Tor. I'm dead broke."

The bartender scowled at him. The two women strolled closer.

"Dang it all, Junior," whispered Tor, reaching into his pocket, "you're bound and determined to get me into a whole pile of trouble." Tor pulled the three silver dollars and the thirteen cents from his pocket. He placed the dime on the bar. "Drink down your dang beer and let's get out of here."

"Hi, fellas," said one of the women, putting her arm around Junior. The other took hold of Tor's hand before he could return his silver to his pocket. She grabbed the three large coins.

"Sakes alive! Looks like you men came to town lookin' for a good time. Well, you two can have a *real* good time with all this money." Tor reached for the coins but the woman quickly pulled away, turning around.

"Give me back my money!" he ordered. The other woman was already nuzzling Junior's cheek. Junior had a wide-eyed look of shock on his face. The woman with Tor's money smiled at him, then slid the coins into the top of her dress. "Dang it all, Junior!" Tor snapped. But Junior heard not a word.

"Here's the deal, Sonny," said the woman, "You want your money? Well, you'll just have to reach right in and take it."

"Listen, ma'am, I'm not reaching down your dress for my money. Either you are going to give it back to me right now or I am going to find the owner of this hotel and he'll settle this. Now—give—me—back—my—three—dollars." The bartender looked on with a wide grin. Two of the men at the poker table turned and stared.

"Shush up, Sonny. I was only joshin' you. I'm just warmin' your money up for you, that's all. How about you fellas buy us a beer. You know, boys, the four of us could have a real good time on your three bucks."

"Just—give—me—back—my—three—dollars! Look, it is *my* money and *you* stole it." Tor raised his voice. "If you don't give it back right now, lady, I swear I *will* report you."

"All right! All right! Don't get in such a huff about it," she said, looking toward the poker table. "I'll give you your three dollars back. Just quiet down, Sonny." She moved toward him seductively. "Here, go ahead." She pressed in close to him, trapping him against the bar. "Just reach down there and you'll find your money, Sonny." She smiled broadly and rotated her shoulders. "Go ahead. If you want your three dollars so bad, just take them."

The bartender laughed. Junior couldn't move. The woman next to him now had one hand on his thigh, the other around his neck. One of the well-dressed poker players walked toward them.

"C'mon, Sonny, reach in and you'll have your money and maybe more."

Tor, still trapped against the bar, moved as far back as he could. The well-dressed man was close now.

"You got a problem here, girls?"

"Why, no, Bill, not at all. These boys just came in for some fun and we're bound to oblige them."

"Lady, we didn't come here to spend our money on you. Now, for the last time, give—me—back—my—three—dollars."

The woman reached deep into her dress and pulled out two of the three coins, shook them in her outstretched hand, then dropped them into Tor's palm.

"Now the other dollar," he snapped.

"All right, all right. Don't get in a damn fuss. I was only foolin' with you. I wasn't gonna keep your dang money, Sonny. Can't a girl have some fun?" She dug down again and pulled out the third coin. But, instead of giving it to Tor, she slapped it into Junior's hand.

"There, Junior, see how nice and warm that dollar is?"

Junior couldn't speak.

"You want to warm your hands up on me and Mabel? It seems like your friend here ain't quite man enough yet. You know, for that dollar there, Junior, you and me and Mabel can have a real good time. *Real* good, Junior."

"He's dead broke," snapped Tor, grabbing the coin from his friend's hand. He dropped the coins in his pocket.

The man in the neat clothes stepped closer. "Gertie, that's enough. Find some other shanty boys to work on. These fellas are not your type."

"Whatever you say, Bill. You're the constable." She turned away. "Just tryin' to take care of the men, Bill. That's our job, you know."

Mabel, now on Junior's lap, slid off seductively, the expression of shock and surprise still painted across the young man's face. His jaw dropped as she vigorously rubbed his thigh. She pulled away laughing.

"Next time you're in town, Junior, you bring some money and be sure to look up Miss Mabel Durst at the Merrill Hotel. You and me can have a few beers and a whole lotta fun, Junior." She sauntered off, joining Gertrude near the poker table. Mabel turned back, adding "And Junior, next time you better leave your pal with his nanny until he grows up to be a man like you."

Tor ignored the insult. Junior was in shock. The constable remained.

"What camp you from, boys?" said Bill Burns.

"Namakagon Timber Company," said Tor. "Came to send a telegram."

"There's no telegraph office, here, Son. Olaf Loken probably figured you'd know enough to go to the train station."

"Yes, sir, we stopped there first. My pal, Junior here, got us sidetracked on the way back to camp."

They both looked at Junior who was finally recovering from his overwhelming exposure to Mabel Durst.

"You all right, boy?" said Burns. "You look like you been face to face with a she-bear."

"I think maybe I were," was all Junior could muster for a reply. He fumbled for his beer, took a gulp, spilling some on his shirt.

"Boys, the sporting gals have a job to do, just like you shanty boys, the gandy dancers, the miners, the businessmen, the preacher, and the undertaker. Don't hold it against the gals if they get a bit over-ambitious now and then. They don't mean no harm. Just want to show the men a good time and earn their pay." Gertrude, overhearing this, nodded and smiled at them.

"No hard feelings," said Tor, loud enough for Gertrude and Mabel to hear. "Let's get going, Junior!"

"What's your name, Son?"

"I'm Tor, this is Junior."

"Tor what?"

"Tor Loken. My pa is Olaf and my uncle is Ingman."

"Well, I'll be danged!" replied the constable. "You're the lad who has the whole pinery buzzin' like a bee hive. You and that old Indian Chief. You helped foil those two train robbers the other day, right? You're sort of a hero around here, Tor." He turned. "Two more beers for these good citizens, Pete!"

"No," said Tor. "We are obliged, sir, but we gotta get goin'. It'll be dark before we get home as it is, thanks to Junior, here."

"Pete," said Burns, "let me see that newspaper." The bartender handed Burns the hotel's copy of the *North Country News*.

"Here, Son, take this back to your camp. Find someone to read it to your shanty boys. They'll get a big kick out of it."

Tor read the headlines.

BOY AND INDIAN CHIEF FOIL TRAIN ROBBERY. One outlaw presumed dead. Other shot and stabbed. Governor to honor heroes for ridding pinery of dishonorables.

"Holy jumpin' Jehosaphat, Junior! Take a gander at this."

"What does it say, Tor?" said Junior, finally regaining some composure.

"It says you won your gol dang bet, that's what it says." Then, to the constable, "Is Chief Namakagon all right?"

"Fit as a fiddle, according to the paper. Says there that he got beat up and left to die but the tough old rooster wouldn't hear of it. Why, I expect to see ol' Namakagon back in town any day now."

"Junior, I do believe I'll be drinking that beer, now. Wait till Pa and Uncle Ingman see this!" Tor folded the newspaper and stuffed it into a coat pocket. "Thank you for helping us out of our tangle, Constable."

"Bill, Bill Burns, Railroad Constable. If ever you need my assistance, young man, you just ask away. It's a pleasure to know the fella who helped hog-tie those hoodlums."

"Let's go, Junior."

Junior gulped down his beer, slamming the mug on the bar. As they turned to leave, two more lumberjacks entered the hotel bar. Mabel and Gertrude were at their side before the boys reached the door.

Tor untied the mare and climbed into the cutter. He did not hand the reins to Junior. With the sun just over the treetops, the long-legged mare trotted down the street. Before turning onto the east road, the cutter pulled up in front of the big windows of the general store.

"I'll be back, Junior. Now, wait right here!"

Tor ran up the steps to the large front door. He returned moments later, jumped back into the cutter, and they soon sped toward Lake Namakagon.

"Tor," said Junior, "soon as I get paid some of my winnin's, I'm comin' back. Yep, I'm comin' back and goin' straight into that hotel bar again."

"That's a fool's way of thinking, Junior. You and all your money will be soon parted."

"I don't have no choice in the matter. Tor, I—am—a—man—in—love."

124

Interlude
May 18, 1966
Late afternoon

    I put the college theme book marked 24 onto the pile and carefully re-tied the string. From out on the lake came calls from the loons. I watched them from the window as they splashed and dove, surfaced and splashed again. It was mating time. Their tremolos carried from shore to shore, inspiring other loons from faraway bays to answer their calls.

    The ladies from the Cable Congregational Church were finished for the day. The back seat and trunk of their green, four-door Plymouth was packed full.

    Waving to them as they pulled out of the yard, I lugged the full wastebasket out to the workshop. As I dumped the trash into the stove, the old buckskin pouch fell on the floor. I picked it up and brushed it off.

    "Your old Indian friend must have given this to you, eh, Grandpa Tor? Why else would you have kept it?" After dropping it into my shirt pocket, I tossed a lit match into the stove and shut the cast iron door.

    Inside the lodge again, I poured a cup of leftover coffee and put some cornbread on a plate. I found no butter, no honey, but did find some molasses.

    "Grandpa Tor, didn't you write about you lumberjacks using molasses on your johnnycake?"

    The coffee, cornbread, and molasses went well together. Before I realized it, I had finished the entire pan. Still hungry, I looked through the cupboard and found a can of stewed tomatoes. Ten minutes later it was gone, along with two cans of beans, and a can of creamed corn, all eaten straight out of the containers. I found a package of chipped beef to go along with the beans and washed it all down with the last of the coffee and a bottle of beer.

    "Grandpa Tor, I haven't eaten this much for years. Must be this fresh, northern Wisconsin air." The only reply was the ticking of the large clock on the mantel.

    I returned to Grandpa's easy chair and the second bundle of books. Darkness approaching, I turned on his reading lamp, wondering how the old lodge might have looked back in the old days with the only light coming from kerosene lamps. After starting a fire in the large, stone fireplace, I untied the second bundle of theme books. Taking the top one, I sat back in his chair and opened the book, saying, "Tell me more, Grandpa. Tell me more."

Chapter 25
King Muldoon

A steel-gray winter sky lay over the snowy December landscape. Ingman Loken and Blackie Jackson crossed the lake in one of the Namakagon Timber Company's cutters and headed west to the dam. With a snap of the reins Ingman urged the horse up the bank. He pulled alongside the dam tender's building.

Two other rigs were tied in front of the fieldstone structure. One was an enclosed cutter, fashionably trimmed. Hitched to it were two handsome white stallions sporting black harnesses with silver trim. Through the building's frost-covered windows Ingman could see two oil lamps glowing. He stepped out of the Loken cutter, wrapped the reins around a nearby post, and entered the office. Blackie followed.

"Good afternoon. I'm Ingman Loken, woods boss from across the lake."

The three men there, two standing and one seated at a roll-top desk, turned. One spoke. "Who did you say you are?"

"Ingman. Ingman Loken. I'm with the Namakagon Timber Company. This here is Blackie. We got wind that somebody bought up the dam and we came to bid you folks a welcome."

"Well, well," muttered the short, white-haired man seated at the desk, "so you are Ingman Loken, are you? Hmm. My name is Muldoon, *King* Muldoon. I own this dam. There! Now we know who we are, don't we."

He peered at Ingman and Blackie. His neatly pressed business suit looked out of place this far back in the woods. "So then, you have bid us your welcome. Now, Ingman Loken, say goodbye." He turned back to his desk.

Ingman and Blackie stood silent for a moment before Ingman spoke. "Me and Olaf, my brother, would like to invite you to our camp for a glass of brandy and some neighborly talk, Phineas. We're not ten minutes by sleigh."

"Not interested," said Muldoon, studying his ledger. "And you would do well to call me King. King Muldoon is how I am regarded, Loken. I have no time to waste talking with you or your brother. Now get off my property."

"Phineas, we have better than two million board feet of pine layin' on the ice and we expect to put up three times that by ice out. We want your word that our logs will make it over the dam. Why not come to the camp and we can talk things over like good neighbors, eh, Phineas?"

"Good neighbors? Now you see here, Loken, you and that cripple on the other side of the lake hoodwinked me out of those six sections of timber north of here. I know you did and you'd be a fool to deny it. Now, you come here, asking me to sit by your fire sipping brandy with you like we are dear friends. Just who the hell do you think you're dealing with? I—am—*King*—

126

Muldoon. I buy and sell outfits like yours just for my amusement. You want to meet, Loken? Well, fine! Bring along the deed to your camp. Now, get out."

"We bought legal claim to those six sections by outbidding you. We didn't do anything you haven't done a hundred times before. No reason our two businesses can't show some mutual respect, Phineas."

"Mutual respect, indeed. There is not one damn thing *mutual* about our businesses. I am King Muldoon. I own more lumber camps than you have shanty boys. I own four mills, two boom companies on the St. Croix and, now, Ingman Loken, I–own–this–dam. You want to talk business, *neighbor,* well here it is. You can float your pine down this river. I won't stand in your way. In fact, I welcome you, just like a good neighbor should. Bring your pine, Loken. Bring it across the lake, down the narrows and over the dam. I'll show you what a good neighbor I can be. But I will also show you just what a good businessman I am. Each log will cost you forty … no, fifty cents, Loken. So bring your pine and bring your money or, if you want to be put out of your misery like the lame horses you Lokens are, just bring me your damn deed. Now get off my property or I'll have you arrested for trespass."

"Ya, ya, ya—*King* Muldoon. You're a big businessman with a lot of land and mills and camps, and now a dam. But you don't own the water. Nobody owns the water—*King*. And, as big as your outfit is, it ain't never gonna be bigger than the government of the State of Wisconsin—*King*. You yust go right ahead and try to wring a quarter, even a penny out of us for our saw logs and you will find yourself in an arm-wrestle you can't win. Mind my words—*King*, the only arm that's gonna get broke is yours. Ya, sure, you own a lot, but you got it off the sweat and blood and backs of others. You cheated your way to fortune. Well—*King,* you ain't gonna increase your winnings by bilkin' us, you puny, slicked-up swindler."

Muldoon turned back to the desk. The old man opened a drawer and pulled out a large revolver. His two men dashed to the far corners of the room. Blackie stepped closer to the door and pulled it open.

"What do you think you're gonna do with that, Phineas?" said Ingman.

"King!" the old man screamed. "You–will–call–me–King!"

Bang! Bang! Muldoon shot into the wall behind Ingman.

Blackie dove through the open doorway, over the steps, into the snow.

Bang! A third shot rang out, the bullet ricocheting off the ceiling and shattering a window.

Ingman stood his ground. "Looks to me like you're one of them businessmen who can't succeed without the help of a revolver. 'Round here, we have a name for them, *King*, we call them outlaws. You shoot me and you'll be in prison until you die."

Muldoon stepped closer, pointing the pistol at Ingman's chest and shaking with rage. "Get off my property, Loken. Next time I see any of your shanty boys on my land I swear to God I will have them shot dead for trespass."

Ingman turned, calmly walked out, then turned again. "We're not done,

127

Phineas. You don't own the gol dang water and you will *not* levy the Namakagon Timber Company a tariff for floating our pine over the dam."

Bang! Bang! King Muldoon shot twice more into the ceiling as Ingman walked out, leaving the door wide open.

As they crossed the lake toward the camp again, Blackie turned to Ingman. "That ol' fool damn near shot you, Boss."

"Wrong on both counts, Blackie. First, he had no intention of goin' to yail for shootin' a competitor. And, second, Phineas Muldoon is no fool. No siree, my friend, Muldoon is no fool."

Junior saw to it fast work was made of his supper chores. He had good reason to rush tonight. He helped Zeke and Zach as they cleared the long dining tables after the lumberjacks' meal. Junior grabbed a four-gallon copper stewpot and a wooden spoon and jumped onto the table, beating the bottom of the pot. The clanging of the copper pot immediately captured the men's attention. Hearing the alert from the horse barn, four teamsters quickly crossed the camp yard and joined with the others to hear Junior's announcement.

"All right, now, listen here!" yelled Junior. "It's news from Hayward that you fellas don't want to miss. Light your pipes, shut your yaps and hear the news." Junior jumped down, pot and spoon in hand.

Ingman stepped up on the table. "Men, my nephew Tor and Yunior went to town earlier today. While there, they picked up this newspaper," he said, waving it above his head. "Before I give you the story, though, I need you to think back to last night when many of us cast our doubt on young Tor and his story about him and Chief Namakagon being robbed on the Omaha. Men, it turns out that, not only was the story true, but it seems the Governor of Wisconsin will be coming to Hayward to honor them for spoiling the holdup."

A noisy rumble came from the men. Junior banged on the copper pot and Ingman continued. "Let me read you the headline. It says here, 'Boy and Indian chief spoil train robbery. One outlaw presumed dead. Other shot and stabbed.' Then it goes on to say, 'Governor to honor heroes for ridding pinery of dishonorables!'" He held the paper up high.

"Now, fellas," Ingman continued, "you will recall some of you placed bets last night, laying odds that the whole tale was yust a big cock-and-bull story, a lumber camp yarn that didn't hold a pinch of truth. Fellas, I admit I, too, was eyeballin' this with somewhat of a squint. But the newspaper bears out the story. Meaning that, if you laid a bet down, then you owe young Kavanaugh his money. Fellas, this deal was done on the up and up. I want you to know that if any man here tries to weasel his way out of his sum obliged to Yunior or Sourdough, I will see to it that it goes against that man's year-end wages."

Olaf wheeled his chair nearer the head of the table. "Men, I have some other news that I know you will like to hear. You all put in a good first month in the woods. The weather's been good to us and we are already well ahead of the game. I doubt that any other camp can hold a candle to you boys. To show you our appreciation, Ingman and I decided to give you a five dollar advance against your spring pay so you could have a night in town."

The room erupted in cheers and laughter. Junior banged on the stewpot.

"Tomorrow is Saturday, men. We are gonna knock off early. Three-fifteen. If you want, you can draw your five dollars from the office starting then. Three-fifteen. No sooner. Blackie will have two sleighs hitched up and ready to leave at four o'clock sharp. Those of you going to town can jump onto one of the rigs. But mind you, keep a close eye on Blackie. When he heads back to camp, you best be on the sleigh or you'll be a-walkin'."

"Now, men," said Ingman, "I need to give you a word of caution. There will be a hundred miners, twice that many gandy dancers and even more lumberyacks in Cable tomorrow night. Stay out of yail and don't get beat up or so drunk that you can't find your way back by Sunday noon because we're going to have a fine Sunday dinner waiting for you at one o'clock sharp."

"Mind you," shouted Olaf, "we're bound to have some guests in camp so you better turn up sober and presentable. And put forth some good manners."

Ingman spoke again. "Some of you may decide to stay here in camp and save your money instead of donating it to the poker tables and sporting gals in town. Well, that's fine, too, and we're planning something special for those who want to stay in camp. We're gonna set up a checkers tournament and we'll crack open a case of whisky yust for this occasion. Olaf has agreed to back off on the rule about no drinking in camp, but just for the night. All we ask is that, if there's any brawling to be done, you take it outside so we don't bust up this high class hotel here."

Laughter and cheers flooded the room. Junior jumped up on the table again, banging the copper pot. "I got something to add," he shouted. "Anyone here who owes me and wants to pay early, well I'd be grateful for it and I'll knock four bits off. That's a half-day's wage, fellas."

Ingman stepped up on the long wooden table next to Junior. "Men," shouted the woods boss, "pipe down whilst I read you the whole story about the train robbery and such. Pay attention, now. You can be sure this here will be the talk of the town tomorrow night!"

With that, over a hundred lumberjacks fell silent while Ingman read the feature story in the December 8, 1883 edition of the *North Country News*.

Chapter 26
Goin' to Town

Tor was back in the woods with Mike Fremont and his men the next morning. Charlie Martin, a sawyer for the crew and a seasoned lumberjack, gave Tor a few tips on how to use a two-man crosscut saw.

"Now, Tor," said Charlie, "usin' a two-man crosscut is like waltzin' with a pretty gal. Only difference is that you gotta look at Leroy Phipps on the other end of the saw, and, Tor, ol' Leroy ain't all that pretty a sight."

"You best mind your clever tongue, Charlie," groused Leroy.

"Tor," said Charlie, "you right handed?"

"Yessir. I am."

"Good. Leroy's a southpaw. That works out best. He will keep his left hand to the outside and his right hand near the steel. You do just the opposite. After you and him set the cut, you just follow Leroy's lead. First, I will whittle out the notch."

His double-bit ax in hand, Charlie Martin stepped closer to the near-perfect white pine. Almost four feet in diameter, it stood over ninety feet tall and would easily scale more than three thousand board feet. At the mill it would bring about twenty dollars—nearly three week's pay for a pinery lumberjack.

"Five trees like this could build you a comfortable house in Chippeway Falls with enough left over to build a two-story privy out back," said Leroy. "Yesiree, it will fetch a good dollar at the mill."

"They call these pines green gold," added Charlie, "and there's so much of it in the pinery, they say it will take a thousand years to cut it all. Think of it, Tor—a thousand years."

"Yep, green gold," Leroy repeated. "More money out here than in half a dozen California gold mines and you ain't gotta be no gol dang woodchuck to get your share of it."

"All right," Charlie said, "first, make sure there ain't no brush in your way." Looking up, he walked around the tree again. "If your pine's got a lean to it, then that is the way you wanna send her. Don't never go agin' the law of gravity. Next thing you look for is a widowmaker—that's any dead limb what can come back to swat you when she falls. Tor, I seen good men sent home by widowmakers. Some of 'em went in coffins, boy. You watch yourself.

"Now, you see that dead limb up there? Looks pretty small from here, but, when it strikes you down, you will find out it's a good eight, maybe ten inches thick and near to a hundred pounds." He studied the tree again.

"All right. The notch goes here—same side where you want it to drop. If you notch your tree in the right spot and then make your saw cut opposite the notch, well, you can drop a tree just about anywhere you want. I'll show you."

Charlie snatched Tor's hat, walked about thirty paces, and laid the hat on the snow. Coming back to the big white pine, he laid his ax in the snow, handle pointing toward the hat. The woodsman bent down low, sighting down

130

the ax handle. He looked back at the tree, picked up his ax, kicked some snow out of the way, and looked up again, then down. Charlie Martin established his stance by digging in with his boots. "Here goes, boys. We'll send her over there by Tor's hat."

His ax angled slightly upward, Charlie took five swings. He then took six more bites a bit higher and with a downward pitch. Large wood chips sailed through the air, landing in the fresh snow. The veteran woodsman then shifted his position, stepping to the other side of the notch. Ten more swings of his ax and the notch was cut.

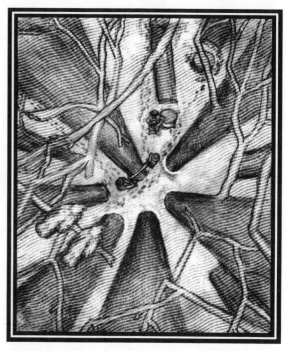

Two blue jays flew into a nearby birch, scolding the loggers with their screechy calls.

"Tor," Charlie said, "there is something else you need to do 'fore you start your saw cut. Figure out just where you are gonna run when she comes down. You make dang sure there ain't nothin' in your way. You do not wanna be anywhere close when she falls, just in case she bucks back toward you. All right, boys, time to take your turn."

Tor followed Leroy to the base of the tree. Leroy swung one end of the long, limber saw to his partner. They placed the teeth chest-high against the bark, opposite Charlie's notch. Leroy pulled the saw toward him. Tor pulled back, starting the cut.

The tall, stately tree hardly noticed these small men at its base. Had they stopped now, it would have sent its pungent sap into the wound and lived another hundred years. But the lumberjacks didn't stop. Leroy stepped up the pace. Tor followed.

"Tor," said Charlie, "yer usin' your arms too much. Keep yer knees locked and bend at your waist more. Just let the saw flow back and forth, Son."

The sharp crosscut saw sang out as it sliced through the pine. Sawdust, ripped from the cut, soon covered the deep snow around them, sending the fragrance of white pine into the icy air. Tor began to sweat.

"Too much steam, Tor," shouted Leroy. "Ease up. Just let the saw do the work." Tor relaxed, following the rhythm of the saw.

Charlie Martin looked on as the saw swept back and forth, back and forth, back and forth. "There you go, Tor, now yer goin' to town."

As though the giant white pine was defending itself from this attack on its clear heartwood, the tree pressed its enormous weight down, closing the saw cut just slightly, and stopping the blade. But it was not enough.

Leroy jammed his sharp, steel wedge into the kerf. He gave it a smack with the side of the hammer that hung from his belt. This opened the cut just enough to allow the saw to move freely again. Back and forth, back and forth again went the saw in rhythm. Suddenly, from deep within the tree, came a loud, solid *crack*. The white pine was losing to this assault on its life. And the men kept sawing. Back and forth. Back and forth. Back and forth.

"Watch her now, fellas."

Tor noticed the kerf was getting wider. The tree now leaned away from the cut slightly. Leroy's steel wedge, no longer pinched in place, fell to the snow below. Back and forth, back and forth, back and forth, and another solid *ca—rack* came from deep within. Leroy stopped, pulling the saw free from the kerf and from Tor's hands. He carried it away from the tree. Tor, seeing his partner move back, did the same. They watched in silence for a moment.

Leroy cupped his hands around his mouth, shouting, "Tim—berrrrrrrrr."

Tor looked up. The tree didn't seem to move. Leroy and Charlie quickly stepped farther back. Tor followed, still looking up.

"Keep yer eye on the kerf, Tor," said Charlie.

Tor watched as the saw-cut widened ever so slowly. Another loud *crack* came from deep inside the stump, then *crack————crack——ca-rack—crack, crack, crack* and the tree was on its way down.

The top moved slowly at first, then gathered speed, soon plummeting earthward, faster and faster, snapping limbs off nearby trees. Snow fell from the upper branches, creating a cloud of white above the men. The huge tree plunged down and down and then smashed to the ground with a thunderous crash. Snow and pine needles billowed high into the air. Twigs and small branches flew in every direction before raining down around the men.

Recoiling from its impact with the frozen ground, the great white pine gave a final shudder and then lay silent, motionless, dead. Never again would it sway in the wind.

The blue jays that had been scolding the lumberjacks took to the sky, piercing the cold morning air with high-pitched screams. They disappeared into what remained of the pine forest as the sound of the fall echoed off the nearby hills. Then—all was silent.

The stately, three-hundred year old pine now lay before the lumberjacks. Its seed had sprouted before the pilgrims gathered for their first Thanksgiving. Full grown when the American colonies declared independence from English rule, it withstood many fierce summer windstorms and winter blizzards. It survived forest fires, droughts, attacks by insects. But, like all the others, this grand white pine was no match for the sharp crosscut saws of these modern day lumberjacks. No longer a tree, it was now just more timber bound for the mill.

The forest was still until Charlie Martin broke the silence with a belly laugh, saying, "Sorry 'bout yer hat, Tor."

"Dang it all, Charlie Martin. I better get that hat back!"

"You might find it after you and Leroy buck up this pine. I will mark your cuts for you and swamp her out."

Leroy pulled a brown glass whisky flask from his back pocket, removed the cork, and poured some on the long crosscut saw, then flipped the saw and sprinkled on more. He stood the corked bottle in the snow and, pulling a rag from his pocket, wiped down the saw.

"You gotta buy this good ol' girl a drink now and then, just to keep her happy," Leroy said straight-faced. "It is a lumber camp tradition to give your saw a shot of good rye whisky now and again." He put the rag back in his pocket, then grabbed the bottle from the snow and held it out before Tor. "Here you go, Tor. High time to celebrate your first felled pine. Have a snort!"

Tor Loken was no fan of straight whisky. Still, he did not hesitate. Here he was, working alongside members of one of the best cutting crews in the camp and they were welcoming him into their group. By making this offer they were telling him he was a man, not a boy, and that he was a lumberjack now. No, he didn't want a drink of whisky, but how could he turn them down? He had to take a drink just to show them he was one of them, one of the crew. Tor snatched the whiskey flask from Leroy's hand, pulled the cork with a soft *pop* and, as all the others watched with wide grins, Tor took a big swallow.

"*Yechhh!*" he rasped, spitting what he could onto the ground. "Achhh—kaach-kaachhh!" he coughed, trying to spit and clear his throat at the same time. The men around him were already doubling over with laughter. Tor fell to his knees, coughed and coughed, spitting and gagging, then spitting more.

"What the heck is that?" Tor tried to say, his throat not cooperating. "Achhh! Tastes like … like boot polish." he gasped.

"Kero … kerosene!" said Leroy, trying to catch his breath. "We use it to keep the pitch off the saw so it don't slow us down." He began to laugh again.

"I ain't seen nobody fall for that in a coon's age," Charlie said.

Tor was on his hands and knees in the snow now, trying to retch up what he'd swallowed. Leroy fell to the ground, overtaken by laughter.

"Dang it all, Leroy Phipps, you are *not* going to get away with this, I swear." He gasped, retching again. "I'll get even, Leroy!"

"Whatever you dish up I will accept with pure pleasure, Tor Loken," shouted Leroy, clutching his belly. "Ain't nothin' … ain't nothin' you can do to me that measures up to this one."

"Say, how 'bout' we get back to work, boys," barked Mike Fremont. "Here it is, almost seven-thirty and the sun's already comin' through the tree tops. In no time we'll be eatin' our noon dinner and then already the day's half shot. 'Fore ya know, it's quittin' time and look here, we only got us one dang tree on the ground. At this rate, by the end of the week we will all be in the poor house. We got a reputation to protect, fellas, and we ain't gonna do that by sittin' on a stump and howlin' at the moon."

In spite of Mike Fremont's prodding, it took a while for the crew to settle down and get back to their work. Still coughing and gagging, and still drawing bursts of laughter from the others, Tor teamed with Leroy to buck the tree into four, sixteen-foot logs.

Using his ax, Charlie cut off the branches and top. The sawyers bucked two more eight-foot logs from high on the fallen pine. The teamster chained and dragged the logs out to the sleigh trail to be loaded onto one of the timber sleighs. Tor found his hat as the horse team pulled out the last log. He brushed the snow and pine needles from it, and then tried, without success, to shake it back into shape. He pulled the tired, old hat on his head.

Preparing for the next tree, Leroy reached into his back pocket and pulled out the flask of kerosene. "More whisky, Tor?"

The men broke into laughter again. "Drink 'er up! I hear there's a fifty-five gallon drum full of this delicious brew back at the camp."

Tor laughed along with the others now, even though the putrid taste of the oily fuel was still in his mouth. "Dang it all, Leroy, I'm tellin' you, I'll get even up. You just wait. Some day you will find a pine snake in your union suit or worse. Three months till the spring drive. I have plenty of time so don't plan on gettin' any sleep betwixt now and then, mister."

By ten forty-five, the Fremont crew caught up to their usual daily quota. The two-man crosscut had exhausted Tor. His back ached. His arms were sore. He was happy to see Junior bringing out the flaggins sled at eleven o'clock.

"Come—and—get it!" shouted Junior. "Best eatin's in the pinery. And, fellas, those words come straight from Sourdough. Get it while it's hot!"

The Fremont crew stopped their work. Another crew, working nearby, joined them. Junior dished up bowls of venison and baked beans and gave each man a large slab of bread slathered with bacon grease. They sat on the huge pine logs, eating their dinner as Junior brought around the coffee. Next he brought each man a pie.

"What kind of pie you peddlin' today, Junior?" asked Charlie.

"Apple, I think."

"This real apple or another one of Sourdough's counterfeits?"

"Danged if I know, Charlie Martin."

Charlie sniffed his pie. "Junior, when you get back to the cook shanty, you tell ol' Sourdough that peaches make far better apple pies than do prunes."

"Best remember what Sourdough says, 'first to complain is tomorrow's cook', Charlie Martin."

"Complain? Not me, Junior. I'll eat whatever that ol' hash-slinger sets out. He's a sight better than most other camp cooks, he is."

"What's this prattle I hear about kerosene?" asked Junior.

"Ain't you heard?" said Leroy. "Tor here ain't satisfied with regular corn whisky. No! He drinks straight kerosene to warm his belly. Ain't no other man in the pinery what can say that." The crew broke into laughter again.

"Takes a gol dang tough lumberjack to drink kerosene for a mornin' eye-opener," added Charlie. "Gol dang tough."

Tor, overcoming his embarrassment, doffed his hat at the men and laughed along with them.

After dinner, Tor and Junior took the flaggins sled to the other crews where Junior was certain to repeat the story.

By one-thirty, the two boys were back in camp helping with some kitchen chores. Tor, still tasting the kerosene from earlier in the morning, went straight to the water pail near the door, grabbed the long handle of the dipper, scooped up and gulped down a full dipper of water.

"You're goin' to town tonight, right Tor?" asked Junior as he rinsed a stack of tin plates.

"Going to town? No, sir. I'm content to stay here and save my money."

"Really? You gonna pass up a Saturday night in town?"

"I can do without. Besides, I want to be rested up for Sunday's dinner."

"Well, I'm sure goin'. Pa said I could. I'm gonna go have me a real good time. I'm headin' straight for Merrill's Hotel. Gonna find Miss Mabel Durst and we are gonna drink beer and dance the polka. You should go, too!"

"Naw, I'll stick around here. Besides, Pa wouldn't let me."

Sourdough entered through the kitchen door, carrying half a hog. He dropped it on the worktable with a thud. "Junior, when you're done there, how about you fetch me three more hog sides, will you?"

"Sure will, Boss." Junior answered. "Sourdough, did you know I was goin' to town tonight with the other men?"

The camp cook tipped his head down and peered at the sixteen-year-old over his glasses. "Junior Kavanaugh, what in the devil are *you* goin' to town for? There ain't nothin' for a whippersnapper like you in Cable on a Saturday night. You mark my words, young man, you will just lose all your money and get your skinny butt caught in a bear trap."

"Well my pa says it's all right and I plan on havin' me a good ol' time with the boys."

"Is your pa goin' along, too?" Sourdough said, dumping fifteen pounds of flour into a large bowl.

"Yeah, Pa's goin'," said Junior with less enthusiasm. He put a large stack of rinsed tin plates in a clean flour sack then shook the sack vigorously before dumping the plates onto a table.

Tor put the spoons and forks in a second flour sack, shaking them.

The camp cook poured a large saucepan of melted lard into the mixing bowl, added salt, sugar, and water and gave it to one of the cookees to mix. "Junior, if you have any sense at all, you'll stick close to your old man, 'specially since this is your first time out on the town."

"Well, Sourdough, this ain't my first time. Me and Tor was ..."

Tor kicked Junior in the shin.

"Ow! Dang it!"

135

Sourdough looked at them over his glasses. "You and Tor was what?"

"We were in town just yesterday to send a telegram, Sourdough," said Tor, staring at Junior.

"Well, Junior, you do what you want," said the cook, now dumping a large pile of dough onto the table, "but, if you have a lick of sense at all, you will take my advice and stay out of them pinery taverns on a Saturday night, … least till you're older. I've seen many a man lose all his pay and come back too hung over or too beat up to work. Ain't much to gain. Plenty to lose. Your pa should've told you that much."

"Well, I'm goin' anyway. You and Tor and the other wallflowers can stay in camp and play checkers and dance man-to-man. I'll be pinchin' the gals and kickin' up my heels in town tonight."

Sourdough began rolling out his pie dough, one ball at a time. Zeke and Zach greased a large stack of pie tins with lard and laid Sourdough's pie crusts into each tin. The head cook then put eight large scoops of brown sugar and some spices into a pot of boiled pumpkin and stirred it well. Junior took the dipper from the water pail and, with Tor carrying the hot pot of pumpkin filling, he put one large scoop in each of thirty of the pans.

The empty pot went into the washtub. Sourdough soon had it rinsed and filled with a mixture of raisins, stew meat, apples, sugar, and spices—his own mincemeat pie filling recipe. He added some water and put it on the stove. Dried apple slices, boiled with sugar and spices until thick, then filled many of the remaining pie shells. When Sourdough and the cookees finished, they had more than one hundred pies ready for the ovens. Each man in camp would have his own pie at tomorrow's special Sunday dinner. Sourdough was soon baking eighteen of the pies in the big cook stoves on special racks built by Gust Finstead, the camp blacksmith.

Junior worked in the cook shanty until shortly after three o'clock when some of the men started to come in from the cuttings. Many changed into their Sunday clothes which, in most cases, looked no different than their work clothes. Several of the men wore dark wool suits and could have been mistaken for businessmen, except their suits were badly wrinkled from being rolled up and used as pillows for the past month. Their boots also betrayed them. Some wore their shoe-pacs, hoping to keep their feet warm on the long trip to and from town. Others wore their driving boots, knowing the steel calks might come in handy in a fight.

A few of the men lathered up at the camp washbowl where several shaving mugs, brushes, and a bar of lye soap were set out for their use. Using their straight razors, they shaved off a month or more of beard growth. Most of the men preferred to keep their beards for insulation against the cold.

At a quarter past three, Junior was first in line to draw his five-dollar advance pay. He buttoned the bill into a pocket and took a seat on the pine bench near the door of the camp office, waiting to collect money owed him. As soon as he had twenty dollars, he left the lodge and ran straight to the horse barn. Blackie Jackson and one of the teamsters hitched up two teams of four Clydesdales each to the largest two sleighs in camp. A wooden nail keg served as a seat for the teamster on each rig.

Junior grabbed a hay fork and pitched a good foot of straw onto each sleigh, both to soften and warm the ride to and from town. He then jumped up on the bed of one of the sleighs, grabbed the reins, and guided the horses as they pulled the sleigh into the yard and up to the sleep shanty. "All aboard for Cable!" shouted Junior in his high-pitched voice. "C'mon, pinery boys. Daylight's a-wastin'!"

Minutes later, two horse-drawn timber sleighs, carrying fifty-four of the Loken camp's lumberjacks, slid smoothly across frozen Lake Namakagon. Blackie Jackson drove the lead rig and Swede Carlson the other. Three latecomers ran behind trying to catch up. When they did, the men riding toward the back of Swede's sleigh gave them a hand up.

"They gonna give us a hard time when we cross King Muldoon's land by the dam, Blackie?" asked Junior.

"Muldoon knows better than to try to stop a gang like this from goin' to town on a Saturday night. He'd surely have a hornets' nest to deal with. No, I don't 'spect we'll see no problems till spring, Junior. That's when we might get into a real row. Gives a fella like me somethin' to look forward to."

The two sleighs passed by the dam without event and ambled through the woods toward town, the men singing songs to pass the time. To Junior, it seemed to take forever to make the trip. They crossed over Five Mile Creek and the Namekagon River and finally pulled into town, well after dark.

As they neared First Street, Junior sprang from his seat and jumped off the moving sleigh. "Join you boys later," he shouted. He ran across the street, jumped onto the plank sidewalk and disappeared into the general store.

Minutes later he came out wearing a new, wool suit, shirt, and a brown derby hat. He still wore his shoe-pacs, knowing the trip back to camp would be too cold for Sunday shoes. Junior ran down the street with his old britches, shirt, and hat rolled up in his red and black mackinaw coat. He saw four other sleighs tied up along First Street. When Junior got to the first Loken sleigh and team, he threw his bundle onto the bed and ran straight to the biggest building in town, the Merrill Hotel. He sprang up onto the boardwalk, pulled open the door, crossed the lobby, and entered the busy saloon.

A thick, blue haze of pipe smoke filled the room. Lively piano music came from the back corner. The bar stools were all filled, as were the tables. Ten or twelve Loken camp lumberjacks crowded the bar, waiting to be served. The others had drifted off to explore other taverns, poker rooms, stores, and sporting houses.

Looking for Mabel, Junior stretched, trying to see over the big men,. He pushed his way through the crowd and shouted to the bartender, "Where's Mabel?"

"Who?"

"Mabel. Mabel Durst. Don't she work here?"

The bartender studied the crowd. "She must be upstairs, Sonny," he said, pointing to the staircase. "You here to order a drink or just ask questions?"

"Here's a silver dollar. I'll take a mug of beer and you give each of them Loken men over there a drink on me. Keep the change for yourself."

"Yessir, young fella. You betcha!" The bartender slid a mug of beer to Junior. He gulped it down, slamming the empty mug on the bar for a refill.

Junior was jammed between two large men wearing dirty blue denim coats and overalls. "You fellas rails?" he said.

They continued their conversation, ignoring the skinny barn boy between them. Then one looked down at him.

"You some kind of a peddler?"

"Nope, lumberjack."

This brought a big belly laugh from the railroad man. "You? A lumberjack?" He laughed again. "Why, you look more like a choir boy than a shanty boy!" Both men were laughing now.

"I hail from the Namakagon Timber Company, out east of here. It's run by the Lokens. How 'bout you fellas?"

"Us? We are deadheaded up here with ten flat cars of steel rail for King Muldoon. He's gonna lay tracks out to his camps next summer. Seems he got tired of drivin' logs down the river. Plans to haul 'em out by rail."

"That'll take all the fun out of it." shouted Mike Fremont, who pushed his way over to thank Junior. "Ain't no challenge or sport in it if you just toss them pine logs onto flatcars. The river's got some life in it—some adventure!"

"You call it adventure?" said the other rail. "I call it plum foolish. Why, last spring there was ten log drivers what drowned down by Chippeway."

"That's the risk," shouted Mike in reply, "but the pay is double, the food is good, you're in a different town with different women every night. If you're good on your feet and the Grim Reaper ain't got it in for you, hell, you might even live to get your pay at the end of the drive."

"Plum foolish," shouted the rail again. "Friend, them jacks what run the pine out by rail, they are the smart ones. The only risk they have is from getting poisoned by the camp cook or shot by a jealous husband."

Junior looked up to see Mabel Durst descending the stairway with a drunken miner on her arm. Slugging down his beer he rushed over to her.

"Good evening, Mabel."

"Well, Junior, look at you! All dressed up like you was goin' to church. You goin' to church, Junior?" She leaned the woozy miner against the wall.

"Nope! I'm not even thinkin' about goin' to church. Remember them three silver dollars from yesterday? Well, I got a whole pocketful. How about me treatin' you to a good supper in the hotel restaurant? What'a ya say, Mabel? Will ya have supper with me?"

With those few words, Junior Kavanaugh and Mabel Durst began one of the most remarkable evenings of Junior's young life.

Chapter 27
Nice Night for a Scuffle

Ingman Loken swung open the heavy wooden door and walked into the Namakagon Timber Company lodge, stamping his feet to remove the snow. He hung his wool mackinaw on the back of a chair and joined his brother near the fireplace.

"So, Ingman, what should we do about Phineas Muldoon?" Both men stared into the fire. "Looks like he might be holding all the cards. He bought the dam. Gives him the right to control both the level of the lake and the amount of water that goes downriver. When time comes to drive our pine over the dam, all he has to do is shut down the gates. With no flow, our logs will sit in the riverbed and rot. Ya, looks like Phineas Muldoon is holding all the cards."

"Olaf, doesn't that mean he will not be able to drive his own logs to the mills? Why, he be cuttin' his own throat.

"Muldoon has so many camps, so much timber, he can afford to abandon what he has laying here on the lake. He would do it solely to ruin us. He knows if we don't drive our pine, we go bankrupt."

"It simply does not seem proper that he can claim rights to the river flow. It's God's water, not Muldoon's."

"Ingman, they call him King for good reason. He's the biggest lumberman from Minnesota to Michigan to Manitoba. Why, Phineas hires lawyers like we hire lumberjacks. Plenty of politicians in his pocket, too.

"It does not seem right. Sure wish I knew what it is he wants."

"What he wants is for you and me to go bust. Then he could step in, take over the company, claim our timber rights. He's already a rich, old man. He's not looking for profit. He wants control. He wants revenge. He wants our outfit and doesn't give a tinker's damn about how he goes about gettin' it."

Ingman leaned forward, grasping the handle of an iron poker. He stirred the fire as his brother continued.

"There's talk about Phineas laying rail through the woods come summer. I am sure our holdings are in his sights for that, too. Ya, old King Muldoon wants our company, wants to see us lose everything. He knew he'd be sittin' pretty when he bought that dam. As I see it we have but two choices."

"And what might they be?"

"Ingman, we need to work on finding ourselves an ally in the statehouse. A fella with political aspirations. Somebody who knows he could get more votes by siding with us instead of Muldoon. We need someone who values what is right for the workers of Wisconsin more than the money Phineas slips under the table. We need a man of the people who is able to force Muldoon to open those gates."

"Sounds like a tall order, Olaf."

"Tor and Namakagon might have us on the right path. The new governor is due in Hayward soon to give Tor and Chief a pat on the back for

139

catching those thieves Phineas hired. Maybe we can get some help from him. There's always another election coming up. Perhaps we can get him to see that, to best serve the voters, he should insist all waters of Wisconsin be shared with the people, not reserved for the rich."

Ingman stepped to the wood box and picked up two large maple logs, one in each hand. He placed them on the andirons and laid a third log on top. "Olaf, you mentioned two options. What was the other?"

Olaf turned his chair toward his brother. "If Muldoon tries to stop our drive, we take the dam by force. We have enough men to do it and I think our jacks would stand by us."

"Muldoon would have the sheriff on us."

"I know."

"Take the dam by force. Hmm. Ya. All right, let that be our ace in the hole. And, Olaf, let's hope to heaven it don't come to that."

Mike Fremont and his crew sat at the end of the bar in the smoke-filled River Pig Saloon. They were drinking beer and singing along to tunes from the tinny-sounding piano. Six of the ten oilcloth-covered tables had poker games in play. At the other four tables sat a mix of railroad men, miners, lumberjacks, and working girls, all enjoying this Saturday night on the town. Two bartenders did their best to keep up.

The room was filled with music, laughter, and loud voices. It smelled of cheap tobacco smoke and beer. A dark-haired woman in a bright red dress climbed onto the bar and danced, bringing cheers from the men. One of the rails reached up, grabbed her around the waist, and swung her down into his arms and onto his lap. Laughing, she grabbed his beer and drank it down.

"Wish I would've had a chance at her," shouted Leroy to the crew. "She's a real looker."

"You'll get your chance, Leroy," shouted Mike, "long as you keep a dollar in your pocket."

"Mike, by the time I drink up my other four dollars, I'll be too dang drunk to remember her, anyhow."

Fremont knocked back his beer and slammed the mug onto the bar. He turned to the two men next to him. "What camp you boys hail from?"

"Ay?"

"I say, what camp you from?" he shouted.

"We're workin' the silver mine south of Pratt."

"Anything worth lookin' for up there?"

"Mostly rock and mud."

"Any silver?" Mike persisted.

"Enough to keep us workin'. We get paid a dollar twenty-five a day and don't have to wait till the spring log drives to get our money. Tony's my name," he said extending his hand.

"Mike Fremont. That's pretty good pay, Tony. They hirin' now?"

"We have twenty-eight men in the diggins as of today. We usually see one or two come and go each week. You lookin' for work, Mike?"

"A fellow always needs to keep a lookout. I ain't much for grubbing' in the ground, though."

"Well I ain't much for freezing' my arse off, Mike. Ain't one of you bark eaters what don't have swollen ears and frost bit noses. Where I work, it might be dark, but it's always above freezin'."

Charlie Martin was sitting at the far end of the bar next to the wall. A drunken lumberjack tried to spit his tobacco into the spittoon on the floor at Charlie's feet but missed. He sent a dark brown stream of tobacco spew across the right cuff of Charlie's britches, then broke into a loud belly laugh. Instantly Charlie sent his massive, clenched fist into the drunk's face, knocking him off his feet and onto the barroom floor.

The music stopped. Everyone turned. The lumberjack lay there, clutching his bleeding nose. Charlie turned back to the bar as though nothing happened.

The bartender poured him another beer, saying, "This one's on me."

"Dang it all! Now I gotta wash my britches before tomorrow's dinner." complained Charlie.

Another jack helped the man with the bleeding nose to his feet. "You gonna let him get away with that, Chester? Looks like he broke your dang nose again." The injured man turned and stumbled out of the bar. The piano player picked up where he left off, and the drinks flowed again.

Across the street at the Rail Inn, three Loken boys and several railroad workers sat around a poker table. This bar was just as crowded, loud, and smoke-filled as the others. The piano was far out of tune, but no one seemed to care. Stacks of silver coins and paper bills showed two of the Loken camp loggers, Rusty O'Hara and Klaus Radlinger, were on a winning streak. Next to them, Swede Carlson was holding his own. A brown-haired woman stood behind Rusty, massaging his neck. The game they were playing was five-card stud poker.

Rusty turned up his hole cards, exclaiming, "Three sixes, fellas."

The others grumbled and swore, tossing their cards on the table.

"Damn! You're awful lucky," said one of the railroad men, reaching for his beer. "I can't figure how you get cards like that time after time."

"Born with the luck of the Irish," quipped Rusty. "Blame it on me dear mother and father, bless their hearts."

"Ya, I must'a been born mit da Irish luck, too," said Klaus with a grin.

"Sure is somethin' how you always get those good cards, O'Hara," said one of the railroad men. "You ain't no professional gambler, is you, now?"

"No, I ain't. And you best be watchin' how you talk. This is a square game, friend, at least it is from the loggers' side of the table."

"You gotta admit, you two fellas been just a bit more than lucky tonight."

"I don't much care for your tone of voice, friend," replied Rusty, quickly stuffing his winnings into his pockets. "Fellas, like I said, me and my mates here have been playin' fair and square. Now if you're gonna accuse us of somethin', then you best be doin' it right here, right now. If not, ante up. Maybe you'll get back what you lost."

"Well, this here switchman is plum tapped out," said one of the players. "Deal me out."

"Ya, better youse deal me out too," mumbled Swede. "Uttervise I will be yust too dang broke to fill me belly mit beer." He pushed his chair back and took his last dollar bill to the bar.

The other two railroad workers stayed at the table. Three more rails sat down. Klaus took his turn as dealer. Each man tossed a dime into the middle of the table.

Rusty handed the woman behind him a fifty-cent piece. "Get us two more buckets a beer, darlin'. Keep the change."

Klaus slapped the deck of cards in front of the man to his right for the cut. Dealing to the left, Klaus gave each man two cards down, then one card face up, naming the cards as they fell.

"Ace, tree, tree, seven, jack, queen, four," said the dealer. "Bet's up to you, O'Hara."

The Irishman peeked at his cards, then laid them face down on the table again. "I'll bet a dime on my ace of clubs," he said. "Now I surely hope you won't be tossin' around more of your accusations just because sweet Lady Luck had the good graces to deliver me another ace."

No one spoke. Each player pitched in another dime. The brown-haired woman delivered the beer.

"Beer's on me, fellas," said Rusty. "Dip in if you want." They did.

"Pot's right," said Klaus, as he sent each player another card, face up. "Ten, tree, five, queen, jack, eight, king. Da bet's to you, Rusty."

"Two bits," said the Irishman, tossing a quarter into the pot.

"I'll see your two bits, O'Hara, and raise a dime," said the rail to his left.

"I'm out," said the third player.

"Me, too," said the next.

"Thirty-five cents," said the rail with the pair of jacks as he tossed in a dime and a quarter.

"Too rich for me," said the next player.

Klaus pitched in two coins and Rusty a dime to even the pot.

"All bets in. Da pot's right," said Klaus. "Time to face da music." He dealt each man the last card, face down. Each man picked up his card, placed it with his other two hole cards and peeked at them. Rusty studied the faces of the other players.

"Still your bet, O'Hara," said Klaus.

"I bet one dollar, fellas," he said. Each of the other players looked at him, then at his ace of clubs and ten of hearts lying face up on the table.

"Have ace under there, eh shanty boy?" said the rail next to Klaus.

"Well now," said the Irishman, "me sweet mother always told me not to speak at the table, so, considerin' her good advice, I guess you will have to pay the piper to find out." The next player tossed in his cards. The rail with the two jacks showing was next.

"O'Hara, I don't think you have two more aces under there. And two more aces is what it will take to beat my three boys, here. I raise a dollar."

They all looked at Klaus now.

"Dat's two bucks to me, ya?" he said as he tossed two silver dollars into the pot.

"Klaus," said Rusty, "that's two days' pay. You must be hidin' some good cards there. Here's the dollar and I'm raisin' four more."

The table was silent. The three remaining players studied their cards and the faces of the other players. With too little money on the table to cover the four-dollar bet, the rail with the pair of jacks showing peeked again at his cards. He examined the table once more before reaching into his vest pocket, pulling out a gold coin. He stared at it for a moment before laying it in the center of the table.

"Irishman," he said, "here's a double eagle that says my three jacks will beat any cards you can show. You want to see my three jacks, well, toss another sixteen dollars into the pot, pinery boy." He leaned back in his chair and grinned, folding his arms and resting them on his belly.

"Lord above and Devil below, that is quite a wager," said Rusty. "Surely you must've had a bout of good fortune, the way those cards fell for you, friend. Maybe me good Irish luck is rubbin' off onto you, too."

"Vell, I ain't riskin' dat much on dese cards, fellas," said Klaus. "Youse high rollers can play mit out me." He tossed his cards onto the table.

"Sixteen bucks to you, shanty boy," said the rail. The other players watched in silence as the crowd around the table began to grow. Rusty gulped down his beer, handing his glass to the brown-haired woman who scooped another from the tin bucket.

"Well, now, friend," Rusty finally said, "That is quite the bold wager you are makin'. Way I see it, you are figurin' I have me a pair of aces. And you believe you can beat my aces with your three jacks. Now a man does not get three jacks all that often. I don't blame you for bettin' them up." He studied his hole cards again. "But, on the other hand, maybe you don't have three jacks. Maybe all you have is those two on the table there. Maybe you're supposin' your double eagle will scare me out like it did ol' Klaus here."

Rusty reached into his pocket, pulling out several wrinkled bills. "I have a notion—a suspicion, you might say, that you don't have that third jack. Don't ask me how I know, friend, I just have that feelin'. So, here is the sixteen you raised and here, friend, is another twenty dollars back to you and your jacks, however many there may be."

143

Forcing a grin, the railroad man stared at Rusty, then reached into his vest, pulling out a pocket watch. He opened it, looked at the time, closed it again. Disconnecting the watch from its chain and fob, he placed it on the table. "This here's a fifty dollar watch. I'm seein' your twenty dollars and raisin' thirty more."

Rusty picked up the gold watch, opened it, snapped it shut, then placed on the pile of coins and bills. "That don't look to me like no fifty dollar watch. I'll spot you the twenty bucks for it. No more."

"All right, then, twenty bucks it is. I call." The railroad worker laid out his cards one by one, showing an ace, a six and another six. "Two pair, jacks over sixes, shanty boy."

Rusty studied his opponent's cards. Then, next to his ace and ten, he laid a jack, then another jack and another ten. "Jacks over tens, me friend."

As he reached for his winnings, he glanced up at his opponent. The man's face was turning bright red. Rusty pocketed the watch and stuffed his coins and bills in his shirt pocket, then stood up. Klaus grabbed his coins, dropping them into his pocket as he got up from the table.

"Ain't you gonna give me a chance to win back my watch?"

"Well, friend, it appears to me like you ain't got enough money to stake another hand. I'll do you this favor, though. If you want to buy the watch back for the twenty-dollar bet it covered, I'll be happy to oblige. I can be found 'most every night at the Namakagon Timber Company camp, east of here."

Rusty and Klaus grabbed their beer glasses and moved closer to the door. Swede joined them. Klaus looked back to see the rails huddled together. "Rusty, I tink ve best be ski-daddlin'," said Klaus. "Der's a dozen gandy dancers in here dat don't no more look so friendly."

Rusty glanced across the big German's shoulder and agreed with a nod. All three loggers guzzled their beers and left, crossing to the other side of the frozen, rutted, street. Before entering the River Pig Saloon, Klaus looked back to see twenty or more men pour out of the Rail Inn. He pushed his way past his friends and into the River Pig.

"Hey fellas," he yelled across the room. "Der's a whole pile a dem rails headed dis way, lookin' to give a lickin' to some miners!"

Several men near the tavern's front windows scraped frost from the glass and peered out at the railroad men lining the boardwalk across the street.

"Let's go give 'em what for, boys," shouted one of the miners. Half of the men piled out of the bar. Miners and lumberjacks soon stood shoulder to shoulder, filling the boardwalk in front of the River Pig Saloon. Across the street, the crowd of rails grew to more than forty.

A shout came from one of the miners. "Which one of you bone-headed gandy dancers wants your ugly face bloodied first?"

The rails charged into the street, shouting and swearing, as did the miners and lumberjacks. They met in the middle like two ancient armies fighting over distant kingdoms. Fists flew. Feet lashed out. Lit only by the now-

144

rising moon and the soft glow of oil lamps in nearby taverns, the hardened men fought. More workers streamed from other taverns and joined in.

For twenty minutes the clash continued in the snowy street. Some men, either injured or too tired to fight any longer, went back into the taverns. More men gathered on the boardwalk to watch and cheer the others on. Occasionally one would join the battle, perhaps not caring what started the brawl or for which side he was fighting.

Constable Bill Burns watched from the boardwalk. Next to him stood Mike Fremont, Rusty O'Hara, Charlie Martin, and Leroy Phipps enjoying the late night entertainment.

Blackie Jackson came down the outside stairway of a sporting house down the street. When he saw the midnight mêlée, Blackie gave the woman with him a passionate kiss, then left her on the stairs. He rushed into the jumble of brawling men.

Jackson slammed two men to the frozen ground and smacked another in the jaw with his huge fist before finding himself knocked face down onto the frozen street. A big calked boot came down near his chin as he ducked and rolled across the snow and out of the way. He stood up and grabbed the big fellow by the collar and belt, picked him up, and threw him over the mass of men, sending four others to the ground. Blackie ducked a punch from another man, socked him in the face, then stepped out of the fight and up onto the boardwalk next to Constable Burns.

"Nice night for a scuffle," said Blackie, brushing snow from his mackinaw.

"It surely is, Blackie," replied Bill Burns. "Looks like the boys are havin' a grand ol' time." Burns reached inside his coat. From a vest pocket, he pulled out his gold watch. "Well," he said with a yawn, "looks like this will be simmerin' down soon. I may just as well call it a night."

With three dozen men still brawling in the snow-covered street, the constable looked up at the moon, now rising above the rooftops. "It looks like it's going to be another fine winter's day in the pinery tomorrow," he said as he turned and strolled off down the boardwalk. "G'night, fellas."

Chapter 28
Whoopin' it up

The Namakagon Timber Company cook shanty was usually crowded with hungry men when the Saturday night supper bell rang. Not tonight. More than half of the lumberjacks had gone into town, a rare chance to blow off a head of steam, so said the woods boss, Ingman Loken. He knew most of the jacks would be back by early Sunday morning with less money in their pockets and more tall tales to tell.

Those who chose to stay in camp that night did so for a variety of reasons. Mason Fitch was still laid up from the leg injury he suffered earlier in the week. Sourdough had sewed him up as best he could, but it would be a good while before he would walk. You can be sure twenty-year-old Mason would have preferred a night on the town to lying on his straw-filled bunk in camp.

Sourdough couldn't go. He had to cook for the men and prepare more than one hundred pies, two roast pigs, three hundred biscuits, beans, and plenty of other fixin's for the Sunday dinner. Guests were coming and the company boss wanted to make a good impression.

Sourdough had help from Zeke and Zach, his cookees. All three would be up most of the night stoking the big cast-iron ranges and baking rack after rack of pies, bread, and biscuits. They would also tend to the sides of pork roasting on a spit outside the kitchen door.

In spite of his strong desire to spend Saturday night with his men, Ingman remained behind. His brother had no choice. Wheelchair-bound, Olaf

had not been out on the town on a Saturday night for more than two years. He wondered if he ever would again.

Other men stayed behind, too. Some had hired on hoping to earn enough money to keep their farms. They knew a Saturday night in town could leave them dead broke. Others stayed back to rest up and enjoy a taste of Olaf's whisky, a rare treat in any dry camp.

Kelly Thompson and Whistlin' Jim Engelbretson had a different reason. Ingman promised them an extra day's pay to provide music that night. Kelly boasted he could play more than thirty songs on his banjo. Whistlin' Jim, who deserved his nickname, also played the concertina.

Tor would stay behind tonight. He wanted to go but knew better than to ask his sheltering father for permission. Tor would sing along with the shanty boys, play some checkers, eat Sourdough's supper, listen to the tall tales, and maybe have a sip of whisky if his pa approved.

"Play us a polka, Whistlin' Jim," shouted Sourdough as he placed a large platter of smoked venison and ham on one of the tables. "Let's get this ballyhoo a-goin'!"

Whistlin' Jim, a chain-haul man by day, stomped his foot four times and squeezed a series of notes from his concertina. Kelly joined right in on the banjo, and most of the forty men who stayed in camp that night clapped to the beat. Sourdough began dancing around the tables, waving a wooden spoon over his head.

"Ya-dah, ya-dah, ha-ha-ha. Ya-dah, ya-dah, ha-ha-ha," he sang. As he rounded the kitchen worktable, he grabbed hold of both of his cookees and the three of them danced around the tables again. Zeke and Zach laughed so hard they could barely stay on their feet. Whistlin' Jim played and whistled while Kelly strummed his banjo. Sourdough sang louder now.

> "Ya-dah, ya-dah, ha-ha-ha.
> Ya-dah, ya-dah, ha-ha-ha.
> La la la.
> La la la.
> Loken's lumber camp. Ya!"

The cook shanty door swung open as Ingman wheeled his brother into the room. He stepped back outside and quickly returned, carrying a wooden whisky crate. He set the box on Sourdough's chopping block and snapped the lid from the crate. Tin cups, half filled with the amber liquid, were soon being passed around the room.

As the cups were relayed down the deacon's bench, Tex Ketchum, the oldest man in camp, took a small sip from each cup before passing it on.

"Hey, Tex!" came a shout from the end of the bench, "what the hell you doin'?"

"Just testin', just testin'," replied the old fellow as he took another sip. "Don't want you boys to get no loco weed juice."

The men laughed and sang. Two lumberjacks stepped up onto a table and danced around each other, clapping and stamping their feet. Whistlin' Jim continued playing as he stepped up onto a bench, making up a verse for the lively tune.

> "Grab your mop or grab your broom.
> Dance around the gol dang room,
> Sing a tune,

147

Shoot the moon,
At Loken's lumber camp. Ya!

See that fella on your right,
How he smells is such a fright.
Chew your snoose,
Spit your juice,
At Loken's lumber camp. Ya!"

Red Olsen, a big, burly Dane with a long, red beard, jumped onto the table next to Whistlin' Jim, making up another verse.

"Sourdough is our camp cook.
Biscuits harder than a book.
Punkin' pie,
In your eye,
At Loken's lumber camp. Ya!"

Everyone laughed, clapped and stamped feet now. Sourdough stepped onto the table. It bent in the center under the weight of the short, fat man in the white apron. When the tune came around, the head cook added his own verse.

"If you don't like my table goods,
I'll pitch your dinner in the woods.
If you're rude,
You'll get no food,
At Loken's lumber camp. Ya!"

The men howled with laughter. Sourdough stepped down onto the floor again and grabbed a whisky cup as Zeke and Zach each brought another tray to the men. Max Wiley jumped onto the table.

"Pinery boys who go to town
Lay their hard-earned dollars down.
Drink and smoke,
Come back broke
To Loken's lumber camp. Ya!"

Before Max could finish the verse, Red Olsen was on another table to take the next. He looked toward Olaf and Ingman as he sang.

"Muldoon ain't no friend of mine.
We'll breach his dam and drive our pine.
If he fights,

148

We'll douse his lights.
We're Loken's lumber camp. Ya!"

The entire room erupted with cheers, hats flying through the air. Tex Ketchum leapt onto the middle table, shaking his fist in the air while jumping up and down. One of the tossed hats landed on Olaf's lap. He threw it back into the air with a grin. The music played on.

Ingman sat on the bench nearest his brother. Leaning toward him, he peered into Olaf's deep blue eyes. With the men all cheering and laughing in the background, Ingman spoke. "There is no way you and I can let these boys down. If Phineas Muldoon gets his way, not one of these fellas here will get his winter's wages. Olaf, these boys will fight tooth and nail for us and, gol dang it, we are going to fight for them! The water in this lake belongs to these men yust as much as anybody else. So do the pines. Muldoon might own the dam, but we have rights to the water and, by God above, we are going to use that water to drive our timber to the mills and that, my brother, is that!"

Olaf nodded. "I agree. This camp and that timber out there on the ice belong to our men as much as us. We owe it to them to get our timber to the mills in the spring, whatever the cost. And, some day I want to turn this outfit over to Tor. Can't do that if Muldoon squeezes us dry. With a hundred Namakagon Timber Company men behind us we can overcome Muldoon. If that's our only choice, then so be it."

The musicians played one snappy tune after another while the men played cards, checkers, sang, and danced. Each time the musicians took a break, someone bounded onto a table and spun a yarn or told of an adventure. The case of whisky lasted well into the early morning hours.

Sourdough took the last of more than one hundred pumpkin, squash, mincemeat, and apple pies from the oven, and locked them in his pantry to cool. He knew the men coming back from their Saturday night on the town would be hungry. The pies would be safe tonight. Returning shanty boys would just have to wait for breakfast like everyone else.

Ingman, Olaf, and Tor crossed the yard to the lodge. Tor placed several logs on the fire and turned in.

Tor stared out his window as he lay in bed, the stars sparkling in the clear December night sky.

"Rosie's coming to camp tomorrow," he said to himself. "Sweet Rosie." Tor drifted into a sound sleep.

Junior Kavanaugh woke with a start, lying on the floor in total darkness and head spinning from all the beer he drank earlier that night. Hanging onto the wall, he slowly stood, then checked his pockets. He found nothing left but a few matchsticks. He couldn't remember anything, other than having dinner with Mabel Durst and drinking beer after beer after beer. "Why did I drink so much?" he muttered.

149

Junior had no idea which building he was in, how he got there, or what had happened. All he knew was that his head was spinning, his money was gone, and he felt sick.

Junior struck a match. In the corner, next to his shoe-pacs, lay his new, derby hat, crushed. Holding the match high above his head, he tried to shape the hat with his free hand, then plopped it on his head. He pulled on his shoe-pacs before opening the door. Dim light flickered from the kerosene lantern hanging over the staircase. The match burned his fingers, He tossed it onto the floor and stepped on it.

His attention turned to the window. Looking out, he realized he was in a third-floor room. He gazed at the quiet, moonlit street below. From his vantage point he could see well beyond the Merrill Hotel and the general store. He stared for a few seconds before it struck him. The Loken sleighs were gone.

The shock of the absent sleighs shook sense into the boy's foggy brain. He dashed out the door and down the two flights of stairs to the bar below. He burst into the barroom, seeing Mabel Durst at the far table with a tall, thin, redheaded lumberjack.

"Gotta go, Mabel," he yelled across the half-filled room, turning every head. "Hope I didn't spoil ya for the other fellas!"

Derby-topped and wearing his new, now-wrinkled suit and old shoe-pacs, Junior sprinted down the street past a small group of men standing near the hotel. "How long since the Namakagon Timber Company boys pulled out?" he yelled as he ran by.

"Ten, fifteen minutes, I'd say," called back one of the men.

"Thanks, pal," he shouted as he disappeared around the corner and down the moonlit street. He knew Blackie wouldn't be in a rush to return to camp. The two, four-horse teams would be taking it easy. He might be able to catch them at the river bridge, about three miles to the east. The beer was wearing off. Although his head pounded, he kept up his pace.

About two miles out, Junior saw something cross the narrow road ahead. When he neared the spot, he found the tracks from the animal that had crossed those of the sleighs. He studied them in the moonlight until he was sure, then sprinted down the trail again.

Picking up his pace, the boy shouted into the dark forest, "You dang wolves better not be lookin' at me for your next feast." He ran faster. "I ain't your Sunday dinner!" The woods were silent. "Go find some other bones to chew on, varmints. You don't want me," he shouted at the top of his lungs.

On down the snow-filled road he ran, shouting at the wolves, hoping to keep them at a distance. His imagination and the shadows caused by the bright moon inspired him to run faster and faster. As he rounded a bend in the road, he saw something on the trail ahead. Something large and dark. He kept running.

A shout came from ahead. "Who's on the trail?"

"It's me! Junior. Junior Kavanaugh. Hold your horses, fellas!"

Junior sprinted up to the back of the sleigh, reached up, and grabbed a large wool-mittened hand that swung him up and onto the sleigh into the straw, right on top of a whisky-spent lumberjack.

"Well, if it ain't the barn boy in the derby hat," yelled Charlie Martin. "We figured with all our money to spend that you'd be livin' the high life in town all winter. So how was your first Saturday night in Cable, Sprout?"

"I tell ya, fellas, it-was-somethin'. First I bought me this here Sunday suit. Then I treated my best gal to a fancy hotel supper and beer, plenty of beer."

"That's the lot of it? A suit and a supper and some beer?"

"Well, fellas, let me put it to you like this: I had plenty of money when Mabel and me left for supper. Five hours later I got me a big grin on my face, and I'm plum broke. Now, fellas, you figure it out!"

Blackie let go a belly laugh that echoed through the woods. "Junior Kavanaugh, you are some bullshitter, you are."

"Well, that is for me to know and for you fellas to ponder," said Junior with a grin. Then, "Blackie, there was a wolf on my trail back there!"

"It's your imagination, boy. No sensible timberwolf wants a skinny little runt like you."

"No, really, I saw him. I saw his track, too!"

"I am tellin' you," said Blackie from his nail keg seat, "it was just your imagination. Bein' alone in the winter woods at night will do that to a fella. Happens all the time."

"Ya, I s'pose maybe you're right, Blackie. Maybe it weren't no wolf after all."

Eight Namakagon Timber Company horses plodded down the snowy trail in the bitter December air. They pulled two sleighs of contented lumberjacks back toward their camp. The snow squeaked and squealed under the ironclad wooden runners, masking the lonely, eerie howling of six hungry wolves in the nearby pines.

Chapter 29
Sunday at the Loken Camp

In the Namakagon Timber Company camp, morning came early if you wanted breakfast. Sunday, December 9, 1883 was no exception. More than half of the camp's one hundred men were in town the night before, in the taverns, gambling halls, and sporting houses until the early morning hours. Dawn was breaking as the large timber sleighs returned to camp. Just as the men fell into their bunks, the camp cook gave the breakfast call, banging on an empty pot, perhaps a little louder than usual.

"Get up you lazy drunks! Get up if you want your beans and biscuits or go hungry till dinnertime," he shouted. "Coffee's hot and the day's a-wastin'. Rise and shine, men. Come—and—get it!"

Grumbling and cussing could be heard up and down the row. Many of the men were quick to leave their bunks, knowing if they missed breakfast, their first meal of the day would be the noon dinner.

"Sourdough," called out one of the lumberjacks, "you, sir, are a cruel and heartless man."

"Call me names if you want, Charlie Martin, but I am the fellow who keeps your belly full. And don't you by God forget it!"

As some of the rising lumberjacks pulled on their boots, others were already stumbling down the trail leading to the latrine. Soon most of the men lined the tables for their morning meal. About a dozen stayed in their bunks, sleeping off their Saturday night on the town.

Sourdough sent his cookees over to the lodge with breakfast for the Lokens. When breakfast was done, Ingman and Tor helped Olaf across the yard to the cook shanty as the lumberjacks set about doing their Sunday chores.

Eight buckets of water had been placed on the hot kitchen range. While they heated, Sourdough's sewing kit was passed up and down the deacon's bench for use by those who needed to sew up tears in their clothing, either from their week in the woods or their night on the town. Yarn was used to darn holes in their wool socks. Buttons were stitched back onto coats, shirts, and britches. By seven o'clock, the water in the buckets was boiling.

The two cookees carried the steaming buckets outside and dumped them into four washtubs. Men, now wearing only their union suits, lined up to wash their britches, socks and shirts. After thrashing their clothes on the scrub board and rinsing them in near-scalding water, they wrung the woolens out and hung them on a rope above the pot-bellied heater at the far end of the sleep shanty. The skylight above the stove was opened wide in a vain attempt to freshen the air.

Ingman poured two cups of coffee, handing one to Olaf. "Did everybody make it back safe and sound, Blackie?" asked Ingman.

"All present and accounted for, Boss. Ernie Milton has a pretty good cut on his chin, and Red Olsen got his arm waffled, but they will both be on the job tomorrow. All in all, Boss, the boys had a rip-snortin' time with little harm done."

Blackie put his arm over Tor's shoulder. "This young fella here and ol' Chief Namakagon sure were the talk of the town. Seems like every man and woman there was askin' about the robbery and them outlaws and such. Tor," he said with a grin, "you, young fella, are a pinery hero."

"Hero?" said Tor. "I don't believe I'm any such thing. I didn't do anything that anyone else wouldn't have done."

"Be that as it may, Tor," said Blackie, "you and old Chief were the fellas that saved the day. If I was you, I'd be holdin' my chin up real high. Ain't every day you get such a pat on the back. Enjoy it with pride, young fella, while folks still remember."

Sourdough stood up on a nearby bench and shouted across the room, "All right, shanty boys, finish up your chores and clean off the tables so as I can fix up our Sunday dinner. I don't need to remind you that we expect company in camp today, but I will anyhow. The boss is hopin' you'll do your best to make a good impression on our guests. Hold down your cussin' and show off your good manners, those of you who got some. Once Olaf Loken's guests leave camp, you can resume your gol dang distasteful, disagreeable, and downright disgusting ways."

As the Lokens left their table, Junior came through the kitchen door, eyes bloodshot, straw clinging to his new suit, and hat wrinkled. He went straight for the water pail, grabbed the dipper, tipped it up, and drank, water spilling down his shirt.

"You got some pretty fancy clothes there, Junior. You runnin' for mayor?" quipped the cook.

"Sourdough, I spent every last penny I took to town last night and all I have to show for it is this here suit and a throbbin' head. But, oh by golly, it was worth it!" Junior then recalled the evening's events, omitting his lapse of memory brought on by too much beer. He artfully embellished other parts of the story, as a young man might. His tale ended with his race to catch the sleigh back to camp while being chased by a pack of hungry wolves. Junior's story had the beginnings of a fine lumber camp yarn.

By eleven o'clock, Sourdough and his cookees were ready for the big meal. They knew the pork sides on the spit would be done to perfection just in time for dinner, as would the venison and bear roasting in the oven. Bowls of molasses, butter, brown sugar, and bacon grease sat on the oilcloth-covered tables. Knives, forks, and spoons stood in the center of each table in large tin cans. A hundred tin plates and cups were in place. The camp cookees put trays stacked high with fresh biscuits and bread up and down the tables, leaving room for the large platters of meat, potatoes, gravy, and squash soon to be served.

Back in his room, Tor changed into his best britches. He buttoned the shirt, fastened his suspenders, and pulled on his leather boots. Next he reached under his bed and pulled out his green wooden box. Flipping open the lid, he pulled out another box, white, about the size of a deck of cards. He placed it in the pocket of his shirt and buttoned the flap, then slid the green box back under the bed.

Tor crossed the small room to his dresser. Pouring some water into the washbowl, he washed his hands and splashed some water onto his face and hair before fumbling for a flour sack towel. He looked into the small mirror hanging on the wall, opened a small tin of lard, scented with wintergreen leaves, scooped some onto his finger tips and, with both hands now, vigorously rubbed it into his hair.

Tor stared into the wavy reflection in the mirror as he combed his hair, parting it straight down the middle. As he finished, he noticed something far across the lake. "Rosie!" he said. He dropped the comb onto his dresser next to the open tin of hair grease and ran down the stairs.

"Somebody's coming!" he shouted to his father who sat at the office desk. Snatching his father's field glasses from the mantle, he rushed to the large window overlooking the lake and peered through the binoculars. "Oh," he grumbled, "it's just Chief Namakagon."

"You don't sound very eager to see him, Tor. I should think you would want to hear his account of his capture of that escaped train robber."

"What? Oh, no, Pa," said Tor, hiding his disappointment, "I *do* want to hear his story."

Tor watched through the field glasses, following as Namakagon came closer. The chief, pulled by Waabishki and Makade, stood tall and regal on the back of the sled's runners. They skimmed across the snow and soon ascended the trail leading up to the lumber camp.

Namakagon jumped off the runners but hung onto the sled, running behind and giving it an extra push up the bank. At the top of the hill he jumped back on and they sailed into the yard with flair. He unfastened his small pack from the sled and released the dogs, letting them explore the grounds as he walked to the lodge. Tor was there to open the door as Ogimaa Mikwam-migwan entered the room. He tossed off his bearskin robe, leaned his walking stick in the corner, and gave the boy a hearty hug. "Good to see you, young woodsman."

"Mighty pleased you could join us," Tor replied. "We've been on pins and needles, waiting to hear the tale of you and that runaway villain, Percy Wilkins."

Tor's father wheeled away from his desk, joining the others. "Namakagon! Welcome back to our camp. We have been wondering when you would return."

"Olaf, between the hunt for the thief and the pestering from the newspaper men, these old bones got weary. I needed to rest."

"Will you stay awhile?" said Olaf.

"I can. Perhaps I may even provide some fish for your table. Maybe your son would like to join me?"

"Oh, I doubt that I can find time," said Tor, staring out the window again. "I'm sawing for Mike Fremont's crew."

"Only half days," said his father. "You haven't tried fishin' through the ice. You'd enjoy it, Son. I surely used to."

"I don't know, Pa," replied Tor, peering through the binoculars, "I'm awful busy these days. I just don't know if I can find the time."

Olaf Loken looked at his son with a raised eyebrow. Namakagon smiled.

"I have heard this many times before," said the chief. "People say they do not have time for this, time for that, time for the things that may be most important in their lives. Young friend, let me explain something I have learned in my many years. Time, Tor, is the *only* thing we mortals are given by Gitchee Manitou. We do not own the earth, the trees, the waters, the animals, the stars. Even those material things we bring into our lives are not really ours to keep, but only to use during our stay here. No, Tor, when you look closely at life, you come to understand *time* is the *only* thing we have. Some of us use it wisely. Others waste it by wandering the wrong trails—chasing fortune rather than contentment. Time is all we have, young woodsman. It is life's most precious gift and we must make the best use of it until it is gone and our dust again mingles with that of our Earth Mother. Until then, as I said, *time* is all we have."

"Good advice, Tor," said his father. "For the last two years I have thought about my past. I realize now how much I regret many choices I made back when I still had my legs—many things I did not do that I could have done. Many places I never saw—places I may *never* see. Listen to Chief Namakagon. He is right, Son. Time truly is life's most precious gift."

"Tor, you are very fortunate," said Namakagon. "You have something we have lost."

"I have?"

"Yes. You have youth. You have many years ahead. You have opportunities to choose your trails. Learn all you can about this land. Make this a better place to live, young woodsman. Care for the land and it will care for you, young woodsman."

Namakagon walked to the door. He put two fingers to his lips and gave a shrill whistle. His two dogs bounded in and sat at his feet. "Are you two beggars behaving yourselves?" he said, scratching their ears. The chief spread his bearskin robe on the floor in a corner of the room. With a snap of his fingers, his dogs were sitting on the robe. "Makade, Waabishki, stay." he ordered.

Tor stepped to the window with his father's binoculars again just as the door swung open. Sourdough stepped in. "Olaf, you want your dinner here or with the men?"

"In here, Sourdough. No need to expose our guests to the unique fragrances of the bunkhouse."

"How many you expectin'?"

"Let me see. Tor, Ingman, and me," Olaf counted, "then Namakagon, that is four, then Oscar, that comes to five. If she makes it, we may have Adeline Ringstadt and maybe two of her three daughters here, too. Better have your cookee set the table for eight, Sourdough."

"Make it nine," said Tor, peering across the lake through the field glasses. "They're comin' around the point right now, and I see the three Ringstadts and Oscar Felsman, and one more fella."

"Wonder who it is," said Olaf.

"Looks to me like a preacher," Tor replied.

"A preacher?" said Sourdough, looking out the window. "Not often we see a sky-pilot out this far." Olaf wheeled closer to the window. The chief looked over his shoulder.

"Looks to be Reverend Spooner," said Olaf. "Must be escorting the Ringstadts."

"Say, Boss," said Sourdough, "maybe Adeline has some plans for you. Maybe she brung along her own preacher to do the last rights and matrimonials."

"Bite your tongue, Sourdough. I am not in the market."

The five guests entered the lodge, Zeke and Zach right behind. The cookies wore clean, white aprons and carried a large platters of roast pork, venison, and bear. Soon they had the table set with a basket of biscuits, bowls of butter, molasses, honey, Sourdough's cranberry chutney, a bowl of squash, another of baked beans, and more. Apple, pumpkin and mincemeat pies were delivered next, along with a pitcher of milk, a big pot of coffee, another of tea and a third of hot cocoa. By the time the food was on, Oscar had set up a wooden keg filled with his home brew. He drove the spigot into the bung and a loud *fisssss* alerted the group this Namakagon Timber Company dinner party had officially commenced.

Chapter 30
The Dinner Party

Tor had planned this for days. His father would take the chair at the head of the table, as usual. Uncle Ingman would sit at the opposite end. Tor would sit in the corner seat next to his father, and Rose would sit beside him. He didn't care where the others sat as long as he could be near Rosie.

As she neared the table, Tor pulled out a chair. She smiled at him, but before she could step forward, her younger sister Daisy slid into the seat. Tor did not flinch, at least not outwardly. He looked at Rose, then moved around to the other side of the table and pulled out another chair for her, thinking he could sit near his uncle and still have Rosie by his side.

"Why thank you, Tor," said Adeline as she plopped down in the chair. "How very polite. Olaf, I see you have raised a well-mannered gentleman."

Tor rushed to the other side of the large pine table where two more open chairs stood. "One for me, one for my Rosie," he said to himself. Reverend Spooner stepped in front of him, taking one of the chairs, Oscar the other. Back he went again, but too late. Namakagon pulled out a chair and motioned Rose to sit next to him. She did. Tor took the last seat, between Chief Namakagon and his father. His plan had failed. He would not sit next to the girl he longed for. He glanced toward Rosie. She looked back with a hint of sympathetic sadness in her eye after seeing her would-be beau work so hard to be near her.

"Excuse me, Sir," Rose whispered to the chief, "would you mind switching places with me?"

"Of course. I was wondering which of you would ask first."

"This is such a delightful treat, Olaf," said Adeline. She wore a long, gray wool dress and had her dark hair tied up in a tight bun. White silk handkerchiefs peeked out perfectly from under each of the tight cuffs on her long sleeves. Her daughter, Rose, sitting across from her, also wore a long-sleeved dress, but the color was a better choice for her age—a bright red and green plaid. She wore a red ribbon in her long brown hair.

"I am so pleased you could join us, Adeline. Don't get many visitors out this far," said Olaf, reaching for the biscuits.

"Perhaps it would be good to give thanks for these gifts before we indulge," said the Reverend. Olaf drew back his hand.

"Dear Father who art in Heaven," began the preacher, "we miserable sinners deserve neither your graces nor this bounty of food you have sent down to us from above. Please have mercy on us when our judgment day comes and reward most those of us who have given generously to your house of worship so that your will may be done. May each bite of this, your food, remind us that those who honor you by giving most charitably are those most likely to have their prayers answered. Amen."

"That was so moving, Reverend," said Adeline, reaching for the apple butter. "You are so clever with your words."

"I agree," said Namakagon. "I cannot recall when I heard such words." Then, whispering to Tor, "Perhaps the last time was during that holdup on the train." Tor forced back his laughter.

"Say now, Olaf," said the preacher, "as long as I have ventured out this far, I would like to hold a church service for your men after dinner. I would imagine they haven't uttered the Lord's name for a while."

"Oh, no, Reverend," said Tor, "I hear the men use the Lord's name mornin' noon, and night."

"Reverend, you are welcome to use the cook shanty after the tables are cleared," said Olaf. "I have no objection. Surely can't do much damage."

"Ya," added Ingman, "I suppose some of the fellas might appreciate some words from the good book. Those who don't want to listen to your talk, well, that is their choice. I have a feelin' most of our men are not the prayin' type."

"Maybe not," said Olaf, "at least not till a man sees a big pine falling toward him instead of away."

"Tor, did you know you are a hero in Hayward?" interrupted Daisy. "Everyone is talking about you and how you saved the Omaha."

"Saved the Omaha?"

"Saved it from being robbed, Tor."

"That's not quite how the story goes, Daisy. It wasn't a train robbery at all. And I sure didn't do a whole lot to help."

"That does not liken to what the *St. Paul Pioneer Press* professed," said Reverend Spooner. "We brought you a copy. Tor, they have you and Chief Namakagon portrayed as quite the champions. They filled four entire pages discussing the glories of your noble battle with those hooligans. They have artist's depictions of you wrestling the revolver from the thug's hands, of the train, the trestle, and even one of the villain all bandaged and shackled up in the county jailhouse. The paper says they haven't found the other hooligan yet. Seems he was lost to the icy Namekagon River for eternity."

Chief Namakagon interrupted, sternly. "No battle. No glories. We were victims. We used our heads, turned the tables. One man is now crippled for life and will spend much of that life in prison. The other is lost under the ice. The word *glory,* Reverend, does not apply. Perhaps it should be saved for your sermons."

"Whether it applies or not," said Rose, "it pains me to admit that my little sister is correct. Chief Namakagon, Tor, they do speak of you two as the heroes of the pinery. The paper says the new governor thinks so, too. He'll be coming soon—all the way from Madison, just to honor you. Pretty good evidence you are heroes, I would say."

"When is he coming?" said Ingman.

"Just before Christmas, or so the paper reports," said the Reverend.

"Is the governor coming here for us?" asked the chief. "Or for himself."

158

Olaf answered. "There are thirty, forty thousand lumberjacks and miners up in this country now, and another twenty thousand to the east, near the Wisconsin River. More and more come every day. He is wise to visit the north if he values their votes."

"That story in the *Pioneer Press* was the work of the railroad company," said Oscar, stabbing a large piece of roast pork with his fork. "The head office knows it's good for business to get a railroad adventure story in the paper. Over the next year we will probably have hundreds of folks voyaging up here—each, mind you, at four cents a mile, just to see the bridge where that fella met his maker. And they'll be searchin' every passenger car to look for bullet holes and bloodstains. Tor, you and Chief here, could not have done better for the rail business unless you captured Jesse James himself, by God!"

Reverend Spooner shot him a piercing stare.

"Rose," said Adeline, "how 'bout fetchin' up a round of beers to celebrate our pinery heroes."

"I'll help!" said Tor, almost knocking over his chair as he stood.

"Good idea," added Oscar. "I brewed that beer myself, and brought it along just to mark this event. I have no intention of takin' back more than the empty keg."

Ingman held his glass high. "Well, here's to our two pinery heroes, whether they like being called that or they do not."

"And here's to the charming ladies seated at our table," Tor said, looking at Rosie. "May they return again, and gol dang soon! Uh, oh, sorry, Reverend."

In the cook shanty, the empty bowls, platters, and dishes were cleared and the tables wiped down. Reverend Wilmer P. Spooner soon stood before the men, bible in hand. He offered a rousing service, inspiring the thirty-two men who attended to put any pocket change they had left from their Saturday night fling into the hat he passed. His sermon was so moving that four of them pledged to swear off cussing until Christmas.

The rest of the men went down to the lake for their usual Sunday afternoon game of lacrosse. They broke into teams, divided up their homemade equipment, and played in the deep snow covering the ice. Those unwilling to suffer the punishment of the rough game cheered others on.

Tor did not play today. Instead, he gave Rose a tour of the camp.

"Me, too," shouted Daisy. "I want to see the camp."

"Daisy, you stay here with me," said Adeline. "Let Tor show your sister around."

"Mother," cried Daisy, "that's not fair! I want to go, too." But her pleas did not work and, much to her dismay, she stayed in the lodge with the adults, silently pouting.

Tor gave Rose a complete tour, showing her everything from the filing shed and blacksmith shop to the tool shed, horse barn, pigpen, corral, and woodshed. He pointed out the dynamite shack far up on the hill, and they ended in the cook shanty, just as the reverend finished his service.

"Don't mind the smell in here, Rosie," said Tor, "most of the men don't take a bath until the spring drive. In fact, most are convinced it is bad for your health to take a bath in the winter."

"Tor, how can anyone stand to eat in here?"

"Oh, you get used to it."

"So they wait until spring to take a bath?"

"Well, the men that drive logs fall in the river enough to get a good washin'. Most of the others don't like mosquitoes much, so, come spring, they still don't take a bath. They think if they can keep up a good stink it'll keep the bugs away. I don't think it works, much. They still get bit. Graybacks get 'em in the winter, mosquitoes and ticks in the summer. It's a wonder they have any blood left, come fall."

"Tor," Rose said quietly, "I think I had too much of Mr. Felsman's beer. I need—I need to go."

"Go where?"

"I need to *go*, Tor. I need to *go!*"

Tor looked puzzled, then suddenly understood.

"Oh, oh, I see," he said, turning red. "You need to see a man about a horse."

"A horse? Lord, no, Tor, I need a privy. And gol dang soon!"

Tor was shocked to hear such language used by a girl, especially his Rosie. He whisked her out of the cook shanty and escorted her down the trail behind the lodge to the outhouse used only by the Lokens and their guests.

"Here you are, Rosie. I'll keep a look out and fend off any train-robbin' hooligans who come this way."

"See, you are a hero—*my* hero. Now you go way up on the path. Way, way up."

Minutes later, Rosie and Tor walked down to the lake. Watching the men play lacrosse, they talked and laughed. It seemed only moments before Daisy called down from the porch to tell Rose it was time to leave.

As they walked back to the lodge, Tor reached into his shirt pocket and pulled out the small, white box. "Here, Rosie, this is for you." He placed the box in her hand. "Remember the light blue ribbon you gave me to remember you by?"

"Yes?"

"Well, this is so you don't forget me, Rosie."

She opened the box and pulled out the small, heart-shaped, gold locket.

"Tor, it is lovely! I've never had such a wonderful, thoughtful gift." She pulled it carefully from the box and held it in her hand. "And I have never known such a nice boy. You *are* my hero, Tor Loken, and you always will be." She leaned forward and kissed him on the cheek.

Stunned and thrilled, Tor was speechless once more. And relieved when, right then, Uncle Ingman opened the door to say, "Better get a move-on, you two. Nephew, we don't want our guests to miss the southbound."

Before entering the lodge, Tor put the chain around Rosie's neck and found his voice again. "I'm comin' to see you just as dang soon as I can. I want to hear you play your piano and sing your sweet songs. I'm comin' to see you, Rosie. You have my solemn word on it."

"I will measure every day until you do, Tor Loken," she replied, taking his hands in hers. "And don't you worry about my little sisters. I'll lock them in the attic when you come—or maybe I should forget about them, and we can just lock ourselves in the attic!" Rose leaned in and gave him another kiss on the cheek.

Tor's heart was racing when they entered the lodge. Ingman sat at the table enjoying the last of Oscar's home brew. Chief Namakagon's dogs were still sitting on the bearskin robe. The traveling dinner guests wore their coats and hats. Olaf wrapped a long scarf around Daisy's neck and face. Tor handed Rose the floppy felt hat she wore on the trip to the camp.

Farewells were exchanged as the Lokens' guests boarded Oscar's sleigh. Tor stood on a runner, riding alongside as it traveled down the hill in front of the lodge. When it reached the lake he jumped off, shouted his goodbye, and waved as Oscar's horses picked up speed. The sleigh skimmed across the snow-covered ice.

With the mid-December sun still high above the tree tops on the southwest shore, Tor sprinted back up the hill. He rushed into the lodge, grabbed his father's binoculars, and ran up the stairs, two steps at a time. From his window he watched as the sleigh appeared to get smaller and smaller until it rounded the point and disappeared from sight.

"I'm comin' to see you, Rosie," he whispered. "You have my solemn word on it."

Chapter 31
Modern Times

Flames in the fireplace licked high, crackling and snapping as the Loken brothers warmed their feet on the hearth. Turning to Olaf, Ingman declared, "What this timber company needs is a gol dang steam enyun!"

His brother gazed into the flickering fire, pulling his old walnut pipe from a shirt pocket. "A what?"

"A steam enyun. A steam enyun."

Olaf opened his tobacco pouch, dipped the bowl into the soft, shredded tobacco, and tamped it with his thumb. He pulled the strings on the pouch, cinching it tightly before dropping it back into his pocket. "A steam engine?"

"Ya, Olaf, like I said, a steam enyun."

"You got a matchstick?"

Ingman stepped onto the hearth and reached for the tin matchbox on the mantle. He struck a match on a stone and held it to Olaf's pipe. Olaf drew hard, blowing smoke into the air as Ingman sat down. The brothers gazed into the flames again.

"A steam engine," repeated Olaf.

"Ya."

"Ingman, either you drank too much of Oscar's home brew today, or you have completely lost your wits. Which is it?"

"Neither. I've been ponderin' this for a good while, now. I know where I can get us a donkey enyun on the cheap. The Douglas outfit over on the St. Croix River is pullin' up stakes. They are movin' the whole camp down to Ghost Lake. Their woods boss, Andrew Price, tells me they have no use for a donkey enyun down there. We should make them an offer."

Olaf drew in on his pipe, leaned back, and blew the smoke into the air. "We can get along fine without a steam engine. The men know their way around the hills. Not a pine in the woods we cannot haul by horse or oxen."

"Ya, ya, Olaf, we can get along fine. But you are not lookin' at both sides of the coin. I'm thinkin' we can pick it up for three hundred dollars, maybe less. If we set it up on that ridge north of the creek, back where Mike Fremont's crew is working, why those sleighs won't have to cross the swamp. Won't be takin' the long way around, neither. I ciphered this out. By February, half our crews can be making use of the donkey enyun. I am of the mind that, by usin' a steam enyun, we can put up two million more feet come spring. Maybe three. That alone is reason enough to give it a try."

"We have done fine without. This is folly. No need to change horses in the middle of the stream."

"Confound it, brother, you cannot move forward by usin' backwards ways. By gosh! This is eighteen eighty-three. Eighteen eighty-three! These ain't the good old days anymore. No siree. These—are—modern—times!"

Olaf drew in on his pipe again. "Well, if we do buy this donkey contraption, and I'm not saying we should, who is going to run it? You?"

"No, not me. Best bet would be the fella who runs it now."

"So … what you are sayin' … is that I have to lay out three hundred dollars for this here contraption and then hire a man to run it, and feed him, and put him on the payroll. Are you sure you didn't drink too much of Oscar's beer?"

"There's another reason we need to do this, Olaf."

"And what might that be?"

"Come spring, it can push our pine across the lake to the dam."

"Across the lake? How do you figure?"

"We build a boat."

"A boat? Pshaw!"

"Ya, Olaf, a boat."

"Ingman, this is getting better and better. First you say you want a dang donkey engine. Now you want us to build a boat?"

"Ya, that is what I said. We build us a boat. While the donkey is pullin' our pine up the hill for us in the wintertime, we will be buildin' our own sternwheeler right here in camp. Later on we move the steam enyun onto the boat and use it to push the log booms across the lake to the dam."

"We have the wind to do that."

"Olaf, how much pine did we have on the ice last spring? Do you remember? Three and a half million board feet. This year we will have seven, maybe eight million with help from the donkey. Maybe more. We cannot count on the wind. I'm tellin' you, I been ponderin' this over and over and over."

"You have, have you."

"Ya, I have. First, we buy the donkey. We use it till March. Then, on the day the ice goes out, we use it again, this time to push our timber across the lake, down the narrows, and right over Muldoon's dam. And nobody beats us to the punch, Olaf. Nobody. Not even Muldoon's own camps will have the edge on us. What's more, nobody's logs get mixed in with ours and we are first to the mills. I tell ya, Olaf, I have been ponderin' this. It will surely succeed."

Olaf stared at the fire for a few moments. "Ingman, I must have had too much of Oscar's home brew too, for I think I see a slight glimmer of logic in your plan. Ya, by golly," he drew again on his pipe, "I believe I, too, have lost my wits. All right. You go ahead. Head on over to the St. Croix. Take a gander at this contraption. And, Ingman, you dang better do this quick before Oscar's beer wears off and I come to my senses."

They stared at the flames in silence for a moment. Olaf slapped his pipe against the palm of his hand, sending tobacco ashes onto the hearth. "A boat," he muttered, "a gol dang, steam-powered, stern-wheeled boat."

"Not just any boat," said Ingman. "It will be *the Loken's* gol dang, steam-powered, stern-wheeled boat."

Olaf dropped his pipe back into his shirt pocket. "Well, ain't that something. Just how big is this contraption, anyway?"

"I figure half a ton."

"Half a ton? Gonna take a good-sized boat just to bear the weight."

"We can have Louie Thorp start work on it. Louie's as good a carpenter as you'll find. And I remember Max Wiley sayin' he did some steam fittin' in St. Paul. Maybe he can help out some."

"Put young Kavanaugh to work on it, too. Ask around the camp. See how many of the men have experience with boats, sailing, and such. Who knows? Maybe there's a ship's captain in that bunch."

The lodge door swung open. Chief Namakagon walked into the room with his two dogs at heel. Leaning his walking stick against the wall, he peeled his bearskin robe from his shoulders and spread it on the floor. A snap of his fingers had both Waabishki and Makade lying in the center of the bearskin. The tall, buckskin-clad woodsman crossed the room and joined the Loken brothers before the fireplace.

"Namakagon," said Olaf, "what would you say if I told you that, come spring, we may have us a gol dang, steam-powered, stern-wheeled boat?"

The chief grinned. "I was wondering how long it would take you."

"We are building it right here in camp," said Ingman. "I'm heading over to the St. Croix River tomorrow to look at an enyun."

"Enyun? Oh, yes—enyun. I will go with you."

Olaf pulled his pipe from his shirt pocket again, raised it high, and exclaimed, "Well here's to the Namakagon Timber Company's gol dang, stern-wheeled steamboat."

"Tim-berrrr," yelled Tor at the top of his lungs. The ninety-foot white pine started its fall. He and Leroy stepped back quickly and turned to watch the three hundred-year-old forest giant crash to the ground.

No sooner had the snow settled than the young men were bucking it into sixteen-foot logs. Mike Fremont positioned the team of Percherons and wrapped the chain around the butt end of the first log. "Giddup," he said softly. Mike and the handsome steeds dragged the thousand-pound log through the snow on down to the ice road.

Charlie Martin and Sven Olson used another horse team to cross-haul the huge pine logs up the ramp and onto the sleigh. This first load of the morning was more than twenty feet high. They hoisted the last log on before Charlie, standing on top, threw down the chains. Sven secured the chains and tightened the binders. Charlie jumped to the ground below. He hooked the horse team to the sleigh and gave a sharp whistle, smacking the rump of the horse nearest to him with his hand. The horses strained to move the sleigh forward but the load would not move. Charlie pulled a peavey from its place on the side of the sleigh and gave the steel-clad oak runner nearest him a solid rap. With a slight jerk, the sleigh began to move forward down the ice road winding toward the lake. Sven and Sonny Vinskoog each guided one of the two workhorses down the trail a few yards, then Sven came back. The next sleigh was pulled into place, and Sven, the chainman on this job, and Charlie, the sky-hooker, continued their work.

For the next several days, Tor worked with Leroy each morning, returning to camp with Junior at midday. On Wednesday, when Junior and Tor stepped into the cook shanty for their dinner, they found the new company blacksmith, Gust Finstead, and Chief Namakagon sitting at a table with Tor's Uncle Ingman. Olaf's wheelchair was pulled up to the end of the table.

Junior and Tor heaped their plates with venison and baked beans, grabbed a cup of Sourdough's strong tea, a fork and a spoon, and sat down at the next table as the men reported to the head push.

"I tell ya, Olaf," said Ingman, "this machine is yust what we need. We saw it on the yob. They had a sleigh loaded high with timber, sittin' at the bottom of this rise. I tell ya, brother, a dozen oxen couldn't have pulled that load up that grade. Well, this here fella runs a long chain down to the sleigh. He hooks it up and gives a wave. This other fella up by the donkey enyun, he throws the chain around the windlass and locks her in. Next, he throws a lever and we watch as the chain slowly tightens up and pretty soon the whole gol dang load is yust a-slidin' up the hill like nobody's business. By and by that sleigh is standin' right there in front of us at the top of the rise! I tell ya, this donkey enyun is gonna double the pine we can bring out of the north forties."

"You have not told me what it might cost us, Ingman. Is there a reason?"

"Two hundred, less the chain. Gust, here, figured he could make up the chain cheaper than what they wanted for it."

"That's it? Two hundred?"

"Yust be patient, now. You see, I didn't figure in the spare parts their blacksmith had set aside."

Olaf took a sip of coffee, putting his tin cup down on the oilcloth. "Spare parts cannot be too costly, right?"

"Three hundred."

"Three hundred. Three hundred dollars? Ingman, that is more than two mans' winter wages! That's … that's …"

"That's what they had to have. That's what I offered."

"How the hell can parts cost more than the whole dang steam engine?"

"Now, don't go off half-cocked. The bargain we made includes an extra boiler and more than enough spare parts to build a second enyun. That way, if one machine goes to pot, we have a spare salted away. Think about that. Next spring, when we're counting on this steam enyun to move our log booms across the lake and down to the dam, we don't have to worry about her brakin' down."

"Gust, can you put all these parts together to make a second engine?"

"You betcha. I can do that in a week and still have a pile of parts left over. I worked on the same machines in Minnesota last winter. It's a mighty good bargain, Boss."

"And we didn't have to hire a man to run it, Olaf," said Ingman. "Gust here says he can train one of our boys to do that. Could save us plenty."

"All right then, we'll buy it. When can you pick up this contraption?"

The men were silent. Tor and Junior looked on, wondering who was going to speak first.

"Olaf," said Chief Namakagon, "you will see your apparatus sooner than you expect."

"In fact," added Ingman, "it's in the horse barn."

"In the barn?"

"Ya, Olaf, in the barn. I knew you'd be excited to hear that."

Olaf shook his head in disbelief. "Gust, you dang well see to it this here donkey contraption is pullin' those timber sleighs up the hill by this time next week. You'll need a man to work with. Maybe Mason Fitch, if he is up to it with that bum leg of his.

"Ingman, get some plans going' for that boat. No point waiting around till the loons come back. If I'm goin' to the poorhouse, might as well be sooner rather than later. Now I would like to go have a look at this gol dang donkey."

In the coming days, Gust Finstead devoted most of his time to the project. Tor, having more free time than the others, assisted Gust each afternoon, as did Mason. Junior spent as much time as he could with them, between barn chores and hauling the midday meal. Three days later the donkey engine was ready. Ingman decided to wait until Saturday to take it out to the cuttings.

Meanwhile, Tor and Junior helped the blacksmith assemble the second engine. Like the other machine, it had a single, large cylinder and piston and a three-inch drive shaft that drove a one-hundred-fifty pound flywheel. A belt from this flywheel could easily propel a paddlewheel. They would need only bearings and seals. Gust could build the rest. The system was simple. The boiler could be fired by coal or wood, either able to produce a flame hot enough to make plenty of steam. The coal would burn hotter and last longer, but would have to be hauled in from the port at Ashland. Firewood was plentiful and free for the taking but would burn faster. They chose wood.

The whole camp took interest in the machinery. Many of the men dropped in to watch or help during the evening hours. Kerosene lamps were hung to give them extra time with the machines.

With the help of Max Wiley, a swamper with experience as a steamfitter, and Buster Seeley, a teamster who had worked in the Milwaukee shipyards, a design was drawn up for the boat. After lengthy discussions and many changes, Louie Thorpe, camp carpenter, showed the plan for the boat to Ingman. Two days later, the oak needed for the hull was being milled. Work would begin on the day of its delivery.

Saturday morning, as the crews left for the cuttings, the donkey engine, too, was on its way into the woods. Gust and Tor mounted it on two old sleigh runners. A single workhorse was sufficient to pull it along the tote road. They set the engine on the crest of a ridge between two spruce swamps. Gust double-chained it to a pine stump so the heavy sleighs would not pull the engine down the hill.

Junior joined them after he finished his morning chores. He helped

166

clear the new sleigh trail leading up to the engine and down the other side of the ridge toward the lake. A pile of dry oak, ironwood, and maple was stacked near the boiler, along with some pine knots for kindling. In the late afternoon, with the donkey engine ready, Junior, Tor, and Gust returned to camp.

CLANG, CLANG, CLANG, CLANG, CLANG, rang out from Junior's stewpot as he rapped it with a wooden spoon. Ingman stepped up onto the table.

"Men," he shouted, "we're gonna fire up our new donkey enyun tomorrow. If you want to see her do the work of a dozen horses, well, here's your chance. I figure if we don't let you get a look-see at her tomorrow, you'll be sneakin' off the yob all week.

"Blackie Yackson will have a sleigh ready to haul you up to the cuttings at one o'clock sharp. Be in the yard then or plan on hoofin' your way up the ridge." He stepped down and then back up. "And I want to thank all of you who have helped with this proyect and are helpin' with the boat. Olaf, Tor, and I appreciate it. We think this will be good for all of us come spring when we expect to drive maybe eight million board feet down the river."

The entire company of men cheered, knowing this was three times what they sent to the mills a year before.

The next day, the Loken crew wolfed down Sourdough's Sunday dinner. When the sleigh left the yard it was jam-packed with lumberjacks. Another twenty walked ahead. More walked behind. Three miles up the trail they climbed the long grade to the top of the hill where the steam engine stood.

A sleigh stacked high with pine logs stood at the bottom of the hill. Blackie tended the sleigh's team. Junior watched from the crest of the hill as Blackie unhitched the horses, leading them a safe distance from the trail.

The Loken lumberjacks all gathered around the donkey engine, studying, analyzing, and inspecting both the machine before them and the heavy sleigh at the bottom of the rise. Ingman and Olaf pulled up in the camp's one-horse cutter. Ingman jumped down. Junior and Gust filled the boiler with water. Tor struck a match and threw it into the firebox, slammed the door, and soon a plume of white smoke was coming from the stack. Gust watched the pressure gauge slowly rise as the smoke turned black and billowed out.

It took ten minutes to build a head of steam. Junior stepped back as the blacksmith cranked open a valve and gave the flywheel a spin. Chug————chug——chug—chug, chug, chug came from the engine, bringing cheers.

Now the flywheel turned rapidly, smoke and steam rising skyward in the frigid winter air. Junior reached up, and with a grin even wider than usual, pulled a small chain connected to a large brass whistle atop the engine. "Shoooooo, shoo, shoo," screamed the machine, bringing more cheers.

Ingman cupped his hands around his mouth. "Blackie Yackson, are—you—ready?" he called from the hilltop.

"Ready, Boss."

Tor moved back through the mass of men and climbed up into the cutter with his father. There, they had a good view of Blackie, below, and the

167

hot boiler before them, now spewing smoke, and the pulsing engine. Tor stood and steadied himself by placing a hand on his father's shoulder.

"Gust Finstead," shouted Ingman, "let 'er go!"

Flywheel spinning now, the blacksmith threw the chain around the windlass and slowly pulled back on the large, oak lever. The belt tightened, slipped at first, but slowly began to grab, turning the windlass.

With the steam engine laboring under the load, the chain pulled taut and straightened out. Onlookers, seeing the tremendous tension on the chain, backed away, sensing that if a single link broke, the chain could shoot through the air like a hundred pound bullwhip. Far below, the sleigh began to inch up the trail. The men cheered again. Minutes later, the huge sleigh load of logs crested the hill, and Gust eased off on the oak lever.

The job was done. A fourth round of cheers went into the cold air, along with half-a-hundred hats. A two-horse team, taking the long way around, would have taken more than an hour. The donkey engine accomplished the task in just six minutes.

"Gust," cried out one of the sawyers, "can you hitch that contraption up to my crosscut so as I can doze off in the woods now and then?" Another yelled "Gust, how 'bout hookin' one end to the Merrill Hotel and draggin' it out here so we can have cold beer and warm women in camp tonight?" The lumberjacks howled with laughter. Junior blew the engine's whistle again and again.

As the men began filing back down the trail to the camp, Gust pulled the fire from the firebox with a scoop shovel, throwing the embers into the snow. Blackie disconnected the chain from the sleigh. Men stepped off the trail as the horse team slowly moved the heavy load of logs down the ice road toward the lake. A dozen men climbed atop the big load. Gust pulled a brass handle on the donkey engine, blowing off the rest of the steam. He opened a petcock and a stream of hot water shot from the bottom of the boiler, melting the snow where it fell. A cloud of steam rose into the sky. Gust, still grinning, turned the flywheel by hand to clear any water in the engine that could freeze during the night.

Tor, Ingman, and Olaf took the long way home, not noticing the single set of snowshoe tracks they crossed on the trail. The Lokens' horse-drawn cutter glided silently through the snow-covered pines in the late afternoon sun.

Chapter 32
The Inside Man

The Lokens took their seats near the coal-burning stove in the Chicago, St. Paul, Minneapolis, and Omaha passenger car. Chief Namakagon and a dozen Loken lumberjacks filed in after them. They were taking two days off work to witness the Governor of Wisconsin pay tribute to Tor and Chief Namakagon for their heroism. Behind the crew came a crowd of townspeople.

Conductor Clyde Williams began working his way up the aisle, calling for and punching tickets. He finally reached the warm end of the car. "Land's sakes! It has been a good while since you rode our train, Olaf. Grand to see you are out and about."

"Well, Clyde. You and the missus doin' all right?"

"Fine, fine. Say, that was some fancy footwork done by your boy and the Chief here. Those two scalawags should have known better than to tangle with the Loken camp, ay?"

"Well, I don't know about that. What I do know, Clyde, is that the new governor thinks this is a fine opportunity to gather some pinery votes. It's high time we see someone from the statehouse up here in the woods."

The conductor punched the last of the tickets. Thirty minutes later, the train rolled into the Hayward yard. Ingman hired a cutter and he, Olaf, Tor, and Chief Namakagon were soon at the front door of Adeline's boarding house.

Ingman dropped his bag in his room and headed downtown again. Namakagon and Olaf stayed in the parlor. Tor found Rosie and her mother in the kitchen, preparing supper.

"Mrs. Ringstadt, well, um, I was wondering, ah, if you would let Rosie, um, take a walk with me. It's such a nice winter afternoon and all. It truly would be a shame to waste such a fine day, Mrs. Ringstadt."

Rose looked at her mother with pleading eyes.

"Without a chaperone?" Adeline replied. "Oh, my. How would that look to the neighbors? I suppose I could come along, just to make it proper."

"Oh, ah, no, ma'am," said Tor. "I wouldn't want you to take time from your good cookin' and all. Um, I'll look out for Rosie. I'll be a fine chaperone!"

"Oh, my, my. I just don't know, Tor."

Rosie looked at her mother with the same pleading expression.

"Well, I suppose it would be all right, considering you are known by all

169

as a champion, Tor. Now, you will need to keep your distance, though. I do not want to hear a word of gossip. And, Rose, you be certain to keep your face and neck covered up against the cold. I cannot have you catching the grippe, young lady. It's going around, they say."

A light snow began to fall as Tor and Rose walked down the steps onto the street. They strolled up the road, passing new homes, each with its own small barn in the back yard. As soon as the boarding house was out of sight, Rose untied her long scarf and let it hang off her shoulders. She took Tor's hand, pulling him closer. They walked arm in arm past home after new home.

"Rosie, are you going to the Governor's talk tomorrow morning?"

"Going? Why, I wouldn't miss it for all the world! After all, the hero of the day is my beau, you know." Tor was speechless once again.

Ingman walked down the frozen, rutted street toward the Lumberman's Bank, then stepped up onto the boardwalk dodging Christmas shoppers. He opened the bank's heavy door. Four kerosene lamps hung from the high, tin ceiling, illuminating the lobby. Ned Dearborne stood at his usual post behind the iron-barred teller's window. Ingman approached, placing a five-dollar bill on the counter.

"Say, Ned. Give me five silver dollars."

Ned Dearborne looked up. His eyes widened. "Yes Sir, Mr. Loken," he said, reaching for the coins. He placed the silver on the counter. "Mr. Loken, that is some story I read in the paper about your nephew and the old Indian."

"Yes, yes. Ain't it somethin' they were in here pickin' up the money for the Loken camp right before it happened? Why, that is some rare coincidence. Wouldn't you agree, Ned?"

"I'm not sure what you're saying, Mr. Loken. You don't thing *I* had anything to do with it, do you?"

"How else would King Muldoon have known about the money my nephew withdrew?"

"See, here, Loken, I would have long ago been handed my walking papers if ever I told *anyone* about *anybody's* banking business. I *never* discuss bank business, Mr. Loken. That includes the money your nephew drew out last week. What makes you think the boy didn't shoot off his own mouth?"

"So you did not speak with Muldoon in the hotel on the evening before the robbery?" persisted Ingman.

Dearborn drew back, eyes wider than before. "I'm telling you, Loken, I don't discuss bank business with anybody."

"Then you *did* meet with Muldoon."

"No. I did not!"

"Are you telling me you were not in the hotel bar after work that day? You were not engaged in conversation with King Muldoon and Sam Rouschek at the far end of the bar?"

"No. I was not."

The bell above the front door rang as a man entered from the street.

"So, Dearborne, if I asked the hotel bartender, he would tell me that he did not see you talkin' to Muldoon and Rouschek that day?"

"I have another customer to take care of," said the teller. "Meet me in the hotel bar after the bank closes. I'm sure we can settle this."

Ingman stared coldly into Dearborn's eyes as he picked up his coins one by one. "Yes. I am sure we can. I'll be waiting for you, Ned."

Dearborn's hands were trembling and his face beaded with sweat as he watched Ingman leave the bank. Ingman crossed the street to Pete Foster's Saloon. Blackie Jackson and seven Loken men lined the bar, eager to hear what Ingman had learned.

"Give my boss here a beer, Pete," Blackie called to the bartender. "He's lookin' pretty dang thirsty." Then, to Ingman, "So, Boss, is Dearborne the one?"

"No question he tipped off King Muldoon, Blackie. He wouldn't say it straight out, but he might as well have. He was squirmin' like a night crawler in a trout pond."

"Want me to square things up, Boss?"

Ingman looked into Blackie's dark eyes, then at the other Loken camp men in the bar. He took a long pull from his glass of beer, set it on the bar and wiped his mouth with his sleeve. "Not yet. Dearborne wants me to meet him after the bank closes. I want to hear what he has to say. Then we'll decide his fate."

"Where's this meetin' gonna take place?"

"In the hotel bar."

"We'll go with you."

"No. No, I'll handle it myself. No point in scarin' him half to death, at least not yet."

"You figure he's alone in this deal?" Charlie Martin asked.

"That, Charlie, is what I need to find out. I want to know if our spat is with a ten-dollar-a-month teller or the bank president himself. Either way, somebody from that bank over there is goin' to pay dearly for this."

"I say we handle this behind the hotel, not in it," said Blackie.

"Ease off on the throttle, Blackie, 'fore ya jump the track. Right now, what I want to know is who all's involved. Once we know, then I will decide if we let the sheriff do his yob or tend to this ourselves."

"Boss, no pinery lawman is gonna go up against King Muldoon. I say we give 'em a taste of jackpine justice." He tipped back his beer.

"We will see what comes of this. You may well get your wish, Blackie."

At three o'clock, the shades at the Lumberman's Bank went down. Ned Dearborne emerged from the narrow alley next to the bank at five past. Ingman and Charlie Martin followed him into the hotel. Charlie took a seat in the lobby and looked on as Ingman spoke with the teller in the hotel bar.

"What do you want from me, Mr. Loken?"

"You know what I want, Dearborne. I want to know who tipped off

171

Sam Rouschek and Percy Wilkins about the money my nephew withdrew from the bank where you work."

"All right. All right. King Muldoon does business in our bank. In fact, it was Muldoon who got me my job. I regret I am beholdin' to him, but beholdin' I am.

"A while back, oh, say six or eight weeks ago, he asked me to let him know anytime the Namakagon Timber Company made a big deposit or withdrawal. I thought he was just keeping track of a competitor. I did not know about any robbery. I would not be part of any such crime. You must believe me."

"Was your boss in on this?"

"Mr. Forbert? Oh, no, no. This here was my doin' alone, I am sorry to say. Why, Mr. Forbert would fire me on the spot if he knew."

"So it was you who told Muldoon, and his thieves about my nephew making the withdrawal?"

"No. Well, ah, yes, ah, Muldoon, but not the thieves. No, not the thieves!"

"Ned Dearborne, I know for a fact you were right here in this bar that night with King Muldoon and Sam Rouschek, the man now sittin' in the yailhouse and surely prison-bound."

"No, no! Well … ah, yes, Sam Rouschek was here, but I never talked to him. You must believe me, Mr. Loken. You must!"

"You are yust as guilty of this robbery as if you, yourself, held that revolver on my nephew."

"No, no, I tell ya. I had no idea what was being planned. Please, you've got to believe me."

"I've a mind to turn you over to the sheriff."

Dearborne reached into his pocket for an envelope. "Here, Loken. I knew it might come to this so I pulled all my savings out of the bank. You can have it all. Just spare me and let me keep my job."

"You think you can pay your way out of this? Why, you don't make money enough in a year to buy yourself a ticket out of this fix."

"Be reasonable, Mr. Loken. Please. I have two hundred for you in that envelope if you just forget about the whole deal."

"Two hundred? Why I spent that much on beer yust this past week.

"That's all I can muster. I have no more."

"Maybe you need some time off in the state penitentiary."

"Show me some mercy, Mr. Loken. Think of my little ones. I can't go to jail."

Ingman stared coldly into Ned's eyes. "I think it's time we stop this folly and go see the sheriff," he said, grabbing his hat from the table and pushing his chair back.

"Wait, wait," Dearborne pleaded, putting his hand on Ingman's arm. "I'll give you my savings and something else."

"What?"

"I'll give you any information you want on King Muldoon."

"Well, now. That seems to be your way, Ned. The way I see it, you are in a real pickle. A real pickle, indeed. If your boss gets word of this little indiscretion of yours, you'll be out of a yob. Never work in any bank again, most likely. If the sheriff hears tell you were in on this with Sam Rouschek, you'll end up in yail. If King Muldoon hears you told me he is involved, well, Ned, you will likely become food for a pack of wolves out in some swamp. Ya, Ned Dearborne, you are in a real pickle."

"Please, show me mercy. Please, Mr. Loken. Be reasonable."

"Reasonable?" said Ingman. He opened the envelope and thumbed the edges of the twenty-dollar bills. "I will show you yust how reasonable I can be. I will take this as your contribution toward the capture of the criminals who tried to rob Chief Namakagon and my nephew last week. I'll see to it they get it. You damn well better have learnt your lesson, Ned, and when ol' Phineas Muldoon comes to you for information on the Loken account, you tell him we've pulled our money out and put it all into a bank in Chicago."

"Oh, thank you, Mr. Loken. I never meant to cause your outfit or anyone else no harm and it'll never happen again. Thank you, Mr. Loken. Thank ..."

"I ain't quite done," interrupted Ingman. "I want you to tell me if Phineas Muldoon gave Sam Rouschek the go-ahead to rob my nephew. Did he or didn't he?"

"I can't say for sure. I left before they had their conversation," he replied, shaking. "But I know King Muldoon would have few other reasons to speak with a ne'er-do-well like Sam Rouschek."

Ingman silently considered these words before emptying his glass. "Dearborne, we are not finished with this. And don't you ever forget how close you came to yail or worse—or how yenerous the Lokens are bein' to you." He stood, pulled on his mackinaw, and put on his hat.

The bank teller breathed a sigh of relief. "Oh, no, Mr. Loken, I won't forget. No sir. Thank you. Oh, thank you so much!"

Ingman smiled at a fashionably dressed young woman who was sitting on the piano bench near the window. He tipped his hat, gave her a wink, and left the bar. Charlie Martin joined him in the lobby. Ned Dearborne remained at his table, shaking and wet with perspiration, as Ingman and Charlie left the hotel, crossing the busy street to Pete Foster's Saloon.

Chapter 33
The Governor's Ear

Tor opened the boarding house door for Rosie. She hung their coats and her scarf on the hall tree. He took a seat in the parlor along with Chief Namakagon, Willard and Mildred Rogers, and his father. Before them, near the front window, stood a ten-foot Christmas tree decorated with hundreds of tiny paper snowflakes. On the end of each branch perched a single, white candle. A satin angel looked down from the top and a bright red ribbon spiraled, around to the bottom. The fresh scent of balsam filled the air.

Rose went to the kitchen to help her mother prepare supper while Tor picked up a copy of Harper's Weekly from the window sill. He paged through it, thinking more about Rosie than the words and pictures in the magazine.

A half hour later Rose returned to the parlor. Seating herself at the piano, she entertained the guests with her songs. Ingman returned from Pete Foster's saloon, joining the others in the parlor and singing much louder than the rest. Supper was served at five o'clock sharp.

The next morning, bright red and green ribbons decorated the depot platform. The governor was coming.

Hayward's own five-piece marching band was warming up in the waiting room when the train arrived. They rushed out onto the platform and lined up against the depot wall in the frigid morning air.

Four stomps from the right foot of the tuba player and they all broke into *The Battle Hymn of the Republic*, the only tune they knew. Blowing off steam, the locomotive rolled to a stop, brass bell ringing. A large group of onlookers stretched to see the governor through the frosted windows of his brightly painted car.

The conductor stepped out of the next car, followed by three uniformed policemen. Two newspaper reporters emerged. One set up a large camera on a larger wooden tripod. He fiddled with the equipment before giving a wave to a man looking on from the governor's private car.

Out stepped Governor Jeremiah Rusk, waving his top hat at the cheering crowd and smiling for the camera.

Pffft. The flash powder ignited, sending a puff of smoke into the air and bringing more cheers.

"Noble citizens of the great Wisconsin pinery," he began, quieting the audience, "as your duly elected leader, I welcome this opportunity to inform you that your futures, as well as the very futures of your children and grandchildren, are in the safest of hands under my new administration. Your wishes and needs will always receive the highest priority in my office as I make decisions that will …"

On and on he rambled, illuminating every corner of his long career in government. An aide, realizing the governor had lost the crowd's attention, gave him a nudge, prompting him to finish his long talk with, "…and, good

174

citizens, every attempt will be made to make the future of this part of Wisconsin as bright as these two, newly minted, medals of honor." His aide held two sparkling gold medals high in the air, re-capturing the onlookers' attention.

"And now," shouted the governor, "just where might I find these two heroes of the people of the great State of Wisconsin?"

"They're standin' right in front of you, Governor," came a shout.

"Well now, so they are. Come up and be recognized!"

Namakagon and Tor stepped forward. Examining the chief's bearskin robe, the governor exclaimed, "So, you must be Chief Namakagon, the man who single-handedly brought the murderous villain to his just reward?"

"Let us just say I attempted to bring him in," replied Namakagon. "It seems he chose his own reward."

"Well, Chief," he bellowed, waving a single finger in the air, "I hereby declare that you are a marvelous, brave, and courageous man, you are."

He turned to Tor. "And you, young man, you must be Tor Loken, the young champion who disarmed the despicable desperado who would have taken your lives if not your money."

"Well, sir, I just hit him with my knapsack, sir. I don't know that he was so bound and determined to shoot, but I wasn't willing to wait around to see."

Governor Rusk laughed along with the crowd, Olaf, Ingman, and Rose looking on with pride. Nonetheless," shouted the statesman, "I am here today to decree and declare," he said, raising his index finger high in the air again, "that this day will be forever known to all who bear witness as that day when Governor Jeremiah McCain Rusk, Chief Executive and Pilot of the great State of Wisconsin, came to the pinery to honor Ogimaa Mikwam-migwan, also called Chief Namakagon, and Master Tor Loken as two courageous heroes who did, between them, upset the plans of two dastardly criminals to rob the Chicago, St. Paul, Minneapolis, Omaha, and Northwestern Railroad train near this fine metropolitan community. Furthermore, I do declare that these medals I now proudly bestow upon you do hereby and forever designate you as being officially regarded and respected by all who look upon you as trustworthy, upstanding representatives of our citizenry and genuine—bona fide—heroes!"

Pffft. The flash powder ignited as the Governor placed the ribbon and polished brass medal over Tor's head. The crowd cheered. Tor's father looked on from his chair, eyes moist with pride. No one cheered louder than Rosie.

The governor turned to Namakagon to hang a medal around his neck. Instead, the old Indian held out his hand. Governor Rusk shrugged his shoulders, grinned, and dropped the award in Namakagon's palm. He turned back to the crowd, smiling and waving again.

Another tray of flash powder went off, bringing more cheers.

Following the ceremony, the steam locomotive pulled out of the Hayward station, leaving a long black plume of coal smoke in the icy air. The train carried twenty-three passengers including six in the plush, private car used by the governor on his tours of the State of Wisconsin.

175

Accompanying Governor Rusk were the two heroes of the day, Tor Loken and Chief Namakagon, along with Olaf, Ingman, and Rose, all invited to attend the seventeen-mile journey north to Cable. There, the Cable rail yard turntable would direct the engine back toward Madison for the Governor's return.

The six passengers sat around a mahogany table in comfortable parlor chairs upholstered in red velvet. A porter brought tea and an assortment of fresh pastries.

"This is some fancy outfit you have here, Governor," said Tor, taking a bite out of a doughnut.

"Yes," the governor replied, "this is a fine car. It is made available by the railroad company so I can visit our Wisconsin towns and cities. It is not altogether different from an Indian chief riding from village to village on a beautiful white horse. Wouldn't you agree, Chief Namakagon?"

"Perhaps, Governor," he replied, "it is better to walk a hundred miles than to ride a borrowed horse."

The statesman bristled. "Chief Namakagon, I am not now, nor have I ever been, inclined to exchange favors for political advantage. It's true, I admit we barter on the floor of the legislature, but, I can say with pride, no railroad car could *ever* sway me, no matter how comfortable."

"Well *I* think it's simply wonderful," said Rose. "Why, I would ride around and around the world if I had such a luxurious carriage." She pointed out the large window. "Look, we're coming to the railroad trestle."

"So this is where the criminal met his just fate?" asked the governor.

"Yes," answered Namakagon. "But justice had little to do with it. Had Wilkins given himself up, I believe then we would have seen justice done."

"He chose his own trail," said Olaf, "as do we all. He had no way of knowing the outcome of his journey any more than do we."

As the train crossed the trestle, Governor Rusk slid open a window, removed his beaver skin top hat and poked his head out, inspecting the river below. His bushy hair and long beard waved wildly in the wind.

Tracks left in the snow from the previous week's incident were faint but visible. The governor pulled in his head, pushed back his ruffled hair, and popped his hat back on. "I must declare! That is quite a drop to the river below," he said to Namakagon. "Now where was it you captured this devil?"

"Beyond that ridge," said the chief, pointing.

"Quite a hike without snowshoes in this deep snow," said Tor. "And you can see another ridge behind it. That's where the outlaw bushwhacked the chief. Right up here is where the train was stopped and the holdup took place."

176

Olaf, Ingman, Rose, and Governor Rusk heard the tale as told by the heroes of the day. As the train passed over the Pac-wa-wong Springs, smoke from the Indian lodges drifted high into the sky. The train later crossed another large trestle and began the final, uphill climb to the next lumber town. They soon pulled up to the Cable depot where Blackie, Charlie Martin, and the rest of the Loken camp workers disembarked.

The governor and his guests remained in his private coach while other cars were switched for the return run. The gigantic turntable rotated until the engine faced south again. The cars were coupled again and the train was soon rolling back toward Hayward.

"Governor," said Olaf, "I wonder if you could help us with a legal matter."

"Well, now, I don't know … I don't deal with legal advice any more. You would be better off hiring …"

"Governor," interrupted Ingman, "this is a matter of great importance to yust about every lumberyack in the north. Thousands upon thousands of men and yust as many votes, sir." The governor's bushy eyebrows rose.

"Governor Rusk," Olaf explained, "this has to do with using our rivers and lakes to carry the logs to the mills. It affects every citizen from the northern corners of the pinery all the way to the Mississippi River."

The politician leaned back in his chair. "Tell me more, Loken."

"There's a fella up here by the name of Phineas Muldoon who bought up the Lake Namakagon dam. He now claims the right to charge half-a-dollar for any log that crosses his dam. I say the water belongs to the people and he has no right to lay a tariff on logs run downriver."

"This must be *King* Muldoon you speak of."

"Then you know him?"

"No, but I know of him. He has influence among the legislators."

"Does he have enough influence to stop us from using the river?" Ingman demanded. "Can this single man decide which lumber outfit goes bust, which lumberyack gets paid for his winter's work? Does Muldoon have influence over what is right and what is wrong?"

The governor paused, looked at Namakagon, then Tor and Rose. "Mister Loken …"

"Ingman, sir."

"Ingman, it is true the people own the waters of Wisconsin. But the state also gives permits to operate dams, and some of the dam owners have sought financial contributions from others to help offset their investments in the dams, investments that benefit *all* who drive logs to the mills."

Ingman spoke deliberately now. "Governor Rusk, the small lumber outfits, the ones who employ most of the lumberyacks in the pinery, make very little profit from each stick of pine. A big operator, a fella like King Muldoon, could easily buy up the dams, and then, by charging for the right to use the rivers, quickly force the small outfits into bankruptcy. That would mean the

177

men in the camps, *all eligible to vote, mind you,* might not get their pay in the spring. The State of Wisconsin needs to stand tall for these small camps and the many lumberyacks who work there. It's only right, Governor."

The train rumbled over the Mosquito Brook Bridge. Its whistle echoed down the valley.

"Ingman, Olaf, I am not in a position to give you my answer here and now. Let me have my office look into this question. I promise you I will have an answer for you soon. For the time being, let me leave you with this. The Northwest Ordinance, created almost a century ago, clearly states 'the waters of Wisconsin will be forever free,'" he said, slamming his fist on the red velvet arm of the chair. "And, by God, our state constitution uses the very same language to give the citizens of Wisconsin the undeniable right to use our lakes and streams without tariff, tax, toll or duty. I believe King Muldoon would not win his argument in a court of law.

"The challenge," he went on, "might be getting this into the courts before your company runs out of time. It would appear Muldoon knows well that if he stops your timber from reaching the mills, he wins. His next step would be to purchase your holdings and those of all the neighboring camps. He would buy them for pennies on the dollar, if that. All the timber, whether on the ice or still on the stump, would be his and his alone."

"Governor," asked Tor, "shouldn't it be up to the State of Wisconsin to arrest Muldoon if he doesn't let our pine go over the dam?"

"Well, Tor, the law says until he actually commits a crime, there is nothing that can be done."

"Does the same go for my men?" asked Olaf. "Do we have any laws protecting us like the laws that protect King Muldoon?"

Governor Rusk considered this. "The same goes for you and your men, Loken. The problem, my friend, is, the moment you run that first log across the dam, Muldoon will claim you are guilty of trespass. Muldoon could have you arrested easier than the other way around."

"That just doesn't seem fair, Governor," said Rosie.

The train crossed the last trestle before Hayward, sounding another double whistle.

"Fair?" he replied. "Young lady, we try hard to make laws that best serve the citizens of this state. It is not always easy, miss, and the laws we create, although fair to most, are not always seen as fair to all."

Chief Namakagon stood. "There is deep wisdom in your words 'the waters of Wisconsin will be forever free', Governor. These words should be the first spoken whenever your legislators meet. You see, Governor, the waters of Wisconsin are the blood in the veins of this land. Our waters must always be protected for the benefit of all those who come.after we are gone."

The train began to slow as it approached the Hayward yard. The smell of freshly cut white pine filled the air again. With a rush of steam and the squeal of steel brakes, the train pulled up to the Hayward station.

178

The governor shook the hands of everyone on the platform. "I shall return, good citizens. Your kindness has made this enchanting metropolis my paramount favorite of all the cities and towns in the great State of Wisconsin!"

Governor Jeremiah M. Rusk departed. The whistle blew, the engine's bell rang, and soon the train thundered toward Madison with stops at the Governor's many other paramount favorite Wisconsin cities and towns.

The Lokens, Rosie, and Namakagon crossed the tracks, and headed for downtown Hayward. Ingman and Olaf stopped at Pete Foster's Saloon while the others continued down the sidewalk, crossed Second Street, and headed up the hill toward the boarding house.

"Chief Namakagon, I've been meaning to ask you something," said Tor. "Last month, when Sam Rouschek had us pinned down before the muzzle of his revolver in that passenger car, his partner, Percy Wilkins, said something about you and some silver mine. Do you recollect that?"

"All too clearly, my friend. All too clearly."

"So, is there silver to be found around here?"

"Far more than most people realize, Tor. There are several mines in the area that are producing copper and silver, and I am aware of one that may yield a fair amount of gold."

"I've heard the men in camp talk about the iron mines up near Hurley," Tor said, "but I didn't know there was silver. What did Wilkins mean when he said you had a silver mine?"

Namakagon stopped, considering the question. "Many years ago, when I came here, I was given a great, great responsibility," he explained. "I was shown to a cave where there are outcroppings of silver, ready for the taking." He pulled up his left sleeve and showed his silver wristband. "This is from that cave. I have shown no one the way, and I have removed only a small amount of the silver to purchase supplies for those in need."

"Why, Chief," declared Rose, "you could be rich! You could be as wealthy as a king."

"Young lady, I may not have a private rail car with velvet curtains, but I am already *rich*, as you say. I have the trees and the sky, the rivers and the lakes. I have the birds, the fish, the deer. I have a warm lodge, dogs who love me, friends who tolerate me. There is food on my table. I have my freedom and no amount of money could inspire me to trade places with another."

"Rosie," said Tor, "Look at King Muldoon. For all the money and lumber camps and mills he owns, he is still not satisfied. He won't be until he owns it all, and even then he will want more."

"But, still, wouldn't it be better to take the silver from the mine and put it to good use—just like the pine in the forests is being put to good use?"

"The silver is far safer where it lies now than in any bank vault," said the chief. "When my people need it, it will be there for them. But if I were to turn it into dollars, it would soon be spent. When it is gone, then what? No, Rose, it is a treasure now. Once spent, it is no longer a treasure. It is nothing

179

more than a memory. But you are right, it is like the pine. Few lumber camp owners care about the future of the land. They do nothing to plan for the future of our forests. They cut, cut, cut. This is a disgraceful way to serve our Mother Earth. No, Rose, the silver is better left where it lies."

"What if someone else finds it?" asked Tor.

"Young woodsman, only a few forest animals and this old Indian know the way. It is safe. Now I must count on you both to help me keep it forever safe by never speaking of it again."

Rose, Tor, and Namakagon climbed the steps of the boarding house, greeted by the aromas of the balsam Christmas tree and freshly baked bread.

Ingman and Olaf arrived just as the others were sitting down at the supper table. Adeline carried out two large platters, each bearing a roasted Canada goose. She placed them on the table with mashed potatoes and gravy, squash, cornbread muffins, cranberry relish, baked beans, and mincemeat pie.

After supper, the guests all met in the parlor to sing while Rosie played Christmas carols on her mother's upright piano. They sang and danced, on and on, celebrating well into the night.

Far across town, in a grand Victorian mansion, a single light shone from Phineas Muldoon's third story window. The short, white-haired man sat alone in his library before a large, roll-top desk. On the desk, a kerosene lamp illuminated the map of Lake Namakagon that lay before him. Squinting through the lens of a magnifying glass, he studied the lands surrounding the lake.

The old man placed the glass on the desk and opened a drawer. He picked up a pen, dipped the tip into the inkwell, and then drew a circle on the map around the land owned by the Loken family.

"Come spring, Olaf Loken, you and your pitiful Namakagon Timber Company will be at my mercy. You will see what happens when you interfere in my business. And you will learn why I am called *King*. For, you see, Loken, I—have—you—now."

Phineas Muldoon laid his pen on the blotter and capped the inkwell. Pushing his chair back, he stood, staring at the map with a grin. He leaned over his desk, cupped his hand around the glass chimney of the lamp, and, blowing into the chimney, he snuffed out the flame.

As the room went black King Muldoon repeated his words into the darkness. "I have you now, Loken, I—have—you—now."

Chapter 34
The Loken Camp, January 1884

"Gee!" shouted the young lumberjack as he guided the team of Percherons. He followed Charlie Martin's sleigh through the yard and out onto the frozen bay, already crowded with logs. "Whoa," Tor ordered, before jumping from his roost atop the massive load of timber. "Good boys. Good boys," he said, unhitching the horses. He walked them a few yards ahead.

Clouds of steam drifted from the large animals into the frigid sky. Behind them stood a sleigh loaded with fifteen white pine logs, each twenty feet long and from three to four feet in diameter. Tor released the safety chains from the side of the load and climbed to the top again. He pulled the heavy chains up, heaving them over and onto the ice below. Descending again, he grabbed his peavey, jammed it behind the chock holding the bottom log in place and gave a hard pull on the handle. The chock fell free and Tor stepped back as the huge load of logs thundered down onto the ice.

The young lumberjack climbed back onto the sleigh. Using the peavey again, he rolled the remaining three logs onto the frozen lake. He jumped back down, secured his peavey, threw the heavy log chains back up onto the oak bunks of the sleigh, stepped up to the horses, and grasped the reins.

"Back, back," he said softly. The horses slowly backed up to the sleigh. Tor hitched them up, climbed aboard and, standing on the sleigh's front bunk, gave his steeds a *giddup*. The horses pulled the empty sleigh across the bay and up the bank, then down the slick ice road to the cuttings.

Blackie Jackson, top-loader on this job and Mason Fitch, the chainman, were topping off another load as Tor came around the last bend in the trail. When the sleigh ahead of him moved out, Tor pulled his rig alongside more logs left by the trail.

"Time to stop your loafin', fellas. I'm ready for another load of toothpicks," shouted Tor.

"'Bout time you got here, boy," replied Blackie. "You been sittin' with your feet by the cook stove again?"

Blackie hooked a long oak pole into the rear bunk of the sleigh. The other end was laid perpendicular to the sleigh and rested on the frozen ground. Mason Fitch, still limping badly from his leg injury, did the same with a second oak pole. With these two heavy oak rails now forming a ramp, the two men used their peaveys to roll a pine log up and onto the bunks. Mason set the chocks and the log was secure.

Meanwhile, Tor unhitched the team and took the horses around to the side of the sleigh opposite the oak ramp. Mason laid a long chain on the ground between and parallel to the oak rails. One end of the chain was hooked around the center of the log they just loaded. Next, the standing end of the long chain was stretched straight out between the rails. With their peaveys, Mason and Blackie wrestled another log over to the ramp. Blackie jumped onto the sleigh. Mason threw the end of the chain over the log to Blackie. It now ran under, up, and across the center of the big log that lay on the ground. Blackie threw the chain down to Tor who secured the chain to the team's whiffletree. With one hand on the halter and a soft *giddup*, Tor walked the horses ahead slowly. The chain pulled taut, and the eleven-hundred-pound log rolled effortlessly up and onto the sleigh bunks. The log was chocked in place, the chain set for the next log, and the process was repeated again and again until the sleigh held twenty-three logs. The sound of Sourdough's loud gabreel announced dinner.

Tor took his team to the front of the sleigh while Mason gathered up the chain and threw it up to Blackie one last time. Blackie slung it over the top log and down the side. He jumped to the ground, grabbed the chain end, securing the front end of the load. Mason threw another safety chain across the back end of the load. Blackie snapped the chain binders down and climbed to the top of the logs. With the team hitched again, Mason, too, scrambled up next to Blackie, followed by Tor. A sharp whistle and a flip of the reins from Tor and the sleigh slid slowly down the ice road toward the lake. As the horses pulled they exhaled large clouds of vapor into the frigid air—clouds reminiscent of those left by steam locomotives.

The young teamster brought the load along the shore and nearer the camp than usual. With a *whoa boys*, they came to a stop. The men jumped down. Tor unhitched the team, leaving the sleigh load of timber on the ice. Following the others, he brought his team up the bank and into the lumber camp yard. The men entered the cook shanty for the midday dinner. Swede Carlson, a Loken camp teamster, followed them in.

Ingman stood by the stove warming his hands. He joined the other lumberjacks. "How's them logs a-haulin' today, fellas," asked Ingman.

"Plenty cold out there," answered Tor. "The ice roads are slicker than glass, Uncle Ingman. A star load floats down the trail like a dry leaf on a pond."

"Ya," said Swede, "youse can hear da sleighs a-comin' from vay up in da voods. Dat ice she squeals plenty loud under dem runners, ya."

"How cold do you figure it might be, Ingman?" asked Mason.

182

"Must be ten below zero or better," said Blackie, grabbing a piece of bread and smearing it with bacon grease.

Swede dipped a piece of blackjack into the pork gravy on his plate. "I yust for da life a me can't understand vy youse camp bosses don't have a dang termometer 'round, yust to check now and den."

"There's good reason for it, Swede," said Ingman. "If you lumberyacks knew how cold it really was out there, you'd all be crowdin' 'round the cook stove all day and you'd get no work done at all. The trees don't care how dang cold it is, Swede. Neither should you."

"Vell, I'm yust sayin'," groused Swede.

"Uncle Ingman, I saw two eagles workin' on that nest on the north shore. They were carryin' some pretty big sticks up to it."

"First sign of spring," said Blackie. "Speakin' of spring, how's that towboat comin' along?"

"Good," said Ingman. "Dang good, in fact. Louie Thorp has her built and ready to paint. Louie and Gust have been puttin' in some long days. Gust has the second steam enyun yust about ready for a test run. He tells me that as soon as he finishes the paddlewheel, we'll be in business. Ol' Gust seems to know his stuff, all right. Good blacksmith, he is. Knows them dang contraptions inside and out. The boat should be done by the end of February, I'd say."

Swede laughed. "Lotta good dat is ven da ice she don't leave da lake till April or May, en so? I tink a good ox team iss da best vay to move timber. Don't need no dang boat."

"Swede, you cantankerous old farmer," said Ingman, "you show me how them two oxen of yours can push a million board foot of pine across this here lake and I'll wash your socks for a year." Ingman gave Swede a stout pat on the back.

"Vell, Boss, I'm yust sayin' …"

"You best catch up with the times, Swede," said Mason. "Machines are replacing animals. We now have steam power from the Atlantic to the Pacific. The days of horse teams and ox teams will soon come to a close. Steam engines will do all the work. Mark my words. Steam power is the way of the future. You best start thinkin' about that. This is eighteen and eighty-four!"

"Young vippersnappers like youse, Mason, ain't never gonna see da day ven ox teams don't do farm verk an' loggin'." Swede snapped. "Ain't no machine dat can hold a candle to ox. No sir! Dem ox, dey go anyvair. Dey move mountains. If yer *modern times* means no ox, Mason Fitch, den youse can yust count me out."

Blackie changed the subject: "Any more talk about Muldoon's claim that he can charge us to float our pine across the dam, Boss?"

"Not since the letter we got from Governor Rusk sayin' we have free right to use the water. That letter will save us if we end up in court. Problem is, by the time it gets to court, there won't be enough water level to drive our timber. We need the runoff from the spring rains and snow melt to get our pine to the mills."

"So, what's the worst Muldoon could do?" said Tor, plopping a large scoop of beans onto his plate.

"Here's how I figure it," said Blackie. "Spring comes, the ice goes out and the Loken boat pushes our pine into the bay near the dam. Muldoon brings all his men down from his East Lake camp and they hol' up at the dam waitin' for us. We show up with our jacks, each man at the ready for a brawl. Them and us scuffle a bit, we push them aside and take control of the dam. Two days later, our timber is headin' downriver and we're whistlin' *Oh Susannah* in Johnny Pion's hotel bar."

"Better off usin' ox team dan boat," mumbled Swede.

"I don't figure Muldoon will give up that easy, Blackie," said Ingman. "You heard what he said about being in charge of the law in the pinery. He will probably hire some lawmen to guard the dam."

"Then why not bring in a couple lawmen of our own?" said Tor. "Uncle Ingman, if Muldoon's lawmen are face to face with our lawmen, and our lawmen show off the letter from Governor Rusk, well, don't you think it would turn the table?"

"Well, that's a good thought, Tor. Let me hash it over with your pa."

"Lot less trouble if you yust use good ox team instead of boat," said Swede as he stuffed a square of johnnycake into his mouth.

Mason shook his head in amazement. The others laughed as the cookee took their empty plates. Ingman headed for the lodge, Tor crossed the yard to the horse barn, and the others left for the cuttings again.

In the barn, Gust and Louie were finishing the large oak braces which secured the engine to the boat's hull. Gust flipped open his wooden rule, took some measurements, and made some notes on a slip of paper. "I'm gonna need those four roller bearings for the paddlewheel," he said. "Here," he said as he handed the slip of paper to Tor, "you get this to your pa or Ingman, and get me these parts."

"Need anything else?"

"No ... well, tell them we will need a bottle of champagne to smack against her hull when we launch her."

"Don't hold your breath, Gust. You know my uncle."

Tor crossed the yard again. He climbed the lodge steps, stamped the snow off his boots, and walked in, closing the big door behind him.

"Pa," he said, handing his father the slip of paper, "Gust says we need some parts for the boat. I'd be willin' to take a run to Hayward to pick them up."

"Sounds to me, Olaf, like someone is eager to see his gal, ya,?" said Ingman."

"I'm not keen on the idea, Son. It might not be safe. I won't risk sendin' you into town right now."

"But, Pa ..."

"No. You're not going, Tor. And that's that."

184

"I can send Blackie," said Ingman. "Ya, he'd go for a night in town."

"How about Gust?" said Olaf. "He knows what he's lookin' for. Maybe we should just send him on this trip."

"I could go with Gust or Blackie if you want," said Tor.

"I must say, Olaf, that boy of yours is a stubborn one," said Ingman. "Wonder where he gets that?"

"Must be from his mother," said Olaf.

"Then I can go, Pa?"

"No. Tor, you are not going. Don't ask again."

Tor went back to the horse barn feeling dejected. "Drat that dang King Muldoon!" he shouted across the yard. Two draft horses tied to a post near the filing shed turned their heads to look at him. They watched Tor open the small door at the corner of the horse barn and step inside.

"Gust," shouted Tor, "Pa and Uncle Ingman are workin' on gettin' those bearings for you." He hung up his coat, grabbed a plane, and spent a few minutes touching up some rough spots on the boat. He could not get his Rosie off his mind now, knowing he came close to seeing her again. He put down the plane, grabbed his coat again, and left the barn.

The bright sunlight reflecting off the white landscape made Tor squint as he stepped out into the still air. He walked past the filing shed and out the gate, following the north trail up to the cuttings. Within minutes he could hear the chug, chug, chug of the donkey engine through the cold, still air. He followed the sound back into the woods and up the hill. Bright yellow letters on the side of the steam engine spelled out *CLEMENTINE*.

"So, how are you and your best girl, Clementine, gettin' on, Junior?" Tor teased, slapping the engine's hot boiler with his chopper.

"Clementine? Why, she sings sweet as bluebirds in springtime and she don't ask me for no money or free beers."

Junior waved, hailing Elmer Schmidt, the teamster waiting at the bottom of the grade. Elmer motioned and Junior threw the big oak lever. The long chain tightened and the donkey engine labored as the log sleigh began to inch toward them. Once on its way, it climbed the hill at a steady pace. A column of smoke from the boiler stretched straight up into the cold, blue sky.

"Here comes one hell of a big load of pine, Tor," shouted Junior. "Biggest one yet. Elmer's toploader wouldn't stack 'em so high if not for ol' Clementine, here."

They watched as the load crested the hill. Junior eased off the steam.

"The sleigh track is plenty slick today, Elmer," shouted Junior. "We got a sand man waitin' for you near the bottom of the grade if you get goin' too fast. Just give Ole a wave if you want him to slow you down some."

"Slow down my sweet Aunt Fanny," shouted the teamster as he hitched his team and climbed to the top of the load. Tor jumped onto the sleigh, climbed to the top, and stood next to Elmer for the ride down the hill.

Elmer gave a whistle and off they went, slowly at first. The huge load picked up speed as they descended the slight grade. Ahead was the sand man, leaning on his scoop shovel.

"Gimme some sand, Ole," shouted the teamster with a wave.

The man with the shovel didn't move.

Faster and faster they descended until the two-horse team was no longer pulling the load.

Tor could see the horses would be crushed if they couldn't keep up. "Sand! Sand! Sand!" he cried out.

The man stood motionless as the sleigh picked up more speed. Tor heard the horses' hooves striking the front bunk of the sleigh.

"Sand! Sand!" screamed Tor and Elmer.

The man dropped his shovel and stepped back into the thick grove of spruce trees behind as the sleigh raced past.

The grade flattened out now, but Tor could see the turn in the ice road coming up fast. Nothing could slow the huge load as it skimmed across the slick, frozen trail. The horses raced to keep from going under.

"She won't make da bend!" screamed the teamster. "Yump for yer life, Tor!"

Tor looked at Elmer, realized he could do nothing to help, and jumped with all his strength, but slammed into balsam limbs that bounced him back into the logs on the runaway sleigh. He landed at the side of the track. The rear bunk brushed by his shoulder, tearing his mackinaw. The steel runner missed his left hand by less than an inch.

"Giddup! Giddup! Gee!" screamed the teamster trying to keep the team ahead of the sleigh. Into the curve they flew, a storm of hooves, snow, and ice flying in all directions. "Heeyaa. Giddup. Giddup! Giddup! *Giddup!*"

The sleigh groaned as the huge load leaned far to the left. The right runners lifted a foot off the trail, then two, then three. Just as the load was about to tip, the steel safety chains snapped, each with a rifle-like *crack!* The thousand pound logs thundered off the sleigh and into the brush along the trail. The teamster deftly sprang from log to log as they dashed out from under his feet. The sleigh shook violently as the timber flew off, then slammed back onto the sleigh track with a crash. Elmer calmly brought his team to a stop. He jumped down and ran to the horses, reassuring them with his gentle hand and soft words. Looking back, he saw his boss' son lying motionless along the ice road. Beyond, running down the sleigh trail toward them, came Junior Kavanaugh.

"Tor! Tor!" screamed Junior as he raced down the hill. Elmer reached him first. He pushed some of the snow off Tor's face and neck.

Tor looked up. "You all right, Elmer?"

"Me? God almighty, Tor, iss you hurt?"

The boy slowly sat up, wiping more snow from his face. "Find my hat," was all he said.

Junior ran up to them, sliding to a stop on the slick ice road. "Tor, what the hell you doin' sittin' in a snow bank when there's work to be done?"

Unamused, Tor slowly stood. Elmer kicked around in the snow finding Tor's hat, a piece of the brim cleanly sliced through by a steel runner. He shook it off and handed it to Tor who was now standing.

Tor slapped snow from his britches and coat. He tried to dig the snow out of his collar, then looked down the trail at the pile of logs scattered into the woods. "Elmer, your horses, they get busted up?"

"Horses all right, tanks be to God an' good luck. Ya know I gotta have dat team to put crops in, come spring."

"What the hell happened, Elmer?" shouted Junior. "I ain't never seen you drop no load of pine before. You fall asleep?"

"You best you shut yer mouth, Yunior, or I shut it for ya. Dis iss no fault of mine. Goddang Ole Hanson didn't do his yob. A shovel of sand, and I'd been fine all da vay to da lake."

"Where did he go?" yelled Junior, looking back up the grade. They walked up the hill to the shovel and sand barrel. The sand man's boot tracks led them back into the thick, short spruces. There, lying in the snow, head bleeding, was Ole Hanson. A three-foot pine limb lay next to him.

"Someone must've bushwhacked Ole," shouted Junior.

The boot tracks led farther into the pines before changing to those left by a man on skis.

"Junior," ordered Tor, "you get back up to the donkey, fast. This fella might have bigger plans than upsetting just one sleigh."

Junior raced up the grade, grabbed a shovel and stood watch.

Below, Elmer and Tor looked at the tracks in the snow. Unable to follow a man on skis in the deep snow, Tor and Elmer helped Ole down the trail to the empty log sleigh.

Elmer used the horses to clear the trail of logs. The skilled teamster then hitched the team to the sleigh again and took Tor and Ole down the ice road toward camp. As the horse team pulled the empty sleigh onto the frozen lake, the men saw the plume of black smoke coming up from the yard.

"Fire!" shouted Tor, pointing toward the barn.

Elmer snapped the reins, gave a shrill whistle, and yelled, "Heeyaa! Giddup!" The horses galloped across the ice and up the bank to the camp.

Sourdough was already in the yard blowing on the gabreel. Tex Ketchum pounded on the dinner bell with a hammer. A dozen men had already assembled to fight the blaze.

The cloud of smoke coming from the barn grew larger. Tor ran through the open barn doors and led the last of the horses out before dashing off to the filing shed where he grabbed a mall. He raced back to the barn where he broke enough fence rails out of the hog pen to let the pigs escape from the fire.

Tor then joined the others who were carrying water from a hole cut in the ice. Lacking enough men to form a bucket brigade, they ran up from the lake with water sloshing from their buckets. Each man threw what water remained onto the fire, now growing too fast for the small crew.

Then, racing down the trail, fishtailing through the gate, came Blackie Jackson on a timber sleigh filled with men. Behind him was Swede Carlson with the tanker. A dozen more men soon showed up. Within minutes the fire was out and the men began rounding up the animals, repairing the hog pen, and cleaning up the wet, black mess.

Tor ran to the lodge where his father had watched the events unfold through the window. "Pa," he shouted as he entered the lodge, "we got bushwhacked up on the trail!"

Olaf Loken looked at him, puzzled.

"Somebody tried to wreck us, Pa. He took off on skis. Whoever it was, he must've set the barn afire, too!"

"Somebody tried to wreck you? What? What do you mean?"

"Ole Hanson got beat over the head and wasn't there to sand the ice road. Elmer's sleigh got goin' so fast it couldn't hold the track. We lost the whole dang load. We could have lost the whole rig, horses, Elmer and all."

"And you say this fella was on skis?"

"Yes, Pa, skis. There was no catchin' him. We were on our way back here when we saw the smoke. He probably stopped here to set fire to the barn before he skedaddled."

Olaf looked at his son, considering what had transpired. "Tor, saddle your mare. Get over to Chief Namakagon's camp. Tell him what happened. Tell him about the man on skis. He'll know what to do. Go, make haste!"

Minutes later Tor raced across the lake to the nearby island. Chief Namakagon was already hitching his dogs to his sled. Tor rode up to the dogsled and told the story.

Namakagon said a few words to Tor, pointed toward the dam, and grabbed the handrails of his sled, shouting "Mush!"

Waabishki and Makade raced down the hill and onto the ice with the sled and their master behind. Tor jumped from his horse and entered the chief's lodge. He emerged in seconds, carrying Namakagon's long, blackpowder rifle.

The black mare took Tor across the lake. Following the chief's instructions, he headed for the cattail marsh upstream from King Muldoon's dam. There, he waited.

Namakagon's dogsled sped through the Namakagon Timber Company yard. As he passed by the cook shanty, he saw men hauling out wet, smoke-blackened hay through the large, open doors of the horse barn. Rounding the barn, the chief quickly found the tracks of a single skier. He followed.

The trail took Namakagon and his dogs southward along the lake shore where the skier's tracks crossed the narrow bay and disappeared into the woods.

With a whistle and a "*mush,*" his dogs pulled the sled up the bank. The track wound back behind the cuttings, far from where the loggers worked.

Chief Namakagon continued through a stand of uncut pines. They towered above, blocking most of the light. With far less snow cover here,

Makade and Waabishki had better traction, picked up speed, and closed in on the culprit.

The skier's tracks turned back onto the lake. Across the ice raced Namakagon in pursuit. He followed the sign as it edged along the west shore, heading toward the narrows. With the sun now nearing the treetops, he spotted the lone skier ahead.

"Mush!" shouted Chief to his eager team.

Seeing the man ahead, the dogs picked up the pace. They rounded the point near the narrows with their quarry before them, unaware he was being pursued.

Suddenly, out from the brush a hundred yards away, stepped Tor Loken, brandishing the long rifle.

The man looked up, stopped, and turned toward shore, hoping to escape into the woods. Seeing the dogsled racing toward him from behind, he kicked off his skis, tried to climb the bank, but the drifted snow gave him no footing. He slipped and slid back onto the ice just as Chief Namakagon reached him. He fell under the dogs, screaming and swinging his arms.

Makade and Waabishki tore into him before their master could call them off. By the time he did, the man wanted only to surrender. The sleeves of his mackinaw were shredded. He had deep bites on his face, wrists, and hands. His boots, britches, and coat concealed more. Bright red blood was spattered across the snow under the cold, blue, late afternoon sky.

Namakagon jerked the man's knife from its sheath, pitching it far into the woods. He was shaking from fear and gasping for breath when Tor approached.

"Who sent you?" shouted Tor with authority.

"I don't ... I don't know what you're talkin' about, Sonny," gasped the fallen man. "Who the hell are you, anyway?"

"I am Tor Loken and I am about to release those dogs on you again unless you give me the truth. Now I will ask you only once more— who sent you? *Who!*"

The man looked up at Tor, then at Namakagon, then the dogs. "Muldoon. King Muldoon."

Chapter 35
Preparations

A light snow drifted down onto ice-covered Lake Namakagon. Olaf and Ingman sat before the large fireplace in the lodge. The fire crackled as the flames licked around the maple logs that lay across the andirons.

"Ingman, I think you should head into town first thing in the morning," Olaf said. "Telegraph the sheriff. Tell him to get out here and pick up this gol damn, dog-bit scoundrel. Take the south tote road so you do not have to cross Muldoon's dam. Then, after you send the telegram, I want you to talk with Bill Burns, the constable employed by the Omaha line. I doubt he has any obligations to Phineas Muldoon. Feel him out. Ask who he would recommend to help us keep the camp safe and secure, at least through the spring drive."

"I can make Cable by nine o'clock tomorrow mornin'. I know Burns from across the Cable House poker tables. I'll talk to him. Olaf, I'd say we best let the men in on what's goin' on here. They have a right to know."

"I agree. Yes, right after supper."

One hour later in the cook shanty, Junior Kavanaugh rapped a wooden spoon on a soup kettle to get the men's attention.

Blackie and Ingman each grasped a side of Olaf's wheel chair and lifted Olaf, chair and all, onto the center table. The camp boss spoke to the lumberjacks in his booming voice.

"Men, I do not need to tell you we have some trouble brewing with King Muldoon. You all know he bought the dam and is threatening to stop us from driving our pine to the mills come spring. Now today, he sent that fella who dang near killed both Elmer and Tor on the north ice road. This is the same scalawag who ambushed Ole. We know he did all this as a diversion just so he could wreck the donkey engine. Chief Namakagon tells me he tried to break into the dynamite shack, to boot. Lord knows what he was plannin' there. Then there is the fire in the horse barn—his handiwork, too."

The lumberjacks grumbled at Olaf's words. Ingman nodded to Junior who banged on the pot again.

"Men," Olaf continued, "Chief and Tor captured the culprit out on the ice just before sunset. He is now hogtied in the filing shed." A cheer went up from the men.

"Give me three minutes with him, Boss," shouted Red Olson over the noise. "I will learn him not to mess with the Namakagon Timber Camp."

"There'll be none of that, Red," said Ingman. "We are going to let the law deal with him."

Olaf continued. "Tomorrow we will deliver him to the law. This rascal will not be bothering us anymore, but, fellas, he is not likely the only hoodlum in Muldoon's employ. We have to be watching our backs from here on out."

Lester Moore stood. "Boss, just what are you plannin' on doin' if King Muldoon don't give way and don't let us drive our pine over his dam? Are we gonna get our winter's pay?" The room became silent.

"Lester, that is a fair question. We know Muldoon would like to see us all go bust. He would like nothing better than to take over the Namakagon Timber Company and add it to his string of camps. I want you to know right here and right now we are not going to let that happen."

"Men," shouted Ingman, "we have near to eight million board feet laying out on that ice and we're not done cuttin'. Every man-jack in this camp has an interest in that timber and, by God, we are gonna see to it every stick gets to the mill come hell or high water. If Muldoon tries to stop us, then we plan on taking the dam by force. That is, if you're with us. Each man in this camp will then be sure to draw his full pay, maybe then some."

Leonard Lewten stood. "We Lewtens are behind you full steam, Boss."

"Goes for me and my boy, too, Olaf," John Kavanaugh shouted.

"Me, too," yelled Elmer Schmidt. "I got a score to settle."

"Ya, ya!" added Swede Carlson. "Count me in."

"Same here, Olaf," yelled Sourdough from the kitchen.

Within seconds every employee in camp was on his feet, shouting his pledge. The Namakagon Timber Company would not go down without a fight.

By the end of March, the short days of early winter gave way to much more daylight and warmer temperatures. February's knee-deep snow dropped to less than a foot in the woods now. Keeping the sleighs moving along proved difficult, especially in the afternoons when the ice on the roads melted and the runners dragged in the mud. Ingman put several men on road monkey duty, throwing shovels of snow onto the ice road as the sleighs moved by. Without a good late March snowstorm, the sleighs would have only a few more days in the woods before being put up for the season. All through the cuttings on this pleasant March day, mackinaw coats hung on low branches in the afternoon sun.

Clementine, Junior Kavanaugh's donkey engine, had been drained for the last time this season and covered with an oiled, canvas tarp. She served her purpose well and would be put into service again in December. Junior was put to work with three other lumberjacks building log booms far out in the bay.

Although Junior's steam engine had been secured in the horse barn for the season, another was being readied for a maiden run. The lumberjacks had mounted the machine on the new, flat-bottomed boat housed in the fire-scarred horse barn. The craft was twelve feet wide and twenty-six feet long with an eight-foot-wide oak paddlewheel.

Tor had almost finished the third coat of paint when the camp

191

blacksmith entered the barn. "Tor, how long you gonna be at that paintin'?"

"Ten minutes should do, Gust," he answered, using a rag to wipe a drip of white off the red deck. "Why?"

"I'm thinkin' about firin' up the engine to make sure everything's workin' right."

"Don't you mess up my paint job."

"Aye, aye, Captain Loken," Gust said with a salute. "Tor, I'll finish up there. You go give Junior a holler. He is still out on the ice, working on the booms. He should be here to see this."

Tor left the barn, crossed the muddy yard, and followed the path past the cook shanty. When he neared the lake, he put his cupped hands to his mouth and shouted at the top of his lungs. "Jun—yer!"

Junior looked up from far out on the ice.

"We're—firin'—up—the—en—gine."

Junior dropped his tools and broke into a run.

Gust was cleaning the paint brushes as Tor and Junior walked in, followed by Ingman.

"How's the boom work coming, Junior?" said Ingman.

"We're dang near done with the last one. None too soon, neither. The ice is getting' a pretty good sag in her under all that timber. Must be a foot of water out there in spots. She won't last long if this weather holds out."

"We got a good three weeks until ice out, Junior," said Gust.

"I'll go you a sawbuck the ice will be out in two weeks, Gust ol' pal."

"You're on," Gust replied immediately. He stretched his big hand out to Junior who shook it with a grin. "Maybe I can win back some of what I owe you on the snookerin' you gave us last December."

"Gol dang it, Gust, that was fair and square and you dang-well know it. 'Sides, nobody ordered you to lay any money on that bet."

"Take it easy, Junior. Take it easy. I don't mean nothin' by it. You won fair and square all right. Don't mean I gotta like it, though."

"Let's get this contraption fired up, Yunior," said Ingman, slapping the boiler. Tor's pa is waitin' to hear it run."

"She's gonna get plenty smoky in here," warned Tor, climbing a nearby ladder. "I'll open the door to the loft. Junior, you get the barn door. Wide as she goes." Tor jumped down again. "We'll need water for the boiler."

"I beat you to it," said Gust. "Boiler's full. Firebox is ready to light."

Junior opened the firebox and saw a mix of kindling and birch bark. He reached into his shirt pocket, pulled out a match, struck it on the side of the boiler, shouted, "Here goes, boys," and tossed the match into the boiler.

He slammed the firebox door and adjusted the door vent and damper. A thin wisp of smoke came from the stack. It soon turned into a black column of thick smoke as the birch bark caught fire. Gust and Tor stood next to Junior watching the gauge on the side of the boiler creep up.

"If she runs like Clementine, we'll need ninety or ninety-five pounds when she's towin' a load," said Junior, "but fifty should be fine for a dry run."

"Fifty pounds it is, Admiral Kavanaugh," said Gust.

They watched the needle on the pressure gauge climb. The smoke turned from black to white as birch gave way to maple in the firebox. Junior closed the damper and firebox door vent.

"Fifty pounds. Right on the money. Send her some steam, Admiral."

Grinning, Junior threw a brass lever from left to right and gave the heavy flywheel a spin. The piston, responding to the steam pressure, pushed the long rod that connected it to the flywheel. The flywheel began to turn on its own, slowly at first, then faster and faster.

"Ready, Gust?" asked Junior.

"Let 'er go, Admiral!"

Junior pulled back on the oak clutch handle. The white paddlewheel behind the boat began to spin to the cheers of the woods boss and his three self-taught engineers. The small amount of kindling in the firebox had done its job and was already burning out. The pressure began to drop. Junior disengaged the clutch and the paddlewheel slowed to a stop.

"One more test," said Tor, reaching for a brass knob. A deafening *screeeeet*, came from the brass whistle Gust had built for the boiler.

"Dang!" said Ingman, "That whistle's bound to wake the dead, Gust."

Junior released what remained of the head of steam and locked the release lever open. The fire was out now. Gust reached under the boiler and turned the petcock. Boiling water streamed onto the dirt floor, and a final cloud of steam rose to the rafters.

"So what are we going to call this rig?" asked Gust.

"How about Mabel?" suggested Junior. "Mabel of Cable. Ya, Mabel—of—Cable. I think that's a good name for a boat. Mabel of Cable."

"Dang it all, Junior," snapped Tor, "don't you start carrying on again about that gal who cleaned out your pocketbook. We've heard your crowin' too many times already."

"No, Tor, I mean it. Let's call her Mabel of Cable."

Gust and Ingman laughed at the discussion.

"Junior, we are *not* going to name our Namakagon Timber Company boat after some sportin' house woman and that's the end of that."

Junior glared at Tor.

"How about we name her the *Namakagon Queen*, Tor?" offered Gust.

"See, Junior," said Tor, "now *that's* a good name for a boat."

"I've been givin' this some thought, Tor," said Ingman. "I think your pa would be honored to have this boat named after your mother."

"Karina?" Tor smiled. "Uncle Ingman, that is a gol dang good idea. Let's call her the Empress Karina."

The next morning, Ingman laid two dimes on the counter below the iron-barred ticket window at the Cable depot.

193

"Here's for the telegram and a three-penny tip for you, Sonny," he said. "And here's another six bits for passage to Hayward."

"Well, Ingman Loken!" came a loud voice from the back of the office. The stationmaster walked into the waiting room. Polished brass buttons stood out sharply against the dark blue wool fabric.

"What brings you to town on such a fine spring day?"

" Oscar, good to see you. I'm here on business, but that does not mean we can't find time for a couple of hands of pinochle before I leave for camp. I'd love to take home some more of your Omaha Railroad Line money."

"What would a high-roller like you want with my meager earnings?"

"Oscar, you old mudpuppy, if I had your money, I'd burn mine!"

Ingman took the stationmaster by the arm and moved away from the window. "Say, Oscar, you may have heard the scuttlebutt about some trouble we expect with King Muldoon. Olaf sent me to talk with your watchman, Bill Burns. He seems to be a straight shooter and is doin' a good yob keepin' a lid on things in Cable. Tell me, if I were to ask him for some advice, do you figure he could be trusted to not give up our intentions to Muldoon?"

"Completely. Bill has no patience for King Muldoon and the low-down way he finagles his way around the pinery, not to mention the way he treats his men. Why just last month two of his workers were killed on the job. They say it was due to Muldoon's orders to increase the camp's daily cut. Happened up near the White River. Terrible shame, it was. Two men dead and Muldoon refused to send their pay home with their remains. He said they violated their contracts by not finishing out the season. The crooked old skinflint wouldn't as much as pay the railroad freight to get the poor fellas back home for burial. I covered it myself. No, you needn't fret about Bill. He's your man, all right. Right now he should be over at the hotel reading his mornin' paper, I'd say."

Knowing the southbound train wouldn't pull out for a half-hour, Ingman crossed to the hotel. As Oscar guessed, Bill Burns sat at a table with a copy of the *Pioneer Press* in one hand and a cup of steaming coffee in the other.

"Why, sure I'll help out," said the constable, "but if you want to go one more step and show Muldoon you really mean business, well, I have a suggestion." He pulled a pencil out of his coat pocket. "You send a telegram to this fella," he said as he scratched a name and address on the corner of the newspaper. He tore the corner off and handed it to Ingman.

"So, Bill, who is this fella, Earl Morrison?"

"Well, he started out as a bouncer for a tavern in Racine. From there he was hired away to head up as a watchman for a small shipping company in Chicago. That was a few years back. Now Ned's a Captain in the dang Pinkerton Detective Agency. I met Ned when he and two of his men came up here trout fishing. I took them out to Cap's Creek. Olaf, they caught over eighty brook trout in just two days. Nice ones, too. I think I made a friend for life that day. You let Earl Morrison know you talked with me, Ingman. He's your man. Not even King Muldoon will go up against a Pinkerton badge."

194

"I appreciate this, Bill."

"Ingman, I'll ride out to the camp tomorrow to look things over. Anyway I'd like to see that bay full of logs I hear your outfit put up this winter."

"Best take the south road. No need to tip our hand to Muldoon. 'Sides, the ice ain't safe for both a man and a horse these days. There ain't been a drownin' in the lake for two years now. I don't suppose you want to be the one to spoil the record, ay, Constable?"

Minutes later, Ingman sent another telegram. This one went to the Pinkerton captain, Earl Morrison, in downtown Chicago. Ingman paid the telegrapher, then dashed out the door, across the platform, and jumped onto the train just as it started to pull out from the station.

A half-hour later he walked down the pine-plank walkway in Hayward and through the doors of the Lumberman's Bank. The lobby was empty. He walked up to the teller's window. "Dearborne," Ingman said quietly, "time for me to make a withdrawal, and I am not talkin' about money."

"I – I don't follow you, Mr. Loken," the teller said in a whisper, looking over his shoulder at the open office door behind.

"The hell you say. You and I both know the only reason you still have your yob here is because I didn't turn you in to the sheriff. You agreed, Ned, and now I'm here to collect."

"All right, all right. Just pipe down some. I could still get the sack, you know. What is it you want?"

"What's Muldoon plannin' out east of Cable?"

"I don't know anything about any of his plans, Mr. Loken, but I do know Muldoon withdrew a thousand dollars. All in five-dollar bills. Just last week. Two hundred five-dollar bills. The only other camp that ever did this is yours. Made me think those five-spots were for his men."

"Anything else?"

"No ... well, only that Muldoon's walkin' boss took the train to Chicago three days ago," Dearborne whispered. "I didn't think nothin' of it at first, but then I got to wonderin' why, when all of Muldoon's camps need to be buttoned up for the season, why would the walkin' boss of those big camps be goin' on a holiday? It just don't make sense, Mr. Loken. It just don't."

Ingman left the bank and caught the midday train back to Cable. He rode into camp just before Sourdough rang the bell for supper. The air was warm now, and the snow gone around camp. He walked his horse to the barn and crossed to the cook shanty. The setting sun peeked out from behind the clouds. A beam of orange sunlight flooded the western horizon. In the distant twilight he heard the call of a loon—the first loon call he had heard since fall. He stopped to listen, then watched it fly over the frozen lake, looking for the first open water of the season.

"Yust be patient, Mr. Loon. It won't be long now."

Chapter 36
The Empress Karina

A gray, windy, April morning found a light but steady drizzle falling across the Namakagon River Valley. The snow was all but gone. Across northwestern Wisconsin, skid trails and tote roads had turned to mud from five days of rain. The Namakagon Timber Company yard was no different. There would be no more timber cut this season.

Tor stood before the large windows of the lodge surveying the scene before him. Several inches of water stood on the lake's diminishing layer of ice, now darkened by the warm temperatures.

Inside, the fire crackled in the fireplace, warming the room. Tor's thoughts wandered to Rosie sitting at the family piano in Hayward, then to their gathering at Christmas. He hadn't seen her in more than two months. It wouldn't be long now. The log drive would start soon, and Tor was determined to ride the pine to Hayward with the river pigs.

"I'll see you soon, Rosie," Tor said quietly, gazing across the black ice now covering the lake.

"What's that, Son?" came from the desk across the room.

"Oh, nothing, Pa, I was just thinking out loud."

"About what?"

"The drive."

"The log drive?"

"Ya. I talked with Blackie Jackson yesterday. He's gonna put me with Lloyd Olson and his men on the front end."

Olaf wheeled his chair closer. "I need you here, Son. I need you and Junior to push the log booms down to the dam with the Karina. You cannot be on both ends of the drive at the same time. Besides, it is too dangerous out there on that river when it is filled with those half-ton logs."

"Pa, I have a fine pair of calks. I've been practicing. I can walk the logs as good as any blackbird in camp. And I know how to swim, too. Most of your drivers don't, you know."

His father wheeled his chair out from behind the desk and joined Tor at the window.

"Son, this winter you learned plenty about the timber business. In spite of your age, you are becoming a damn good lumberjack. I do not blame you for wanting to be part of the drive, but you have more important work to do. Some day you will run this outfit. Let Blackie and Ingman and the boys drive the timber to the mills. You will be far better off here."

"Let me have my say, Pa," Tor said, turning to face his father. "First off, I'm seventeen now. Second, if you and Uncle Ingman want me to learn this business, then I need to be in on the drive. Just like I needed to be on Mike Fremont's saw crew. Just like I needed to be with Swede and Blackie on the cross-haul. Just like I needed to work with Elmer Schmidt and his Percherons, pulling sleighs down the ice roads. Pa, if I'm to learn this business, you need to let me be part of the drive, too."

Tor turned back to the window, waiting for his father's reply. He and Olaf stared in silence at more than a hundred thousand pine logs out in the bay.

"Those logs look friendly enough now, just lying there calm and quiet. They are not so friendly once in the river though. They turn mean and nasty. They do their damnedest to make trouble. They trick you. They hide in the brush and try to sneak into backwaters never to be found. They wait till they're in the worst possible place, then they jam up on you. The other logs cannot wait to make the jam bigger and more dangerous. Sometimes the only thing that will break those jams up is dynamite."

"The old timers say the logs seek revenge for being plucked from the forest. Son, there have been many a river pig who have been walking the logs with confidence one moment and drowned or crushed to death the next. I've seen it happen. A mean log will hunt you down and, when you least expect it, put you under. When the other logs rush in to close over the top of you, well, that's it. You're fate is sealed. Nothing left but your hat floating betwixt the logs. You're gone. Gone forever." His father's voice trembled. "Son, last spring ten drivers drowned in one week on a two mile stretch of water upstream from Chippewa Falls. Ten good men. Strong, experienced drivers. Whitewater men. All dead and soon to be forgotten."

"I have to do this, Pa."

"Tor, you have no idea how much power the river has. Look at this lake—more than three thousand acres. And Phineas Muldoon has it dammed up eight feet high. Once that dam is opened, there will be millions and millions of gallons of ice cold water blasting down that river and carrying with it thousands of angry logs. It only takes one of them to kill you, Son."

"Pa, I know you're concerned about me. I know you want to keep me safe. But you know I have to do this. Just like you and Uncle Ingman had to."

Olaf sighed. "All right. Once you and Junior get the log booms into the bay near the dam, you can join the drive. But, only if you stay close to your Uncle Ingman. You will get your bellyful of river pig work by the time you reach Hayward. You will be cold and wet and hungry and tired and sore. You will want to get yourself up to Adeline Ringstadt's Boarding House to rest up. Then, when you are shaped up, catch the train and get back to camp so I can hear your stories."

"I'll take care. I promise. I'll come back safe and sound with tales taller than ol' Paul Bunyan himself." He bent down and hugged his father. "Thanks, Pa. Thanks for having faith in me."

They both stared out the window through the dreary sky. The large bay in front of the Namakagon Timber Company camp was packed with huge pine logs. They were joined together in six large log booms built by Junior Kavanaugh and several other lumberjacks. The ice had given way under the extreme weight of the pine, and the entire bay was now free of ice. The rest of the lake could go out any day.

"This rain will help melt the rest of the ice," said Tor's father as he rolled his wheelchair closer to the window. "Our timber will be bound for the mills before the week is out."

"Junior and Gust ought to have the Karina going today, Pa. We're figurin' on launchin' her later this mornin'. There's enough open water for her now," he said, nodding at the bay in front of the lodge. "Sure would be good if the rain were to let up some so we don't get soaked to the bone when we launch her."

"Soaked? Tor, you best get used to the idea. There is no such thing as a dry river pig."

"You're going to join us when we launch her, right, Pa?"

"I wouldn't miss it for the world, Son, wheelchair or no damn wheelchair!"

Tor crossed the muddy yard to the horse barn. A dozen men examined the boat, still perched on its supports.

Gust was polishing some of the brass on the engine. "She's fit to launch and all set to sail, Captain Tor," shouted Gust with a salute.

"Charlie Martin," said Tor, "how 'bout you and a few of the men lay down some of those tamarack fence posts 'cross the yard to help skid the boat down the hill. I'll hitch up a couple of hay burners and we can have her launched by dinnertime."

"Leroy, Mason, Red," yelled Charlie, "grab some picaroons out of the tool shed and meet me outside. We're gonna lay some corduroy, boys."

Elmer Schmidt walked his two Percherons to the boat. Rusty O'Hara helped hitch the team to the boat's bow. Ernie Milton and Frank Anderson pitched a dozen fence posts onto the barn's dirt floor, making a bed of rollers leading to the door. Six long, oak poles were lashed to the supports below the hull and angled down to the ground.

More lumberjacks gathered to watch. Gust had the men line up along the boat, a dozen on each side. Grasping the gunwales, they steadied the craft as Ole urged the horses forward. The steamboat slowly slid down the poles and onto the tamarack rollers. Inch by inch, it followed the horse team out the door, crossing the corduroyed yard, and slowly sliding down to the lake. Ole walked the horses out into the water a few yards before unhitching and leading them back to the barn.

The rain turned to a light mist as nearly one hundred Namakagon Timber Camp lumberjacks stood on the shore of the gray lake. The small steamboat was eased into the bay. Gust, Junior, and Tor jumped up onto the deck of the long, wide boat. The blacksmith opened the door to the firebox, struck a match, and soon a coal-black cloud of birch bark smoke spewed from the stack. Four men hoisted two large boxes onto the deck, each filled with hard maple firewood. Tor and Junior slid the wood bins toward the stern, nearer the large firebox door.

"Gust," shouted Tor, "she's drawing only about a foot of draft. That's less than we figured."

"Any leaks?"

"None yet," yelled Junior.

Tor looked up toward the lodge to see his father being carried down to the shore in his wheelchair. Blackie and Ingman were on each side and Chief Namakagon behind, steadying the chair as they crossed the soggy slope. With them were four other men, dressed too well for lumber camp work.

"Friends of your Uncle?" Gust asked.

"Must be, Gust. Probably came to witness the big event." He tapped a gauge lightly, watching the needle rise.

With pressure in the boiler, Junior pulled a chain, and the sound of Gust's whistle split the air, echoing back from across the lake.

"Let King Muldoon try to figure what that bird call was, eh fellas?" shouted Junior above the laughter of the other lumberjacks. *Screeeeeeeeet, screet, screet.*

"Where's Louie Thorp?" yelled Tor. "Louie, get up here where you belong."

As Louie climbed aboard, Tor spoke to the men. "Fellas, this here boat would not have been built without the skills of our carpenter, Louie Thorp, and those of Gust, here.

"Junior had a good hand in it, too," shouted Gust, "and don't leave yourself out, Tor, and your Uncle Ingman for comin' up with this lame-brained idea in the first place." The men laughed and cheered, some waving their hats.

Tor shouted above them. "Many of you others helped out, too. Now it appears we have ourselves a mighty fine, steam-powered sternwheeler to help us do our work." More cheers came from the band of lumberjacks.

"Men," shouted Olaf, "this is a proud day for me and my brother Ingman and, as you can tell, my boy, there. But there is an even greater day ahead as you well know. Just as soon as the ice goes out, our pine is bound for the mill. Now you know I generally offer double pay for each day spent on the drive. Well, men, that's out the window."

The men grumbled as the camp boss continued.

"Pipe down, men. Let me finish. This year, the Namakagon Timber Company will pay not two, but three dollars a day for every man who helps us get this timber over the dam and down to A. J. Hayward's new mill."

The lumberjacks cheered and cheered, waving their hats in the misty spring morning air.

"Fellas," shouted Olaf, "I have one more thing to say. We have no way of knowin' just what old Phineas Muldoon has in mind. What we do know is that he is not gonna show us any hospitality. There might be trouble. Ingman has learned Muldoon may have hired some Chicago ruffians. We figure, too, Muldoon will have his East Lake camp boys greet us at the dam. Now is your chance to bow out if you have a mind to. As for me, well, you know I am not one to back down."

"We ain't backin' down, neither, Boss," came a shout. "We're with you, thick or thin."

A roar of cheers and raised fists filled the air.

"Fellas, fellas," yelled Ingman, "listen. We don't want to be the ones who start the fight, should there be one. Like the fine gentlemen we are, we will wait for them to make the first move. When they do, though, there's no holdin' back. We have our rights, men, and, by golly, we are bound and determined to drive our logs, come hell or high water!" The men cheered again. Another *screet, screet* pierced the air.

"Time to launch this boat, pinery boys," shouted Tor. "Grab on and give a shove." While the others cheered, a dozen men waded into the icy water and gave the boat a mighty push. She slid out into the bay gracefully.

Tor pulled an empty wine bottle from the wood box, shouting, "I christen this boat the *Empress Karina of Lake Namakagon.* Long—may—she—sail!" He smacked it on the boiler and it shattered, falling back into the box.

Another round of cheers went up. Junior sent the head of steam to the engine, reached up, gave the large flywheel a spin, and released the clutch.

The paddlewheel turned slowly, then faster as the boat glided into the bay. Tor pulled the tiller to the far right and she turned easily to port. He then moved the tiller to the left and completed the figure eight before coming back to shore.

The lumberjacks on shore laughed and cheered, waving their hats.

The gray clouds now gave way, letting a thin stream of sunlight fall onto the bay of floating timber. Smoke billowed from the stack of the brightly painted Karina as she gently nosed onto the beach again. Tor and Junior stepped onto the bow rail.

"She waltzes as smooth as the gals in town, fellas," yelled Junior, laughing and wiggling his hips.

"Say, Leroy," Tor shouted, "Leroy Phipps. You should step up here, too."

Leroy jumped at the chance, bounding from shore to deck with a grin.

"Leroy," said Tor, "grab a couple of sticks of wood for the firebox, would you?"

"Hang on, Gust," whispered Junior.

Gust grabbed the rail. Leroy bent over to reach into the wood bin.

"Now, Junior!" ordered Tor.

Junior engaged the clutch and the boat lurched back, tossing Leroy into the ice-cold lake. He sprang up and ran to shore, drenched, muddy and sputtering, his wet hat in his hand.

"Leroy," yelled Tor above the laughter of the men, "I waited four months to get even with you for that kerosene whisky of yours!"

The men laughed and cheered again, but not loud enough to drown out Leroy's long string of cuss words.

Just as Junior nosed the sternwheeler up onto the beach again, Zach

Rigby blew the gabreel. The mass of lumberjacks climbed the slope, crossed the muddy yard, and piled into the cook shanty. Chief Namakagon, Tor, and Ingman helped Olaf back to the lodge. Soon the beach, shore, and yard were quiet again.

"Olaf, Ingman," said Chief Namakagon as they sat down around the dinner table in the lodge, "this is a very fine spring day, very fine indeed. And, Olaf, this son of yours, well, I have come to believe he is meant to be a leader of men." Tor beamed with pride.

"I agree, Olaf," said Ingman. "Tor has earned the confidence of the men. He's been workin' shoulder to shoulder with them all winter and become quite the lumberyack." Ingman reached over and patted Tor soundly on the back. "This boy is growin' into quite a man, I'd say."

Tor was at a loss for words.

"Well," offered Olaf, "it is good to hear such kind words. I am very proud of my boy."

The lodge door swung open. Both of the camp cookees came into the lodge lugging wooden shipping crates filled with tin dishes, food, and coffee for the noon meal. The aroma of Sourdough's freshly baked bread soon filled the air. Zeke set a platter of roast bear and a pot of baked beans in the center of the table. The next platter carried stacks of both blackjack and yellowjack squares. A bowl of molasses and a tin plate of butter came next, followed by a stack of quarter-pound sugar cookies. As the men filled their plates, Zach filled their tin cups with hot coffee while Zeke placed a squash pie on the table.

Through the lodge windows, Namakagon noticed the sky now clearing. Soon sunlight glistened off the softening, black ice.

"Yes indeed," said Namakagon as he stabbed a large piece of roast bear with his knife, "this is truly a very fine spring day."

By the time Ingman finished dinner, sunshine flooded the bay. He spent the rest of the day overseeing his crews as they turned in their equipment for storage until the next logging season. The tool shed was soon stuffed with crosscut saws, double-bit axes, and cant hooks, all protected by a coat of linseed oil. The peaveys and pike poles were leaned against the outside wall, waiting for the drive to begin.

In the blacksmith shop, Gust had three men cutting and bending steel links to build logging chain for the next season. He joined the links by heating and hammer-welding each red-hot link.

Junior and Tor spent the afternoon on the Karina, checking every valve and gauge, polishing her brass, and preparing for her first day of work.

The boys secured the bow of the Karina to an oak tree near shore. The stern was fastened to the dock. Tor put two pike poles, a peavey and several coils of rope on board while Junior covered the engine and boiler with an oiled tarp. Beyond, the ice turned darker and darker in the warm April sunshine.

By the time the sun met the tops of the trees on the western shore, the Karina was ready, the Namakagon Timber Company camp was in order, and the men were all hungry. Sourdough rang the supper bell. They gathered for another good meal.

After supper, like so many evenings before, Kelly Thompson reached for his banjo and Whistlin' Jim his concertina. Most of the men joined in tonight, knowing this would be one of the last times they would all be together at the camp. Tall tales and lively songs filled the air, as did thick, blue smoke from the lumberjacks' pipes. Ingman's four guests sat with him at the end table.

"Tor," said Junior, "that fella sittin' next to your Uncle Ingman down there, isn't he the constable we met in the hotel bar last December?"

"Shush your mouth, Junior. I do not want that story to get spread all over camp. I don't need the razzin'." He looked at the stranger across the room. "Ya, maybe you're right. He does sort'a look like the same fella."

"I'm pretty dang sure that's him, Tor. I'd even put a dollar on it."

"Junior Kavanaugh, you ain't pinchin' me for another gol dang buck. I am not interested in any more of your wagering."

Tor and Junior each grabbed a molasses cookie and left the cook shanty. They headed straight for the Karina for another inspection, then sat on the dock listening to a loon calling in the distant twilight. The wind picked up.

"Junior, do you hear something?"

Junior pointed across the bay. "Look at the ice! There, just off the point."

They watched as, far out on the lake, driven by the breeze, a large section of ice separated from the rest, slowly colliding with the logs in the bay. As it broke into millions of tiny crystals, it gave off a strange hissing sound.

"Go find my uncle. Tell him he should come and look at this."

Junior sprinted up to the cook shanty and disappeared inside. Almost one hundred curious loggers soon poured out. Chief Namakagon and Olaf looked down from the lodge windows.

Ingman made his way through the mob of men, stepping onto the dock. He felt the wind on his face and saw a large section of the lake now open.

"Sourdough," he shouted, "I want breakfast at four. Not a minute later. Men, you show up at the table with your calks on. Tomorrow we drive logs!"

Tor had trouble getting to sleep that night. In the dark, his thoughts drifted back to the time when he lived in New York with his mother. His mind then wandered to the train derailment and the horrific crashing of passenger cars, one after another. Next, the orphanage, followed by his time in the coal yard. He remembered the thrill of meeting his Uncle Ingman and, after so many years, seeing his father again. He tossed and turned. Tor's thoughts roamed to the train robbery, to Rosie, to his experiences working in the woods, to the train ride with the Governor, and to Rosie again. He was finally drifting off when it happened.

The sudden blast from a shotgun shattered the stillness of night.

Tor jumped at the shotgun's report.

Then, from out on the lake—another shot—and another!

Tor recognized them as rifle shots. He threw off the quilt and, in his long, white, wool underwear, ran to the window. A flash of light near the dock illuminated the Karina, immediately followed by another shotgun report.

"The boat!" he shouted. "Pa, Ingman, the boat!" Tor pulled on his shoe-pacs, grabbed his hat and his deer rifle. He opened a drawer, pawed around, then pulled out a box of shells.

Another rifle report tore through the night air—this one from the lake.

He frantically ripped open the box. Cartridges flew across the floor. Tor fell to his knees and, in the darkness, found one shell, then a second. He slid them into the rifle's magazine, levered one into the chamber, and lowered the hammer. Down the stairs he flew in the darkness, two steps at a time. In the dim light from the fireplace he saw his father coming from his bedroom in his wheelchair. Ingman was putting on his coat.

"What is it?" shouted Tor.

"Trouble!" answered Ingman. "You stay inside, Nephew." Ingman rushed out into the yard, shotgun in hand.

"Stay inside? Uncle, if somebody's tryin' to wreck the Karina, then I'm gonna try and stop 'em!"

"Tor," snapped his father, "if there is someone out there with a rifle and you step outside wearin' that white union suit of yours, you'll be a fine target. Now you get upstairs, put on your britches and a shirt, and then stay put until we know what the shootin's all about."

"Pa, I gotta protect the boat!"

"Dang it, Tor, three of those friends of Ingman's are Pinkerton detectives. The other is Constable Bill Burns. We hired them to keep an eye on things. Let them do their jobs and, for St. Peter's sake, boy, do not get in the way! Now go get your dang britches on."

Tor raced back up the stairs, rifle in hand. He laid the Winchester on the bed, put on his shirt, and kicked off his shoe-pacs. He pulled on his wool britches, whipping the suspenders up over his shoulders before peering out the window. In the dim starlight stood the Karina, boiler and engine still covered. He saw a flash near the dock and heard another shotgun blast, quickly answered by two more rifle reports from the log booms.

Fifty yards to the left he saw another flash, followed by another report!

Tor raised the window, shouting, "Uncle, is the boat alright?"

"She's fine, Tor. Stay inside. We got two culprits out on the log booms and one more most likely shot or drowned off the dock."

Tor reached over to his dresser and fumbled for his father's binoculars. He scanned the log boom. In the dim light he made out the shape of a man in a rowboat. In a forced whisper he spoke to his uncle again.

"Uncle, is anyone from our camp out there on the lake?"

"No. Why?"

"I think I can see one of your culprits in a rowboat."

"Can you get your sights on him?"

"I think so."

"Then take a potshot at his boat, but get away from the window in case he shoots back."

"Uncle Ingman, what if I hit him?"

"Aim low and to the side, Tor."

"All right, but I surely hope I don't hit him."

"I'll take the responsibility, Nephew."

Tor knelt, resting the Winchester on the windowsill. He looked through the field glasses again, set them down, then squinted, peering across the iron sights of his rifle. He pulled the hammer back with a soft *click—click*. He squinted, adjusting the aim of the rifle, hoping to place the bullet through the boat. Carefully steadying his rifle on the sill of the window, Tor Loken slowly squeezed the trigger.

The stock pounded against his shoulder and the report echoed through the trees. Tor pulled his Winchester and the field glasses from the sill and rushed to the other window.

204

A voice came from the middle of the log booms. "Don't shoot! Don't shoot no more, I surrender. I ain't gonna die for no lumber tycoon."

"Pipe down, you fool," came another voice through the darkness.

"I'm givin' up, Horace," the first man said. "'Tain't worth dyin' for."

Lumberjacks were pouring out of the bunkhouse now. Ingman stopped them. "You men sit tight. We don't know how many there are and they got deer rifles."

Through the binoculars, Tor could see the other man now. He raised the window, knelt down and took aim.

"Uncle, I got the other fella in my sights. He's hunkered down on one of the log booms. Should I fire?"

"Ya, Tor. Shoot. Shoot!" answered Ingman.

Tor squeezed the trigger and another rifle blast cut the night air. He rushed back to the first window and peered through the field glasses.

"Horace?" shouted the first outlaw.

Silence.

"Horace!"

More silence.

"My God, my God! You sent Horace to his grave! Now don't shoot no more. I ain't gonna shoot and don't you neither."

"Boss, look at this," shouted Gust Finstead from the dock, holding something in the air. "Dynamite. They were tryin' to blow up our boat."

"You on the lake," came a new voice from near the boat, "I am an officer with the Pinkerton Detective Agency, and I hereby place you under arrest. Now, I want to hear each and every cartridge come out of your rifle, mister. If I don't hear your gun empty out, I will order my sharpshooter to put his next round straight through your gizzard."

"For Almighty's sake, don't shoot no more," came the voice through the darkness. "I surrender! I am unloadin' right now."

From the lake came a series of *click-clack, click-clacks*. "There, it's empty. I couldn't shoot now if I wanted to. I am layin' my rifle down and I'm comin' in. Don't you go shootin' me. I ain't gonna be no more trouble."

A leaking rowboat soon approached the dock. The man rowing was pale and shaking. The instant his boat reached the dock, two Pinkerton men yanked him from the boat by his collar, dragged him to shore and slammed him face-first into the wet, muddy ground

The third Pinkerton put one knee on the middle of the captured man's back. "How many are you?"

"Three. Just the three of us."

"Where are the others?"

"Others? There ain't no others. Just me and Horace and Smiley, I told you. You must've shot Horace 'cause he ain't out there no more, and I seen Smiley go down off the dock there. Must've shot him, too. My God in heaven. It weren't s'posed to turn out like this."

"Where's the fourth man?" said the detective, putting all of his weight on the knee that dug into the outlaw's back.

"I'm tellin' ya, there ain't nobody else."

"Four men got off the train. You and the two we shot make three. Where's the fourth?" shouted the Pinkerton, now bouncing on his knee.

"Stop! Stop!" cried the bandit. The detective eased off. "Four of us hired on all right. But only three of us came to lay wreck to the boat."

"Where's the fourth man?"

Ingman didn't wait for a reply. He turned and raced up to the lodge.

"Olaf, Tor, watch yourselves. There is one more on the loose!"

Tor moved from the window to his bedroom door and peeked onto the floor below. The light from coals glowing in the fireplace barely illuminated the room. Tor saw the silhouette of his father, pistol at the ready, peering out the window.

Ingman stepped onto the porch. Just as the door began to open, a loud *snap* sounded as something cracked across Ingman's shotgun.

Crashing into the room came Ingman and a large man, both thrashing and punching in the dark. The fireplace coals offered too little light to distinguish one man from the other as legs tangled, arms and fists flew.

In the dim glow, Tor made out the form of a big man, his arm high above, holding a broken nightstick. Tor then realized his uncle was pinned to the floor, looking up, waiting for the jagged end of the club to descend.

"I've been waitin' six months to even the score with you, Norski," said the big man. "You know who I am?"

Ingman was silent.

"I'm the man from the Chicago coal yards who you sent to the hospital, Norski. I'm the man who lost his job because of you. I'm the man who's gonna make your face so ugly that nobody will ever be able to look on you again without retching."

Tor noticed his father inching closer.

"Jake Riggens!" shouted Tor, stepping out of his room and onto the top step. "Jake, don't do it."

"I'm gettin' even, boy," Big Jake replied into the darkness.

Tor raised his rifle. "I got you in my sights, Jake. I don't miss."

"You won't shoot me, boy. We both know that."

Bang! The bullet's impact sent Big Jake Riggens back out the door. He scrambled to his feet but collapsed. The bullet from Olaf's revolver had shattered Riggens' hip. He tried to stand again but the pain was too great. He tumbled off the porch onto the wet ground. As he tried to stand a third time, two Loken lumberjacks tackled him, pinning him to the ground.

Ingman lit an oil lamp and stepped outside. Tor joined him, leaning his rifle against the outside wall. Olaf rolled his chair up to the door to get a look at the wounded intruder. Every Loken lumberjack was in the yard now.

"Get these fellas chained up for the night so we can get some sleep," said Olaf. "Big day tomorrow."

Bill Burns soon had handcuffs on Big Jake Riggens. Both he and the other man were chained to a tree in the yard for the night.

"The boat's fine, Boss," shouted Gust from the lake. "Still fit to sail in the morning. Nothing askew. And, I have the coward who tried to dynamite her. Ingman, you peppered him good but he'll be fit enough to stand before a judge."

The man called Smiley was chained to the tree with the other two assailants. The Loken men filed back into the bunkhouse.

In the lodge, Bill Burns, the Pinkertons, and the three Lokens discussed the attack. Ingman poured each man a glass of whisky. Tor turned his down.

"Richard, you and Archie keep an eye on the boat till dawn," said Morrison. "We stopped 'em once. Don't want to let 'em sneak up on us again."

"I doubt Muldoon will send anyone else," said Burns. "We got his hired henchmen. When it gets around his camp that these thugs ain't comin' home tonight, well, let's just say no man-jack in Muldoon's outfit will have the gumption to show his face."

"Wish I could've seen the look on that fella's face when he heard the word 'Pinkertons'," said Tor. "Do you think we should let the rest of Muldoon's jacks know we have Pinkertons working for us?"

"Shouldn't be necessary, Tor," said his father. "After this, we don't even know if any of his men will show up tomorrow."

"Where's Chief Namakagon?" asked Ingman. "I didn't see him at all tonight. He missed a good scrap."

"Namakagon left camp right after supper," said Olaf.

"Well, that figures." said Archie, "Probably don't have the stomach for a good tussle."

"You don't know Chief Namakagon," snapped Olaf. "He would not leave without good reason."

"I'll put a sawbuck on it that he left to save his own skin," said Archie.

"You'd lose that bet, mister," countered Ingman. "Chief ain't one to run from a fight if the cause is right. Not Chief Namakagon."

"Archie, you and Richard best get down to your posts," said their boss. They turned toward the door.

Just as Richard lifted the latch, the door flew open with a crash, kicked in by a large man holding a cocked rifle. Archie and Richard fell to the floor.

"I am Horace Walters, the man you thought you'd done in out there on the log boom. And I am here to git my partners and git out of this corner of hell for good. Now you all step over there. I swear I will shoot any man who don't give way. Now git!"

Archie and Richard slowly stood, hands held high and eyes wide. All of the men stepped back except Tor.

"Son, do as he says."

"No, Pa," said Tor, "I ain't raisin' my hands to some no-good, mud-suckin' scum from Chicago who points my own gun at me. No sir, I won't!"

"Tor, don't be foolish," said Ingman. "Do as he says."

"Reach high, Sonny, or, God help me, I will pull this here trigger."

"You won't shoot me, Horace Walters. You won't shoot anyone. Now ease off on that hammer there and hand my Winchester over to Archie or Richard there. They're from the Pinkertons, and they will show you where you're bunkin' tonight."

Horace pointed the rifle at Archie who turned white with fear. "What makes you think I won't shoot, Sonny? None of you mean more to me than a skunk in a woodpile."

"I'll tell you why, Horace," said Tor. "You see, I put two cartridges in my rifle. One hit your partner's boat and the other one I shot at you. That rifle is empty."

Silence.

Seconds passed.

Click.

The hammer fell on the empty chamber. Immediately, five men tore into Walters. Ingman grabbed the big man by the wrist and gave it a sharp twist, fracturing the man's arm with a *snap.*

Still, Walters thrashed and fought, freeing himself. But, as he was about to make a run for the yard, he was whisked to the floor again. A large, calked boot pinned his right hand tight to the floor as Pinkerton handcuffs closed on his wrists. Minutes later he was chained to the same tree as his partners.

Horace Walter's left forearm was broken and his bloodied right hand would carry, far beyond his long prison term, the telltale scars from Ingman's calked boot.

"Those fellas do not know how lucky they are," said Bill Burns. "If they would have got mixed up with most other camps around here, they would all be drowned like leg-trapped rats by now. Nobody would ask questions or give a damn about the answers."

"That is not the way things work in this camp, Bill," said Olaf. "We do not make the laws, we do not judge, and we do not choose the penalty. Someday this will be a civil and settled land. It might just as well start with us."

Archie and Richard posted for the rest of the night near the Empress Karina. Ingman, Bill Burns, Earl Morrison, and Olaf went over the night's events and morning plans. Tor took his Winchester back up to his room, stretched out on the bed, and immediately fell into a deep, sound sleep.

Chapter 38
Camp vs. Camp

There was no need to wake the camp this April morning. Every lumberjack was out of his bunk and ready for the day long before the four o'clock breakfast.

"Eat hearty, river pigs!" cried out Sourdough. "I don't want nobody complainin' about not getting a good bellyful today."

"We know better than to complain, Sourdough," came a shout from the back of the long room. "Danged if any jack amongst us wants to find one of your pet mice in his mincemeat pie."

The men laughed as they filled their plates with flapjacks and pork sausage, spread lard across their biscuits, and dipped huge molasses cookies into their steaming coffee.

"Boys, I'm sendin' two wannigans out for your dinner today," shouted the cook. "One will be two miles downriver from the dam. I'll send another over to the river crossing south of Cable, under the railroad trestle. Those of you working upstream from Mosquito Brook can count on breakfast tomorrow at the Pac-wa-wong Indian camp.

"You drivers who make it farther downriver might need to look for a meal at some other camp or in Phipps, or go without. By tomorrow night, I'll have a supper camp set up near A. J. Hayward's mill. Any driver who makes it there before my cookees and me will have to find his own food till I get there. I'll do my dangdest to keep you fed, boys, but only if you look me up. I ain't no hotel waitress and I sure ain't gonna come lookin' for you."

Ingman stood up on a table. "You that are drivers, listen good now. Blackie is your yam crew boss. You do as he says. I'll be workin' all up and down the line, too, if you need help. Other than that, yust keep them logs a-floatin', boys. Keep 'em out of the backwaters and the brush, too. We didn't cut that pine yust to have it rot in the weeds."

Blackie took the floor. "Let's talk more about jams, men. Any driver who sees logs startin' to tangle up needs to get right in there and bust 'em up. And I mean right now—well before they jam up good. Now, if you should get a jam you can't break, you get ahold of Ingman or me straight away. We'll each be carryin' dynamite to loosen her up for you. But don't you go doin' that on your own. It's risky business and if it ain't done just right, it wastes good pine."

"Now, here's the plan for this mornin'," said Ingman. "Tor, Yunior and Gust will be on the Karina. They will bring the booms across the lake, around Bear Point, and clear down the narrows to the dam. The Karina can carry near to thirty men. The first thirty men to board will be dropped off on the shore up from the dam. Gust will split the boom, and the boat will send the pine down the narrows toward the dam, with help from the current. You first men yust bide your time until the second boatload of drivers comes along. Then you should follow the shoreline to the dam or yust ride down on the pine. When you reach the dam, you should go ahead and send our pine over the top and down the river. I will be comin' by way of the south road with the rest of the men.

"Men, I am still figurin' Muldoon could have his East Lake boys there. If they get in the way, you will have to move 'em, but, like I said before, if it's a fight they want, let them make the first move. When they do, you show 'em what for. Our pine is goin' downstream today, come hell or high water."

"We have the law on our side," Ingman continued. "Olaf and I will be there. So will Bill Burns and the Pinkertons. They will make it clear to anyone who gets in our way that we are acting within our lawful rights. So, like I said, our pine is gettin' drove today, come hell or high water."

"Ingman," shouted Blackie, "I reckon it's bound to be some of each. Today ol' Phineas Muldoon is gonna see both hell *and* high water!"

"Fine with us, Blackie," came a voice from the back. "We're ready to play to whatever cards is dealt."

"Men," shouted Ingman again, "you take care out there. Watch out for yourselves and watch out for each other. I want every man to show up in one piece to claim his pay. You fellas make this a gol damn good lumber camp. Olaf, Tor, and I are proud to work with such a good crew. Come fall, each and every one of you have a yob waitin' for you at the Namakagon Timber Company. Well, I guess that's it. Good luck!"

Junior jumped up on the table and cried out, "And those of you who owes me money on various bets here and there, well, don't forget me cause I ain't gonna forget you!"

"Junior," shouted Sourdough, "I don't know if you'd make a better tax collector or a preacher. Neither one leaves you with much in your pocket." Laughter rolled across the room.

"Any last questions?" shouted Olaf.

The room was silent.

"Then it's hell and high water, men. Let's have at 'er!"

Cheers filled the room as a hundred lumberjacks rose from the tables and rushed out to get their pike poles and peaveys.

A faint, peach-colored glow was beginning to show in the eastern sky. In the dim, morning twilight the men made their way to the shore.

Gust Finstead pulled the chain on the steam engine's whistle and a loud *screeet* split the air. Junior counted as thirty-four men boarded.

Within minutes, the Namakagon Timber Company's Empress Karina made her maiden voyage, pushing a large boom of logs across the open lake, wind at their backs. The engine ran smoothly, the paddlewheel slowly moving the boat and the great mass of pine slowly forward.

By the time they rounded Bear Point and moved into the narrows above the dam, the sun was breaking over the eastern horizon. A pair of loons flew overhead, their calls masked by the noise of the powerful engine.

As the log boom neared the dam, Gust split a link on the boom, setting the logs free. Junior backed off on the throttle, letting the timber drift toward the dam in the current. He turned the boat and nosed onto shore.

"Take your leave, fellas," shouted Tor. "We'll join you soon. Good luck to every last one of you."

Thirty-four Loken men jumped onto shore, each carrying either a peavey or a pike pole.

Junior brought the Karina about. Eager to fetch the next boom of logs, he opened the throttle wide. Smoke billowed from the sternwheeler's stack and water flew into the air behind as she crossed into the rising sun. Gust looked back to see the Loken timber drifting down the narrows with the current. "There goes our pine, boys! Tor, looks like your Uncle's plan just might work."

As loons called and sunlight filtered through the trees, two Loken wagons rounded the south end of the lake. Ingman and Olaf were in the lead rig, along with four security men, Blackie Jackson, and five more lumberjacks. Ten men rode in the next wagon. Others walked behind.

The roads were soft, but passable, and the horses sure-footed. Olaf knew they would have no trouble getting to the dam. "The trouble," he said to his brother, "will come after we get there."

As they passed the southwest corner of the lake, the Lokens looked far across the lake to see the Empress Karina, laden with lumberjacks and pushing the second boom out of the bay.

"They are makin' good time, Olaf," said Ingman. "Now let us hope Muldoon don't bring out an army of men. I am concerned about what Dearborne said."

"Dearborne?"

"About Muldoon's withdrawal."

"What of it?"

"Dearborne said it was all in five dollar bills. Two hundred of 'em." Makes me wonder."

"Two hundred?"

"Ya, Olaf. Two hundred."

"No reason to ponder it now, Ingman. The die is cast. Our boys will do fine. They are strong, smart, and determined. Our timber will get to the mills."

The Loken wagons soon tied up south of the dam. Ingman and Olaf watched as the men moved quietly through the woods toward their fellow workers. They emerged, finding a hundred men from King Muldoon's East Lake camp guarding the north side of the dam. Another hundred from Round Lake guarded the south. Muldoon's men carried peaveys, and ax handles.

Farther beyond, some walking along the shore and others riding the pine, came sixty-four of Olaf Loken's men. As they neared the dam, a shout was heard as King Muldoon's men attacked from the shoreline above. They jumped down onto Olaf's workers, shouting, and swinging their weapons.

In spite of being outnumbered, the Loken men fought back. They retreated onto the floating pine logs where their calked boots gave them a great advantage over the shoe-pacs worn by many of their opponents.

Within minutes, a dozen of Muldoon's men were neck-deep in the icy water, trying to dodge the great pine logs. The Loken men coaxed more of their opponents onto the timber as the battle between the camps raged on.

Ingman helped Olaf down from the wagon and into his wheel chair. He pushed his brother up to the door of the dam tender's office. From there they could see the men fighting all along the waterfront and out on the logs in the bay. They also heard Earl Morrison, the Pinkerton Chief, give the order for the rest of the Loken men to attack, shouting, "Lay into 'em, boys!"

Thirty-six Namakagon Timber Company lumberjacks rushed out of the woods, running to rescue their fellow workers. Attacking from behind, their peaveys and pike poles quickly laid low many of the Muldoon fighters, but they remained far-outnumbered. The Loken lumberjacks fought all the harder.

The sound of the pitched battle echoed off the trees that lined the shore. Peaveys struck cant hooks. Ax handles and pike poles flashed in the April sunlight. Men splashed into the ice-cold river while others held their positions atop bouncing, turning logs. The Loken men fought hard but could not overcome the overwhelming number of their opponents. They were losing the fight—until …

A blast from both barrels of a shotgun shattered the morning air.

"Olaf, look!" Ingman pointed to the opposite shore.

There, on the north side of the dam, was Chief Namakagon. Behind him stood more than a hundred Ojibwe men brandishing bows, clubs, shotguns and rifles. Namakagon gave a wave of his hand and three rifles were fired skyward. The fighting stopped. All attention shifted to the Ojibwes. Another

wave from Chief Namakagon and three shotguns discharged, their smoke shooting straight up into the air.

The Muldoon men lowered their weapons and began working their way from log to log, back to shore where they stood in silent submission. Not one Muldoon worker was willing to fight on. The battle was over.

Chief Namakagon raised his walking staff high in the air, knowing the Loken camp had prevailed. King Muldoon's attempt to stop the Namakagon Timber Company from driving their pine downstream had failed. Ogimaa Mikwam-migwan gave a loud victory cry, quickly answered by his men, then followed by a roar of cheers from the Loken lumberjacks.

The conflict over, eyes turned to the windows of the dam tender's office and King Muldoon staring down on them all.

Chapter 39
Hell and High Water

Phineas Muldoon and two of his men peered down from the open window as the battle came to an end. The office door flew open. Ingman Loken entered, followed by his wheelchair-bound brother.

"Muldoon, you are done," shouted Olaf. "Your men are defeated. Your Chicago henchmen are at my camp, chained to a tree by my Pinkerton men."

The old man turned away, staring out the window in silence.

"Phineas, your boys have no more gumption to fight," said Ingman. "Admit it, Muldoon, you have lost."

King Muldoon turned, "Now you listen here, and you listen good. You Lokens are not driving your logs across my dam. You are no more than immigrant trash. I buy and sell better men than you two every day. By the time I am done with you Lokens, you will be lucky to get work throwing slop to my hogs."

"You can't stop us, Phineas," Olaf said. "We have the law on our side, and, like it or not, we are taking our pine down this river."

"Law on your side? Humph. Loken, I–am–the–law! You are more of a fool than I thought. Why, I own every politician and lawman from here to Chippewa Falls. Law on your side, indeed. There is not a lawman in northwest Wisconsin who will stand against me."

"You are wrong," replied Olaf. "I may not have the legislators and the lawmen on my payroll, but I have something better, old man, I have *right* on my side. Phineas Muldoon, you—do—not—own—the—water."

Olaf reached into his coat pocket, pulled out an envelope, and waved it in the air. "This is a letter from Jeremiah Rusk, the Governor of Wisconsin. It says we have every right to send our pine down the river."

"The die is cast," said Ingman. "You have no right to stop us. Look out that window. We have over nine million board feet of prime white pine headin' for the spillway and you, you small man, you cannot stop it."

Muldoon rushed back to the window. The bay was thick with pine logs. Namakagon Timber Company drivers rode on top of them, working the logs toward the dam. The Loken pine stretched as far down the narrows as could be seen. To the east, smoke rose from the Empress Karina as Junior positioned the next boom of pine logs. Her shrill whistle pierced the air.

"Those are all our logs," said Olaf, pointing past the window. "And I have a hundred men, each determined to see to it every log reaches the mill."

"Phineas," said Ingman, "you have no more hired henchmen left to do your dirty work. You have lost. And next year you will lose again. And the next, and the next, and every year after."

"Fifty cents per log, Loken. That's my fee. Your letter does not say I cannot charge you a toll. You want to drive your pine? Then pay me for the privilege of crossing my private dam."

213

"Muldoon," Olaf shot back, "you cannot assess fifty cents a log any more than I can charge you a dollar for every breath of air you take! The Wisconsin Constitution clearly states that the waters of Wisconsin are forever free. You need to get that into your thick, greedy head. Forever free! Our timber is going downstream today and you have nothing to say about it. Nothing!"

"Wilson! Show these immigrants why they will gladly pay me."

King Muldoon's assistant opened a desk drawer, revealing a rack bar detonating device. Its wires led across the desk and out the nearest window. He placed the device on the desk just as the door swung open. Tor rushed in, crossing the room to his father's side.

"Now, you fools," said Muldoon, "you will see why they call me King. Yesterday, I had my man set two charges below the spillway. Either you accept my terms, or I will blast this dam sky-high and send the entire head of water down the river valley, leaving your pine behind, high—and—dry. High and dry and useless, just like you, Olaf Loken. I will waste every stick of your pine unless you agree to my terms."

Ingman rushed for the detonator, but stopped when Ed Wilson pulled up the handle, threatening to plunge it down again.

King Muldoon grinned. "Fifty cents per log, Loken."

"Never!" replied Olaf.

"Now, Wilson!"

"Wait!" shouted Tor. "What about the people at Pac-wa-wong? You'll drown them all."

"I care not about a handful of Ojibwes! You're as foolish as your father."

"You can't do this!" Tor shouted. He dove through the open window and rushed down the steep bank toward the base of the dam.

"Tor!" shouted Olaf. "Good Lord! No!"

Ingman bolted out the open doorway.

"Mercy's sake, Muldoon!" shouted Olaf.

"You see, Loken? I win after all, you miserable, cripple."

He turned to his hired man. "Wilson, set off those charges—right now—before the boy reaches them."

Wilson didn't move.

"Wilson!"

"No!" shouted Olaf. "Wilson! Don't do it. Are you willing to rot in jail for this twisted old man?"

Wilson still didn't move.

"Wilson!" screamed Muldoon, "These men are trespassing. I have every right to protect my property. Set off those charges. Now! That's an order!"

"I ain't no killer, Boss," Wilson cried, tearing the wires free and thrusting the rack bar box into his employer's hands. "I ain't gonna be party to killin' no boy and drownin' no Indians and I sure ain't goin' to prison for the likes of you."

Ed Wilson rushed out the office door with King Muldoon shouting,

214

"Wilson, get back here. Wilson!"

Outside, Tor scrambled down the steep bank following the wires toward the charges. Ingman rounded the building just in time to see his nephew slip on one of the large rocks and fall to the water's edge. Tor regained his footing and climbed up the rocks. Seeing the bundled sticks of dynamite, he fumbled for the wires, wrapped them around his hand, and gave a quick pull, snapping them from the first of the two charges.

With Ed Wilson gone, only King Muldoon and Olaf Loken remained in the office. Through the open door, both men could see Constable Burns and Earl Morrison running toward them from far down the shore.

"Well," said Muldoon, "it seems I will just have to set the charges off myself. It will be more satisfying this way."

"No!" shouted Olaf. He wheeled his chair as close as possible to Muldoon but, with the large desk in his way, could not reach him. "Phineas! My God, Phineas! You cannot do this!"

"Loken, you miserable cripple, look at you. How do you plan to stop me? Insignificant pawns like you will never stop men like me."

Laughing, Muldoon turned his back to Olaf and twisted the wires back onto the magneto contacts. He jerked the tee-handle up.

Olaf reached down, grabbed the leg of the large desk, and, with a mighty rush of adrenalin, flipped it onto its side, scattering papers and a large pile of five-dollar bills across the floor. He wheeled his chair into the back of Muldoon's legs, causing him to drop the rack bar box. The plunger went half way down but did not set off the remaining charge.

Grinning now, Muldoon kicked the wheelchair over. Olaf flew across the papers and bills that lay on the floor. The old man turned back to the window. He picked up the rack bar and placed it on the windowsill. Looking below, he saw Tor moving across the face of the dam toward the second dynamite charge. Muldoon pulled the plunger up.

Just as he was about to push it down, a large, powerful hand grabbed his shoulder and turned him around. There, with his left hand clamped like a vice on Phineas Muldoon's right shoulder, stood six-foot-four-inch Olaf Loken. The Norwegian's huge right hand was clenched and drawn back like a catapult waiting to be released. Muldoon's eyes and mouth opened wide in disbelief.

Chief Namakagon came through the doorway just in time to see Olaf's large fist strike Muldoon square on the chin. The blow lifted him off his feet and sent him sprawling across the office floor.

Olaf stood above him for a moment before turning to the window to look for Tor and Ingman in the rocks below.

The chief rushed around the overturned desk and wheelchair, joining Olaf at the window. Both men searched below for Tor and Ingman.

Muldoon lay on the floor looking up at a fire ax hanging on the wall. Scrambling to his feet, he pulled it free and ran toward Olaf with the ax held high. He swung the ax down toward Olaf's head, but the big man sensed him coming and ducked away from the window. The momentum of the ax carried Muldoon past Namakagon and Olaf, flipping him out of the open window and down onto the rocks below.

Chief Namakagon reached out to catch him, but Muldoon was gone, the rack bar with him.

Olaf watched the rack bar bounce down the steep, rocky bank, knowing each time it hit the rocks, the dynamite might go off. Again and again it bounced, clattering down the boulders. Olaf watched in horror as it tumbled out of sight. His son was nowhere to be seen.

Suddenly, the blast shook the nearby woods and waters, echoing across the lake. Olaf was thrown back into the room by the terrific explosion. Namakagon caught him, and they both landed on the floor. Far below, timbers flew into the stream, washed by torrents of water. A deep rumbling sound came from within the dam.

Chief Namakagon helped his unsteady friend to his feet. They returned to the window to see a large stream of water shooting straight out from the left-center of the dam.

"Tor!" screamed Ingman from the rocks above.

Chief pointed at the spillway below. "Look! Tor! And Ingman! There!"

Tor climbed out from between two large boulders. As he ascended the rocks, he spotted Muldoon lying in the rising water only yards away.

"Stay there, I'll help you," Tor shouted.

"No, Son!" yelled his father. "It's too dangerous!" Get out of there before the whole dam gives way."

The water's rush and roar above drowned out his father's words. Tor scrambled down, nearer to Muldoon.

A second, deep rumble shook the dam. Several logs washed over the top and were immediately whisked downstream by the raging water. Another support timber gave way and a huge stream of water blasted through a wider breach in the dam. A score of men, unable to help, looked on from above.

"Phineas! Grab my hand!" screamed Tor over the roar of the water.

Muldoon tried, but could not reach the boy's hand.

"Tor," screamed his father, "the dam is givin' way! Save yourself!"

The rumbling grew louder. Tor peeled off his shirt and flipped one end to Muldoon who grabbed for it, missed, then caught it, clutching tightly. Tor pulled Muldoon from the water.

They both climbed up the rocks, Tor in the lead, and the icy water rising fast. More logs drifted into the breach above, some dropping over the

216

dam, others jamming in tightly.

Muldoon, hunting for any handhold as they climbed, found Tor's ankle. Grasping it, he pulled himself up, causing Tor to slip and fall. Muldoon glanced down at the boy, grinned, and resumed his ascent.

But Tor was lean, strong, and agile. He quickly scrambled up and beyond the old man, and reached the top of the wall.

More logs plugged the breach. The rumbling ceased. An eerie silence followed.

From far within the dam wall came another deep, earth-shaking rumble, then a thunderous roar as the other side of the structure collapsed, sending an enormous torrent of water rushing through the dam. With the water came tens, then hundreds of white pine logs, eight to twenty feet long, two to five feet in diameter. The water flooded both spillway and channel, engulfing Muldoon, and throwing his frail body into the icy, white, swirling vortex below, now crowded with logs.

"Muldoon!" Tor screamed. He climbed down toward him again. "Muldoon!"

The old man struggled to swim. Within seconds, a dozen huge pine logs surrounded him, bobbing and slamming into each other with extraordinary force. Horrified, Tor watched as the logs closed in, crushing King Muldoon.

Within minutes, a thousand logs washed over the dam as raging ice water blasted violently into the gorge below. It tore trees from the banks, moved large boulders and turned the clear river into a dark, muddy torrent, destroying all hope of finding any remains of Phineas King Muldoon.

Tor rounded the building and ran into the dam tender's office, Ingman close behind. There, standing near the window was his father, his wheelchair still lying on the floor.

"Pa! Look at you!" Tor ran to his father. "Pa! You're standin' up!"

"Dang well about time, Son. Took me a good long while to get out of that insufferable chair. Now, maybe we can get some work done around here."

Chapter 40
The Spring Drive

The shrill whistle of the Karina echoed across Lake Namakagon. Junior Kavanaugh, pilot, and Gust Finstead, camp blacksmith, released the fourth boom of logs. Junior brought the steam-powered sternwheeler about and headed back across the lake for another log boom.

On the west end of the narrows, Earl Morrison, Pinkerton Detective, stepped into the dam tender's office along with Constable Bill Burns. "We watched it all from the far side of the dam," said Morrison. "Tor, you did all you could to save Muldoon I doubt many others would have risked themselves for the old scoundrel. I surely know I wouldn't."

"He was a fella in trouble," said Tor. "I should have done more."

Tor's father spoke. "Had Phineas Muldoon not come at me with that ax, he never would have ended up in the river, Son. He chose his own trail."

"We each choose our own trail," said Namakagon. "What we do along the way determines who we are. Muldoon could have done so much more with his life—so much good. Yet this is how he will be remembered. Only this."

"Namakagon," said Olaf. "How can I ever thank you? The outcome would have been so much different without you and your people. You saved our camp."

"My friends needed no persuasion, Olaf. They knew what was right. They also desired to protect their village."

"Ingman and I will see to it they are rewarded," Olaf said. "And Bill, the money for Muldoon's men is there on the floor. Be sure every one of his men who came here today gets his pay. I am sure they were promised it. Let's see to it that they get it."

"I will do that, Olaf," said the constable. "Then I'll head back to the camp to get those hog-tied hoodlums off to the sheriff. I'll let him know about Muldoon and what went on here. He'll be up to talk to you, Olaf."

"Ya. Fine, Bill. Say, you better get hold of Muldoon's walkin' boss, too. He needs to let all of Muldoon's lumber camps know what happened here today and reassure them they will get their winter's pay when their timber reaches the mills."

"As for us," said Ingman, "our pine is already on its way downstream. Blackie and his crew have moved out. Our other drivers will be close behind. We have a good head of water and should make quick work of this drive, Olaf. Tor, say so long to your pa. Yust you wait, nephew, by nightfall, you'll be soaked through and worn to a frazzle—a bona fide river pig!"

"Yes, sir, Uncle Ingman!" Tor reached out and shook his father's strong hand, then hugged him tightly. "Thank you, Pa."

"Take care, Son. You pay close attention to what your Uncle Ingman and Blackie tell you. Take no foolish chances, now. I expect you back, safe and sound, in a few days with tales to tell. And bring me the latest copy of the *St.*

Paul Pioneer Press, Son." He reached in his pocket, pulling out a double eagle and, handing it to his son, "Here, take this. High time you traded those tattered britches of yours for some new ones. Something tells me we'll be getting around more."

"Thanks, Pa!" Tor slid the coin into his back pocket, fastening the button.

"And, Tor, when you call on that gal of yours, give my best to Mrs. Ringstadt. Let Adeline know I shall be walking up her front steps one of these days to enjoy one of her home-cooked dinners."

By late afternoon, the Namakagon Timber Company drivers were stretched out along the untamed river for fifteen miles. Ingman, Tor, Rusty O'Hara, and Mason Fitch made their way downriver on the large logs, passing under the Omaha Railroad trestle near Cable. As they did, the sound of rushing water mixed with the calls from a flock of northbound Canada geese. Tor looked up.

"Tor, you keep your gol dang eye on the river, Nephew," shouted Ingman, "and watch that bend ahead. Looks like they're bunchin' up."

"I'll loosen 'em up, Boss," yelled Rusty. Using his twelve-foot pike pole for balance, he sprinted downstream across the logs. Before the others could catch him, he broke up the beginnings of a jam.

"Mason, you best hang back here to keep the pine from yammin' up on this bend," shouted Ingman over the roar of rushing water.

As the other three worked on downstream, the river narrowed. Banks on both sides rose sharply and a loud roar came from the rapids ahead.

"Best yump off here, fellas," shouted Ingman. "This next stretch is a man-killer."

They jumped onto shore and followed the riverbank downstream. Below them, they watched the pine they had been riding on only moments before. The raging current now tossed the large logs as though they were mere twigs. Some flew end over end, smashing into each other and the rocky river bottom. Minutes later, in calmer water, the three drivers stepped onto the logs again.

By nightfall, they reached the Ojibwe village at Pac-wa-wong. Fifteen other Loken camp river pigs sat around a large campfire, hoping to dry off before turning in. They let Ingman, Tor, and Rusty get close to the fire. Of all the men, only O'Hara was dry above the waist.

"I don't see how you do it, Rusty," said Tor. "I must've been dunked a dozen times or more. I lost count somewhere below the railroad trestle."

"Simple, Tor. You gotta be smarter than the log you're ridin'."

"Ya, O'Hara, yust you vait," said Klaus Radlinger. "You'll get your bath, too. Lord knows you needs one 'fore you reach dem Hayvird dance halls."

"Don't mock me, fellas," smiled Rusty. "I'm the only one here who's bearin' dry tobacco." He filled his pipe and passed his can of Plowboy to the man next to him. Three women from the village brought the men smoked suckers and cornbread for their supper.

"You figure Blackie made it all the way to Hayward before dark set in, Uncle Ingman?" asked Tor.

"I wouldn't be surprised if they're walkin' into town right now. Blackie is a determined fellow when it comes to whisky and women."

"We'll catch up with them in the sweet morrow," said Rusty.

In the crisp, April night air, the Loken lumberjacks sat by the fire, steam rolling off their wool shirts, hats, boots, and britches. It drifted up into the moonlit sky. All the men grew quiet now, thinking about the day's events and wondering what tomorrow would bring. They all slept soundly that night, their calked boots and socks drying before the coals.

As the eastern sky began to show its first faint glow of daylight, Zeke and Zach Rigby arrived with two other Loken men. They rekindled the fire, put on the large coffee pot, and opened the wannigan sent by Sourdough.

The men filled up on smoked pork, blackjack, and cold beans, grabbed their peaveys and pike poles, and headed for the river. They found it thick with logs floating downstream in the high water. The men stepped out onto the logs and worked their way through the slower reaches of the river, breaking several small jams. Some drivers hung back at sharp bends to keep the pine moving. At a quarter past nine, the logs ahead slowed, then stopped.

"Log-yam ahead'," shouted Ingman.

The water rushed up and over the logs as they piled into each other. Rusty O'Hara, walking the logs spryly, rounded the next bend to see two men far downstream.

"Ingman," shouted Rusty back to his boss, "if I ain't mistaken, that be Blackie and Mike Fremont ahead."

"They should be far downstream by now. Must be a pretty good yam."

Tor and Ingman crossed the river, stepping from log to log. They climbed up onto the riverbank, joining Rusty and soon reached the two men at the sharp bend, seven miles upstream from the new Hayward millpond.

"Blackie," shouted Ingman, "I figured by now you'd be tryin' to win back your winter's wages at some poker table."

"Mornin', Boss. 'Bout time you got here. We been fightin' this dang jam all night. Each time we bust her loose she jams up again. I figure it's that boulder there," he said, pointing below the logjam. "It must've been rolled out here by the rush of water yesterday. No matter what we do, it's gonna keep jammin'."

"Can we blast it out of there?" asked Ingman.

220

"I thought about that. But I lost my rucksack to the river yesterday. I see you still got yours."

Blackie, Ingman, and the others studied the jam. Klaus cut a ten-foot sapling and trimmed off the branches. Ingman wired two sticks of dynamite to the end, inserted a blasting cap, cut thirty seconds of waterproof fuse, and his men all stepped back. He lit the fuse and jammed the pole under the logs, just behind the boulder, then ran for the woods.

Ingman counted out loud as he ran. "Fourteen Minnesota, fifteen Minnesota, sixteen Minnesota, seventeen Minnesota," He ducked behind a large maple tree and peered around the trunk at the river. "Keep your heads down, fellas," he shouted. "Twenty-seven Minnesota, twenty-eight Minnesota, twenty-nine Minnesota—heads down, men."

Nothing happened.

Seconds lapsed. Still nothing.

"Ingman," shouted Rusty, "did you remember to light it?" Some of the men stepped out from behind their trees.

Suddenly, the dynamite exploded, echoing down the river valley.

The shock from the blast knocked Lester Moore back over the fallen log he hid behind moments earlier. He did a backwards somersault, landing in shallow, black, backwater muck.

"Must've cut your fuse a bit long there, Ingman," Blackie shouted.

Disgusted, Lester sat up, covered with black mud. "If you don't mind, Boss, you'd better have Blackie cut your fuse from here on out."

"Don't you be worryin' about it, Lester," yelled Rusty. "You'll be washed clean a dozen times 'fore we again reach civilization." The roar of the rushing water masked Lester's reply, but the howling laughter of the other drivers carried well up and downstream.

The blast had lifted the boulder onto the bank, but the logjam held fast.

"Let's loosen her up, boys," shouted Blackie.

With pike poles and peaveys, they worked the jam, looking for the key to the tangled mass of pine. Ice-cold water sprayed out below, between, and above the logs, making the search difficult and soaking the men.

Upstream, the water was rising fast. Here, more and more logs piled up.

"Stand aside, men," yelled Blackie above the rush of water. "I think I got 'er figured out."

The men backed away as Blackie thrust the handle of his peavey between two logs and gave a good pull. The log moved slightly. Then, under the enormous pressure of water upstream, the sixteen-foot log shot out into the air, flipped end for end, and splashed into the pool below. The twenty-foot-high logjam let loose with a thunderous roar and rush of pine and water. Giant logs were hurled, and flipped through the air. Blackie dashed across the logs toward shore but lost his footing on the wet, shifting timber. Caught in the rush of pine and water, he was thrown into the pool with the logs.

The men all raced toward him, but Blackie Jackson immediately disappeared below the churning mass of wood and muddy water.

Hoping to rescue his friend, Rusty risked joining him by running the logs to the opposite bank of the wild and powerful river. The lumberjacks stared helplessly into the violent pool.

Seconds stretched into minutes. Silent now, these great, robust men, these bulls of the woods, now stood motionless—weak and helpless before the furious caldron of ice, water, and wood. No one spoke. The only sound was the roar of the river and the bashing of timber against timber.

Above it all came a shout. "What's the gol dang holdup, fellas?"

Downstream, peavey in hand, thoroughly drenched and missing his hat, stood Blackie Jackson on the far shore.

"Yackson! For Saint Pete's sake, we thought the dang devil had ya!"

"Who do you think threw me up on this here riverbank, Boss? I would've showed up sooner, but I lost my gol dang peavey and had to go back into the drink for it. A man ain't worth much on the river without his peavey."

Throughout the week, the men, now stretched all along the river, guided the great pine logs downstream. By dusk of the fourth day, most of the Loken timber was nearing the new sawmill at the Hayward dam. A. J. Hayward's mill hands would take it from there.

That evening, those log drivers within walking distance of any Hayward saloon made the trek. Most had their money buttoned into a pocket to prevent it from being lost in the river, but no button would keep their money from disappearing in the saloons, poker rooms, and sporting houses of Hayward. Tonight, like most spring nights, this pinery boomtown was packed with thousands of lumberjacks.

In the light of the rising moon, Tor Loken jumped from log to log, crossing the wide millpond some now called Lake Hayward. Reaching the shore, he climbed the steep bank and followed the trail into town. The around-the-clock clouds of smoke from the sawdust burners led the way. He crossed the railroad yard. Hundreds of empty boxcars lined the sidings, each waiting to be filled with pine lumber.

As Tor walked up the street, music poured out from the many, lively saloons along Iowa Avenue. Men, celebrating the end of the winter cut, filled the taverns now, spilling out onto the boardwalks and muddy streets. Every store was open, catering to the rush of lumberjacks looking to spend their winter earnings.

Wagons, buggies, horses, and oxen occupied most of the hitching posts along the deeply rutted street. The odors from the animals mixed with those of the sawed pine and smoldering sawdust. "The smell of fortunes being made," Tor recalled from his time in the Chicago coal yard.

Tor went directly to Callahan's Mercantile. Three clerks were there to assist the lumberjacks now exploring the store. Tor picked out a white cotton shirt, a matching Arrow collar, cotton britches, leather shoes, socks, underwear, and a smart, dark blue jacket. He removed his damp, ragged hat, studied it with

222

affection, and stuffed it into his back pocket, trying on several from the shelf of boxed hats. He chose a blue derby, similar in every way but the color, to his Uncle Ingman's.

Tor approached a clerk. "I'd like to put these on."

The clerk motioned toward the back room.

Minutes later, Tor returned, looking and feeling like a new man.

"I'll take a dime's worth of peppermint sticks to boot," he said as he handed his double eagle to the clerk, "and, could you put those in three bags?"

The clerk grinned. "You tryin' to sweeten up some young ladies?"

"Well, one bag's for Mrs. Ringstadt. She owns the boarding house up on the hill. The second bag is for her daughter and she is far sweeter than any old peppermint stick. I hope to use the third to coax her little sisters to make themselves as scarce as feathers on a fish. Say, which way's the closest barbershop?"

"Around the corner," said the clerk. "But you'll have a good long wait with all the lumberjacks in town tonight."

The clerk gave Tor his change before wrapping his work clothes and boots in brown paper tied with cotton string.

Much later, Tor emerged from the barber shop, well-groomed and smelling of wintergreen tonic. He turned up the boardwalk, clutching a bundle of work clothes in his right hand, candy in his left. Whistling, he walked gingerly up the street, soon reaching the boarding house steps.

The sweet sound of soft piano music drifted through the open window. He listened for a few seconds before knocking on the door. The music stopped. He heard footsteps. The corner of the curtain moved. The door flew open. Tor Loken dropped his packages and wrapped his arms around Rosie, hugging her as though he would never let go.

Chapter 41
The Way of Wenebojo

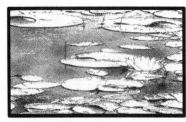

On the last day of April, Tor's cedar strip canoe glided smoothly and silently across the bay in the early morning light. A warm, southern breeze brought with it the fresh scents of early spring. Reaching his destination, Tor rested his paddle and drifted into position. Then, with a single, strong thrust, the bow slid up onto the sand beach on the west end of the small island.

Stepping out, Tor noticed another canoe slowly skirting the far side of the lake. He gazed at it for a moment, then turned as Makade and Waabishki, tails wagging, bounded down the bank to greet him.

"Chief Namakagon," he called. The old Indian stepped into the sunlight, squinting and shading his eyes with his hand.

"Welcome, young woodsman."

"Boil up some water for tea, Mikwam-migwan, I brought along a hunk of Sourdough's yellowjack and some molasses cookies." He grabbed his pack and climbed the hill, the dogs in the lead. The tea was soon steeping.

"Most of the men in our camp are gone now," said Tor as he helped himself to a piece of yellowjack. "Junior and his pa left two weeks ago. They have crops to put in. Junior says, come November, he'll be back for his third year in the pinery. Now, other than Pa, Uncle Ingman, and me, there's only Sourdough and Gust Finstead left to mind the camp."

"And the animals?"

"Well, we kept a couple of good teams and four ridin' horses. The rest of our workhorses we sent along with the men to use over the summer. They'll bring them back next fall, fat and sassy, pa says. Sourdough had a say in things too. We kept a boar and four sows and two milk cows. We'll have plenty of cream and milk for cookin' and butter and such, and I expect we'll get plenty of pork for next winter, the way those swine have been acting.

"Pa put in a bid for the Bass Lake Camp. Plenty of good pine and hemlock left to harvest up there. My uncle says we're likely to win the bid."

"Good land," said Namakagon. "Good pine. Needs to be treated with respect. I hope your father wins the chance." He paused in thought. "Tor, some see our Earth Mother much like your basket of yellowjack, there. Some think they were given life so they could take without giving back. They think not of the future. Others, like your father and uncle, work to protect the land so those who come later can enjoy the richness of nature. You, Tor, are one of the protectors." He paused again. "There is something old Mikwam-migwan needs to share with you. Many years ago a wise old man who watched over this land placed his trust in me, just as I now trust in you. He was called Old Bear. He took me to a hidden cave where silver garnishes the walls like stars grace the black winter sky."

"Yes, I remember you speaking of it."

"It is time for me to pass this knowledge on to the person I trust most."

"You mean me? Isn't there someone else who should know about this?"

"No. I have searched my mind and my heart. There are others who want to know but you are the one I have chosen."

"I have heard some of our jacks talk about the secret silver mine. I think they figured it was just another yarn told to pass the winter nights."

Namakagon laughed. "This is the work of Wenebojo. He confuses any who might abuse nature's gifts. I am off to Marengo Lake today for spruce roots and birch bark to build a new canoe. Come with. I will show you the cave."

"I am honored to have your confidence, Mikwam-migwan. Yes, I will go along with you. But, first, tell me more about this Wenebojo. I have heard you mention him before. Who is he?"

"Wenebojo?" Namakagon paused again. "Some say he is a spirit. Some say he is a man. Some say both. Wenebojo wanders the land, eager to teach us the lessons of life. Sometimes he guards us from each other and, sometimes from ourselves. He plays tricks on us to help us remember exactly who is in charge. At the same time, he works to protect nature and his grandmother, the Earth. Some say he can change from man to animal to plant to rock and back."

"So Wenebojo is made up, like Paul Bunyan?"

"Oh, no. You see, Tor, Wenebojo is more than just stories. He watches us. He could be watching us now. He can lead you to safety or into danger. He can make you lost in the forest one moment and tell you where you are the next. He brings the frost to the ferns each autumn. In the winter, just when you plan on traveling to town for supplies, he brings you a blizzard. When you think the winter will never end, he brings you warm, sunny days to melt away the snow. When you have fished in the cold rain for hours without a bite and are ready to quit, it is Wenebojo who will tug on your line to make you stay and suffer longer. In the summer, if you are not paying attention, he will make the sun so hot it will make your skin burn all night. You never know with him. Listen closely to the wind in the pines, Tor, you might hear Wenebojo laughing at us. Oh, no. Wenebojo is more than stories. Much more."

"Then, you say he is real?"

"Wenebojo is what he wants to be. He is real and he is not. He is always there and he is never there."

The two friends finished their food. Before leaving the island, Tor helped Namakagon hang a dozen large, slabs of pike in the old Indian's birch bark smokehouse.

Tor dropped one onto the dirt floor. "Don't blame me. Wenebojo made me lose my grip."

"Young woodsman, do not use him to explain your own mistakes. If he likes you, you will do well. If Wenebojo does not like you, life can be miserable.

I once heard of a dozen Frenchmen who made a latrine on a riverbank.

When rain washed it all down the bank, spoiling the water, they blamed it on Wenebojo. That day, seven of them, those who had used the latrine, drowned in the rapids. The men who had not used the latrine survived. No, Tor, never mock Wenebojo. He can be your friend, but you do not want him for an enemy."

Namakagon threw a hatful of tag alder chips onto the coals and closed the buckskin flap, tying it tightly to retain the sweet smoke. There would be plenty of smoked fish to put in the ice house when they returned.

Tor and Chief Namakagon stepped into the canoe followed by Waabishki and Makade. A quick push and they were out onto the lake. They paddled north, far up into the creek until brush and windfalls blocked their way. Namakagon found his old portage trail.

After lashing their paddles to the thwarts, Tor raised the light canoe onto his shoulders. With the two dogs and Namakagon in the lead, Tor followed the well-tramped trail to the next lake. They crossed the lake and portaged again, skirting the next small lake and crossing a bubbling creek.

Tor noticed steep ridges on either side of their trail now. Rocky outcroppings faced the trail from both sides. Neither Tor nor the chief noticed the dark shape moving quietly behind them.

A shadow flashed across the trail.

"Look. Our brother the eagle is here to show us the way."

Tor rested the canoe's stern on the low limb of a tree and looked out from under. Above, a bald eagle flew so close that each wing beat could be heard.

"We are near, young woodsman. We have but one more lake to cross."

They crossed the last lake, paddled up the creek that fed it, and pulled the canoe onto shore. The last leg of the trek would be without a canoe on Tor's shoulders.

They hiked fewer than a hundred yards when Tor heard a faint noise in the brush. The dogs froze, staring down the trail. The hair on their backs and necks stood on end. They growled a warning to the menace ahead. A huge bear stepped out onto the trail. Tor and Namakagon remained motionless.

"This could be Wenebojo now," whispered the chief.

The bear turned toward them, stopped, and then stood up on its hind legs. On its chest was a large, white, diamond-shaped blaze. The deep growls from Waabishki and Makade grew louder and more threatening. The bear stood frozen for a moment, before it ambled down the trail away from them.

"Wenebojo? Really?" asked Tor, heart pounding.

"Who can say? Wenebojo may have revealed himself to us as a makwaa. Perhaps, like the eagle, he shows us the way. We are very close."

They continued down the trail, following the bear through another steep ravine before it disappeared into the thick woods. Both dogs suddenly spun around, looking behind. Makade growled again.

Namakagon turned, looking back down the trail just as a black-bearded man holding a double-barrel shotgun stepped out. "Animosh, hide!" said the chief to his dogs in a strong whisper. Both dogs dashed into the underbrush.

"Stand tall and reach high," shouted the short, heavy man. Both Tor and Namakagon obeyed. "Where'd them two dogs go off to?"

"You scared them so bad they ran off, mister. We have no money to rob," shouted Tor.

"Sonny," came the reply. "I ain't after no small change."

Namakagon recognized his voice. "Tor, I believe we are in the company of Percival Wilkins."

"That bandit who drowned under the Hayward trestle?"

"That's me, Sonny, the one yer Indian friend, here, left fer dead under the bridge. Well, no—such—luck. You see, Indian, there was a pocket of air under all that snow and ice. I laid there in that freezin' water till I heard the train pull off. Then I broke through and climbed out of that icy grave you left me in. I been fixin' every day since to square up, Indian. And to learn the whereabouts' of yer silver poke. High time we even up the score. Show me to yer mine or the boy, here, won't see hisself another sunrise."

"There is no silver, Percy, just the tall tales of lumberjacks," said Namakagon. "You have wasted your chance to put your past behind."

"Lies!" shouted the thug, pointing the double barrel at Tor and pulling back one of the hammers. "Show me the silver, Chief, or I pull this here trigger!"

"All right! I will show you the way if you let the boy leave."

"I'll let the both of yous go when you show me the silver. Not before."

"How do we know you won't kill us both?" said Tor.

"You ain't no good to me dead, Sonny. After I fill my bags with silver I'll be needin' the both of yous to help me pack it out. Now, Indian, what's it gonna be? Do I kill the boy or do we go get that silver?"

"This is the place. The cave is right here."

The bandit's eyes searched the surroundings, seeing no cave, no silver.

"You takin' me for a fool?" The gunman thrust the gun barrel forward.

Chief Namakagon pushed aside the lower branches of the closest balsam tree to reveal a large, flat, knee-high boulder with a shallow opening under its center. "It is here. It's at the foot of any passerby."

The bandit moved toward the cave entrance, keeping his gun trained on Tor. He bent down, looking into the opening. "Well, so it is. Now, just how are we gonna to go about this? You, boy. You first. Git in there, find me some silver and git back here fast."

Namakagon nodded, and Tor obeyed. Kneeling down before the entrance, he gave Namakagon a quick glance and then slid head first on his belly, wiggling through the shallow opening. His legs and feet disappeared.

Inside, the cavern's interior was totally black. Waabishki and Makade startled him, licking his face in the dark. Soon, the cave took on form as his eyes adjusted. Only a soft glow came from under the cave entrance.

"What do you see in there, boy?" came a voice from outside.

"Nothing. Too dark."

"Strike a match, then."

"I have none."

"You, Indian, you got matches?"

"No," replied the chief, "Flint and steel."

"Well, reach it under there. Hand it to the boy."

Namakagon pulled a small buckskin pouch from his belt, knelt, then reached under the large rock with his fire kit. The thug eased the shotgun's hammer down.

"I cannot reach him," said Namakagon.

"Get on yer damn belly, then."

The chief flattened out, reaching far under the rock with both hands.

"Boy," shouted Wilkins, "can you reach it?"

"No."

"Farther. Reach farther," shouted the bandit. Namakagon crawled forward into the cave.

"Now, boy?"

"Nope. Still can't."

"Damn it all! Reach farther in there."

Chief Namakagon slid farther under the rock. Now, the gunman could see only his calves and feet sticking out.

Inside the cavern, Tor could now make out the hands and wrists of his friend. He reached down, grabbed onto both of Chief's wrists and shouted "I think I can reach it now. Should I take it?"

Namakagon answered, "Do you think you can, Tor?"

"I know I can. Should I take it?"

"Well, 'course you should, Sonny," shouted the thief, resting his gun against the trunk of the balsam.

"Namakagon," called Tor, "should I?"

"Pull," bellowed the chief. "Pull!"

That was all Tor needed to hear. He tightened his grip on Chief's wrists and lunged back into the darkness, whisking Chief Namakagon into the black cavern with him. Both dogs greeted him with wet tongues as they had Tor.

Outside, Wilkins saw the chief's legs and feet disappear under the rock. He reached for his shotgun, pulled back the hammers but no target remained.

"Damn you. Damn you both!" he screamed. "Don't think fer one minute that I won't wait here till you both starve yourselves dead or come out with my silver. Damn you both."

"Good work, young woodsman. We are safe from the slow-witted hoodlum, for now."

"Chief, with that bushwhacker out there and the four of us in here, well, just what are we gonna do? We sure could use some help from ol' Wenebojo."

"Wenebojo. Yes. It would be good if we could call on him in this time of need. Yes. Wenebojo."

Chapter 42
The Cavern

In the absolute black of the cavern, Namakagon opened the leather pouch containing his fire kit. He fumbled through its contents, finding some fine birch bark tinder and the flint and steel. Over and over he struck the two together, trying to ignite the tinder. With each strike, the flash from the spark bounced off the cavern walls showing countless veins of tarnished, black metal. The spark took, and the tinder began to glow. As Old Bear did so many years before, Namakagon blew life into the fire and held it high as the flame grew.

The flickering light allowed Tor to make out a narrow cave with tall sides and a rocky, uneven floor. The walls were wet with condensation—the air musty and cold. Pools of water helped cast the firelight onto the silver veins reflecting from the walls. The glow from the flaming birch reached far back into the cave, reflecting off more and more and still more of the dark metal.

"Chief, it's …it's amazing! Now I see why you protect this place."

"The silver has been safe here for many thousands of years. I did not think old Mikwam-migwan had the right to change that. Or to take more than that needed to help others. I hope you will follow this philosophy, my friend."

"You can be sure I will—if we ever get out of here."

"We will get out.

"You, Bushwhacker, you still out there?" called Namakagon.

"I'll be here till the winter snows come, Indian."

Namakagon searched the cave floor near the entrance finding some dried leaves, small sticks, and dried moss. He pushed them into a small pile and dropped the glowing tinder onto it. Soon a small fire lit the cave.

"Is there another entrance?" asked Tor.

"I have searched twice and found no other opening."

"What should we do?"

"Nothing. We will wait Wilkins out. He carried no pack and will need food. I have a bit of pemmican. There is good water farther back in the cave. The advantage is ours."

"Indian!" came a shout from outside. "I'll make you a bargain. You send out a hundred pounds of silver, and I will be off for good."

"All right, Bushwhacker, but it will take us a week to collect that much."

"A week? I ain't gonna wait no week."

"That's up to you, Percy," yelled Tor. "We got plenty of food and water in here. You go back to your camp. We'll gather up a hundred pounds and put it outside. When you get back, you cart it off, and we'll never cross paths again."

"You're takin' me for a fool again, boy. If I leave, even for a minute, you'll skedaddle, and I'll be on the run again. No sir. I ain't leavin'."

"What about tools?" shouted Namakagon. "We need picks and shovels."

"Confound you! Maybe I'll git some dynamite. Seal this cave for good!"

Namakagon pulled a three-inch shard of silver from the cave wall.

"Percy, this is why you won't do that." He flipped it out into the daylight.

Pulling his knife, Wilkins scraped the metal, exposing pure, shining silver. He sighed, then sat down to wait. Hours passed. Shadows darkened the ravine, and cooler air soon had the thief shivering. He built a fire.

Inside, Namakagon took another small piece of silver from the wall. He pulled a pinch of tobacco from his pouch and sat down across the small fire from Tor. Chanting softly, he dropped the small bit of silver into the fire, then offered tobacco to the flames. His dogs sat nearby, watching their master in the dim firelight. The smoke from the tobacco rose straight up in a single wisp—a thin, white ribbon, slowly turning in the dark cavern.

"Young woodsman, I have something for you." The old Indian removed his silver wrist band. "This was given to me by my friend Old Bear on the day he showed me this place. I have worn it for many decades. Now it should be yours, young woodsman."

"I am honored, Ogimaa Mikwam-migwan. But why not keep it?"

"No. The time is right for me to begin passing my few earthly possessions to those who can keep them alive. I have lingered here for more than one hundred years. The day will come when the morning sun no longer lights my way. Carry this for me. As long as you do, I will continue to roam these woods and waters with you. It is right."

Tor placed the band on his wrist. "I will, Namakagon. I will carry it all my life. I will pass it to someone trustworthy and strong. And I will do the same with this place. If we get out of here in one piece, I pledge to you, as long as I am alive, no one else will ever know of this cave, and no silver will leave here unless it is to serve someone who really needs it."

Chief Namakagon extended his right arm across the smoldering fire, as did Tor. They each grasped the other's wrist and held tight. The tobacco smoke encircled their hands before rising to the ceiling.

The old man nodded in approval as they both leaned back against the wall, staring at the glowing embers. Putting another pinch of tobacco onto the coals, the old Indian resumed his chant. As before, a thin ribbon of white smoke rose gracefully. Tor stared at the rising smoke, mesmerized by it and by Ogimaa Mikwam-migwan's somber song.

Tor jumped to his feet. "Namakagon, the smoke! Where is it going? There must be another opening." He tried to follow it in the darkness, the chief close behind. "We need more light."

A flash from Namakagon's flint and steel abruptly lit the chamber for an instant. Tor saw the trail of smoke snake around a huge boulder and rise high into the cavern. A second flash was followed by a third and a fourth and a fifth. The smoke snaked deeper and deeper into the darkness where more blackened silver glimmered from the wet cavern walls. Tor followed the smoke.

"You must stop," said Namakagon, grabbing the boy's shoulder. "This cave goes many ways. It has places as high as the tallest pine and as deep as Gitchee Gumi. You are young with much to lose, should something go wrong. I will see where this leads."

"And isn't this more dangerous for an old man?"

"You have many years left. I do not. I will take the dogs with me. Maybe they can help find where the smoke goes. Return, Tor. Make more smoke. I will follow it to see if it will lead us out."

"But, we should go together."

"Tor, if we both leave the entrance, Wilkins could enter and capture us again. If that happens, he is sure to kill us both. We cannot give him that opportunity. Besides, one of us must feed the fire, keep this smoke rising. You must go back. Take this," he said, handing Tor the pemmican. "Make it last."

Tor said nothing. He gave Namakagon a bear hug and took the pemmican. Chief Namakagon disappeared into the black of the cavern.

Moments later, through the darkness Namakagon heard, "Ogimaa Mikwam-migwan, may Gitchee Manitou and all the spirits walk with you."

Tor fed what few dead leaves and little moss he could find to the fire, sending white smoke toward the ceiling. The light near the cave entrance was growing dim. He waited impatiently, tending the smoky fire, searching for any scrap of fuel, wondering where this smoky trail might lead his friend.

Chief Namakagon followed the smoke. Each flash from his flint and steel gave him another look down the narrow passages. He watched the smoke rise high, beyond several large boulders protruding from the cave wall.

Makade and Waabishki climbed the rocks, their master laboring to keep up. The smoke snaked along. "Where do you take me?" he said into the darkness. "What spirit must I call upon to find my way?"

He struck the flint again. As before, the thin ribbon of smoke silently twisted along another passage. Namakagon followed.

Tor moved closer to the cavern's entrance, feeling April's cold evening air enter the cave. His fire was almost out. He had no more fuel. Tor knelt, looking out, but could see only the dim reflections of Wilkins' campfire. "You still out there, Bushwhacker? Halloo. Somebody there?"

"I'm still waitin' for you, boy," came a calm voice from outside. "You had enough? You comin' out? I won't harm you, boy. Come on out."

"Why don't you come in here, instead?" shouted Tor. "We have dried apples and smoked venison to share with you. And the water in here is clear and cold as the night sky in January. Come and join us for supper, Bushwhacker."

"Sure I will, Sonny. I'll just send my shotgun in ahead of me, then slide under this here rock, and you can give it back to me, right? What kind of fool do you take me for, Sonny?"

"The ordinary kind, Bushwhacker."

"You won't mock me when you're starvin' to death, boy. You and your Indian friend soon will be beggin' me for any scrap of meat."

"You been visited yet by that big ol' bear?"

"What bear?"

"The big boar with the white, diamond blaze on his chest."

231

"You're mockin' me agin."

"You look on the trail, Percy. You'll see his tracks. Better keep a sharp eye out for him. He's been trained by the old chieftain to guard the cave. Why, he's probably watchin' you right now."

Wilkins shuddered. Pulling a burning branch from the fire to use as a torch, he studied the trail, finding the track of the large bear. Rushing back to the fire, he threw his smoking tree limb into the flames and frantically added more wood. The fire blazed. Wilkins watched the trail, shotgun at the ready.

Far back in the depths of the cave, by the flash of his flint and steel, Namakagon followed the trail of smoke. He climbed over rocks and slid through narrow openings, moving only a few feet between flashes. The smoke grew more difficult to see. He found himself in a dead end corridor. Backtracking, he tried again to locate the trail of smoke, his dogs just ahead of him. The old man tripped on Makade, falling to the cave floor, dropping his flint. On hands and knees, he searched between the rocks for the small stone.

"Oh, Wenebojo, why do you do this? Why must I suffer so? Why won't you help me?" His fingers found the flint. Stiff from the cold, muscles aching, the old Indian stood in the sheer blackness of the cavern. Striking out another flash, he tried vainly to locate the trail of smoke.

Tor's fire was out. His fuel was gone. Now, the only light in the cave was the dim glow at the entrance that came from Wilkins blazing fire outside. Tor taunted him again. "Did that big ol' bear stop by for a visit yet, Bushwhacker?"

"There ain't no bear, Sonny."

"I see you got your fire just a blazin'. You saw his tracks, didn't you? You sit tight. He'll be along any time now. It's his suppertime, Percy."

"Enough of your mockin' me!" screamed the thug. He jumped to his feet, his shotgun in hand. In anger, he kicked the edge of his fire toward the cave opening. Hot coals flew everywhere. As they did, some of the dead leaves and pine needles under the cave entrance caught fire. Air currents near the opening fanned the flames, carrying smoke into the cave. Seeing this, Wilkins pushed more grass, pine needles, and leaves into the entrance. The fire grew. Wilkins grinned. Leaning his shotgun against a tree, he snapped off three balsam branches, and tossed them in. They cracked and popped as they burned, sending thick, white smoke under the rock and into the cave.

"Say, Sonny," shouted the bandit. "Hows about a good snout full of pine smoke? Maybe that will bring you out. No?"

Wilkins pushed the burning bows farther into the entrance. The flames lit the chamber. Tor watched the thick cloud of white smoke rise to the ceiling and drift above, far back into the cave. It did not affect the air where he sat.

"Stop! Stop the smoke," Tor called. "We are choking to death in here. Oh, Mister Wilkins, have mercy. Please stop."

Percy Wilkins snickered and threw more pine boughs onto the fire. "What's that, Sonny? You say you want more smoke?"

But, as the thief snapped branches from the balsam tree, a large shadow fell on him. He turned and froze when he saw before him the great bear. It rose to its hind feet, dwarfing the bandit. Wilkins slowly inched toward his shotgun. His eyes shifted from those of the bear to the diamond-shaped, white blaze on the bear's chest. It stared down on him.

Just as Wilkins' hand touched the gun barrel, the bear's huge paw slashed through the air. He screamed as the bear's paw hit him squarely across the face. Knocked to the ground by the blow, the bear pounced on him.

Tor heard the shrill scream. "Bushwhacker," he called. "Bushwhacker!"

There was no answer—no sound outside.

"Percy Wilkins!"

Again, nothing.

The smoke from the fire in the entrance stopped. Tor heard a dog barking beyond. Then two.

"Tor Loken, are you there?" came a call from outside.

"Chief! Is that really you?"

"It is, young woodsman. These two fine dogs and your plumes of smoke brought me out high on the ridge." He pulled the last coals away from the entrance. "Tor, Percy Wilkins is no longer a threat."

Tor scrambled out of the cave, across the hot ground. Makade and Waabiski rushed to him.

There, in the firelight, stood Chief Namakagon. Tor grabbed him around the neck with one arm and patted him on the back with the other. "Good to see you, old friend. I figured you'd find your way out."

Tor then saw Wilkins' body, face deeply slashed by the claws of a large bear and his skull crushed. Blood covered his torn clothing. The stock of his shotgun, lying on the ground, showed deep bite marks.

"Percy Wilkins won't return this time," said the chief. "It appears he angered a large makwaa."

"You think it was that bear we saw earlier?"

"Who is to say?" replied the chief as he sat down on the large rock near the fire. Seems as though he just showed up out of nowhere. Perhaps this was the work of old Wenebojo. Who knows? No matter now. Wilkins is gone."

Tor searched for bear tracks but, other than tracks from the dogs, the only footprints he found were from his own boots, Wilkins' boots, and Chief Namakagon's moccasins. "Seems as though the makwaa left no tracks."

"No tracks? How curious," replied Namakagon.

"Chief, tell me more about this Wenebojo you speak of so often."

"Someday, young woodsman. Not tonight. I'm a bit weary. It must be this fine spring air."

Chapter 43
May Day

Every northern Wisconsin lumber mill was working at full capacity on the first of May, 1884. Like most pinery boomtowns, Hayward's streets were crowded with horses, wagons, and many lumberjacks eager to celebrate the end of the logging season. The smell of fresh-cut white pine filled the air. Plumes of smoke from the sawdust burners billowed into the clear blue sky.

The continuous whine of gang saws ripping through pine logs filled the air and echoed off each new brick building. Tall stacks of rough-sawn lumber filled every vacant lot, field, unused street, and open space. The large lake created by the new dam was choked with green timber. Long lines of railroad cars flanked each sawmill. More lumber-laden cars stood in the yard, ready to ship. Wagons heaped with hardware, furniture, food, beer, and other goods rolled from depot to downtown.

Carpenters and masons feverishly built homes, offices, and stores as fast as the fickle spring weather permitted. Every hotel and rooming house sported a sign declaring, "no vacancy". The restaurants, barbershops, bath houses, poker rooms, brothels, and saloons were crowded. Lumberjacks, flush with winter earnings, shared the boardwalks with shrewd businessmen, sharp-witted charlatans, willing women, gamblers, and others hoping to cash in on the new prosperity—prosperity made possible by the harvest of the great white pine forests. Business was booming. The young city of Hayward, Wisconsin, had the look and feel of a flourishing, modern lumber town. Everyone had plenty of money and wanted to spend it fast.

The two-fifteen from Cable rolled into the Hayward yard. A sudden rush of steam and the squeal of the iron wheels braking against the rails momentarily drowned out other sounds of the city.

One by one, a party of six stepped off the train. Tor, Ingman, and Olaf were first. Olaf carried a cane but did not use it. Chief Namakagon, Constable Bill Burns, and Sourdough followed. The county sheriff, the mayor of Hayward, and the local undertaker met them.

"The outlaw Percy Wilkins is three cars down, Sheriff," said Burns. "I inspected the body. A bear surely killed him all right. No question about it."

The undertaker walked down the platform toward the lone boxcar.

"You say, Mr. Burns, this is the same man who tried to rob the train last winter?" asked the mayor. "The shypoke we all took for being drowned?"

The undertaker slid open the boxcar door as the other men approached.

"One and the same, Your Honor. He so confessed those deeds to Chief Namakagon and young Loken here. And both got a good, long look at him during the train robbery. There is no doubt this fella is Percy Wilkins, the fugitive we dang-near nabbed last December."

"You were the last to see him alive?" the sheriff asked Namakagon.

"We were," replied the chief, placing his hand on Tor's shoulder.

"So, you saw him, too, Son?"

"I'd say so! He held us at gunpoint. Before the bear got him, he explained how he foiled his capture by hiding under the ice near the railroad trestle. Then he lit out to a lumber camp over at Morse. Said he was bent on gettin' even with the chief for all his troubles. That's about all we learned before the bear got hold of him."

"Seems odd that a bear would attack a man at all," said the sheriff. "And odder still a bear would attack a man with two others right there."

"There are many odd things that happen in the pinery, Sheriff," said Chief Namakagon. "I suppose that is why your good service is so valuable and necessary in this country."

"Yes, yes. I suppose you are right," said the sheriff. "Well, let's have a gander at this here dead fella."

The undertaker slid the tarp-covered body from the floor of the boxcar. The corpse fell onto the brick platform, landing at their feet with a dull thud. The sheriff removed the tarp. The mayor gasped when he saw the crushed skull, twisted neck, and severe cuts across the dead man's face.

"Looks like a bear done it all right," said the undertaker with a grin. "Ain't another critter in these parts that will leave a man lookin' like this here, not even a wild cat."

"Well, Clarence, you go ahead and get this fella fixed up for buryin'," said the mayor to the mortician. "But do it on the cheap now. I don't think the voters want to spend a dime on such a ne'er-do-well. I suppose this will cost the good people of Sawyer County two, maybe three dollars, all told."

"Sheriff," said Olaf, "unless you have more questions for us, we need

235

to be off to Adeline Ringstadt's Boarding House now. Oh, and Sheriff, this afternoon I plan to throw a small celebration at Johnny Pion's Hotel. Would you and the mayor like to join us?"

"Why, sure, Loken," replied the mayor. "On behalf of the citizens of the fine City of Hayward, I accept. The sheriff and I would be pleased to share in your celebration. I know folks 'round here are gol dang glad to see this matter put behind us. You tell old Johnny Pion I said to put the first five dollars of the bar bill on the city tab. I do declare it to be a sound investment. Yessiree."

"Tor!" came a young woman's voice from the street.

"Rosie?" He jumped from the platform, racing across the railroad tracks. Turning back, he shouted, "Pa, I'll meet you later in the hotel."

Olaf watched his son cross the railroad yard to the young, dark-haired girl. "She reminds me of Karina when we were their age."

"Tor," Rosie said, "When I heard you were on the afternoon train, I came right away. Do you know what day this is?"

"Sure, Rosie, Thursday."

"No, silly, it's the first of May! It's May Day, Tor. May Day! School has been dismissed for summer, it's a beautiful day, and all my friends are planning to meet in the park. We'll have a grand party with ice cream and fruit punch and even a Maypole. We have a fiddler coming. And a fellow with a concertina. It's May Day! Oh, Tor, you must come."

"You know what else this day is?" Tor said, reaching into his pocket. She watched as he unwrapped a ring crafted from a shard of silver. He placed the ring on her finger. "Rosie, this is the day when I ask if you will officially be my sweetheart."

Astonished, Rosie stared at the ring. Tor, overcoming his shyness, leaned forward, kissing her on the cheek. She looked up into his eyes, said nothing for a moment, then, wrapping her arms around him, gave him a kiss they would always remember.

Olaf, Ingman, Chief Namakagon, and Sourdough looked on from the platform. The engineer gave two blasts from the locomotive's whistle.

"Yust look at those two," Ingman said. "Ain't young love grand today?"

"Yesterday, today, tomorrow," offered Namakagon, "young love always has been, is now, and forever will be grand."

"Oh, but time seems to move so fast nowadays," Sourdough said. "I often wonder if love will be as magnificent in years to come."

"Sourdough," replied the chief, "I will stop by and let you know—the next time I go 'round."

With a rush of steam and the loud chugging of the engine, the Omaha pulled away from the station under a bright sun. The train thundered south, pulling two passenger cars, one empty box car, and sixty-eight flat cars, each piled high with prime, white pine lumber.

The End

236

I closed the last theme book, returning it to the stack. "Well, Grandpa Tor, it's high time I took a closer look at that map of yours."

Untying the first stack of theme books, I opened chapter one. The faded, crumbling, grocer's bill was not there. I flipped through the book. Finding no map, I looked through the second, then the third book. Nothing. I flipped through every book in the stack. Still, nothing. I checked my pockets. I looked on the floor. No map.

Behind the cushions of the old chair, I found only a few tarnished pennies, a fistful of acorns, and a buffalo nickel. Staring at the image of the Indian on the coin, I muttered, "Wenebojo, is this your doing?"

The only reply—the only sounds I heard coming from the old lodge now were the ticking of the big clock and the crackling of the fire in the fireplace.

"The kitchen!" I heard myself speaking louder, now. "Yes! It's on the kitchen table!" I rushed into the kitchen, flipping on the light switch. There, right where I left it, on the table, was the photo of young Olaf Loken, his pretty wife, Karina, and their baby, Tor. Next to the photograph was the old, green, wooden box. I snatched it off the table. Inside was the knife with the broken blade, the worn pocket watch, the blue ribbon from Grandma Rosie's hair, the medal with the broken clasp, the odd, tarnished, silver ring. No grocer's receipt. No map.

I dropped to my knees, hoping to find it on the floor. I searched under the refrigerator and under the stove. Nothing. I checked my pockets again. Still no map. I searched and I searched and I shouted to the rafters, "Wenebojo, is this one of your pranks?"

At first, silence. Then, far out on the moonlit lake, there came a ghostly wail from a loon.

That lonesome, eerie call prompted me to glance out the window into the yard. A thin wisp of smoke ascended above the workshop chimney. I stared at the rising smoke and it came to me. I realized what had happened to the map.

I looked again at the child in the old tintype photograph. "Oh, Grandpa Tor," I whispered, "those nice ladies from the church, with help from ol' Wenebojo, did a very good job cleaning today. You and Chief Namakagon can rest easy now, Grandpa. Your secret is safe—safe forever."

# # #

Glossary to accompany <u>The Treasure of Namakagon</u>

<u>Animosh</u>: Ojibwe word for dog.

<u>Anishinabe</u>: *a-nish-i-NAH-bee*. The original Native American people who lived north and south of the western Great Lakes region. Primarily Ojibwe but also Algonquin, Pottawatomie and others.

<u>Barber chair</u>: Slang for what is created when a tree is improperly notched prior to cutting, resulting in a tall splinter rising up from one side of the stump that makes it resemble a chair.

<u>Bark eaters</u>: Slang for lumberjacks.

<u>Barn boss</u>: Oversaw care and feeding of the animals.

<u>Blackbird</u>: A slang term for a log driver who was skilled at walking on the floating logs.

<u>Blackjack</u>: Gingerbread. A sweet cake made with ginger and blackstrap molasses.

<u>Boom</u>: A large raft of logs that were held together by a ring of logs connected by chains. Boom companies were formed on parts of some rivers to sort logs and direct them toward the right mills.

<u>Boozhoo</u>: *Boo-ZHOO*. Hello. Probably from the French term *bon jour* meaning good day.

<u>Breakup</u>: The spring ice melt when logs could again be driven to the mills.

<u>Bull Cook</u>: A worker who did many camp chores including the feeding of some animals, bringing in firewood, keeping the stoves filled, fetching water for the kitchen, clearing paths through the snow, plus many kitchen chores. Not well-paid.

<u>Calked boots</u>: Leather boots with spiked soles that helped men walk on the floating logs.

<u>Camp dentist</u>: The worker who sharpened the saws and axes.

<u>Cant hook:</u> A tool for rolling logs. Consists of a stout, wooden handle and a C-shaped hook. Similar to a peavey.

<u>Caught in a bear trap</u>: Lumberjack slang for getting into trouble.

<u>Chain-haul team</u>: The men who used horses or oxen and chains to load the logs onto the sleighs.

<u>Chautauqua</u>: *sha-TAHK-wa*. Traveling entertainment troupes that would set up large tents and then offer lectures, music, comedy, burlesque and theater before moving on to the next rural communities.

<u>Chequamegon</u>: *she-WAHM-a-gun. A large bay on th*e south shore of Lake Superior. Also a national forest in Wisconsin.

<u>Chippewa</u>: Originally pronounced *CHIP-ah-way*. Now usually pronounced *CHIP-ah-wah*. French slang for Ojibwe. Also a river in Wisconsin.

<u>Choppers</u>: Heavy leather mittens.

<u>Clydesdales</u>: The largest of the big workhorses.

<u>Cookees</u>: Assistants to the head cook.

<u>Corks</u>: Calked (spiked) boots.

<u>Cross-haul</u>: Loading the logs onto the sleigh by using a horse or ox to pull a chain that would roll the log up a ramp mounted on the side of the sleigh.

<u>Cross-hauler</u>: The man who loaded logs onto a sleigh using horses or oxen and chains that crossed over the load. Chain-hauler.

<u>Cruising</u>: Inspecting and estimating the value of standing timber. Timber cruisers were also called land-lookers.

<u>Deacon's bench</u>: A pine board attached to the ends of the bunks. It ran the full length of the bunkhouse (sleep shanty) and was usually the only seating, other than on the benches at the cook shanty tables.

<u>Deadhead</u>: Make a trip to deliver cargo with no prospect of returning with other cargo.

<u>Donkey engine</u>: A steam engine used to haul full logging sleds up steep hills.

<u>Double Eagle</u>: Twenty-dollar gold coin.

<u>Double sawbucks</u>: Twenty dollar bills.

<u>Double-bit ax</u>: An ax with two cutting surfaces so it will last twice as long between sharpenings.

<u>Dray</u>: Hauling service.

<u>Dressed</u>:, Gutted. Entrails removed. Cleaned.

<u>Flaggins</u>: Dinner carried into the woods for those men who were working too far from camp to eat in the cook shanty.

<u>Four bits</u>: Fifty cents.

<u>Gabreel</u>: A long tin horn often used to call the men in for meals.

<u>Gandy dancers</u>: Slang for railroad construction crews. They earned this name from the repeated, rhythmic stomping on their Gandy brand shovels when tamping crushed rock under railroad ties. This shovel-tamping technique appeared similar to dancing a jig.

238

Gang saws: Powerful, multi-bladed saws that, in one pass, could cut many boards from a single log.

Gee: A signal used to train horses to turn to the right. *Haw* turned them left.

Gitchee Manitou: *GI-chee MAN-i-too*. The Great Spirit.

Graybacks: Body lice. A common problem in the lumber camps.

Grippe: Any of several flu-like illnesses.

Hay burners: Work horses.

Head push: The camp boss.

Iron Belt: The iron-mining region of far northern Wisconsin and Upper Michigan.

Jam crew: A team of log drivers that specialized in breaking up logjams.

Kerf: The groove cut by the saw.

Lac Courte O'reilles: *la-COO-da-RAY*. A major Ojibwe village and a lake in northwest Wisconsin. Also an Ojibwe tribe.

Latrine: A pit or ditch used for human waste.

Log drive: Logs were floated down rivers in the spring. Men would drive the logs to the mills downstream much as cowboys drove cattle to market.

Lumber baron: A wealthy, powerful businessman who prospered from the timber industry.

Makade: *ma-KAH-day*. Black

Makwaa: *MUK-wa*. Bear.

Menoomin: men-OO-min. literally, good grain. Wild rice was plentiful in many Wisconsin waters before the logging boom altered the lakes and rivers.

Mikwam-migwan: *MIK-wam-MIG-wan*. Feathers of ice.

Namakagon: *nam-eh-KAH-gun*. A large lake in northwest Wisconsin and headwaters for the Namekagon River.

Namekagon: *nam-eh-KAH-gun*. An outstanding northwest Wisconsin river. On early maps, some cartographers spelled the river Nam*e*kagon and other map makers spelled the lake Nam*a*kagon. These different spellings remain today.

Ogimaa: *OH-ga-ma*. Chief.

Ojibwe: o-*JIB-way*. Sometimes spelled Ojibwa. Correctly pronounced with the long *a* sound. The French fur traders called most Anishinabe people who lived in the western Great Lakes region either Ojibwe or Chippeway.

Pac-wa-wong: *pa-QUAY-wong*. A rice-rich lake formed by a widening in the river downstream from Cable. An Ojibwe village sat on the west shore until a lumber company dam raised the lake level, killing the rice.

Peavey: A tool used for moving logs. Composed of a stout wooden handle, a C-shaped steel hook and a steel point.

Pemmican: A mix of grains, dried fruit and dried meat. A high-energy food, easy to carry and resistant to spoilage, making it ideal on the trail.

Percherons: Purebred work horses, originally from France.

Picaroon: An ax handle fitted with a short, sharp, steel pick rather than a blade. Used to stab, and then pull or turn logs.

Pinery: The great stand of virgin pines that once stretched from central Wisconsin to Lake Superior, into Minnesota and Michigan. Until 1890 it was, by far, the richest range of white pine on Earth.

Pinkertons: A Chicago detective agency distinguished for investigating and preventing train robberies in the late 1800s.

Rack bar device: A T-handled box containing a magneto that could generate an electrical charge. Used to detonate explosives.

Rail: Railroad worker.

River Pig: Log driver.

Road monkey: A worker who maintained the ice roads, trails and tote roads.

Rut: The deer breeding season when does are in heat and bucks often lack normal caution.

Sand man: The worker assigned to slow down a timber sleigh by throwing sand in the track. Straw was also used.

Sault Ste. Marie: *SOO-saint-marie*. A settlement and military post on the eastern end of Lake Superior.

Sawyer: A logger who felled trees using a crosscut saw. Also mill workers who ran saws.

Shaving the whiskers: Wisconsin's pine was often compared to being *as thick as whiskers*. Clear-cutting a forest was compared to shaving the pine *whiskers* from the landscape.

Shypoke: Slang for a Green Heron.

Sky pilot: Clergyman.

Slats: Lumberjack slang for ribs. Barrels were made of thin, curved wooden slats that were held together by metal hoops. The rib cage was compared to a wooden barrel by some.

Sleep camp: Another term for bunk house.

Sluice: *SLOOSE*. A channel built to control which way a log can travel.

Stamp hammer: A hammer used to mark the lumber camp's name on the end of each log.

Standing part: The free or unattached end of a rope or chain.

Star load: A very large load of the biggest and best pine.

Stove lids: Lumberjack slang for pancakes or flapjacks. Term was inspired by the heavy, circular, iron lids found on old, wood burning cast iron cook stoves.

Swamper: The saw crew member who trimmed branches from downed trees and cut any brush in the way of the sawyers and teamsters.

Top loading: Guiding the logs onto the sleigh while standing on top of the pile. Also called the sky-hooker.

Travois: *Trav-OY.* A device used to drag heavy items. Usually made from lashing saplings together.

Trestle: *TRESS-sil.* A large railway bridge

Two-man crosscut: A 5 to 9-foot-long saw blade fitted with a handle on each end. Perfected in the 1870s, it replaced the ax as the primary tool for felling trees. This greatly accelerated the harvest.

Union suit: One-piece underwear. Longjohns.

Waabishki: *wa- BEESH-key.* White.

Waffled: Refers to scars resulting from being kicked by calked boots during a brawl.

Walkin' boss: A woods boss who managed several camps at once by walking to each.

Wannigan: *WAHN-i-gun.* Company store. Also a portable kitchen that was used to prepare food for workers who were too far from camp to return for dinner at midday.

Wenebojo: *we-ne-BO-ZHOO.* A key spiritual character to many Native Americans, His father was a man. His mother was the west wind. His grandmother the Earth. Wenebojo is often depicted as a half-man, half-spirit, who delights in playing tricks on and confusing people, both to demonstrate his talents and wisdom and to protect all plants and animals. Able to perform miraculous feats, but also vulnerable and capable of making thoughtless errors. He may take the form of animals, rocks and plants. Sometimes called Wenebush. Wenebojo is, to many Native Americans, what Jesus is to many Christians—the worldly manifestation of the great spirit.

Whiffletree: The rear wooden component of a horse team's rigging that connected the team to the load. and evened out the force of the pull from two horses. Also called an evener.

Widowmaker: A dangerous tree or limb that may injure or kill a logger when it falls.

Woods Boss: Foreman of the crews that worked in the woods.

Yellowjack: Cornbread. Also called johnnycake.

Watch for the next book in this series . . . . .

Tor Loken and the Death of Namakagon
by James A. Brakken

According to mid-1880s articles found in the Ashland Daily Press, Chief Namakagon traded unrefined silver for supplies and services in Ashland. Several area businessmen tried to convince the chief to disclose the source of his silver. None did, although one, it's been said, came very close. But, when a large bear blocked their trail, Namakagon took this for an omen and refused to continue. Following a fierce 1886 blizzard, Namakagon's frozen remains were found along a trail that many believe may have been very near his silver cache. Suspicions remain today regarding his demise and of the whereabouts of the lost silver.

In the next adventure, Tor Loken loses his mentor during this fierce snowstorm. The authorities refuse to investigate and Tor is challenged to solve the mystery of Chief Namakagon's death. Meanwhile, new developments, both man-made and nature-made, again place the Loken camp in peril. Learn more about the rich history of the lumberjack days, help solve the mystery, and gather more clues about the likely location of the legendary silver mine of Chief Namakagon.

About the author/illustrator

James A. Brakken was just a boy when he first heard stories of Chief Namakagon and his secret silver mine. Born and raised in Cable, Wisconsin, not far from the Namekagon River where this story takes place, he listened to the tales of the old lumber camps, explored the legendary river, and walked the ice roads in search of Chief Namakagon's treasure.

An educator and active conservationist, James Brakken has earned statewide recognition for his work to protect and preserve the lakes and streams of Northwest Wisconsin through his writing, teaching and leadership.

Share your suggestions

Thank you for reporting to the author any errors you may find so future editions may be improved. Email us or find us on Facebook®. If you enjoy this book, please tell us at BayfieldCountyLakes@Yahoo.com. Let your friends know, too!

Explore Lumberjack Country

Contact the author to arrange for a brief and easy walking tour that includes the site of a 19th century logging camp, a former ice road where thousands of sleigh loads of timber once traveled, the remains of a 19th Century river dam used to hold back water for spring drives, and other historic sights between legendary Lake Namakagon and Hayward, Wisconsin. Includes readings by the author and informal discussion. See TheTreasureofNamakagon.com for details.

Looking for Treasure?

Find examples of THE TREASURE OF NAMAKAGON Study and Discussion Guide, plus maps, new engraved illustrations, and much more.
Visit our website, TheTreasureofNamakagon.com or
BadgerValley.com

What the readers are saying –

"Weaving mystery into history, "The Treasure of Namakagon" vivifies the tu-multuous nature of 19th-century life in the legendary north woods."
Michael Perry, bestselling Wisconsin author

"Open with caution. You won't want to put this one down."
LaMoine MacLaughlin, President, Wisconsin Writers Association

"A twisting, thrilling mix of mystery, adventure and legendary treasure. ...a great fund raising idea for our lake associations. Wisconsin history buffs will find this book a treasure in itself. An exciting adventure for all ages."
Waldo Asp, Northwest Waters President and AARP County Chairman

"... A very talented writer. Consider me fan!"
Jeff Rivera, media personality, bestselling author

"Like a living history lesson, Brakken takes his readers on a ride down North-ern Wisconsin's untamed Namakagon River, back when giant virgin forests lured heroic lumberjacks to seek their fortune. In scene after scene, the reader is surrounded by the beauty of pristine woods and lakes, rooting for the good guys to beat out the greedy ones, even learning step by step how to place the giant saw so the magnificent tree falls in just the right place."
A. Y. Stratton, author of Buried Heart

"Brakken's new book animates the long history of conflicts over Wisconsin's water and mineral resources. The interplay between citizens, corporations and government will be familiar to people following today's debates over mining and groundwater protection in Wisconsin, or energy development in other re-gions."
Eric Olson, UWEX-Lakes Director

Blurbs Wanted: Find us on Facebook® and leave your own review!

James A. Brakken's **The Treasure of Namakagon**

A twisting, turning, thrilling adventure based on records from the great Wisconsin timber boom of the 1880s. Tor Loken and his mentor, Chief Namakagon, join with lumberjacks from their camp to foil a ruthless timber tycoon and protect the secret silver, treasure that truly existed and has yet to be rediscovered. The clues are within.

Treasure of Namakagon Discussion & Study Guide

Discussion questions and projects to accompany THE TREASURE OF NAMAKAGON. 186 questions and projects covering all 43 chapters. This guide will help readers reach an in-depth understanding of the story's foundation—the rich history of the 19th century timber harvest in northwest Wisconsin. Ideal for classroom use* and reading discussion groups.

Item	Price	Quantity	Extended Price
Treasure of Namakagon	$15.99		_____.__
Study Guide	$3.99		_____.__
Study Gd & Ansr Key*	$10.99		_____.__
DARK: A Fireside Companion	TBA See: BadgerValley.com		_____.__
S & H in USA: $4 first item, $1 each add'l item			_____.__
US dollars only. 6% sales tax if shipped to WI address			_____.__
Please provide your email for delivery confirmation:		Total	$ _____.__

Complimentary study guide & answer key with order of 10 or more books. Quantity discounts available at **715-798-3163**.

Prices subject to change without notice.

Ebook versions for all E-readers available atTheTreasureofNamakagon.com

For online payment visit

BadgerValley.com

Mail entire form and check or money order payable to:

James A. Brakken
45255 E. Cable Lake Rd
Cable, WI 54821

Email: BayfieldCountyLakes@Yahoo.com

Brakken's TREASURE OF NAMAKAGON
45255 East Cable Lake Road
Cable WI 54821

Name _____

Address _____

City/State/Zip _____

*THIS IS YOUR **SHIPPING LABEL**: PLEASE PRINT CLEARLY*

The Treasure of Namakagon

This action-adventure is founded on historical facts blended with fiction. Most of the characters in <u>The Treasure of Namakagon</u> are not real, but they could have been. References to the Namekagon River log drives, life in the logging camps, and fraudulent timber sales are based on true events, as is the gunplay that resulted from a ploy to charge for timber floated over a dam near Hayward. The rivers, the lakes, the towns, in this story are all real. So are most of the hotels, taverns, depots, and other buildings mentioned. These and other historical references help bring this tale to life.

Add in historical accounts of silver and gold found in the region and Chief Namakagon trading shards of silver for supplies. Although many still search for Chief Namakagon's secret silver mine, it has yet to be rediscovered. Perhaps, though, the real treasure was the vast white pine forest that, until the 1880s, gave northern Wisconsin its character, its life.

This book will plunge you into Wisconsin's single, greatest economic event—the post-Civil War harvest of the largest stand of white pine in the world. Estimates said that timber would take a thousand years to cut. It was gone in just fifty. Tens upon tens of thousands of lumberjacks descended on the north to harvest the "green gold" and cash in on the wealth. Many northern

Wisconsin towns sprang up in the middle of nowhere and boomed into bustling cities full of life, fast money, fortune seekers, loose women, and lumberjacks. Rowdy wilderness towns quickly gained notoriety—and popularity. In the woods, wasteful harvest practices, poor forest management, and outright greed prevailed.

Most of those boom towns failed soon after the pine was cut, shrinking to impoverished settlements and, in some cases, ghost towns. Our forests will never be the same. The great Wisconsin pinery, as it was called, will never return.

What does remain are the tales of the lumberjacks and those who arrived in the north along with them. This adventure is based on those great men and the hard but colorful lives they lived in the late nineteenth century. This story is also based on the history of Mikwam-migwan, better known as Chief Namakagon, and his legendary lost treasure.

Open this book and step back in time. Share in the rich history of life in the great Wisconsin pinery during the lumberjack days of the 1880s. Share, too, in a great north woods adventure.

Made in the USA
Charleston, SC
24 September 2012